## The Door through Washington Square

"Premier spinner of dark tales . . . as always it's Bergstrom's attention to character that makes her work so intriguing and ultimately rewarding. Not to be missed."
—*Milwaukee Journal Sentinel*

## Leanna

"[Bergstrom] blends successfully the elements of the thriller, the Gothic romance, and the horror novel into a seamless whole which defies simple categorization . . . Page-turners don't come any better than this . . . A dark, erotic vampire story in the Anne Rice tradition."
—*Milwaukee Journal Sentinel*

## Mina

"Chilling, fast paced, a real page-turner."
—P. N. Elrod, author of *The Vampire Files*

"A stunning reading experience . . . This is a most excitingly written adventure story, filled with sensuality, a raw intensity of emotion, and a suspense that will match and surpass Bram Stoker's original story."
—*Affaire de Coeur*

"Takes the Dracula legend beyond its original ending . . . a nicely twisting sequel."
—*Milwaukee Journal Sentinel*

"Throbbing with the rich sexuality that marked Bram Stoker's *Dracula*, *Mina* is an erotic ride through the life of a liberated Victorian woman who no longer desires to repress her dark passion."
—*Shadowdance*

"*Mina* is a tremendous novel that Stoker would have been very proud to have authored. [Bergstrom] successfully incorporates the events of the original novel [and] splendidly goes beyond."
—*The Talisman*

"Destined to be considered a literary classic . . . a wonderful read."
—*Eclipse*

"Strong . . . sensual . . . surprisingly tender . . . *Mina* displays a resonance unlike its source material, humanizing people Stoker merely used as pawns."
—*BookLovers*

# NOCTURNE

## ELAINE
## BERGSTROM

**ACE BOOKS, NEW YORK**

NOCTURNE

An Ace Book / published by arrangement with
the author

PRINTING HISTORY
Ace mass-market edition / October 2003

Copyright © 2003 by Elaine Bergstrom.
Cover art by Victor Stabin.
Cover design by Rita Frangie.
Text design by Julie Rogers.

For information address: The Berkley Publishing Group,
a division of Penguin Group (USA) Inc.,
375 Hudson Street, New York, New York 10014.

ISBN: 0-441-01109-8

ACE®
Ace Books are published by The Berkley Publishing Group,
a division of Penguin Group (USA) Inc.,
375 Hudson Street, New York, New York 10014.
ACE and the "A" design
are trademarks belonging to Penguin Group (USA) Inc.

PRINTED IN THE UNITED STATES OF AMERICA

10  9  8  7  6  5  4  3  2  1

**TO MY FANS**
*I hope this book is as
much fun for you to read
as it was for me to write.*

# PR⊕L⊕GUE

**January 1965**

Dickie sat in the theater box, clutching his adult cousin's hand as the stage lights dimmed and died, taking with them the last bits of applause. The singing had not impressed him; anyone in the family could hit notes far more pure than those of the star soprano on the ornate stage. But the orchestra had played so perfectly, and the color, the dancing, the drama! The audience had been bewitched. Dickie was six years old and had never shared such emotion before.

"Thank you, Laurie," he whispered to his cousin sitting beside him.

Laurence looked down at the boy, his expression almost as excited. "Would you like to go backstage? I could introduce you to some of the singers."

Dickie shook his head. "I'd like to stand on the stage, though."

"Easily done," Laurence said. They sat in silence for a long while, waiting for the crowds to thin, then Laurence led his cousin toward the front of the theater, past a guard who knew him well, and down a narrow flight of stairs to the orchestra level. Once there, he lifted the boy onto the stage and joined him.

They wandered for a time amid the props, Dickie amazed at the backdrops hanging above them, the buildings with their secret staircases, the lights, the weights and the hidden mikes. "It seemed so real," he whispered.

"So it was, for that little time you watched it."

"Will you take me to see your opera when they perform it?"

"If Stephen agrees to the visit, then, yes."

Dickie frowned, thinking of his flight tomorrow. "He will let me come back to Chicago. I know it," he said.

Laurence took the boy's hand, gripped it a moment. —Of course he will. He might even come himself,— he responded, mind to mind, a soothing touch the child was used to, and one that implied so much more. Dickie knew in that moment that Laurence would do everything he could to assure it.

"Could we walk home, down the lakefront? I like the waves."

A frigid night, one that would drive even the hardiest humans to shelter. Laurence and his young cousin would be alone with the waves and the sky and the bright city lights the boy would likely not see for some time. "Of course," Laurence agreed.

At the edge of the stage Laurence hesitated, looking past the open doors and into the lobby. It was still crowded and Dickie was not used to the noise of crowds or to the friendly smiles his dark eyes and silvery brown hair invited. He led the boy to the back and down a narrow flight of stairs leading to the greenroom and rear entrance.

Near the outer door, Laurence stopped to say a few words to the conductor while Dickie went outside. The air was clear and bitter cold. Even though he was used to harsh Canada winters, Dickie caught his breath from the sudden sharpness of the wind then stepped off the exposed metal stairs and moved closer to the theater wall and the shelter it offered. Two old cars, gray with street salt, were parked alongside the theater and he rested a gloved hand on one of them while he waited for his cousin.

A sudden motion caught his eye, and he turned to see a man step into the alley and head toward him. Just a bum, he thought. Remembering what he had been told about the unpredictability of street people, he retreated between the two cars, hoping that if the darkness did not hide him completely he would at least appear insignificant enough to be overlooked.

But the man had already spied him and stood in front of him, blocking any exit unless Dickie wanted to ruin his first set of good clothes by scrambling underneath a car to escape. No need, since Laurie would rescue him soon enough.

"Waitin' for someone?" the man asked.

Not sure whether to say yes or no, Dickie said nothing.

"Sure you are," the man replied for him and moved closer.

It never occurred to the boy to call out for his cousin—either mentally or audibly. Instead he tried to rely on his speed to duck under the man and through the door only a few yards away. But the man anticipated the move and snagged him, swinging him around and gripping him tightly.

"Laurie!" the boy screamed.

"Shut the fuck up!" the man ordered and pressed a knife against Dickie's neck. "We'll wait together and surprise 'im," he said.

Dickie had little experience with an attack, but frequent advice on what to do should one occur. He followed that advice now, staying still and silent as ordered, willing the man to be calm, waiting for his cousin to come out and tell him what to do.

Laurence took in the scene even before the stage door closed, came down the stairs to where the man stood. He knew what the man wanted, knew better than to even ask. —Don't move. You're doing it just right,— he told Dickie instead.

"Whatever you've got, I'll take," the man said.

Laurence reached into his overcoat pocket, realized he'd transferred his wallet to his suitcoat, reached there.

"Hurry up!" the man ordered, gripping the boy tighter. As he did, his foot slipped on the icy concrete and the knife cut into Dickie's throat.

Instinct responded to the pain and triumphed. Dickie, using the strength he had been trained to hide, gave a high-pitched cry of rage then dug his teeth through the tattered cloth of his attacker's coat and bit down hard. The man responded by slicing into Dickie's shoulder and throwing him away with enough force that Dickie's body made a dent in the side of the car he fell against. Dickie bounced off, landing stunned for a moment, then backed away on all fours slowly.

With one of his own injured, Laurence struggled to remain calm. He had the wallet in his hands now but they were shaking with barely controlled rage. As he held it out to the man, he dropped it, catching it before it hit the ground. The man misinterpreted the sudden gesture and lunged.

To Dickie the scene that followed unfolded in delicious slow motion—the narrowing of his cousin's eyes, the tensing of his body, the strength of his kick, the sound of the man's attempted scream, cut off by death even before he hit the ground.

Dickie walked forward and looked down at the still form. His cousin ignored him for a moment, fighting for control, weighing what to do, caught in indecision until he saw Dickie starting to kneel beside the body.

—NO!— he ordered and pulled the boy away before he left some trace of himself for the police to find and analyze. The world had gotten far too complex for simple justice.

With that sad thought dousing his own hunger, Laurence picked up the knife in a gloved hand and wiped it on the corner of Dickie's jacket then dropped the blade in the snow beside the body. Hoping it would be enough, Laurence led the boy deeper into the alley, over the fence, and through to the next street. Dickie was bruised and while the cut wasn't deep, he should feed before morning. But not on the victim.

Somewhere safe, somewhere far away.

By tomorrow, when the police discovered Laurie had used the stage door and showed up to question him about the man's death, Dickie would be long gone, on a plane headed for Edmonton, and from there to the isolation of his home.

Laurence, of course, had long since learned how to lie.

Across the alley from the stage door, on the second floor of an abandoned warehouse—high enough to give plenty of warning should the police get wind of his presence—a young man shivered in his sleep and rolled over on the soiled mattress that served as his bed. His eyelids fluttered but as he started back to a deeper sleep he heard a cry from outside and was instantly awake. Keeping low to the ground, he moved to the window. There a narrow oval had been polished in the fractured glass, allowing a clandestine view of the outside.

The alley was not lit, but he had little trouble seeing in darkness. Peering down, he saw one of the neighborhood junkies, his dirty knife pressed to the neck of a small child he gripped as tightly as his trembling arms would allow. The junkie faced a man in a suit—the child's father perhaps? No matter. The junkie needed a fix, needed it bad. Need made him vicious and unpredictable and the youth guessed that no matter how cooperative the well-dressed man might be, this encounter would end in bloodshed. He ran a dirty hand across his chapped lips, pressed closer to the glass, and watched.

It was over as quickly as it began—a second cry from the child, not one of pain or fear, but of rage. Then the child bit hard into the arm that held him while he pushed the knife hand away. The junkie broke free, sliced the boy with his knife, and thrust him away. A moment later he turned on the man as well.

The speed of the defense, the quick and lethal kick, and most of all the way the child stood there until it was over as if he knew beforehand how the fight would end, convinced the youth that he was witnessing something more than a human struggle. Then, as quickly as the encounter had begun, it was over and, after a quick upward glance from the boy that made the youth back away from the window, his heart pounding in fear, child and adult vanished into the night.

The observer bit back a cry of triumph. He had heard rumors that an old one had been seen at this theater more than once. And so he had moved here to watch. He thought he had only found a secure place to spend the winter. Until now he had only half believed the old tales. Now he knew they were true.

Pushing himself to his feet, the youth stretched his cramped legs and drew the blanket more tightly around himself before going down to the alley where the body lay. The scent of the child's blood hung in the air, sharp as the smell of onions and cayenne in the casseroles his mother used to make. He bent down beside the body and looked at the crescent-shaped wound on the neck, the only apparent damage. As he brushed his hand across it, he noticed that the skin was broken, the bruise seeping blood onto his fingers. He raised them to his lips for a taste. He risked one more, larger sample—such a marvelous treat!—then considered the consequences of the corpse.

There would be trouble when it was found, a lot of trouble. It would not affect the old one and his son; no, they were beyond being affected by the concerns of men. Instead, it would likely descend on him if he remained upstairs.

He glanced up at his window and sighed. After the body was found, it would be the first place the police searched. It had been a good winter home but he would need a different shelter for at least a few weeks.

Falling deeper into the shadows, he followed the alley to the next street and headed south toward the abandoned buildings on the edge of the slums. There were always shelters there, though he might have to share them.

Along the way, he stopped at an all-night diner and treated himself to a hot chocolate, throwing in five creams from the dispenser. He sipped it thankfully, letting it take the edge off his hunger as he continued on.

# PART I

# RICHARD

# CHAP+ER I

I often feel that my twin brother and I were raised not by my own, or by our short-lived friends, but by wolves. I kept the thought to myself until recently then shared it with my cousin Laurie.

He grinned, something we rarely do even when we are only with each other because it fosters bad habits. "It wasn't wolves," he said. "No matter what parents prefer to think, most children raise themselves."

It's the sort of thing he often says, and why he is my favorite relation. Stephen, my father, believes that with only half a century separating us, we would feel a bond of youth the others cannot understand. But we share a different bond as well, one Laurie and I have never spoken of because there is no need. We both know it is real.

It can be seen clearly in my brother and me, twins but so very different. Patrick is small with that deceptive Austra delicacy, his mind nearly as powerful as our father's and full of hellish mischief that he has always managed to compel me to share. I, on the other hand, am stronger and larger. Nineteen now but with five years of growth ahead of me, I am already over six feet, with my strength obvious in my broad shoulders and thicker limbs. My hair is different as well, coarser textured, with silver tinge on brown rather than the true black of the family. Helen, my mother, tells me I resemble her human uncle for whom I'd been named though Patrick prefers to think me a throwback to her Magyar heritage. As to my mind, it is like my cousin Laurie's, with just enough power for me to get by.

As we age, our strengths will determine our destiny. I may become a master craftsman in Chaves or Ireland working to create the colored glass or design the windows that still provide a major share of our sustenance. Or I may find some special talent to excel in and be loved by all as Laurie is. But most likely it will be Patrick who one day leads our firm and, if the firstborn are willing to allow him the honor, fathers our children. These things are denied my cousin Laurie and me. I understood the necessity of this, but not the justice that conceived us the way we are.

But no matter what my strengths might be, I was the instrument for the most important event in the history of the Austra family; one that has altered our future as much as the course of my own life.

Though our family history is by necessity oral, Laurie suggested that I write my story as I recall it now. He said that while my memory of these events will remain perfect, my interpretation of them will alter as I age. He believes my youthful perspective will be valuable to those of my kind born after me. He is right, but this is not just my story. There are some portions of it that I did not live and others that I feel I cannot write objectively. Patrick will set those down. And we have decided that we do not write this just for our own, but in the hope that someday others may read it. After so many changes, so much seems possible.

There are many places I can begin my tale. I have memories of lying beside my brother in the crib and of nursing at my mother's breast. Memories even of the time before birth that were only the contentment of warmth and the comforting ripples of breath and heartbeat. Memories of my first hunt in the wilderness surrounding our isolated Canadian home—the matte silver of the moonlight on the forest mists, the whisper of the pines. The taste of my first kill—the musk of the animal's fur, the heat of its blood, the wolf that watched me devour the small creature with a detached sort of pride as if I were his king not a potential enemy.

Patrick and I were born in the Canadian Rockies. Our births

were registered there so legally we are citizens of Canada. But when we turned five, no official came to discuss our attendance at the local school. I suppose the books my parents had been ordering since we were toddlers allayed some of their concern about our education as did what intelligence we were allowed to display on our rare visits to Dawson, the closest town. And the isolation of our little cabin made travel to any school almost impossible once the winter snows began to fall. And so, my brother and I were homeschooled, receiving an education no human child could ever hope for in this far from perfect world.

Dry words from our books alternated with the perfection of my father's mind. All we need do was shut our eyes and he would take us to the streets of his past. Through his memory, we saw Versailles at the height of its glory, heard the Sun King's voice, saw the poverty outside its beautiful walls, the revolution that followed. As he moved forward in time, he accented the conflicts and carnage, the increasingly effecient methods that humans use to kill.

"Why do people kill each other?" Patrick asked, not an unreasonable question since we are incapable of aggression against our own.

"Perhaps because there are so many of them," Father replied, almost absently, his hand moving east across the globe on our worktable, long fingers brushing Toronto and New York, London and Berlin, Istanbul and Tokyo, those crowded and dangerous centers of the human world.

I stared out the north windows at the snow-covered wilderness. Our numbers were less than thirty and the world grew more crowded every day. A reminder that our most important lessons were in learning to hide.

That education began soon after we began to walk, with instructions in how to stand with our arms slightly bent to hide their length. Later we were trained to smile with our lips closed to conceal the long rear teeth, to move slowly and carefully to give no hint of our speed or strength, and especially to avoid any situation that would arouse our instinctive need to attack.

As we aged, our parents would sometimes drive us into the nearby town of Dawson. We were beautiful children, and people watched us, but though they commented on our looks, they did not see the differences behind them. We passed those early tests, and well.

When we were older, Patrick and I were sent to stay with others in the family. Patrick loved his time in New York, while I was drawn to our cousin Laurie, and his apartment on the lake in Chicago and the music that always filled his rooms. But other than those excursions, we were raised apart from humans and from our own.

All that changed the winter I turned ten years old, not in Canada but in the mountains above Chaves, Portugal, the site of our family's retreat and the current headquarters for the company the firstborn founded some eight centuries ago. I could describe the view of the Cantabrian Mountains as I saw them from the air or my first scent of the thick pine and cedars which grew on the peaks. I could describe the corporate lobby with its soaring windows of colored glass, the firm's alpha/omega symbol inlaid in teak on the marble floor, the paintings, the sculptures—all done by family. But there are coffee table books for that, so I will only say that I was in awe as I saw it all for the first time with my own eyes.

Our firm shuts down from the day before the winter solstice to the weekend after Epiphany to allow those in exile to return for a week with family. Our workers were happy to go home for the holidays with pay, but there were always a few who stayed, close friends who understood what we were. For those few, our difference made no difference.

There were even children, though not many because children are too impulsive to be fully trusted. Conscious of the importance of the ceremony that was to take place that night, I stood apart from the games they played on the sunlit lawn behind the firm, trying to act older than my years. As it grew late, I watched parents come to claim the young ones, and smiled when I saw my mother coming for me, her hair golden in the setting sun. For a moment I was caught in the fantasy of being a human child.

"It's time," she said, then took my hand and led me up the mountain to Father's house. Built of stone, softened only by his windows, with an iron-framed widow's walk at the top and a fireplace inside that Patrick swears was once used for burning witches, it was the most keeplike of the family houses. My mother had prepared for her first family gathering here. It was fitting that her sons did, too. Patrick was already there with Laurie and Denys, wearing an embroidered cobalt silk tunic that was his tenyears gift from Denys. I accepted a similar one in red and put it on.

Mother took my left hand, Laurie my right. And with Patrick flanked by Father and Denys, we walked the ridge to where the solstice fire already burned. Because this would be Patrick's and my first sharing, nearly the entire family had come. They had formed a circle facing the blaze. We stood inside of their circle, at the northernmost point, our backs to the flames. Mother stood in front of me; Father in front of Patrick.

A bit over twelve years ago, in a special summer ceremony to honor her and the one who had died bringing her into our life, it had been my mother standing here—Helen Wells, the first human in centuries able to become one of the family. There was no man there who did not desire her, no woman who did not envy her the power of her once-human body. Of all of us, she alone had the ability to bear children and live.

I looked over my shoulder at them all, nineteen men and six women, their lustrous hair and eyes the same midnight black. I looked at my brother beside me, so much one of them. And I felt my differences too sharply, my huge lumbering body, my coal-colored hair. Then I looked at Mother, her own hair white gold in the firelight, her human eyes so oddly pale. For all her more marked differences, she was one with them, and soon I would be too.

She took my hand, squeezed it, then let it go when she understood that I did not want comfort or reassurance. With a child's impatience, I merely wanted all the fuss to be over.

In the decade since my parents had chosen exile, Father had attended few family sharings. At each, he had led the circle. Not tonight. Tonight his role was as our parent presenting his sons to his kin. This was the Austra equivalent of a first birthday.

We measure our lives in decades because years seem too excessive. I was one. Laurie, five. Small, easy numbers. Father is one hundred twenty-five, Rachel ten decades older, and my uncle Denys a ponderous two hundred seven. But even at one, I would be an adult in their eyes.

The fire had not been built high on this night, nothing that would hinder any of the family's view of us when the moment of first joining came. Denys led the circle. He moved between us and lifted a pair of goblets, their crimson crystal heavy with gold, their onyx rims a mirror for the dancing flames.

*"Ge cres nas gevornes. Cres Aughkstra!"* Denys chanted, the others repeating the words. From blood we are born. Blood of life eternal. Fitting, I would say, for a ceremony so awash in blood.

Patrick and I repeated the words, inflecting them carefully to make it clear that we were not yet part of the group.

The family responded in same, the simple phrase growing softer and softer until it was no longer spoken, only silent and pulsing on the edges of the mind like the ringing of a wineglass.

Denys passed the goblets to my parents, lifted my hand, and bit into my wrist. Not the little nips that my brother and I share, but the sort that brings real pain. He swallowed, then repeated the gesture with Patrick. After, he bit his own wrist—deeply and painfully, for pain is a part of this ritual—and let drops of his blood fall into each glass.

The circle shifted clockwise, so that Laurie stood before us. Again, we offered ourselves and he held a self-made wound in his wrist over each of the cups our parents held. Ann followed, then Daniel and Sebastian, Matthew and Marilyn, until all the circle had stood before us. As they passed us they moved to the next person in line, sharing blood with them. In the end everyone had taken from us and from each other. We the only ones still unjoined.

And through it all, the simple chant rolled through us. *"Ge cres nas gevornes. . . ."*

It is hardly a large family so it was not a heavy blood loss, but enough at my age that I felt light-headed at the end, and hungry too. But that was as it should be to heighten the effect of the sharing that would come.

When the last in the circle had taken life from us and the goblets were passed to my brother and me, there was silence—within and without. We turned and faced the fire. The family waited.

I drank and very nearly dropped the cup, so sudden and sharp was the onslaught of their combined minds. Mother steadied me and, feeling foolish for a moment, I looked to Patrick, pleased to see that in this at least he was no better able to hide the dizziness the rush of feelings and memories brought him.

The last words of the chant repeated one final time, unspoken yet bellowing in my mind. —*Cres Aughkstra!*—

Silence fell over the group. Some stood with eyes closed, others stared into the flames, but the minds, the collective whole of them, meditated on the last year—its tragedies and triumphs, the large and the small.

Nearly an hour passed before Denys raised his right arm—the one he had bitten—now as perfect as the other. With fist clenched, he shouted, *"Na'szekornes!"* The others did the same. Then we raised our fists and repeated the words, our battle cry, our affirmation. *"Na'szekornes!"* We survive.

Only one piece of the ritual remained, and my brother and I bowed our heads so that Father and Mother could slip the pendants onto us, the opaque glass that is more precious than any window, made as it is from the combined ashes of those no longer with us.

I do not know what gives these pendants their power, yet the touch of it against our skin brings peace in the most unsettling of circumstances, the solace of family when we feel most alone.

The circle broke. I felt Patrick leave with Ann and Rachel, but I stayed where I was. There was so much I wanted to understand and this place seemed made for meditation.

I sat until the logs fell into embers, alone but not alone. Their blood was in me and I knew them all—passions, concerns, lusts, hungers. Were I to focus on any one of my family, I could see the world through their eyes. I tried with Laurie, then with Marilyn and Sebastian, whom I scarcely knew. It was the same with each.

It might seem to some that ten is too young for this ritual, for the emotions I shared were adult ones—pleasure and pain beyond anything a child could understand. Yet I did understand. The blood I had shared allowed it. And I realized with sudden sadness that I had lost my innocence that night. I still had much to learn firsthand, but after the sharing, I was a child no longer.

Now merged with the family, that loneliness abated. But the joining had come too suddenly and I needed time to sort my thoughts.

# CHAPTER 2

For my family, the December holiday season has its own tradition. Before the dawn following the long night sharing, the family disappears into the mountains of the Basque country for a long hunt. Though Patrick and I had both been looking forward to it, I decided not to go.

Laurie asked if I would like his company. This was a polite way of saying that he'd stay behind and keep an eye on me. I was thankful, for I suspected I would have many questions and could not think of anyone more patient with answers.

For the next few days I wandered the empty buildings with Laurie. I walked past the pouring tables, the ovens, the lehring racks where sheets of glass are left to cool. I went into the office that one of the family has occupied since the firm moved to Chaves a century before. I sat at the desk and considered how different my life was from my father's when he'd been my age and how far he had traveled since.

When night moved close to morning, Laurie and I would lay in his bed, my back pressed tight to his chest, his arms wrapped around me. I would open my mind to him and he would show me the keep as he had seen it on his stay there thirty years before when he had fled there to escape the horrors of the last great war.

My father had been born there, in the high mountains in what is now Romania. Frn'cs, the Old One, patriarch of our family, still resides in that huge strong fortress he had built before Christ walked the earth. He will not move to the west to be with the others and they will not return to him. So we are separate, no sharing of blood, too distant to touch minds, yet we are never quite apart since his blood flows through us all.

Laurie's house was set some distance below my father's, in a sunlit clearing within sight of the firm. His windows were lighter than I was used to, but the tones of glass imparted the same warmth so that the dazzling brightness seemed more beautiful than painful. Like all of our houses, the layout gave hints of the time when we were more pack than family—a large room with only a few smaller ones off of it for privacy.

It also had a stereo system whose sound seemed to come at me from all directions. There was always something playing, from classical to British rock, except when he worked. The Bösendorfer grand piano that dominated the great room allowed for that.

We'd been alone for four days. During that time, I had gone through the fifth of the training books Laurie had mailed to me some months before. After watching me play for a time, he pulled the sheet music away. "Play it without," he told me.

My memory is perfect. It was a simple exercise. "Now shut your eyes and play it again," he said.

I did, but dropped a few notes. The second pass had only a brief moment of uncertainty. He sat down and played a few bars of something I'd never heard before while I watched and listened. I played it back, not perfectly but as well as I would have done had I been making the first pass from a printed sheet. "Again," he said, softly and I felt the pride rippling through that single word.

I practiced for another hour then began to feel a need for more sustenence than light or water.

"We could join the others. I know where they've gone," Laurie suggested.

"No. But I wish we were in Chicago." I wanted to walk those dark streets with him where he would let me choose someone from the crowd, then hold my choice so I could feed.

He followed my thoughts and I expected him to draw me close and offer himself. Instead, he reached a quick decision. "Come," he said. "I will do for you what was done for me."

I did not ask what that might be. The barrier he threw down between my mind and his hinted that it was to be a surprise.

I followed him up the curving woodland path that linked his house with Father's, where I'd left my suitcase. More rustic even than our cabin, it had no electricity, no heat save that which would be thrown by its fireplace. The only modern luxury was running water—hot and cold—and a tub large enough for two.

He ordered me to use it—something I had not done since the ceremony four nights before. When I came out of the soapy water, I saw that he had laid out the red shirt Mother had made me before we came here, a clean pair of jeans, my best boots. He had already gone, but the order came clearly to my mind,

—Put them on and meet me at the glass house. One hour.—

I was there in half that time, and paced the office alone, wondering what he might have planned for me. Surely not a hunt, not in clothes like this.

If I'd had nearly as much sense as expectation, I would have figured everything out easily enough. But I was ten, and at ten the world is filled with every possibility, no matter how illogical.

He was dressed much as I was. Without a word, he led me down the mountain, past the main offices to a narrower path, this one wilder and steeper than the ones above. I looked through a break in the trees and saw the Portuguese town of Chaves beneath us.

"We're going there?" I asked, concerned.

He stopped, turned to look at me. "You don't want to?"

"Father said I must stay close to the houses and not descend below the firm," I replied.

"Stephen also left me in charge of you. I don't think he would mind what I have planned, since he did the same for me."

"He did?" I asked, curious now.

"You do go into Dawson sometimes, don't you?"

"Only with him." I was old enough to feel sorry the moment I said it.

"Half the town has some idea of what we are. The other half must be blind. You'd pass easily enough even if you weren't so clever," he replied.

Clever! Feeling a bit more confident, I stopped asking any questions, following him through the thinning trees, the fields and vineyards, and into Chaves.

It was dark when we reached the town, but I still kept close to Laurie as we walked the hilly maze of narrow streets, past open doorways that seemed to promise incredible adventure.

—Never alone until you're much older,— Laurie told me and moved more quickly on until we reached a house set off from its neighbors by a wooden fence and a little garden across the front yard and down one side. Before we reached the door, it opened, and a woman came out, stood at the gate, and waited for us.

She was not beautiful as we would judge beauty, or even as humans would. Her lips were too narrow, her body a bit large. But her eyes were nearly as dark as our own, wide spaced and slightly slanted, her skin bronzed by birth and the sun. She wore a loose black skirt, white cotton blouse, and a black scarf over her hair, a scarf she shed once we were inside, then laughed and kissed my cousin.

Crouching before me so our faces were even, she looked at me closely. "So you are Stephen's son? I am Amalia," she said. I knew a few words of Portuguese, enough that I understood and nodded and held out my hand.

"Now that he can stand in our circle, he needs to know more," Laurie explained, mentally translating as he spoke. Not an easy trick, but a quick means of teaching language if you have students with memories as perfect as ours.

"And you thought of me?"

"Someone closer to his own age, perhaps, and as unsuspecting as those he would use would be. Inez?"

The next exchange was spoken rapidly. This time he did not translate. I understand the reason for that now and am glad he did not share that brief conversation. I did not need to know that my night's conquest was the orphaned niece of a woman of the evening who would be purchased for my use. Laurie told me later that he did suggest the money be saved for her wedding.

I think of her sometimes and wonder if she ever did marry. She was certainly pretty enough, I thought as Amalia brought her to me. Taller than I, perhaps four or five years older; young enough that I did not feel too much the little boy.

Inez was dressed like her aunt, but her head was uncovered and her long thick hair fell in a single braid down her back.

Her aunt told her to amuse me for a while, then the adults left us alone in the kitchen.

I looked at her, stammered my name, and fell silent. I had no idea how to begin. I stared at her, feeling incredibly dense. She stared back, then asked if I had Arab blood.

I understood every other word, which was enough. I shrugged, shook my head.

"You must," she said and moved closer to me.

I started to look away when I felt Laurie in my thoughts.—Touch her mind. Like any animal.—

I tried, felt him supporting me at the beginning until my confidence gave me strength. As he retreated, I moved to hold her. She became placid, her expression dreamy. I took her hand, my mind more in her than on the space around me. For the first time in my life, I held human prey alone.

There were many places I could have bitten. The side of the neck is more cliché than common, used as foreplay for sex or a particularly painful death. The inside of the wrist would do but seemed too public. Then there was the shoulder, or . . .

I was trying to recall everything I had ever heard at a time when my mind should have been entirely on her.

—Somewhere she cannot see,— Laurie suggested with not a hint of the exasperation he must have been feeling.

I moved her braid over her left shoulder, brushed my hand across the back of her neck, instinctively searching until I found the place near the spine where the pulse was strong. I sensed him agree.

Holding my calm, I clenched my jaws, felt the heat of her in my mouth, felt her fingers tighten against my palm. She made a small, throaty moan, but did not otherwise move.

I had her and realized that I could keep on having her for as long as she lived.

I swallowed, careful to hold my lips tight against her skin, to allow no mark on the cotton of her blouse.

There are no words to describe the exquisite explosion of life that comes to us through blood. I felt this girl in me, and as the blood allowed a tighter merging with her mind, her fingers relaxed, her pulse slowed to match mine. And I thought . . .

—You are correct. It is time. Leave her, but carefully,— Laurie advised, his voice gentle in my mind.

I kept my hand on hers as I moved my face away. I ran a finger over the single small wound I had made, and held our bond a few moments longer, both because I wanted to savor it and because I wanted the blood to dry before I moved the braid over the spot.

—Now sense the emotion strongest in her. Focus her mind on it and let her go.—

I recalled how she'd looked at my eyes, glimpsed the memory that had caused her interest in them. As I loosened my control of her, I kept gripping her hand. She blinked, sighed, stared at me, and frowned. "I . . . I . . ." She fought for a means to continue something she had not started to say.

"You said you live . . . lived in Morocco?" I supplied for her.

Words I did not understand then poured out of her. But my mind caught images of her, hardly more than a toddler, in her father's arms.

I felt her sorrow at the loss of her parents, and how much she despised the aunt that cared for her. Tears came to her eyes. I drew her close, comforting. As I did, my hand moved under her braid and brushed over the still-wet mark of my use. I wiped my hand against my jeans, a little stain that would be unnoticed on the dark blue denim.

I was with her less than a quarter hour, and though I expected Laurie to come for me, he did not return for nearly an hour more. During that time, we played dominoes, which she thought simple but about right for a child my age.

Though I already knew how to cheat at blackjack, I decided it would not be wise to correct her.

Laurie and I had nearly reached the firm when I felt a familiar presence in my mind and turned and saw Father coming up behind us, a wide-brimmed hat pulled low over his face.

I had not realized how much I'd missed him, and I suspect the girl's sadness coursing through me heightened the emotion. I ran to him and jumped into his arms.

As he held me close, he caught the scent of where we'd been, looked past me at my cousin. "To Amalia? I never would have expected you to do that," he said.

"To Inez. He was ready, past it actually," Laurie replied. I heard the humor in his tone.

"I suppose I should skip a visit to Amalia tonight, yes?"

"I'd wait a day. But I thought you'd be hunting."

Father put me down, moved between us. We walked for some

time before he replied, "Unlike many of the others, I spend a great deal of time in places far wilder than these peaks. A bit of perfume would have been a delightful change."

If I hadn't been so curious about why Father had come back alone, I might have missed the next comment from Laurie. —We need to discuss this child's future. And soon.—

I felt the stab of pain those words gave my father and his almost resigned reply. —Helen agrees. But after the meeting.—

We climbed awhile longer then Father and Laurie decided to return to a tavern in Chaves owned by a discreet friend of the family. I thought they would send me home alone but Father asked if I wished to come. He and I waited near the dark rear exit of an old stone tavern while Laurie went inside and arranged a place for us. The owner himself let us in through the back and gave us a table in a dark rear corner.

"It is a shame you cannot sing tonight," he whispered to Stephen and left us.

—So now you are a hunter, yes?— Father asked me, mouthing the words his mind conveyed. With the din inside, it would have been impossible to speak softly enough not to risk being overheard.

I nodded, my mind full of everything that I'd experienced in the last few hours.

He rested his hand above mine. "Now it is my turn," he said and leaned back, pulled his hat down over his eyes, and stretched out his legs on an empty chair.

The tavern's smoke made my eyes burn. The din made my ears hurt. I was beginning to think this was not at all the sort of place I liked, when someone asked the owner for a song.

I had no clue what the man was singing, only that his voice was passable and the emotions he conveyed sweet. I don't know why everyone suddenly decided to sing along but soon all the attention was on the music and my father drew my mind into his and began his hunt.

I observed as his mind touched likely prey. There were only five women there—three drunk and two nearly so—and minds unfocused are difficult to read or control. And so he studied the younger men, finding one nearly sober at a nearby table. The man had come with only enough money for one beer and so looked for a stranger to turn into a friend.

Father caught his eye, pointed to one of the glasses the owner had brought us. The man nodded and Father ordered him another.

Soon Claudio was sitting with us. He was a student come up from Coimbra to stay with his uncle. He'd drunk only half his beer when he felt a sudden need for air. Father decided to join him.

I stayed behind, but saw him through Father's eyes, leaning against the building, pulling a cigarette from the pack he'd rolled into his stocking cap, his breath as visible in the chilly mountain air as the smoke.

"I should have gone to Nazaré," he said. "I have a girlfriend there."

I shared his memory, then, of a pretty girl with a flower tucked behind one ear. They were in a park, in summer. It was nearly dark and he was thinking how he wanted to kiss her and try to slide his hand inside her blouse and wondering if she would slap his face if he did.

Father caught the wish, granted it. And so, for a little while on a warm summer's evening in a cold alley, the man did kiss and a bit more than that. And yes, she had been willing.

"I should have gone," he whispered as Father's mind slowly released him. "Maybe I should go now."

"Not tonight," Father replied and helped him back to his table. The man seemed a bit unsteady on his feet and apologized for his odd drunkenness.

"That's because you've had nothing to eat," Father said and signaled for a tavern girl to come and take an order.

We left when the meal arrived. Father had part of what he wanted. So did I. For the first time, I felt like the adult the ceremony said I was.

And thankful.

# CHAPTER 3

The family returned before dawn on January 2 to wash and sleep until afternoon when the first sessions of the long series of annual meetings would begin. Since these determined the family's as well as the firm's future, they were vitally important but no one looked forward to them.

Patrick was among the first to arrive. I'd been sleeping with Father, sharing his bed as I sometimes did in Dawson. I'd just drifted off when I felt Patrick brush against my mind, the laughter in his touch telling me that he'd had all the fun he'd expected. —Come down to Laurie's,— he called to me. —Try not to wake Stephen since Helen wants to surprise him.— I slipped out of the bed, greeting my mother quickly at the door then running down the hill to Laurie's, where I found Patrick stretched out in a steaming tub. The grime on him had made the water swampy but at least he was clean. He stood and turned on the shower to rinse off then stepped out of the tub, grinning all the while as if he'd gone completely feral.

"Did I miss so much?" I asked.

He laughed. "You know how it is when we hunt in the mountains, always with that little shred of fear that we might be seen. Up there, all of us together with the firstborn keeping watch, we shed all that care along with our clothes. And there are caves, Dickie, three of them, stocked with whatever we need. We spent our days in them, and the nights under the stars. All those visions Father used to impart, I was there. I know why they do this, I only wish I could find words to explain."

I touched him, shared the memory, the ripples of excitement as he recalled it all.

After he'd finished, I shared what Laurie and I had done. He thought that, even though the hunt had been marvelous, I'd gotten more of an education by staying behind.

"I'll show you how, first chance I get," I said and, moving close to him, drifted off to sleep.

When we woke late in the day, the annual meeting was already under way. We could have gone to it, of course, though our elders had hinted we would likely get little out of it and only be a distraction to them. Besides, what did ten-year-olds care about global warming and the homogenization of seed stock, the threat of nuclear disasters and biochemical terrorism, the future of the world's shifting alliances? We care now, of course, but at the time it was much more pleasant to act like the boys we were.

The sun set. The moon rose. The meeting went on, ending just before dawn on the following day to give everyone a chance to bathe and sleep a few hours before it started up again. No wonder the adults made certain they were well fed before it began.

Though our parents took occasional breaks to check on us, we were mostly on our own. We read and roved the grounds, hung out at Laurie's listening to Hendrix and the Beatles at a volume just shy of pain and later tried to make out the faint words coming through the static from some Basque radio station in Bilbao. We hunted on our land but, though Patrick reminded me of my promise to show him what I'd learned, I would not disobey and take him into Chaves. "When we get home we'll do that," I insisted.

But he would not listen; he started down to the village on his own. I ran after him and grabbed his arm. Furious that I would think to control him, he pushed me away. My temper responded and soon we were our usual tangle of arms and legs. It was a wrestling match born from boredom, little more. We had grown too old to do real damage to each other.

But we had been told to behave, and this was hardly behaving and far too public a display for our elders to ignore. By the time we had broken off on our own, someone on the staff had drawn Stephen out of the meeting. Of course, we could not hide how it started once it came out that Patrick had attacked first. This was all our father needed to know. "Patrick, go up to the house and stay there, alone, until I come up and talk to you. And this is one of those rare times that I hope this meeting lasts another day at least."

Patrick accepted the inevitable and obeyed. I started after him, but Stephen called me back. "I said alone," he reminded me.

So I was to be punished, too?

He caught the unshared retort. "Go down to Paul's and wait for us. Elizabeth is putting out a buffet for those who need to eat. Your mother and I will be there later."

I did as he asked and sat with the adults at the table while they discussed Vietnam and its relationship to the long-term findings of the firm's consultants. Though only a few of the ideas made any sense to me, I was happy to be included in the conversation. As everyone began to prepare to head back to the firm for the evening session, I started up the mountain alone. Stephen had not exactly said I had to stay away from my brother and I missed him.

As I approached the tall carved doors of my father's house, I saw a woman standing on the widow's walk above. I thought it might be Rachel but I could not touch her mind. Curious, I ran up the outside stairs then stopped at the top of them, looking down the length of the roof as the woman came toward me.

She'd walked only a few steps when I realized who this stranger who was family must be. Patrick and I had heard tales of Catherine, the Old One's consort, who sometimes shared the mountain keep with him or wandered off to live alone, often for years. The others believed that she had become too wild to live among men. Yet she had come here.

—For you,— she told me, the thought conveyed in oddly accented English little more than a whisper in my mind.

"But why?" I asked, thinking myself too insignificant to deserve such a long journey.

—Frn'cs takes great interest in you.—

"But how would the Old One even know I'm here?" I persisted, unable to believe that even the most powerful of my family could be aware of anything that happened so far away without a recent bonding.

She laughed silently. The ripple of it in my mind made me shiver with pleasure. —I wish I could say that I know his power to be so great, but there is an easier explanation. The men who ship the water had news of your uncle's death, your mother's rebirth . . . and of you.—

I saw the goblet she carried then, filled with the cloudy Tarda water that flows from a spring near our ancient home. It sustains us when we cannot hunt. The firstborn especially crave it. It appeared that she did as well, for she took a deep swallow of it then moved closer to me. I inhaled the sweet and wild scent of her clothes; odd yet familiar.

She took my hand and led me down the stairs and inside where she had started a fire in the hearth. —For the heat,— she replied to the question I had not thought to ask.

"Patrick," I called when I saw him lying on the sofa, eyes shut. I brushed his mind, felt nothing. The sleep she had ordered was too deep for even a twin to break.

—I am not here for him,— she said, then moved me close to the fire.

I can't say I felt fear as she got down on her knees in front of me. But I did hold my breath as she unbuttoned my shirt and slipped it off. The pants followed. When I was naked, she turned me slowly around and I began to suspect that she was . . .

—That is right. The Old One wants this look at you. And more. . . . —

She rested her palm against my chest then ran her hands down my arms, my legs. There was no gentleness in that touch, it seemed more an examination than anything else. As she did this, I could feel the heat of the fire increase and noted we had moved closer to it.

—Do you fear it?— she asked.

I shook my head. "It will not—"

She pulled me close, my back against her chest and clamped a hand over my mouth. —No words now. Do you fear it?—

—It cannot hurt me.—

—But it will cause pain.—

It was arrogant of me but I could only convey the word of the tenyears celebration, our profession of faith. —*Szekorny.*— I survive.

—Do you?—

Her left hand tightened over my mouth, the right gripped my right hand, pushing it forward into the flames. —Do not call for help, don't even think the word,— she ordered.

As I struggled to escape pain beyond anything I had ever felt, I saw her hand and mine begin to blister but her grip did not loosen, not even when our blood began to flow. And though I wanted to scream if only because I thought the act might lessen the pain, I ceased to struggle. If she could endure it, so could I.

An eternity seemed to pass in those minutes. Finally, satisfied, she pulled our hands away from the heat, but still held mine and watched our burns heal.

—You'll do,— she decided, then slid her dress off one shoulder and pulled me close to her. —Take,— she ordered.

The healing had already aroused hunger; curiosity made it all the stronger. I obeyed, not surprised when she did the same to me (and painfully).

I had expected an explosion of memory; after all, she was far older even than Denys. Yet, though she held me close for some time, there seemed to be nothing conveyed. Nothing at all except a moment of emptiness in my memory.

She pushed me away and poured some water over my hand to wash away the soot that darkened my nails. Standing, she went to the table, returning with a bundle of what looked like cured hides. She untied the rope holding them together and unwrapped an open-sided tunic made of leather trimmed with glass beads. As she slipped this over my shoulders, I inhaled that same sweet scent and understood that it had come from the mountains of my people. The tunic seemed far too large, ending just above my knees. She wrapped a long strip of hide around my waist to hold the garment against me, fastening it with a buckle worked in gold.

—It is from him,— she said.

For a moment I saw myself through her eyes, older and much larger, still wearing this garment, a perfect fit then.

She kissed me, not with passion but with the promise of it. —When you are ready,— she said.

I stared into the flames, trying to think of something to say, questions I might ask. None came to me. When I looked toward where she had been standing, I saw that she had gone.

I wanted to follow after, or seek out the family and tell them about her. But too much had happened too quickly. I felt the same great exhaustion that had trapped my brother. Wearing only the gift Catherine had brought for me, I picked up the goblet from the floor and drained it then stretched out in front of the fire and slept.

I am not certain how long I lay there, but when I opened my eyes, I saw that the logs had fallen to embers. I raised my head and noticed that the main doors were open and it was raining. Too weary to get up to close them, I crawled to the sofa and pressed close to my brother. Stealing his warmth, I returned to sleep.

I woke to my father's angry voice, the slamming of the doors. Looking up, I saw a puddle of rainwater on the wood floor in front of them. Before I could explain—as if I really could—he started toward me, then halted. I had never seen him so astonished before.

"He was here?" Stephen finally asked.

It was the scent not the shirt I wore that told him this, a scent distinctive, even to me who had never experienced it firsthand. "Catherine," I responded.

My mother came and sat beside me, gripping my hand. I sensed she wanted to ask if I was all right, and not certain that she should.

I thought of the fire, shuddered, and leaned against her.

Patrick stirred and opened his eyes. All the sudden attention on him made him certain he must be in far more trouble than before. He sat up quickly and, blinking away sleep, looked from one to the other of us.

Seeing that he was all right, Stephen turned back to me and asked gently, "What can you remember?"

I recalled the details, conveying them through words and shared memory. When I started to speak of the fire, I could not go on vocally. My mother held me tighter. I sensed my father's rage.

"How could someone do that to a child?" she asked.

I don't think she expected an answer, but Stephen provided one anyway. "We value intellect. He values endurance. I had the same done to me. So did the rest who were keep born. He calls it faith. You passed, yes?"

I sat up straighter. "She said I'd do, but . . ." I realized that there was something I had not conveyed because I did not quite understand it. "She watched us both heal," I said, showing him her face when I said this.

"She judged the time it took, just as she had judged your strength and obedience and self-control," he explained.

"Patrick, did you see her?" Helen asked.

He only looked at me, trying hard to remember something that hadn't happened. Without a word, he went to the table and looked down at the hide that had protected my gift. Coarsely cured leather, nothing unusual about it, yet he turned it over, hoping for something.

Nothing. He turned to me. "Why?" he asked.

Meaning why was I singled out? Why one gift, not two? Why no acknowledgment of him at all? He thought himself the smarter, the handsomer, the better. And nothing?

I could feel the anger boiling in him, threatening to surface in a howl of rage. I should have felt some empathy, some concern, but I am honest enough to admit that I relished the anger. Stephen might have diffused it, but more important things were on his mind. "Did she give any hint of how she got here?" he asked me.

"She mentioned the men who ship the Tarda water."

He went to the doors and opened them. Wind-driven rain beat against him, but I knew he did not feel it. His mind was already moving away from this place, down the road that led to the gates and the road to Porto, seeking her.

—How long has she been gone?— he asked me.

"I don't know. But it wasn't raining yet."

"Well over two hours," he said. Far too long a headstart for him to catch her on the road, but if she had to wait for a ship to depart . . .

He was weighing the possibilities when we heard her laughter sharp and bitter in his mind. —Do you really think you could track me if I do not wish it? I carry his power in me, strong as your child.—

Our plane droned overhead and as it headed east we shared her parting words. —Do not try to order your pilot back, lest he meet with an accident.—

Patrick pulled away from the others, tried to join with her mind by himself. She allowed it, but only for a moment, speaking to him quickly. —Do not envy your little brother. You have no need of my gifts.—

He spoke her words aloud, and I saw my mother's expression become troubled, even more than it had been when I'd told her how I'd been burned.

"What did she call him?" Helen asked Patrick, as if the phrase already meant something to her.

I glimpsed something of her past and might have learned more had she been less aware or more open.

"Little brother. That's what he is, isn't he? I was born first. Even if you hadn't told me, I would remember," he said.

She gripped us both tightly, pulling us close. "Promise me something. Promise me that you will always be ready to support each other. Whatever happens, whatever differences you may have. Always."

We were twins! How could we not? We told her so, then sat and watched Father still at the door, looking up at the sky as the rain beat down.

*You'll do.*

The words tore at my brother in a way he had never expected; Catherine's parting comment seeming no more than a bone tossed in his direction. It wasn't fair—not her visit or the gift she had left only for me. Of course, I wore that oversized shirt every chance I had, rubbing in the fact that I had been singled out. And so, for the last few days of shutdown, we stayed as far away from each other as possible.

But it wasn't just jealousy that kept us apart. The glass house drew Patrick like no place ever had. He kept close to Rachel and Denys and Father, watching them during the few hours of shutdown that they worked, asking questions and taking every possible chance to learn something new.

Meanwhile I often stayed with Laurie or Elizabeth to discuss art and music and literature. It hardly surprises me now to realize that Patrick was drawn so strongly to the doers in the firm, while I fell in with the dreamers. Our family has its share of both, though in the two of us the division seems most marked.

But we were in perfect agreement on one thing. The day before we were to leave for Canada, we both decided that we did not want to go, at least not yet. Patrick wanted to stay in Chaves with Rachel and Denys while I had already persuaded Laurie to take me to Chicago with him if our parents allowed it.

Having experienced the sharing, we had tradition on our side. So we behaved like adults, going to our parents with Laurie and Rachel, who had agreed to speak for us if their opinions were needed.

"Your mother and I have already discussed this. Now that you request it, perhaps it is time," Stephen said when we told him, then looked to his chosen to see if she agreed. Whatever he conveyed to Helen in the next few moments seemed to satisfy her because finally she nodded.

"You've been exposed to a great deal in the last week, and it's been made all the more appealing by years of isolation," he said to us. "Of course you want to see more."

"You both agree to it?" I asked, looking past him to my mother.

"For a time, yes," he responded. "Tomorrow, she and I must leave here. But though we will return to Dawson, we'll likely be living in Quebec by fall and there'll be more of the family nearby. It is still wild country but far from the wilderness of Dawson. You'll hardly be isolated any longer."

"What about the cabin?" I asked because I loved it there.

"Laurie is getting a bit too old to remain in Chicago much longer and wants the isolation to work. So there will be a place for you to enjoy a week or two of wilderness freedom if Laurie allows the company."

Freedom; I thought that an odd way to put it.

"You've been spoiled," Stephen said. "You'll understand that freedom soon enough once it's missing from your life."

Patrick and I looked at each other, then at our parents. We had no idea what they meant.

My mother explained. "First, we agree that once we are living in a more crowded place, there will be no excuse for not giving you a proper education."

"School?" I asked, astonished. I could not imagine it . . . not the desks, the teachers, the other students, and especially not lunch. I directed that last thought to Patrick, who stifled a giggle.

Helen laughed. "A tutor, we think, would be a better choice and we will start that as soon as we can. But there will be regular hours and texts you will have to read. And you will both have a chance to pursue your favorite interests, likely with other students."

"The next few months will be a test as well," Stephen added. "I want to see how well you manage apart from each other, and us. I hope that you can master all your lessons to near-perfection during the next few months."

"We will!" I all but shouted then went and hugged my mother.

As I did, I looked past her to Laurie. My bond had tightened with the one person in the family who was most like me. As for Patrick, he did not feel the same toward Rachel or any of them. It was not a person that had pulled him away from my parents, it was a place—the glass house in Chaves.

The next day, we left Patrick standing on the edge of the airfield, watching the plane take off, his mind linked to ours for as long as the distance would allow. As the bond broke, Helen's grip on me tightened. I was the child left, and only for a little while.

# CHAPTER 4

I had thought my parents would say good-bye to me in Chicago, but though their passports were created from the best forged documents money can buy, it was still wise to avoid unnecessary scrutiny. So they left the plane in Montreal. It was a frigid, snowy day and as we pulled away from the terminal, I saw them standing on the tarmac, their unnecessary wool coats making them look like any tourists as they saw us off.

I think my parting was easier on my parents than Patrick's had been. I had visited Laurie many times before and he had often come to Dawson so Mother knew him well. As for me, though I loved my parents, I loved Laurie nearly as much.

Though I would miss them, I was already beginning to view them differently: adult to adults rather than child to parents. And I knew that when I returned to them, I would be ordered never to speak of them as *mother* and *father*. An important piece of my education, since I would look my years and my parents no more than twenty-five or so. We are all cousins to the world's eye, no matter what our relationship might be. And in describing what follows, it is difficult to think of them as my parents at all.

After we left them, Stephen and Helen had no need to rush back to Dawson. They wanted to look at property in the area, and

Helen had never seen Montreal. They checked in to a restored Victorian bed-and-breakfast north of the Quartier-Latin, one with a fireplace, a huge claw-footed tub, and an iron-railed balcony overlooking a tiny city park, star-covered with holiday lights under a fine dusting of snow. In the first hours they were alone, Helen huddled close to Stephen for comfort. But that night as, arm in arm, they walked the snowy streets, some of her misery lifted. Enough that she took his hand, slowed her pace, and thrilled to the life surrounding her.

Montreal was alive for the holidays, with McGill and other Quebec college students on winter break mingling with American expatriots who had fled the draft. In that January of 1969, they filled the taverns and coffeehouses with mumblings of discontent, whispers of anarchy, and the pungent scents of marijuana and opium.

Always chameleon, my parents merged with the life around them, remarkably easy to do when the tribal dance reminded them so much of family. Helen braided her hair, fastening the ends with bright ribbons. They pulled out some of their more colorful clothing; his bead-trimmed, hers embroidered peasant style.

Helen put on the long flowered skirt she had bought in Cleveland before her changing, multiple strands of beads they'd purchased from street vendors in Vieux-Montreal, a pair of lace-up boots.

She sipped a glass of wine and studied how she looked in the long mirror in their room. Stephen came up behind her, ran his hands up under her shirt, and found that, like those of the girls proclaiming their liberation in the nearby cafes, her breasts were bare. She turned and pressed against him, laughing.

He went down on one knee, slipping the skirt off her hips. It fell into a bright puddle on the hardwood floor. His lips brushed her bare stomach and thighs as she stood, finishing the glass of wine, feeling the first euphoria of it bubbling through her, heightening desire. She could share both, and more.

"I thought we were going out," she said, laughing.

He picked her up, dropped her softly on the bed. "We have time."

Later, ardor cooled but hunger rising, they walked down Saint-Denis, stopping finally at a cafe, drawn in by an acoustic guitar, a pleasant voice. They sat at one of the little bistro tables in the back, where the cold air pouring through the half-open door diluted the smoke.

The politics here were leftist, the songs mostly by Dylan or Ochs with an occasional darker piece by an artist they did not recognize. The lyrics distracted Helen as she studied the room, settling finally on a young man in a black turtleneck and jeans sitting at a neighboring table.

She leaned toward him and asked who had written the songs the performer was playing.

"Leonard Cohen. He's a local. You can buy his first album at the store on the corner." He spoke almost absently as he looked past her at Stephen.

She caught his interest, misinterpreted. "He's just a friend," she said.

The young man stared at Stephen with franker interest. "Would you like to join us?" Helen asked.

He did, sitting between them, his eyes moving from Stephen to her and back again. Helen brushed his mind, saw where his fantasies lay. —Yours?— she asked Stephen with a bit of disappointment.

—Ours?— he suggested.

It is not usually done, being a bit dangerous for the one so used. But Helen, able to live in part on more conventional food, needed only a taste of passion to satisfy her needs. And the thrill of them hunting together was too heady for either to resist.

—Like my first time. He reminds me of that,— she responded then smiled and tapped the young man's hand to get his attention. "Do you suppose the record store is still open?" she asked. "We could walk there together."

He scanned the room, glanced at the door. "I was supposed to meet someone, but . . ." He shrugged, a gesture made all the more French when he reached for a cigarette.

Stephen moved faster, picking up the matches, lighting one and holding it up. It was natural, then, for the man's hand to steady the light. And as their fingers brushed, Helen could feel the pleasure roll through their night's choice to Stephen to her.

They would have him, preferably soon. When the song ended, he pushed back his chair and reached for his jacket. Stephen laid some money on the table and they went outside.

An exchange of first names on the quiet street. My parents used their own, no need to lie. Their choice was Henri. "Like the painter, though I am much taller," he said, as he walked between them toward the neon lights of the corner music store.

They did buy the album and two more. And since they were staying in a hotel with no place to play them, it was only natural that Henri should suggest they return to his apartment only a few blocks west. "Besides, it's late," he said. "These days it isn't good to be walking alone."

"It's hard to believe there would be any danger in a place this beautiful," Helen said.

"Deceptive beauty," Henri replied. "There are vampires afoot."

"Pardon?" Stephen asked, a hint of humor in his tone.

Henri laughed, but only a little. "That sounded melodramatic but I do not lie. Read the papers. Four murders in the last two months. One just days ago. The crimes were discussed in this morning's paper."

—Stephen?—

—Impossible. Everyone in the family was in Chaves. It must be some lunatic doing the killing or perhaps . . . —

—Some lunatic,— she replied, her mind closed to any other option.

"So we are lucky to be traveling together," Helen told Henri, and reached for his hand as if she and Stephen were suddenly rivals rather than partners that night.

Henri's apartment was only a short walk away, and they went inside into warmth that felt stifling after the chilly walk. "My landlord lives downstairs. I don't even have to turn on the heat. I suppose I should be thankful the man isn't cheap," Henri said, switching on a single lamp, its shade covered by a red silk scarf to soften its glow.

The apartment was a large single room with a wall painted in a mural of jungle vines, a mattress in one corner, a desk in another, no chairs. Helen slipped off her jacket and sat cross-legged on the carpet, Stephen on the edge of the bed.

Henri offered them wine, which they declined; tea, which they accepted, not because either had any need for it, but because anticipation would increase the pleasure later. It certainly did for Henri, who played diligent host in his galley kitchen, all the while watching Stephen put the Cohen record on the turntable.

"The singer's gotten quite a bit of recognition," Henri explained before the music began.

"Deserved," Stephen said, sitting on the mattress, his eyes closed. At first glance, he seemed to be listening to the music. And a small part of him was, but the rest was already moving through their host, brushing against his fantasies, subtly heightening them.

"Smoke?" Henri asked. "I got it from a friend. It's supposed to be pretty good stuff."

"Wasted on me," Stephen replied then glanced at Helen.

—What will it do?— she asked.

—Make you just the slightest bit giddier than you already are.—

—And him?—

—I can control that.—

She laughed and took the glass pipe Henri held out to her, inhaling as if this were some sort of happy adventure, more intense than any she had experienced before.

Henri had finished two drinks in the cafe, and now this added euphoria. It made him daring, and he sat close beside Stephen, wanting to touch him, not sure how to begin. "So you two are . . ."

"Friends," Stephen finished for him and rested his hand on top of Henri's.

It is an easy thing to take a man who so wants to be taken, and all Henri wanted was that someone else make the first move, wanted it desperately. As Stephen touched him, Henri stretched out on the bed, eyes closed, waiting for the miracle.

It came. He felt Stephen press against him, the woman too. "Thank you," he said in half a whisper, half a thought. One kissed him, then the other. He was past caring which, but the hands, the hands that moved so knowingly to remove his shirt, belonged to the man!

—Now!—

Helen moved closer, her breasts against his back, her lips against the back of his neck. A quick, nearly painless bite and his life exploded in her. Yes, she was so giddy she wanted to throw back her head and laugh. Instead she leaned past Henri and kissed her lover, quickly, playfully, sharing the passion. Another taste of the blood, all she needed, before Stephen pressed his lips over the mark she had made and fed. As he did, Helen brushed one hand down the side of Stephen's neck, the other over Henri's lips and down his chest, stopping at the waistband on his jeans.

But Henri did not know this; he was lost in a dream in which his guests were doing both less and so much more.

The album side finished, and the next record dropped onto the turntable.

"Damn good stuff," Henri whispered, then rolled onto his side and shut his eyes. Somewhere deep in his mind, he felt them still with him, hands and lips and bodies twined. In truth they had already moved away from him to stand together at his door, staying with him as he drifted off to an ordered sleep.

Helen slipped on her coat. Stephen put his over his shoulders, and they left, moving softly so their host would not wake.

They ran back to their hotel. "My Suzanne," he said as Helen fell into his arms and kissed him, Henri's passion heightening what they felt for each other.

Just before dawn, after Helen had turned away from him and shut her eyes, Stephen went down to the lobby and took the day-old *Montreal Gazette* from the coffee shop rack. He glanced over the headlines and found the story Henri had mentioned at the top of the second page. As he read the details, he was hardly surprised. He tore out the story and put it in his wallet. Later he would mail it to Denys in Chaves to place in the family file on practicing witches, psychics, self-proclaimed vampires, and alien sightings; in short, all the possibilities the world dismissed as we are dismissed. Back in the room, he stretched out beside his chosen and went to sleep.

When I was thirteen and living in the Laurentian Mountains, I took my first human lover. Louise and I stole away from her house one night and crawled into the back of her brother's Volkswagen camper with passion on both our minds. After the first awkward fumblings, I relaxed, did as all these shared memories had taught me, and at the end found myself clamping a hand over her mouth lest her cries of passion alert someone from her family on what we were up to.

We only stayed together a few months after that, but I knew when she had found another conquest. She came up to me one night, furious. "You bastard! You lied when you said I was your first," she whispered.

"I didn't lie," I replied, then looked away from her and tried not to smile. The first thought that came to mind was to tell her that I learned it all from my parents.

# CHAP+ER 5

Laurie lived in an airy apartment on the top floor of a turn-of-the-century brick building on Lake Shore Drive just south of Irving Park. It had its original dark woodwork, hardwood floors, and a working fireplace. Laurie had added sliding doors with family windows that altered the room with delicate shades of peach and orange, stunning against the pale green oriental carpets and white walls. At night, we would slide the doors open and sit on a private terrace that overlooked Lake Michigan and the heart of the city to our south. Though the flower boxes were empty and covered with ice, the dwarf trees free of all but a few dried leaves, Laurie had strung his three small pines with tiny white lights so it seemed like Christmas well into January.

We Austras are at our core nocturnal and it was always close to dawn when we went to bed. Four or five hours' rest suffices for an adult. Being young, seven or more felt better for me. When I woke, usually around noon, Laurie would have already left for work.

He spent three days a week at our corporate branch office, where he managed a staff of ten. On the other two days and often Saturday morning, he taught musical composition to a select group of students at the Chicago Conservatory of Music.

Perhaps Mozart was a more accomplished composer than my cousin but I can think of few others living or dead who are. And I know that Laurie's need to stay out of the spotlight grates at him, as it does at all of us who have some special talent for the performing arts, but he understands the necessity of it. We all do.

But his specific genius has made him more fortunate than many. Laurence Austra, the composer who wrote such an incredible wealth of classical music before he was thirty, died at the end of World War II. His nephew, a fiery pianist and one of the few in the world who can play the Austra classics without modification for either pacing or reach, has recorded a number of his famous uncle's unfinished works. Though he is far too shy to tour, he occasionally gives private performances, usually for friends or charity events. And so, Laurie keeps his own reputation alive.

Because of his teaching position, and because he supported a number of the city's performing arts, we had season tickets to nearly every major event coming to Chicago and passes that let us in to the less popular ones.

We went to shows twice the week I arrived. The first was the *Nutcracker* ballet on its last night at the Auditorium Theater; the second at a smaller theater I'd been to before and, because of what happened there some years before, would rather not name.

Laurie had been more protective of me on our last visit. Now that I was older, he let me roam the lobby and gift shop during intermission while he joined friends in the next box. When it was time to leave, we followed the crowd out the main doors into a clear and frigid night so windy that I knew how the city had gotten its nickname. I reached into my jacket for my cap, but when I tried to put it on, a gust of wind blew my hair over my forehead. Laughing, I retreated to the shelter of the doorway, brushed back the dark curls, and slipped it over my forehead. As I did, I noticed a girl two or three years older than I come out the door. She stopped when she saw me, and for a moment her soft brown eyes were wide with surprise. Then she looked away as if she didn't want to be caught staring. I buttoned my coat and went to join Laurie on the street. When I looked over my shoulder, I saw the girl walking away in the opposite direction.

I was used to being stared at. I didn't even think to mention it.

During the first few afternoons I was alone, I would watch TV— a marvelous treat for someone who had grown up without it—

read, or practice one of the classical pieces Laurie was teaching me on the piano. He also kept a naizet, the family instrument my father plays so well, and I practiced chords and strumming the double necks, hoping that one day I could be half as good.

Every evening when Laurie came home, he would ask what I had learned, making no distinction between the music, the information in the books, or the soaps I found myself drawn into each afternoon.

Day's quiz completed, I would lie back on the sofa and listen to him play. Two hours every night of old compositions, impromptu variations, new pieces in progress. I would listen to the chords, the harmonics. On the wilder pieces, I could all but hear the Bechstein's keys stretch and warm, as excited by his skill as I was.

By then it would be dark and we would slip on our coats and walk down streets teeming with life. We went to the movies or to cafes, where I sampled teas until I found one I liked. And so we could sit and eavesdrop on the thoughts of those around us.

It was not long before I became bored with my afternoons, so Laurie arranged passes to museums and theater rehearsals. I thought we would go together until he handed me a detailed map of the city which showed the bus and Metro routes. "Memorize all of it," he said.

I felt a moment of triumph, replaced just as quickly with the certainty that I must be misunderstanding his intent. "I can't go out alone," I said.

"You can. You've done admirably the last few nights."

"But people always look at me."

"That's because they find you beautiful not because they perceive you as different. The only problem you'll likely have is someone asking why you're not in school. Just tell them you're on winter break. As to age, say you're thirteen. At your size, you'll pass for three years older."

So my immensity had some use after all. "Stephen would never let me go into Dawson alone."

"Of course not. You are all too well known in Dawson, and in small towns people have little else to do but gossip about each other. One slip and, yes, there would be a problem. But this is a city and in a city when people notice something odd about someone else, they look the other way."

He paused to let me consider this, then added, "You do know what sort of people to avoid, yes?"

I sighed. "Mo . . . Helen explained all that. In great detail."

"Good." He pointed to the map. I spread it out on the table, found our building, and traced the walks we had taken. I found the places I could visit, noted the easiest routes to get there. Chicago has so many streets that I spent over an hour reading each name and seeing the patterns, committing them to memory.

When he was certain I had it down, Laurie showed me places I had to avoid.

"But why?" I asked, those neighborhoods suddenly seeming far more interesting than the rest.

"These are streets where force rules. I don't want you to be put in a position where you will have to kill."

"Like the man in the alley," I said, remembering my earlier visit and what had happened then. And because I sensed that what he had done that night troubled him, I added, "Stephen says that he would have been on the man the minute he cut me. He marveled at your self-control."

"But it wasn't enough." I sensed his sadness and slid my chair close to his, resting my hand on his knee as he went on. "I think your parents were right to raise you away from people. Keep born, he knew that you must understand what you are before you live among them and see too much likeness. I think that only the children of the Old One are prepared for the rage that fills us when we are threatened. I wasn't."

He did not speak of how he had been forced to kill far more than once in those long years of the last war. Instead he showed me and in the end we held each other. He for the touch of family; me to comfort him.

"They kill, sometimes for no reason. They destroy themselves with as great an efficiency. If I were alive for only a little while, I would cherish every day." He brushed his fingers across my forehead. —I can touch them as I am touching you, and yet when I am as old as your father I doubt I will understand them any better than I do now.—

"I won't go anywhere I'm not supposed to. I promise," I blurted and kissed him.

He looked past me at the terrace, visible through the half-open door. "Look out there," he said.

Snow had started to fall, coating his little trees and undoubt-edly the ones in the park below. Barefoot, I ran outside, leaning over the stone wall to look down at the street. It was after mid-night and the traffic was thin. The park looked empty, the white dusting waiting for some pioneers' tracks.

"Shall we go?" Laurie asked.

I didn't need a second invitation. With a whoop of excitement, I went running for my shoes and socks and the lightweight jacket and thin gloves I had to wear so I would not look too out of place in the cold.

We set out, walking the lakefront nearly as far as Belmont Street. The snow increased. The waves washing the beach grew higher and louder. I stood on a rock close to the water's edge and with arms flung wide, howled back at the growing storm.

The next day I got up just after Laurie left. I pulled on my clothes and coat, grabbed my key and bus pass and the money Laurie had left for me, and set out to explore Chicago.

I thought I would take in so many sights, but as soon as I saw the first exhibit at the Field Museum I was sorry I'd stopped any-where else.

I wandered through the antiquities in the weapons room, past rough-finished armor and medieval swords. I went back further to clubs and arrowheads and shields. I found myself thinking of my father and how he had been alive when men killed with swords and spears, crossbows and clubs. He had seen so much change. And the world moved so much faster now. What would I learn in the next century? In two?

I glanced at the exhibit doors and saw that the guard had stepped out into the hallway. Not certain I would get another chance, I went to an alcove holding an assembled set of armor and a battleax. I licked my finger and, standing on tiptoe and stretching to my full reach, I ran it down the dull edge of the blade.

Moving away quickly, I backed into a shadowy corner and tasted. Rust. And if there had once been something more, some possibility of a bond, it had fallen to dust years ago. Now the only way to touch that past was through our oldest—Stephen and Denys and Rachel.

Suddenly in need of family, I headed for the main entrance. When I reached the lobby, I looked through the doors and saw that it was already dark. I called the conservatory to tell Laurie where I was and caught him just as he was leaving. "Field Museum, is it? I spent my first week in Chicago there," he said. "Come down here and meet me and we'll walk home together."

Moving quickly for the door, I brushed against a sandy-haired man standing behind me, apparently waiting to use the phone. "I'm sorry," he said. He spoke with an accent and stared at the floor.

"My fault," I replied, thinking that something about him seemed familiar.

He moved away from the phones without looking at me, which seemed the way most people functioned in the city. But there was more than disinterest in how he had avoided letting me see his face, as if he knew me already and wanted to hide. Curious, I waited until he'd gone some distance, then followed him toward the rear exhibit halls.

The guard told me the museum would be closing soon. I mumbled something about having forgotten my hat and quickened my pace to keep up with the man, slowing down when I had him back in sight. No need for him to know I was trailing him.

The earlier crowds had thinned, enough that I had to walk softly on the marble floors so he would not hear. Had I been Stephen, or even Patrick, I might have touched his mind without effort. But I am not so strong even now. Then I would have needed to be much closer to him and I feared that he would see me and I would frighten him away.

He went into a washroom while I waited behind a post outside. When I heard the washroom door open, I froze as he all but passed me by and went to a nearby public phone.

The place had become quiet, so quiet I did not even have to strain to hear the coins falling, the man's voice as he said a quick hello, a mention of where he was, then words that seemed so clearly about me. "I've followed him all day. Tell the others that what Irena said was true. The young one has come back."

While I stood shaking at the implications of his words, he hung up and started toward the exit. I couldn't let him go; I had to know why he was so interested in me. Without really thinking about the unfocused state I was in, I thrust my mind out and into his.

I do not have the deft touch that Patrick does, but even without a blood bond, I should have gotten some insight into this man's thoughts. But there was nothing except a brief rush of fear when the man inexplicably sensed what I'd done and swung around to look me straight in the face for the first time.

The fear focused and I saw myself and Laurie through his light brown eyes. He was looking down at us, at the killing in the theater alley several years before. "You were there," I whispered.

When he heard this, his fear grew stronger, so strong I could smell it. He might have been facing Stephen for all the terror he felt. It made me braver.

"Why were you following me today?" I demanded.

He said nothing, only backed away until he'd put a few more meters between us, then turned and fled down a hallway. I ran after him, heedless of the guard calling that we had to leave.

The corridor ended with an exhibit door, already closed and locked for the night. With no place to run, he turned to face me. I repeated the question, demanded an answer.

In response, his hand moved slowly into his coat pocket. He pulled out a knife.

He was far larger than I, and armed. But I'd had the sharing. If I had any doubt what I was capable of, the visions of my family made me certain. Calm for the first time, I stood my ground and waited.

The hall was only a few meters wide, enough that I doubted he could get away. But he tried, rushing forward on my left, almost fast enough, but not quite. I snagged his arm but he was twice my weight and a good foot taller. He kept going, pulling me along with him. Though I did not want to hurt him, I needed an answer and tightened my grip on his arm. He stifled a scream. "I'll crush the bone. I mean it," I told him and squeezed harder.

He stopped moving but said nothing. I tried to convey that he should calm down, that I only wanted to talk to him, but my attempt only made his fear increase. When he saw I would not let go, he slashed my arm then stabbed deep into the back of my hand with his knife, a move he knew was foolish the moment I released him and he heard my cry of rage.

I wanted to lunge for his throat but something held me back long enough for him to take his only chance to survive. He threw the bloody knife on the floor, turned, and fled for the safety of the lobby, its crowd, and the exit.

I felt dizzy, not from blood loss but from emotion, and by the time I thought to follow him, prudence had taken over. I picked up the blade and used my cap to wipe the blood from it, then from the floor.

My arm had nearly stopped bleeding by the time I'd cleaned away most of the traces of myself, but my jacket and shirtsleeve were soaked with blood. I slipped off the jacket and laid it, clean side up, over my wounded arm and the knife I held in that hand. Taking a deep breath, I squared my shoulders and walked slowly past the guards to the doors. They suspected nothing as I left, nor did the cabdriver who took me to the conservatory.

But Laurie knew. Even before I walked into his office he was already on his feet and coming around his desk to catch me as I collapsed, trembling with fear, into his arms.

# C H A P + E R  6

Laurie held me close on the cab ride home, as if by holding me he could stop the shaking that I could not control on my own.

Once we were safely inside his apartment, he took off my coat and shirt and studied the wounds. Though they were nearly healed, he could still see the length of them, and from the blood on my shirt, gauge how deep they had been.

Without a word, he led me into the bathroom where he helped me undress and step into a warm shower. Only then did he leave me.

I came out wrapped in his robe and we sat in the living room in front of the fire that had already claimed my ruined shirt. He took my hand and as softly and gently as his own anger would allow, he merged with my mind.

—Show me,— he asked.

And though it brought a new bout of trembling, I did. Laurie's face grew taut as he watched the man lunge and cut and run. Then I told him how I had seen myself through the man's eyes as he'd watched Laurie and me in that theater alley. I showed his face.

"I know him," Laurie said. "He's been a volunteer usher for conservatory recitals for the past few years." I could feel him try-

ing to come up with some likely explanation but there was none
that made sense. There had been no light in that alley the night
we were attacked, barely enough for my eyes to see the man's
shadow behind the glass yet he had seen me and remembered me.
And how he had reacted to me earlier that day showed he knew
what I was.

"Or who *I* was," Laurie said after he caught my train of
thought. "We're not exactly a poor family, Dickie. He may have
been planning a kidnapping."

Laurie didn't believe it, though, and neither did I. "He knew,
and so I stood my ground, at least until he attacked."

"How did you do it?" he asked me. "How did you keep from
killing him?"

"I . . . I . . . I felt the rage starting in me but I couldn't hurt
him! By the time I thought I could, he'd already run from the
fight." I looked away from him, ashamed for what I hadn't done.

Catherine's words came back to me with a different sort of
understanding. *You'll do,* she had said. I'd been so proud to hear
her say them, but perhaps I had misunderstood. Perhaps I had
barely passed.

"Not true," Laurie said. "Restraint is a gift, Dickie, one we
would all gladly share if we could."

He thought he was making me feel better but he wasn't, not at
all. Something was lacking in me, something important. I did not
question why I had never noticed its lack before since I had never
been called upon to use it.

"Not true," Laurie repeated. We sat without speaking for a
time, then he said, "You've been wounded. You should feed."

"I don't want to go anywhere," I said. "Not tonight."

"All right." He pulled me close, the invitation unmistakable.

One of my human friends speaks of comfort food. For us there
is the blood of family. And as Laurie held me, his warmth filled
me. His life, his love. And I could feel the other emotions he
wanted to impart but could not find for himself . . . calm and
peace. I tried to yield to them, and even succeeded for a time.

"I'm tired," I whispered, though it was early evening, a time I
should have been most awake.

"Then sleep."

I started to move away from him but he picked me up and carried me to bed. Stretching out beside me, he rubbed his hand over

my back in slowly expanding circles until my eyes shut. He was thinking of the boy and girl he had raised after their mother died. They had been fortunate to have him, as was I.

When I woke late the next morning, I heard Laurie's voice. I found him in the study, where he had just hung up the phone.

"I went out after you were asleep," he told me. "The conservatory had a recital last night. I hadn't intended to go but under the circumstances it seemed best to catch the end of the show and see if I could find the man."

He hadn't. His expression made that clear enough. "He knew," I mumbled.

"He did. But since most people guess only part of the truth, I thought I'd try." As I considered this, he added, "I just finished talking to Hunter. He agrees that this is a security matter and will be flying in tomorrow."

Gregory Hunter, the head of our firm's security, was coming here! "It's not that important," I said, wishing for the third time in as many weeks that less of a fuss were being made over me.

"It is important, Dickie. I told you about the war, but I never completely explained why I was taken. They wanted what they called a 'young one' because they knew we are weaker when we are young. That could be what this one wants too."

Laurie had been shackled, tortured, experimented on. I tried to forget the horror of his past but it was threatening to shatter my calm into another fit of trembling.

"So, I am sorry, Dickie, but I don't think it would be wise for you to go out alone for a while. I've freed a few days to see the sights with you. Where would you like to go first?"

I'd picked out a dozen places but answered with the first idea that came into my mind. "I want to go and find the man that attacked me," I said, my voice even, determined. I felt certain my request must be granted since it was what anyone else in the family would do under the circumstances.

I followed his thoughts. A man could easily leave a job, but a dwelling took more time. If we traced him now . . .

"What could Hunter do that we couldn't?" I asked.

"Kill without remorse," he replied, only half joking.

I thought of my attacker's face again, how I could actually see his pulse throbbing in his temple as he looked at me with such terror that . . .

"Very well. Get dressed and we'll try," Laurie agreed.

I'd expected him to put up more of an argument before I won. I suppose he saw the inevitable ending and decided not to bother.

By late afternoon, following a visit to the theater where the man had volunteered, we knew a few important things about him. His name was Lev Konovic. His family was from the Ukraine and he lived alone a few blocks inland from Western Avenue on Devon. The theater manager who told us all of this forgot we'd asked the moment we had the information then poured us each another cup of tea and inquired how we'd been enjoying their latest concert series.

We waited until evening when a visit would be more easily hidden then started for Devon Avenue. Laurie had the taxi driver drop us off on Western and we walked the rest of the way.

As we traveled down Devon, I saw sari shops and Indian food stores interspersed with pizza parlors, Mexican restaurants, and all-purpose grocery stores. A multiethnic neighborhood, and with our dark hair and eyes, skin pale but with a faint tinge of olive, we hardly looked out of place.

Laurie and I had chosen nearly the same clothing, the American uniform of blue denim jeans, black sweaters, and dark pea coats. If anyone noticed that we moved a bit more gracefully than other pedestrians slogging home from work through badly plowed piles of slush, they dismissed it.

Lev Konovic's apartment was on the third floor of a dingy brick building on the south side of the street. A tattered FOR RENT sign with a phone number was posted on the front door. We reached his rear unit by walking through a narrow space between the building and its equally dingy neighbor and up an outside flight of unpainted wooden stairs. As we climbed, I saw that someone had used Day-Glo pink spraypaint to make peace symbols on the first two landings. I wondered if our quarry had done this, and if he thought such a silly thing would protect him.

Each rear apartment had windows on either side of its door which opened onto the stairway. Fortunately, no one was home to notice us. When we reached the landing outside of Konovic's rooms, we saw that his windows were shuttered and drapes were drawn behind these as if even at this height he felt the need for darkness and privacy.

Or perhaps he did not understand everything and thought he was preparing the space for me. Perhaps . . .

—No matter, you're with me,— Laurie said, motioning me to stand between the left side of the door and the window, my back against the bricks. He did the same on the right side and shut his eyes, his mind moving where his other senses could not.

—Don't touch his mind. He'll know,— I reminded him and got a quick wave of his hand in response.

Too unsettled for the necessary concentration, I did not merge with my cousin. Instead I waited, hands flat against the wall, for some sign that the man was inside. A full minute passed before I saw Laurie frown and shake his head as if to clear it.

—Is he there?— I asked.

—He is. He has a gun. I did not touch his mind but he sensed us anyway. He's sitting just inside the door with the weapon aimed at himself.—

—Can you stop him?—

—If I was your father, perhaps. Given his insight, I am not even sure of that.—

I shut my eyes and drew on my best mental strength: controlling others' emotions. I thought, —Calm,— I thought, —Peace,— and I directed it at all of us. I could not sense the man's emotions, was afraid to try.

"We come only to talk," Laurie called. "You have no reason to be afraid of us."

No reply but I heard a click. I guessed what it must be. Laurie knew.

He spun to face the door and gave a hard kick. As the door burst inward, I heard the shot, saw the spray of blood and flesh, hair and bone explode past me to land at my feet and spew over the side of the porch. My left shoe was spattered, my pants as well. I leaned forward and glanced at Laurie, who had managed to jump back quickly enough to avoid most of the mess. Then, because a child's curiosity has to be satisfied, I looked at the victim and felt suddenly queasy.

Sometimes, the oldest say, they can touch a mind after death, but only if there is a mind left to touch. I wondered if the man had known this, or guessed, or merely wanted a quick and painless death.

But I only had time to consider these matters later. Someone was pounding on the man's front door, saying he'd had enough of the man's lunacy and now this shot and no use arguing since his wife had already called the police.

Laurie scanned the dingy kitchen and saw no note. This had not been a suicide, but an act of terror. He backed out the door and leaned over the rail. Sensing no one watching below, he told me to jump. My feet slipped as I hit the snowy ground but he was beside me, steadying me. We kept to the alleys, moving as quickly as we could through the growing dark without attracting attention. Three blocks later, certain we were not being followed, we stopped in a shadowed alley, retreated behind a Dumpster, and used the lining of my coat to clean me off. Presentable enough then, we walked a few blocks and signaled for a taxi.

Once home, Laurie sponged off my dirty coat. Then we showered together and met in the living room in front of the fire, staring into the flames for some time before either of us said a word to the other about the death or anything else.

"It's over," I said, breaking the silence.

He shook his head. "It's likely just begun."

—Irena right,— I thought and felt his troubled assent.

Gregory Hunter arrived from London late the next afternoon, dropped his damp suitcase on the rug in the foyer, and hung his soggy macintosh in an empty corner of the empty guest closet in the smallest bedroom as if he had always lived here. Whatever color his hair had been had long since faded to salt and pepper and his face was lined by too many seasons spent outdoors. He had a scar across one cheek and a nose slightly off center from his beatings by the Gestapo during the war. There were scars on his hands and arms as well and he claimed he could feel the change of weather in the ill-healed cracks in his ribs. But for all of that, I doubted there were many men half his age that would be able to stand up to him.

He was fifty-eight, a few years older than Laurie. We considered him family, especially now that he was Ann's lover, bonded to all of us through her blood and the added years she had chosen to grant to him.

None of which had diminished his taste for good scotch. Laurie poured him a drink and he settled into a chair close to the fire. "On a day like this I feel every bit of that lousy war," he told Laurie then looked at both of us with something akin to paternal affection. Amenities quickly set aside, he focused his attention on me.

"So you've already had your first adventure in the big city," he said. "Tell me about it."

While he sipped his drink, I related everything that had happened from the attack in the alley to the museum to the man's suicide the previous night. Then, because Hunter thought it important, I rested my hand over his and, with the bond strengthened by touch, I showed it to him.

Hunter looked from Laurie to me. Laurie is tall, but like all of us, so deceptively delicate in appearance. I was sixty-one inches and slightly under a hundred pounds. "And so an armed man shot himself rather than face the fearsome-looking two of you?" He gave a grudging smile. "Well, true, you both are fearsome, and I'd expect most people would agree if they knew anything about you. But how did he? And why did that lead to his suicide?"

"And who received his phone call, and who the hell is Irena?" I added. It seemed to be my life most affected by all of this, and I wanted the matter ended as soon as possible.

"It's in our favor that he's an émigré—and from a Communist country, too. If I can't find out enough about him through the usual means, the bureau may have information on him or his family. And immigration reports will likely state exactly where he came from."

"Do my parents know about this?" I asked, certain that if they did my time with Laurie would be measured in days rather than months.

"They're a bit out of reach at the moment. Denys is trying to find them but does not think this so important that we can't handle it on our own. But he did want me to ask you something. He said I must ask how well you can control minds."

"I'm learning. If I touch them, I can make them see what I want and forget me after," I replied.

"And you can read them?"

"Read minds? If I am close to someone, it's easy."

"Easy, is it? Good. Because Denys tells me that since you're the one who's been threatened, you must be involved in this. He said your nature demands it. Is that how you feel?"

As Hunter asked this, I sensed Laurie's relief. If Denys had suggested this, no one in the family would disagree with Laurie's decision to take me with him the night before.

"I need to go," I replied.

"Good. I like having one of the family along. It keeps people honest. And Laurie might be too fearsome, so a small boy is better, yes?" Those last words were a perfect imitation of my father. And he meant most of it. I was glad of that.

# CHAPTER 7

The next morning—far earlier than I was used to and a bit later than Hunter would have preferred to start—I joined him in the kitchen. I hadn't been sure what to wear so I settled for the look of a kid on a school outing—dress slacks and shirt and a V-neck sweater. Hunter looked as if he hadn't changed from the night before. His tan pants were rumpled, the green turtleneck frayed at the cuffs. Comfortable clothes; not memorable ones. He preferred them that way.

He had found the building's landlord through the number I recalled from the vacancy sign of the building and had also started others tracing the Konovic family. Delegated work complete, he sat reading the morning paper, sipping coffee, and finishing the second bagel he'd bought from the little bakery at the end of the street.

He slid the metro section across the table to me, pointing out a brief mention on page three of a body found in a Devon Avenue apartment. A suicide, the one-paragraph account noted. At least we didn't have to be concerned about the police.

"It's time." Hunter started to get up, then glanced at me and stayed in his seat. He pulled up his sleeve and held his wrist out to me.

I took it, thankful I did not have to ask. What we did was a simple thing, a blood bond that required hardly more than a quick taste. I scraped my own wrist and held it out to him.

This should have taken no more than a moment, but I found myself thinking of the dead man's terror and began to shake.

Hunter pulled me close to him, holding me while I drew on his confidence, his strength. If I gave him anything in return for his gift to me, it was likely the terror Konovic felt just before he pulled the trigger.

We went first to the owner of the dead man's building, his apartment only a few blocks away from the place where Konovic had died. After we were buzzed into a dingy lobby, I waited until Hunter had entered the landlord's apartment then followed softly down the narrow hallway, which reeked of cabbage, cigars and damp plaster, and stood outside the landlord's door. His apartment, like the hallway, was chilly and the man stood in his living room, his back to the radiator on the same wall I leaned against. Proximity made it easy for my mind to touch his.

The man had expected to meet a prospective renter for a first-floor apartment. When Hunter introduced himself as a representative of Konovic's family, the landlord did not bother to hide his anger. "In the few months Lev was there, he trashed the place. The day he died, he broke in his own door. Then he shot himself in my kitchen. There's gore everywhere and the damn bullet cracked the tile above the sink. I've been renting in this neighborhood for twenty years and never had anything like this. Tell his family that they won't get any return of his security deposit from me!"

None of Hunter's disgust leaked to his expression as he replied, "They aren't after money but they wonder if they owe you some. For rent, or for damages?"

To the man's credit he did not lie. "He was paid up. But the cleaning will take more than the deposit and I'll have to repair and paint the kitchen."

"Will an extra two hundred dollars do?" Hunter asked.

Twice what the man would have asked for, but money spent gives the best information.

"And I'll need a copy of his lease," Hunter went on.

"Lease? Not a problem. I'd've shown it to the police last night but they never asked for it." He dug through a desk drawer then handed it over. Though Hunter had asked for a copy, the man said nothing as Hunter put the original in his pocket.

"And a key to poor Lev's apartment," Hunter continued. "The family would like to get his photographs and personal things, and perhaps pick up his utility bills so they can pay them. They want to make things right for you. I'm sure you understand."

"I was told to wait until the police said it was all right before I let anyone in. I don't want any trouble with them."

"There won't be any trouble if I go there alone," Hunter explained.

At Hunter's urging, I gave the man a subtle push. "Well . . ." the old man said, wondering if Lev owned anything of value he might have missed in the half hour he'd taken inventory after the suicide.

Another push.

"Well, if you promise to stay out of the kitchen," he decided.

"That room would likely give me nightmares," Hunter replied and the man, suddenly thinking too vividly of the scene, nodded and handed over a key.

The landlord hadn't exaggerated. Konovic's apartment was filthy, the few pieces of furniture old and tattered as if he'd salvaged them from curbs and alleys. It also reeked of stale blood and cigarette smoke. I stood close to the bedroom window we'd opened moments after we arrived, gulping in fresh frigid air while Hunter sifted quickly through the dead man's bureau and desk and a side table next to his wall phone. He found nothing but a stack of utility bills. Hunter scanned the one for the telephone and, though no long-distance calls had been made, put it in his pocket.

When he went into the kitchen, I followed but only as far as the doorway. The smell was thicker there, dead, rancid, and not just from the suicide. One corner of the room had a pile of refuse, dumped it seemed from a metal wastebasket nearby. Hunter reached into the basket and pulled out a piece of paper almost completely burned.

"He must have done this the same night you fought," he said.

But Konovic had forgotten the lease, or else could think of no way to get it back. We had a previous address, which turned out to have been a lie, and the name of his employer.

As before, I waited outside while Hunter went into the offices of the small meat-processing plant where Konovic had worked.

But though Konovic had been working there for almost three months, no one seemed to know much about him.

His employer, an old Romanian who had been in this country since the end of the war, had not known of Konovic's death, but felt no surprise. "He kept his own company," he said. "No family that he spoke of. No friends. Troubled."

He added that he had requested no credentials when he'd hired Konovic. "When I came here, I was thankful when no one asked for mine," he explained. "And given the pigs who control Eastern Europe today, I would be the last to make things hard on another DP."

"Why did he apply here?" Hunter asked.

"Why? He answered an ad, gave someone who works here as reference."

"And that man?"

"He quit."

The old man was lying. I told Hunter so. I decided to give the man a subtle push to be truthful but they were both deep in the building, and I could barely touch his mind let alone direct it. I walked around the corner and saw an employee entrance halfway down the side. As I neared it, I felt my bond with Hunter strengthen. I sat on a wooden bench next to the door and gave the owner a push.

"So you are telling me that after so many months he had no friends in your employ?" A question, but Hunter's tone made it sound like a threat.

"Well, there was—" The man stopped speaking as abruptly as he had begun, but not before he said the name in his mind. I shared that with Hunter as well.

"What about Jules Ruse? He still works here, doesn't he?" Hunter asked.

The man pressed his lips together, thinking it best to say nothing rather than be caught in another lie. "Why do you want to talk to him? What has he done wrong?" he finally asked.

"Nothing. But before he died Lev Konovic threatened my employer. I want to make sure he acted alone."

As the owner considered this, I understood that he knew nothing about us. He would have been this evasive with anyone to protect his own. In an instant, Hunter knew it as well and his tone softened as he continued, "And if I could be assured that those threats were only the ravings of an already insane man, then there would be no need to contact the police or any other authority."

"You swear?"

*"Jur pe mormântul mamei mele."*

"You speak Romanian. Why?"

"My mother was born in Moreni. I swore on her grave." Not knowing the man's politics, Hunter did not add that he had fought in that country with partisans as a U.S. agent during the war.

"And I am from Tinca, which makes me a sometimes-Hungarian. But then, we are all Americans now, eh? You come back tomorrow. You can talk to Jules then."

A dismissal. I took a deep breath and exhaled, untangling my mind from Hunter's.

From somewhere far away, the three o'clock whistle blew and people started coming out of the warehouse across the street. The door beside me opened. Thinking Hunter would be with the group, I looked up but saw only a handful of workers on their way to lunch.

Hunter followed them out. As I stood to leave with him, I saw one of the workers break from the group and head for a rusty yellow car parked further down the street. He'd already put some distance between us and I did not try to touch his mind, not even when he turned to glance back at me as he unlocked the car door. Instead I noted the license plate of his car.

I gave the number to Hunter as we walked around the corner to our own. "I'll have it traced." he said. "If I don't talk to him tomorrow, I can see him at his home. Now, let's stop at Laurie's and see what we've discovered about his family."

There was only one relation, a Ion Konovic who lived a mile or so north of Laurie's, on Sheridan near Lane Park. His phone was not listed, and rather than take the time to obtain it, Hunter decided on the surprise approach.

The man's building, newer than those around it, had a dozen white marble stairs leading up to a lobby with a harlequin-patterned floor in black and white ceramic, white marble walls and ceiling, and a crystal chandelier. A guard about Hunter's age sat at a center desk, the building directory on a console in front of him. "Maybe we should go home and put on suits and ties," Hunter mumbled, then leaned against a post and studied what he could see of the building.

"Can you get me in without that guard buzzing upstairs, Dickie?" he finally asked.

"I can."

We silently went over a quick plan. I went up the stairs alone, kicked the snow off my shoes, and walked straight to the desk. "Excuse me, sir," I said. "Is there a bathroom on this floor?"

"Are you a guest?"

"My father and I are coming to visit my uncle. He wanted me to wait outside while he parked the car but he's been gone awhile and I got cold."

"Who is your uncle?" He was looking at the directory as he asked this.

"Ion Konovic. He's on the . . . third floor. Apartment 306, I think." I covered my hesitation. "I'm sorry if I'm wrong but I've only been here twice."

"Well, you have a good memory. Now if you go to the right . . ." He leaned over the desk to point the way to the bathroom. As he did, I slipped and fell hard against the desk. He reached out to steady me and I grabbed for his hand. Mental bond formed, I willed him to sleep long enough for Hunter to get past him to the elevator, holding the door until I'd joined him. I released the guard as our door closed.

As I had before, I waited until Hunter had gone into the apartment, then moved close to the door. Given how Lev Konovic had reacted when he sensed my presence, I would not touch the man unless I had to. So I watched the meeting through Hunter's eyes.

Even by my family's standards, Ion Konovic's suite was sumptuous. Inlaid wood floors, restored antiques, walls of windows that, like Laurie's, overlooked the lake. Most intriguing were the Helen Wells watercolors in the foyer and the cut crystal AustraGlass bowl on the center of his mahogany dining room table.

Though they lived in markedly different circumstances, Ion Konovic resembled his brother. He was older by at least ten years, with unruly brown hair streaked with gray. But he had the same height and build, the same round face, the same deep-set brown eyes as the man who had died.

But while Lev was filled with nervous energy that rapidly shattered into terror, Ion exuded confidence. It showed in how he invited Hunter into his rooms after only a handshake and quick exchange of names, offered him a seat, and made it clear that he

had already surmised what the visit concerned even before
Hunter gave his brief explanation. Ion spoke with the same Eastern European accent as his brother, but in him it was far less pronounced. I guessed that this man did not associate with others
from the Old Country, and had instead made a place for himself
in the new.

"Lev phoned me the night he died, Mr. Hunter. He told me
everything."

"You must have sensed how desperate he was," Hunter
replied.

"Lev was always desperate. He drank, Mr. Hunter. I suspect
he used drugs as well though drink alone will destroy a mind.
The family offered to pay for a long stay at one of the better treatment centers, but he refused us. He had so many gifts that he
squandered. On his downward spiral, he fell into delusion and
paranoia. He believed in all the legends at the end—the liderc,
the kisassony, the satyr, the old ones. Whenever the family would
meet with him, he would speak of nothing else.

"Eventually, we tried to have him committed, but since he
could seem remarkably lucid when necessary, we were not suc-
cessful. After that, he began avoiding us. I am sorry for how he
died, but I do not mourn him. I believe I speak for all the family
in saying we are relieved his suffering is over except, of course,
for poor Irena, who thinks she was the cause of his sad end."

Hunter, who had not mentioned the woman's name, followed
the next words with particular interest.

"You see, a few years ago, my brother witnessed something—
he never made it clear precisely what—that convinced him that
the old ones existed . . . here, in Chicago. I admit that I have seen
some of the Austra family at events here and in New York. At the
last, I bought my favorite paintings." He waved toward the watercolors in the foyer. "Yes, Lev was right. Your employers do resemble the legends, but that proves nothing.

"What I cannot understand is what he thought he saw. But I
told him this: A wealthy man who does not know self-defense is a
fool. And, given the outcome of that attack, like Laurence Austra,
I would have left that alley as quickly as he did."

Hunter understood the warning in that last comment and
chose to ignore it. A response might silence the man and he suspected that most of what he was learning was the truth.

"Lev could not be discouraged," his brother continued. "He returned to that hovel he preferred to our home. He watched. When he understood that the object of his delusions often attended that theater, he cleaned himself up enough to volunteer, to obtain a name and address. It's a wonder Laurence Austra was not aware of his interest. Lev must have hidden it better than I would have expected."

"Given who he is, Laurence Austra is used to being watched, particularly at classical performances," Hunter replied.

"Of course. And of course, Lev's ravings made us all the more aware of that family. So when Irena was at the theater a few nights ago and saw the boy she believed Lev had mentioned, she made the mistake of telling Lev about it. And so . . ." He ended the sentence with a shrug, a wry smile.

"But why the terror when your brother only faced a child?"

The grim smile vanished, replaced with a look of genuine pain. "He thought the child would steal his life and his soul. So his fear of that boy defied all reason. And yes, it would have been enough to push him over the edge.

"You see, Mr. Hunter, Lev believed."

Konovic stood, implying that Hunter should do the same. But Hunter remained where he was, sending me a warning to retreat, then asking, "May I speak to Irena?"

"She is only a child and most upset. Because of that, no. Now, if you please, I do have to go out myself in a little while. I have a funeral to plan."

At the door, Hunter stopped to ask where the man had come from. "I was born in the southern Ukraine. Spent a bit of time in Romania and then Germany before I saved the money to come here. My family came later.

"Funny. Lev was only a baby when he came to this country. Yet he was the one with one foot planted too firmly in the old soil. In the end it killed him. A pity, yes?"

As we took the elevator down, Hunter was well aware that every part of that meeting to that final cold "yes," inflected in an accent deliberately similar to my father's, had been intended as a polite but firm warning.

He was still mulling over what sort of advice to offer the family when we walked quickly past the oddly distracted guard.

Once outside, he asked that I let him be for a time while he formed his own opinion of how we should proceed.

"Let's walk back," he suggested. As we cut south then across Lake Shore Drive, he automatically reached for my hand as if I were his child and needed protection. It was likely a habit held over from those brief years when Hunter had married, fathered two children, then realized a bit belatedly that a split-level in suburban Virginia and a desk job with Hoover's goons would have left him dead by fifty. By the time the family made him an offer, he had divorced and was holding on to the bureau job only for the security it gave his ruptured family.

We, of course, offered much, much more.

He thought of his family as we walked, contrasting his concern for them with Ion Konovic's lack of it for his brother and our own in which the death of one of us would haunt us all for centuries.

It was early evening and already dark by the time we neared Laurie's building. Since my cousin wouldn't be home for another hour or two, we stopped by a nearby steak house so Hunter could have dinner. The happy hour crowd was starting to grow at the bar so we chose a quiet table in the rear.

Hunter ordered, seemingly for both of us, a trick he'd discovered while dining out with Laurie's sister, Ann. After the waitress left, he fell silent again, lost in thought, finally asking, "Well, Richard, I'd like your opinion. Should I advise your cousin to keep up this investigation or drop it?"

I considered, then thought aloud, "Fa . . . Stephen says one should never ignore a threat that may be serious."

"He's right. I'm asking if you feel this is serious."

"Instinct?" When Hunter nodded, I took his hand again, something that made the waitress just bringing his coffee, "my" chocolate shake, and our glasses of water smile.

As soon as she left us, my mind went back to Hunter's half hour in that plush apartment, listening to that man's voice and Hunter's assessment of it, waiting for some decision to come to me. But there was nothing but what little logic a ten-year-old might muster. "He believes, doesn't he?" I asked.

"That he does."

"And he has for a long time."

Hunter grinned. "Thank you, Richard."

I wasn't certain I'd given him an answer but he seemed to

think I had. I sipped my water while he drank the shake, passing it to me when I asked for a taste. I dipped my finger in the foamy top and licked it. It tasted bitter as my mother's chocolates, and as disgusting as the water in this crowded city.

# CHAP+ER 8

It was fully dark when we stepped outside. At our corner, I glanced across the street. The same yellow car the man from the meat plant had been driving was parked in a loading zone.

I tapped Hunter's arm to get his attention and pointed it out.

"Come on," Hunter said, right hand dipping into his pocket for the building key.

There is secured underground parking for Laurie's building accessed via a steep sloping driveway next to the main entrance. The drive veers slightly to the right and levels out in front of a metal garage door that could be opened only with a tenant's passkey. As we passed the driveway, we heard a man call out from below, "Mr. Hunter, please. I need speak to you. To you and the young one both."

—Hunter?—

—Go upstairs, Richard. See if Laurie is there. If he is, tell him to come down.—

I didn't have to leave Hunter to do that and he knew it. He was afraid that this was indeed a planned kidnapping. It has happened before and those who know what we are—

I cut off that thought. I would not allow Hunter's fears to affect me. —He isn't home yet,— I told Hunter then moved closer to him and studied the man.

Like the one who had died, he was in his twenties; sandy-haired and round-faced, though thin. He wore black jeans, a thin soiled tan jacket. He was visibly shaking, not from the cold but from fright and it was all directed at me. Nonetheless, he did not back away as we approached.

"Shall we talk upstairs?" Hunter suggested.

The man shook his head. "In open where there are people. You name place."

"We speak here then," Hunter said.

The man glanced up at the sidewalk. Though we were in the dark, there were occasional pedestrians passing by. All he had to do was call out to get help. "Here will do," he decided, inhaled, then paused.

I think he'd expected a few more minutes to calm his fear and organize his thoughts, and so had not rehearsed where to begin. Sensing his nervousness, Hunter prodded, "You are Jules Ruse?"

The man nodded.

"And you are related to the man who died?"

"We are cousins, both from Ukraine. From west of the River Dniester. All our families. We are orphans of Stalin and the war; children of storm."

Despite the chilly air, the man's forehead was moist. And though we did our best to make no move toward him, his heart pounded. "What are you afraid of?" I asked.

"We have been warned to never speak of this. Especially not to you. But we must. This is free country. Let us live."

—Richard, does any of this make sense to you?— Hunter asked me. I shook my head.

"You have to be clearer," Hunter said. "We don't understand."

Ruse pointed at me. "He does!"

"I do not!" I retorted.

"Then someone lies . . . lies even to you!"

"No one lies," I whispered, longing to show him what I could of our sharings, to make it clear that nothing could be hidden. I did not dare touch his mind.

"Someone lies," Ruse repeated.

There is only one who does not bond with us, I thought, but could not speak of him. Before I could say anything more, a

large, dark-colored car with four men in it pulled into the drive.
Thinking it belonged to one of the residents, Hunter and I moved
over to let it pass. As we did, it roared forward, slamming into
Ruse, crushing his legs against the metal garage door. The impact
blew out the car's lights but I did not need them to see what happened next. The Ukrainian folded forward, his body resting on
the hood. The car lurched backward, and the victim fell facedown
onto the concrete drive.

I noticed Hunter's right hand instinctively drop to his side for
the weapon he usually carried. But this was Chicago and he was
no longer with the bureau. He had not thought this matter serious
enough to break the law by carrying a weapon.

I thought the driver would take off or hit the man again and
kill him. Instead the passengers on the right side got out and
started dragging the injured man toward the open rear door.

Hunter conveyed a quick plan that might work.

Though I understood, Jules Ruse had stolen my attention. He
hadn't made a sound but I could feel his agony, smell the blood
seeping from his shattered legs onto his black denim pants. And
more: his terror at knowing he had committed some terrible
crime, one that would not be forgiven.

—Dickie!—

The mental cry pulled me back. I bent my arm, tensed it. Running along the driver's side of the car, I swung it hard, using my
elbow to break out the already cracked windshield. Swung again
and the driver's window shattered inward.

The driver thought I was coming into the car and reached
through the broken window, trying to hold me away. Grabbing
his wrists, I wedged my legs against the car door and pulled
him sideways until his upper body was half out the broken window.

The driver's face and mine were only inches apart as he strug-
.gled to escape my grip. I squeezed, hard enough that I could feel
the tiny wrist bones shift under the pressure of my thumbs.

He should have cried out, or at least struggled. Instead, he
went rigid and stared straight into my eyes. I sensed the rage in
him, cold and controlled, and the promise of what he would do to
me and the pleasure he would take in the act if I did not heed this
one and only warning and let him go.

I was aware of Hunter reaching over the dash, hand already
on the keys. Aware of a bystander yelling that the police were

on their way. Aware of the distant sound of a siren. Aware of two of the passengers coming around the driver's side. One reached for Hunter, the other reached for me. I should have ignored them, crushed the driver's wrists or gone for his eyes. Instead, I released my hold then managed a hard kick on the arm of the man trying to grab me. He gave a yelp of pain and retreated a few steps. The last of our attackers had already pulled Hunter away from the car, but too late. Hunter tossed the car keys to me. "Run!" he yelled and ducked as the man swung at him.

I should have done as Hunter asked, or else joined in the fight. Instead I gripped the keys and, trapped by indecision, stayed where I was.

I heard something then, a low, soft growl. Wolf sound. Bear sound. I stared at the driver, the source of it. He stared back at me, his gray eyes cold and slitted, his lips curled into a feral smile.

I could not look away from him, not until I heard Hunter call my name.

Though it was two on one and both his attackers younger men, Hunter fought well until one of the thugs pulled him down. As he fell, the smaller of his attackers kicked him twice in the ribs, swung a booted foot back to kick again.

"—Stop!—" I cried. Mental. Vocal. My right hand tensed and curled, ready to slash if I were not obeyed. My eyes darkened as my vision expanded. I could not tell if they could all see this, but I knew the driver did. He bowed his head, the nod of one predator to another, and barked an order to the others. They rushed into the car and slammed the doors.

The keys might still be in my hand, but someone had a second set. The engine caught, tires skidding as the car reversed up the drive and into the street. Gunning the engine, the driver headed south toward the Loop, away from the approaching police car. I heard tires screech and horns blare as he ran a stoplight. Felt the injured Ukrainian's sudden rush of agony and fear. Sensed a mental cry for help so loud I could not avoid being drawn to it. I entered the man's mind and discovered something else, something so terrible that no matter how much I loved Laurie, I wished I had never come to this city.

—Hunter?— I called, questioned.

—Get out of here now. I'll handle this,— he replied.

I did as he asked, retreating through the gap between the damaged garage door and its frame. Cutting through the dark structure, I took the rear service stairs to our floor and let myself in to the apartment just as the police were pulling up outside.

Their lights flashed against the windows and, without turning on any lights, I went onto the terrace and leaned over the wall to see what was going on.

Hunter sat on the concrete ledge that bordered the driveway, clutching his stomach and answering an officer's questions with short, broken sentences. When the officer left him alone for a moment, I joined with him.

—Are you going to a hospital?— I asked.

His assent was weak, filled with pain and grim humor. —I acted so well the police called an ambulance. I could drive myself if I had to.—

Which made me feel only slightly better about what I had not done.

When Laurie found me a half hour later I was still on the corner of the terrace, knees pressed against my chest, trying to understand what I had discovered.

He knelt beside me and I wrapped my arms around him. "Let's go inside," he whispered. When I would not let go, he carried me and put me down on the couch. Though I moved away from him, I kept hold of his hand—beautiful, delicate, and with a strength I wondered if I would ever possess.

I showed him everything that had happened on the drive below then looked away, ashamed. "I should have fought. Defended him. It was like the museum again. I could barely breathe, let alone move, until it was almost too late."

"You're ten years old. Stop being so hard on yourself."

"Age is no excuse."

"Damn it, Dickie. Our fathers were twelve when the Old One judged them ready, and *they* were firstborn." He considered what had happened, then asked, "Were you ever really threatened?"

I thought of the driver, what he had conveyed to me. There had been no words, only a feeling, but it was so strong. "I can't decide," I said, and shared the driver's threat along with everything else.

Then, because he was family and I would not hide from him

even if I could, I told him what I had kept from Hunter. "As they drove away, one of the men in the back took hold of their captive's leg and squeezed the crushed bones. Ruse was so weak he could not find the breath to scream, but I heard the driver tell him that his entire family would know why he had died. He said everyone would see his agony on his face long after they had devoured the rest of him."

"Dickie, I agree that the man they took away is likely dead by now, but people say things they don't really mean all the time. It could have been a figure of speech, nothing more."

I shook my head. "I was in the man's mind when the driver said it. It was something the victim knew they had done before. He'd been a part of it. And, and . . ."

—Finish,— Laurie ordered gently.

I couldn't speak, thought the words instead. —And they all seemed like one family. Laurie, how could they do that to one of their own?—

This was one of those rare times that Laurie did not try to answer. Instead, he sat silently beside me for a time, then reached for the phone and called Chaves.

Hunter returned by taxi some hours later, favoring one leg and sporting a swollen lip and a bandage on his temple. He sat stiffly in a straight-backed wing chair across from us and looked from me to Laurie as if we were the more injured.

"Are your ribs intact?" Laurie asked, thinking of that last kick I'd shown him.

"I've had worse. The police want to question me again sometime tomorrow to see if I recall anything else. I'd like to tell the locals as much as I can."

"I have already spoken to Denys. He has a number for Stephen in Montreal. I expect he and Helen will be here by tomorrow afternoon."

"Good. Because, unless I want to plead amnesia, which even a rookie cop won't buy, I'll have to give some explanation for the blood on that garage door."

"Blood?" Laurie asked.

"Quite a bit on the pavement, too. Likely some of it is still wet. Can you get something from it?"

"Not likely but I think I must try."

My cousin rummaged in the kitchen and found a sheet of plastic that had been wrapped around Hunter's morning bagels. He took it downstairs.

Hunter waited a few minutes, then asked me, "Can you tell me what Laurie's thinking right now?"

—Without him knowing?—

—That would be good.—

I merged with Laurie as he moved silently through the dark garage to the battered door and through the gap the car had made. Though I had not seen it, Hunter was right. The man had lost some blood, enough that there were streaks of it on the garage door, and more on the pavement. Only the latter was still wet and Laurie dipped a finger into it and tasted.

There would be no life left in it, and likely no mind left to merge with any longer. But as he expected, the taste was odd, nothing he had ever experienced but familiar somehow.

Hoping that Stephen could solve this riddle, he placed the plastic over the wettest spot then wrapped the sample carefully and started back.

"Would you say that Laurie's confused?" Hunter asked while we were still alone.

"Very."

"I think you stumbled onto a real mystery here. I wonder if we'll ever get the opportunity to solve it." He pulled a bottle of pills from his pocket and pushed himself to his feet. "If the boss is coming, I'd best get some rest while I can." He swallowed two pills with a glass of water and limped down the hall to bed.

I'd expected to see both my parents the next day, but in the interest of time, Stephen had taken a commercial flight and there had only been one seat available. And, as he made clear from the moment he arrived, this was a family matter first, a parental one second.

After kissing me, then pushing back my hair and telling me that I looked a bit more mature for the wear, he turned his attention to the events that had brought him here.

Like our family meetings at home, this one was conducted for the most part in silence. We showed him everything in the order in which it had all unfolded, including Laurie's late-night sampling of the evidence.

Stephen asked no questions, but instead took the blood from the refrigerator and held the plastic in his cupped hands, warming the contents while he considered what he had been shown, matching it against centuries of experience.

We were not a part of this process, nor of the conjectures he made when he tasted the blood. But his conclusions were swift and not debatable.

Hunter had carefully constructed last night's story to the police to be as close to the truth as possible. He had seen a man run down and assaulted, had been injured himself when he had gone to help. He'd also provided the make and color of the car. But he had not mentioned our family, except to say he was staying here with Laurie.

"I need to give the police more help, at least the license number of the car. After all, I've been trained to notice these things," Hunter said.

"Did you see this number yourself?"

"Only half of it."

"Give them that. Tomorrow, we may want to provide them with much more. Anonymously, yes?"

Hunter grinned. "So you're going out tonight?"

"I must," Stephen replied and reached for me. I had to fight to keep from recoiling, shaking my head, saying no, I could not face them again, not even with him. But he never said I was to go, only held me close and rested his free hand over Hunter's.

"Realize that my son's fear is perfectly understandable, Gregory," Stephen said by way of warning then showed him every nuance of the driver's threats to me and what they planned for their prisoner.

Hunter looked less shocked than furious. "Why?" he asked.

"That is what I will discover. In the meantime, please find out what you can about that family, especially Ion Konovic and the source of his wealth.

"Laurie, I suggest you go out tonight. Pick someplace where you will be seen and remembered. If you have been seeing someone with nothing to hide, so much the better. Spend the entire night elsewhere if you can, or bring someone here. If anything unexpected happens, you will need an alibi, yes?"

"There's a family resemblance, but you don't look that much alike," Hunter commented.

"For the sake of the life Laurie has built here, they must mistake me for him. You have seen our eyes when we hunt; you've seen my brother's face taut with anger and need. That change is enough, I think, that I can pass as him. When I am through, no one will dare threaten any of us again."

Business finished, he pulled me closer. "Have you gotten any rest at all since last night?"

"Only a little," I admitted.

"Then may I share your room for a few hours? You can tell me all the other interesting things you have discovered in this huge city and I will show you Quebec."

As I led him down the hall, I felt a calm that had been absent for the last few days. Lying close to him, I did tell him all about the music lessons and the theater and the people I had met. He spoke of singers in cafes, and hunting in the Laurentians and an isolated house that Mother wanted to lease. I drifted off to the sound of music and the sight of soft-edged hills fading into the mist.

When we joined Laurie and Hunter that night, my father looked ready for nothing more challenging than a late-night walk. He scanned the astonishing list of names and addresses Hunter had already collected on Konovic's extended family, including those of the driver's. The intriguing pieces still missing were the source of Konovic's wealth and his interest in us.

"He will explain those to me tonight," Stephen said as he spread out a Chicago map on the coffee table. "Please, show me where I am to go."

Hunter read off the addresses and Laurie pointed them out on the map. Other than Ion Konovic's Gold Coast apartment, most of the family lived much further north, closer to the building where Lev Konovic had killed himself. Fortunately, the driver, who did not appear to be a close relation, lived near us as well, off Bryn Mawr west of the Edgewater Hotel.

"Konovic and the driver are the most important," Stephen said. "Time permitting, I'll try for some of the rest."

"There's always tomorrow night," Hunter commented.

"By tomorrow it will not be so easy to find them." Though Hunter said nothing, he could not hide his concern. Noting it, Stephen added, "They frightened my son, but they did not harm him. Fortunate for them, yes?"

He stretched as he said the last words, his body long and lean in the tight-fitting knits he'd deliberately chosen. He would not hide tonight, and had already promised to share with me whatever he learned—or felt—a promise he would only half keep.

# CHAPTER 9

Konovic had fallen into a deep and ordered sleep before Stephen walked past the preoccupied lobby guard to the elevators. He began to dream as Stephen reached his door, terrible dreams of dark and musty places where walls pressed against him and the air was stifling. When he heard the front door frame give way, he tried to break free of the nightmares but something held him rigid, immobile.

It occurred to him that he was likely still dreaming. If so, he could alter the dream or wake. Both seemed impossible so he rolled onto his back.

The unfamiliar position made his pulse more noticeable. It pounded in his ears, harder and faster, and without any warning a feeling, so akin to terror, gave way to something worse. He could no longer breathe.

He was in his late thirties. Didn't men his age have heart attacks? Strokes? He needed a doctor. Soon. He lashed out with his arm, hoping to wake the girl beside him. But she did not move and his arm came away wet and sticky. He held it above his face, forced his eyes to open, and saw that it was covered in blood. He turned to look at the woman and saw her chest, her face, both coated with it; her eyes open, unseeing.

Had he killed her? He could recall slapping her a couple of
times until she'd accepted his advances—no more than a game,
of course, since she was hardly in a position to refuse him anything. One kind of passion always seemed to lead to another so
his last memories were of pounding into her, hearing her cries of
pleasure—or at least of well-feigned acceptance—now this? His
heart beat faster so that his ribs seemed barely able to contain it.
The pressure on his chest increased. Uncomfortable. Real.

He fled the nightmare then, opened his eyes to a dim light
spilling into the bedroom from the hallway fixture and . . .

A sharp angular face only inches from his own, thick curly
hair falling over the high forehead, hair dark as the full-black
eyes that stared into his with an expression of disgust he misinterpreted as interest.

As to the pressure on his chest, it was coming from the creature's hand pressed against his bare flesh, long spread fingers digging into the hollows of his ribs, nails pushing hard enough to
hurt, the fingertips themselves almost as sharp. The first would
break the skin, the second would rip through muscle and bone,
going for his heart or . . .

—As one predator to another, Ion Konovic, we both know
what it means to devour. I doubt you are the expert I am.—

"I . . . I . . ." The words Konovic might have said caught in his
throat, so he thought them instead. —I am sorry I have offended
you, Lord of the Mountain. It was not my intent.—

Urban. Civilized. Yet the man displayed all the faith and def-
erence of an Apuseni peasant of two centuries ago. Another question to ask. —Then why did one of your own threaten our young
one?—

—The man should not have done so. He will be punished for
it.—

—Punished? I would prefer to see him dead.—

Anticipating the reaction, Stephen allowed his victim a moment of relief, long enough for Konovic to draw in a breath and
to speak. "Isn't that something you would prefer to do yourself?"
The driver's name and address rolled through Konovic's mind, a
deliberate offering of information Stephen already knew.

—You must prove that you can keep your own in check.— An
idea came to him. —Tonight. Here. In two hours.—

"Here?"

Stephen pointed to the bedside phone, paid attention as the

number was dialed, listened to both sides of the conversation, intruded on Konovic's thoughts. As he'd expected, the man intended to do exactly as ordered.

As Konovic hung up, he motioned to the girl asleep beside him. "She'll wake eventually," he said.

—I doubt it.—

Konovic studied her more closely, seeing only the bruises on her arms and chest and the bite on her shoulder that he had put there himself some hours before. He assumed that were he to scream her name she would not stir. Yet she would be a distraction.

Obedience had brought him his first reward—a chance to move, to stretch, to gain more favor. He slipped the sheet off the girl's naked body. "This is not a city with the luxuries you must be used to. Allow me to give her to you."

To feast? Yes, Stephen thought, peasant at his core, placating his lord. But the peasants had given their women because they valued them. This one valued no one but himself.

Maintaining the ruse was simple, for it meant that Stephen only had to think like the creature he had once been. He ran one tensed finger down the sleeping girl's torso from neck to pubis, feeling the skin ripple under his touch, watching her nipples harden as if they were already being kissed.

Passionate, even in sleep. Perhaps she was a sacrifice after all.

Though making a pretense of studying the girl, Stephen's mind was with Konovic as the man contemplated the dilemma he thought he faced.

If Ion killed Viktor, as he had already promised his guest, then who would dispose of Viktor and the woman? Konovic watched as the old one ran two taut fingers up the outside of the girl's thigh. He hardly seemed to press at all yet he left scratches on her, deep enough that the tips of his fingers came away red. Konovic licked his lips and hoped that he would at least be allowed to watch.

—Leave us,— Stephen ordered.

Konovic got out of bed. "Please, could I . . . ?" He motioned at his body, as naked as the woman's.

—Take what clothes you need and go . . . quickly!—

Accepting the inevitable, Konovic grabbed his discarded pajamas then stopped at the doorway, waiting for an order. —Back room. Shut the door. I will know if you open it.—

Alone, Stephen returned his attention to the woman. He was well aware of how he looked—the eyes, the lips, the hands, the body.

And her reaction? It occurred to him that either extreme would provide the very torture he wanted to inflict on the bully only now shivering with fear as he sat on the edge of the guest room bed and stared at the closed door.

Stephen turned on the dresser light then returned to the bed and sat beside his offering. He had a role to play this night, and for Laurie's sake especially, it had to be as perfect as his conscience would allow.

He released his mental hold on the woman. As he had done to Konovic, he rested a hand on her chest and pressed insistently enough that her eyes opened. Blue, clear as a summer sky.

She'd expected the brute, but glimpsing a stranger seemed so much worse. She pushed his arm off her and skittered crablike away from him. With her back pressed against the headboard, she hugged her knees close to her body as if she were in a position to defend it.

When he brushed his hand against her ankle, she responded with a brief, startled cry; then, realizing that she did not face one of Konovic's goons, but instead a legend, her expression rapidly shifted from fear to wonder and back again. She crossed herself, right to left, Orthodox fashion. Thinking the action might have insulted him, she started to say something then fell silent.

In response, he reached for her, running a taut hand up her leg. Her body shook as she tried to force it, by will alone, to relax, to accept whatever he would do, to offer herself in exchange for her life as the legends suggested could be done.

He probed her mind, got glimpses of how she had fought earlier, how Konovic had wrapped his hands around her throat. And how only the difficulty of disposing of her body had kept the man from killing her. . . .

No, not yet. He would not think of Konovic yet.

The animal that is so strong in all the family is strongest in the firstborn. It has no conscience, no remorse. It wanted this woman in exactly the way Konovic had offered her . . . body, blood, soul for him to devour.

Stephen gave that beast free rein only when danger made him too weak to fight its release or when a victim truly deserved a horrible end. Neither was the case here and he did not trust his control, so he ordered —Shut your eyes and keep them shut,— the Romanian forming in his mind.

She did as he asked and felt him slide across the bed, press a hand against her cheek, so soft against her. And his body, warmer than she expected, and far gentler than the man had been.

She felt the old one in her mind, touches on her body so arousing they had to be real. She leaned her head back and laughed, a sound that carried down the hall to the room where Konovic waited, impotent fists clenched, fighting fear and rage, even fighting the passion he was being allowed to share.

For Konovic, for the girl, the apex seemed to hold forever until both felt a brief stab of pleasure, another, another. Taut hands moved down her thighs, lifting them for one final thrust. She screamed, the sound ending in a sob, then silence.

Stephen moved away from her long before he released her from the visions he had created. When she opened her eyes, the facade had fallen once more and the beast looked at the blood seeping from the shallow scratches, the bites.

She cleaned the marks with the corner of the sheet. —Get dressed and go,— he ordered then stood and, with his back to her, stared out the window while she pulled on her clothes.

"Pardon me," she whispered to him, the first words she had spoken. "Pardon me. What can I say happened here?"

—You may tell anyone who asks that you were so passionate that a mountain lord denied his need and let you live. The marks on you mean no one must touch you without your permission. Not Konovic, not anyone, unless you wish it, or they will deal with me. Tell them—

"Let me thank you," she whispered and started slowly toward him, arms raised.

—Go!— he ordered without looking at her. She blushed and fled, running through the apartment to the broken door and the elevator beyond. By the time its doors opened, much of the memory of what had happened in the last hour, like the dream it so resembled, had begun to fade. By the time she reached the lobby, only his words remained clear in her mind. She doubted she would forget any of them until the day she died.

Upstairs, Stephen looked in the dresser mirror at the face he saw so rarely, and grinned. In spite of the evening's temptations, he was thinking logically enough to have solved two problems with one swift stroke.

Still grinning, he left the room, shutting the door behind him, and summoned Ion Konovic.

# CHAP†ER 10

During the time Ion Konovic had been in the guest suite, he'd held a thin line between furious and terrified, managing to ignore them both. After all, he'd reminded himself far more than once, he had done nothing to offend the creatures he so admired. His actions had even saved them a great deal of difficulty. All he had to do was stay calm and explain everything.

Prepared to talk, and convinced this feeling came from him alone, Konovic stopped at the closed master bedroom door. The hall light revealed the blood on the doorknob, spots of it on the rug. He reached for the knob and decided to wait. The sight of a savaged body would be too unsettling. Better to keep a clear head and worry about that problem later.

The old one stood in the dark living room, facing the window, his long limbs outlined by the dim light of the streetlamps on the drive below. "Would you like a drink?" Konovic asked; then, realizing how odd that sounded, he added, "I have brandy, excellent scotch, wine."

"That isn't our custom," Stephen replied, using his voice for the first time. Though he matched the pitch to Laurie's, the inflection in it was deliberately thick. The effect was exactly what he'd expected: the man thought he spoke to Laurie and that Laurie was trying to hide his identity. As Stephen had planned, Konovic immediately concluded that Laurence Austra was far more dangerous than he'd ever suspected.

"I'd been given to believe that you did drink. Water perhaps? I rent a cooler with bottled. No one should drink this Chicago crap."

"Then yes. For both of us. We have much to discuss."

When Konovic returned, Stephen was sitting at the glass-topped dining table running one finger along the edge of the AustraGlass bowl in the center of it. Konovic's hands were shaking, but he managed to pour.

"We have been most content to be considered legends. How did you know what we were?" Stephen asked.

"Because I have seen one of you before. More than once, actually, during the war."

"In Ukraine?"

"In Romania."

"Jules Ruse told me that his people were 'orphans of Stalin, children of storm.' Was he speaking of the Ukraine famine?"

Konovic's eyes narrowed. "Yes, but my family had gone to Ukraine from Romania. We were always border people," he replied.

"You were born during Stalin's famine?"

"Stalin's famine? Yes, yes! That's the way to put it! I was born in 1932; I was lucky to be conceived let alone survive my own birth and childhood. My mother's belly had already become so swollen from the hunger of sacrifice for her children that she had not even known I was coming until the labor began. At a year, I weighed what my oldest brother had at birth. I watched my mother bury my four older siblings when they died of starvation. But I survived. She told me it was because—and forgive me for this but you asked for what I know—because I had a different father from our siblings; one that, like her, had the blood of the mountain lords in his veins. She said I was twice blessed with your strength."

Stephen looked from his own hands to Konovic's stubby fingers circling the water glass, to the man's round and florid face and lank hair. There were legends, rumors, even among his own, and once he had met . . .

He pushed aside the memory. "And you believed this?" he asked instead.

"Everyone died of the famine: all the other villagers, my grandfather, my half brothers and sisters. How can you explain that of nearly five hundred people, the only survivors were a rail-thin man and woman and their youngest child?"

"How did you survive?" Stephen prompted.

"I have never spoken of this but I will tell you. You see, the authorities thought our entire village gone. We encouraged this, hiding until Stalin's thugs went away to report that everyone had died from typhus rather than hunger. And so they left us to the peace of our dead." He held up his glass in a silent salute to them and drained it. "I could use a little scotch," he said, and Stephen, suddenly inclined to mercy, told him to bring the bottle.

"You're sure?" Konovic asked, holding out the bottle after he filled his glass.

"I'm sure. Continue."

"At night we would sleep in the root cellar beneath our barn and . . . and we survived by . . . by . . ." His voice broke. He took another swallow from his glass but could not go on.

"By eating your dead, yes?" Stephen prompted. Konovic was right. This news did not repulse him.

Once the words were said, Konovic's voice grew stronger. "In the beginning, Mother made a pot of stew from it, flavored with a bit of salt and dandelion greens. Since I was barely a year old, she mashed mine into a sort of gruel and spoon-fed me. I was too young to know what I ate or if I liked it, but it kept me alive. When what meat we had rotted beyond the reach of even the desperate, Father would go out and hunt.

"Frightened that soldiers would come if they saw our smoke, we cooked only at night. But when the first winter cold arrived, they knew that to live we had to risk the warmth of daytime fires, which would bring soldiers, or risk the border guards and leave. Father had been slipping past the guards for months and so they seemed the lesser threat. •

"He carried a well-sharpened scythe, a vicious instrument when one is truly desperate. He killed two guards and we made it across the border to follow the passes back to the village Mother still called home, a little place some miles east of Borşa.

"We were not the only ones to return. We found cousins there, survivors of Stalin just as we were. Many had survived as we had and we flocked together for comfort.

"When the great war began, I was eight years old. The Russians came. Our young men hid in the mountains, fearful that they would be taken as soldiers or slave laborers. But the soldiers had no interest in them, only in our crops and our herds.

"They took nearly everything they could find and gave us nothing in return but a few armed guards. Fortunately, a good part of our harvest was already hidden away in mountain caves. We had food through the winter but we had to steal into the mountains to bring it down. This was hardly a problem, since the commandant was a drunk and the soldiers quite taken with the village girls. Corruption saved us.

"Then early the following year, with hardly any warning, the Hungarians, allies of the Germans, came and our alliances were forced to shift again.

"There were good reasons for our family to side with the Nazis, if only because they opposed the hated Stalin. While some in the village hung their heads when the Russian soldiers were shot in the town square, my father applauded.

"Soon he was eating at the captain's table, telling them where the Russian garrisons had been when we had lived in Ukraine. He told them of the famine. He said he wished to shoot Stalin himself, starting with his balls, and they laughed and poured him more vodka from the cases they had liberated from the Russians. But drunk as my father became, he always remembered to bring home meat and wedges of cheese in his pockets for us to devour while those around us tried to live on bread alone. He never let us share. "You are no good to anyone dead," he would say.

"The village had over five hundred in it when we first arrived there. By the time the war ended, half that number were gone— Jews lost to the pogroms of the Iron Guard and the holocaust, partisans lost to firing squads, old people and children to hunger and disease. Of our extended family, nearly forty when the Germans arrived, we lost five, and three of those were shot."

"You spoke of seeing my kind," Stephen prompted.

Konovic poured another drink but took only a sip before going on. "I was nine when it happened. I was not at home at the time, but to the south in Bistriţa. My father, who by now spoke Romanian as well as Ukrainian and Russian and a good amount of German, went there to act as an interpreter at a Russian interrogation. He had asked that I be allowed to come along and see a

big city. I do not know to this day if he was trying to harden me—
for he said often that my heart was too soft—or if he really did
not know what to expect.

"The German who drove us there was a red-faced, red-haired
man. He let me sit beside him and wear his hat and taught me a
song that German children sing when they jump rope.

"Bistriţa was not the pretty place I had expected, but instead
seemed sad and gray as a poor man grown old too soon. We
pulled up to a huge brick building with bars on all its windows.

"The driver told me to sit on a bench in a little room off the
lobby while he and my father went down the hallway to one of
the doors. I thought I heard a moan as it opened but then it shut
behind them and everything was silent again. An hour passed and
they didn't come out. After two, the driver returned, took me
down the street, and bought me a bowl of soup and some bread.

"As we ate I noticed there was blood on one of his sleeves and
a splatter of it on his cheek. The Germans always seemed so particular about their clothes that I was afraid to point it out to him
and so said nothing. 'Should we go back for my father?' I asked
instead.

"'No hurry. I don't care how important their prisoner is, I
don't have the stomach for this.' He spoke quickly, more to himself than to me. We sat in the scant shade of a newly planted
sapling and ate slowly so that it was late afternoon when we
started back.

"As we approached the front door, an army truck drove by.
The two servicemen had their hats pulled low over their faces.
The truck took a left at the corner, which would have taken them
around the back of the building. It must have been the usual thing
to do because the German hardly glanced up as they went by. Instead, when he did not see my father waiting, he slowed his pace.

"As a result, we were barely inside when the lights went out
and an explosion rocked the building. A second, closer explosion
followed. I heard gunshots, but thinking they had come from the
street, I fell flat next to a desk and began to slide beneath it.

"When I understood the shots were coming from deeper in the
building, I began to crawl toward the door. As I did, a man ran
down the hallway, dragging what looked like a bloody corpse. I
did not see him clearly, but he saw me. Grabbing me by the waist
of my pants, he jerked me upright and threw me out the door.
'Run!' he ordered.

"Fear gave me strength I did not know I had and I listened, then stopped when I reached the corner and saw the same truck drive past. Its driver stopped at the doorway of the building and the man who had pushed me to safety lifted the limp body into the back.

"That was when I saw him shot at least twice, saw his defense when three guards rushed him. He should have been dead, yet he fought. He should have been overcome and captured, yet he killed two. And the way he killed them with only his hands, then dragged the third into the truck with him . . . My jaw fell in amazement and in the moment he sensed me watching, he turned toward me. There was scarcely a hundred feet separating us. I saw his eyes. And I knew.

"Then he was gone. As they pulled away, two more explosions made the building shake. I moved closer to the door and stared in at the body of the driver who had been kind to me. I tried to rush into the building, but someone held me back. 'My father was in there!' I cried. I had to see with my own eyes what I already knew.

"'Shhh, boy,' someone said and, not understanding, added, 'Hide the grief or the soldiers will kill you, too.'

"Later, other soldiers came and asked me what I had seen. I told them only that I was the son of their interpreter and that he had been inside. I said I wanted to go home but no one listened to me.

"In the morning an old woman came up to me. 'Have you eaten anything?' she asked.

"My father died in there," I replied and she shook her head and took my hand and led me through the narrow streets to the orthodox church. Its priest gave me a bit of bread and jam and let me sleep in his bed until morning. Soon after first light, he took me through the woods to a path that led north. "Be careful. Trust in God," he whispered and kissed my forehead and sent me on my way.

"It took me six days to return home. I walked when I had to, caught rides when I could, and dodged everyone that looked like they were too much a part of one side or the other.

"By the time I reached my family, I was no longer as naive as my father had been. Take no sides, I decided, look out for your own, for they are all that matter. I feel that way to this day."

"Your father saved your life by taking a side," Stephen said.

"An old one saved my life and I have always been thankful to him. As for my father, he only wanted to be a big man, and it killed him. My mother was smarter the second time around. She married my father's brother, who kept his mouth shut and his eyes lowered. All the better to not be noticed while he waited for his best advantage."

"And your brother. Why did he fear us so?"

"I made him fear you. I did the same to the others as well. You see, the one who fought with the partisans was not exactly in hiding. Too many saw and believed, particularly those who held to the dream of an independent Romania.

"Some thought they could simply forget the old pact we made with you; they thought they could climb into that pass to meet the legends and ask for help as if they were petitioning the gods of Mount Olympus. But I had seen an old one fight and I would not lose my brother or any of my own to the one who had ripped that soldier apart. So I told him every detail of what I had seen, added a few of my own. He was young. He believed. So did the others. They believe it to this day."

"As well they should." Stephen noted it was nearly 1:30 and covered the man's hand with his. He felt the pulse quicken, the sudden tensing of the muscles. The fight not to pull away. "It is not easy to get into this country. It is far harder for a recent immigrant to accumulate wealth, yet you have. How?"

"What is my wealth to you?"

"If I am to let you live, I need to see your flaws, and your strengths."

Konovic shut his eyes. Almost smiled. "Very well. I think my strengths will be obvious.

"People looked up to me after that trek home. Eleven years later, my family had saved enough to send me and my oldest cousin to America. Once here, we worked. Sometimes two jobs each, sometimes three. When we had saved enough, we sent for another of family and another—the closest first, distant cousins later. Some escaped, and so we only had to pay for their passage. Others had to be bought from the government, like slaves being freed. Taking care of family first was a trick we learned from the Jews but we were not wealthy like the Jews we'd known at home, and so each that came had to work to pay back the others who had sponsored him and to help bring still another here.

"Now there are sixty of my family here, all the oldest survivors like me. I protect them. I find them jobs. I loan the smartest money to get started in some business and they pay me back plus the cost of their passage here. I use this to start more businesses. We have a diner, two bars, a funeral parlor, a flower shop. A cousin is considering a McDonald's franchise. We do well when we work together."

It was a half-truth, Stephen knew. The man did help his family leave Romania but the price was exorbitant. Once here, only a chosen few prospered. The others were no better than slaves.

"Some of my family work harder than others, but a few cause trouble. That girl I gave to you would not learn English. Would not work. I told her there is only one kind of work for a lazy woman, but she did not even want to act on her back. No, she only wanted to go home, and when we would not allow it she threatened to go to the government. I'm glad someone found some use for her."

Stephen's hand pressed a bit harder on Konovic's. One nail drew blood. "Since you know so much about us, what do you suggest I do with you?"

Konovic stared at the blood a moment, weighing an answer, deciding quickly. "Do? Consider. You came to me. You asked the questions. You could do nothing and it would change nothing. Or if you are concerned about this visit, take the memory of it when you go. It changes nothing."

"I could kill you and so convince the others that no one should meddle in our affairs. It would be a good lesson, yes?"

"Who will control this family then? Someone will have to because you cannot kill them all without the authorities noticing. And my own, when panicked, will talk. It would be dangerous to you."

"And what of the woman? Won't her death cause panic?"

"No one will know but those I can trust. To the others I will say I sent her home as she wished."

Stephen pushed him, a subtle suggestion that he go on. "Of course I have done this before," Konovic continued, almost happy for the prompting. "I am an independent thinker from a soviet state. I do what I must to survive."

Brute. Murderer. But Konovic was right. He was too valuable to kill. Stephen looked at his own hand, one finger bloody from the wound he had made. Blood did not lie. And it would not be wise to avoid the truth. He lifted his hand and, almost idly, tasted.

There had been times in the family's distant past when a hint of their own could be tasted in a peasant. Not unlikely considering the occasional killing of one of their family. In barbarians who ate their enemies to acquire their strength, who better to devour than a mountain lord? Stephen had already detected a hint of his own in the Ukrainian's blood as well as the woman's, so he had expected to find that Konovic told the truth. What astounded him was the strength of their tie!

"What happened to the Ukrainian, Jules Ruse?" he asked.

"I heard he was dead. I didn't ask Viktor for details. The less I know . . ." He shrugged.

So confident and so foolish, Stephen thought. Well, they would both know the details soon enough.

That was the last part of the night Stephen shared completely with me and only, my brother and I think, to put my mind at ease. The rest of the night was conveyed in half-truths, and what he chose not to reveal seemed far more important than the rest. What follows is all of it, or at least as much as Patrick could steal when Stephen's thoughts were unguarded. I owe my brother a debt for how carefully, over the years that followed, he helped me assemble bit by bit the missing pieces on the following pages.

# CHAP+ER II

It did not seem unusual for Ion Konovic to ask for a visit so late, but the strained voice convinced Viktor Celac that something was wrong. He expected that Ion had lost his temper and killed the woman. But Celac was not sure, and so he carried a revolver in an inside pocket of his leather jacket.

On the way into the apartment, he noted the ruined door and the dim lighting and proceeded silently down the entrance hall with his gun in his hand. The sight of his cousin in the company of one of the old ones made him back up a step. But he had faith in his reflexes and strength, enough that he held on to his weapon though he kept it at his side.

"It's all right, Viktor. Come. Sit. He only wants to question you," Konovic said.

Rather than taking the seat his cousin pointed to, Celac walked around the table and stood behind the chair closest to the window. The thin light from outside made it easier to see his adversaries, and his eyes narrowed as he scanned the room, peering even into the darkest corners, making sure the only enemy here sat at the table.

"What in the hell could I tell him at this hour of the night that you couldn't?" he grumbled, looking only at Konovic.

—Why you threatened one of our children.—

Though the question or the manner in which it was delivered troubled Celac, he showed no outward sign of it except that he would not look directly at Stephen. "The brat should learn to stay out of business that does not concern him," he replied. "The same goes for your security man, if that's what he is."

—What happened to the Ukrainian?—

"What the fuck is his life to you?"

—What is yours to me?—

"Answer him, Viktor," Konovic prompted, his voice deceptively gentle.

Celac's pulse increased, more from anger than fear. "Why should I answer? When I have told the truth he will kill me. And for what? I only threatened the brat. Hell, I could have shot him half a dozen times and he would have healed with not even a scratch to show for the pain." There was rage in his tone, cold as his eyes, until he caught enough shreds of the truth to reach the right conclusion. His grip on his weapon tightened. "*You* are supposed to kill me?" he bellowed at Konovic. "You made that agreement, you fucking whore? Well, it won't be so easy to be rid of me!"

As Celac raised his weapon, Stephen entered his mind and found he'd underestimated the man's mental strength. Though Celac's motion could be slowed, he could not be stopped. Stephen pushed harder and Celac seemed to give up the fight. His arm fell slack at his side.

Thinking he'd won, Stephen ordered him to sit. Celac began to obey but in the moment Stephen allowed him to move, Celac stepped back, raised the weapon, and fired, not at Stephen but at his employer.

Konovic dove sideways, and the bullet aimed for his chest hit his shoulder instead. As Celac took aim for a second shot, Stephen abandoned all effort at mental control. Pushing the table out of the way hard enough that the glass bowl on it rolled off the edge and shattered on the hardwood floor, he lunged for Celac.

Celac was no match for Stephen's speed or strength, and he knew it. He jumped backward, close enough to the window that the force of Stephen's attack pushed him through. Stephen caught the frame with one hand, steadying himself at the edge. He watched the fall—how the man tried to twist to land on hands and feet. But he hit hard and lay facedown and motionless.

Over forty feet onto concrete. Likely no need to touch, Stephen thought, but he did and as he did he realized the man was not dead, not even close to it. Celac pushed himself to his feet and, sensing Stephen watching him, steadied himself against a lamppost and looked up at the window. Their eyes locked. Their minds touched. Then, with a defiant snarl, the man broke Stephen's hold and, cradling his left arm with his right, limped away into the darkness.

Konovic, who had moved as close to the window as he dared, watched Celac go with only a trace of surprise. "I am sorry that I cannot honor your request and go after him but I think I need a doctor," he said.

"Your neighbor on the floor above has already called the police."

"Police! But what about Marie!"

Stephen did not answer. Let the man have his well-deserved minutes of fear. He leaned over the edge and, sensing no one watching, followed the driver down.

Stephen might have tracked by sight, for he saw footprints on the newly formed frost on the walk and deserted street. He might have tracked by scent from the trace of it hanging in the still and frozen air. But he needed neither. His mind had already linked with his prey.

Viktor Celac's sight was blurry from the blow his head had taken on the pavement. Blood dripped down his face from the cut on his forehead. He would have wiped it away but he needed his right arm to support the left, which was broken near the shoulder. But at least he was still alive. And if he could ignore the pain and the fear and make it just a few more blocks, he might have a chance of staying alive at least through the night. With a miracle, through tomorrow.

At this hour, there were no well-traveled streets to give him safety. Besides, if an old one willed it, he would step into an empty alley and obediently raise his chin. Best to keep moving on the most direct route he could find.

He could feel his pursuer brushing against his mind and tried to push him out. He had learned that trick well enough to hide from the few of his own with any mental power, but this intrusion was far more powerful. The old one could have him anytime he wished but chose to let him struggle on.

Just a few more blocks. Maybe even two and he would be close enough that the others would hear his cry. But would they even come? Given his odds, he regretted the killing he had done last night.

He cut through an alley bisecting a city block, saw the gate at the far end, and looked for another way out that would avoid backtracking. The doors that opened onto the alley seemed all thick wood, and locked, until he found one hanging open. An inside flight of stairs led only to another locked door.

The old one was closer now, the touch of his mind stronger. Celac descended the stairs as quickly as his body would allow. Seeing the long shadow at the place where he had come in, he made for the gate at the end of the alley, praying that he still had the strength to climb and that the one pursuing him would allow it.

—What did you do to the Ukrainian?—

"Exactly what I told the brat I'd do," Celac screamed without looking back.

The question came back to him, demanding, repeating. —Why? Why? Why?—

"Because it's what I am, you son of a bitch. Given what you are you ought to fucking understand it."

—He was one of your own.—

"No! Not my own!" Celac reached the gate and stopped long enough to undo a center button on his shirt and slide the wounded arm inside. Not much of a sling, but all he had. At least the other three limbs were working. With difficulty, he made the top of the gate, but as he swung his body over, he lost his one-handed grip and fell hard on his injured side. Dizzy from the pain, he forced himself to stand, to breathe. To go on.

Stephen paused at the place where the man had fallen. There was blood on the concrete, more than he had expected. Deciding it was time to take full measure of his opponent as well as strengthen the bond between them, he tasted.

Konovic's blood had been thick with the essence of his family. But this . . . so much more! It was as if the man had somehow found a means to begin the change himself.

But not just him; he had implied there were others. Stephen kicked snow from the edge of the alley over the stains his quarry had left and diluted the blood with the toe of his boot.

—Do you really think there are enough of your own to stand up to a mountain lord?— he asked, the question deliberately subtle.

With logic dulled by fear and pain, Celac considered it. There were only three like him left, but only two of those would come. Would two be enough? Again, he wondered if they could fight.

Only two? Insignificant, Stephen thought. No need to push and make his quarry wary. He would know the names soon enough.

As if reading his thoughts, Celac quickened his pace then turned west. When he crossed under the el tracks, he turned down an access road; one side fields of gravel beneath the tracks, the other closed and boarded warehouses. A pack lost in a city would choose a place like this to hunt, to sleep. Certain they had reached their destination, Stephen closed the gap.

Viktor Celac sensed the old one coming. He tripped as he whirled and would have fallen if Stephen had not been quick enough to catch him. One hand on the back of his neck, the other flat against his chest, Stephen held him upright as if he were a kitten or a doll.

Their faces less than a foot apart, Stephen studied the man, looking for similarities between them, finding few he had not already noted. Celac's pupils were large, and Stephen suspected his night vision was excellent. But the shape of the face was only Slavic; the good arm trying to push his away had only a human's length and a bit of added strength. The wound on Celac's forehead still bled and, judging from the way he had groaned when Stephen grabbed him, his arm gave him agony. But Stephen already knew the main differences lay in his blood and his mind.

—Are the others coming?— Stephen asked.

In response, Celac pulled in a deep breath and howled, the cry of a wolf for his pack. Not at all like the shriek of a mountain lord, but more suited to the man's abilities and his environs. And the effect would be the same. His kin would come.

—While we wait, how precisely did the Ukrainian die?—

"Precisely? I shot the bastard in the face, that precise enough for you? By then his blood was already thick with fear, enough that we could still taste it an hour later when we began to feed."

—Why did you wait to drain him?—

When Celac did not answer, Stephen's grip on his neck tightened. —Why?— he repeated.

Celac moaned then grinned. The teeth were long but human. "We did not need him, we wanted that part of you in him."

And their waiting ensured that the only life left in the corpse would come from the tenacious blood of the mountain lords. With no heartbeat to pump the blood they were forced to suck it from the flesh; so their words to last night's victim were completely true. They had devoured him as they had others, and so were forcing their own change.

—Do you all do this?—

"Only those few with the strength to take. The others must give."

—How many others have you killed?—

Celac didn't answer. Stephen pushed, found a vague number. Dozens.

—Does Ion Konovic know what you do?—

"He pays me to keep order and smuggle troublemakers home. He guesses that I kill some of them, but he does not know."

—And the police?—

"We leave no traces, or if we do, the others handle it. There are no crimes to investigate."

Intelligent, deadly. But Stephen knew their luck would not hold forever. When it faded, they would not be the only ones in danger. Stephen had not intended to kill this night, but he had no choice.

Conscience almost clear, his thoughts on me and Patrick, Helen and the others, Stephen pushed Celac away from him, intending to spin him around and finish him from behind. Celac broke free for a moment. Even in his injured state, he managed a blow that sent Stephen reeling before Stephen found a hold and subdued him. Thinking the others might be as strong, Stephen backed against one of the metal pilings supporting the tracks and gripped the man tightly.

Guessing his end was near, Celac fought in spite of his pain but Stephen had him pinned and it was useless. —And what of your own?— Stephen asked.— Do they know you feed on them?—

Celac's answer was defiant, filled with hate for those born to what he would never possess. "They think it is you doing the killing. And so you are the ones who terrify them all. They would not speak to you about it, or of you to anyone. They know the penalty is a long and painful death—at *your* hands."

Stephen questioned further, the answer quick and so filled with anger he knew the man believed it.

"Why wouldn't they accept it? In the Old Country, it was always you doing the taking. Even now, I read in letters how our strongest disappear."

—We know nothing about that.—

"Liars! All of you!" Celac made one last, futile effort to break free then froze, silent in his killer's arms.

—Why?— Celac asked as his will to fight faded. —What have I done to you?—

—You have taken the worst of what we are and glorified it.—

As Celac had feared, he did obey that final command, lifting his chin, resting the back of his head on his killer's shoulder. That first stab of pain seemed magnified, extended, but though Stephen barely held him, he did not move.

And that was how his little pack found them, the two men in dark coats, pants, and knit caps staring at the old one's display of power. Stephen hoped the two would rush him and make killing them easier. When they did not, he let the dying man fall at his feet and crouched flat-handed beside him, a posture he hoped they'd interpret as a sign of weakness.

The lure worked. They attacked. The smaller man died quickly, his neck broken. Petro Sava, the larger and slower of the pair, saw the lethal defense and backed off. Unsure whether to run or to beg for his life, he wished most that he possessed enough power of his own to have resisted Viktor's call.

He had known Jules Ruse, had liked him, and the torment Viktor had put the man through had been all the more terrible because it had not been necessary. It had even sickened Wolfe, who had tried to leave before it was over. Wolfe had promised to tell no one, but Viktor detected the lie and so Wolfe had died, too, and Petro could only stand and watch, frozen by the power of his leader's mind.

Once there had been six of them, then four, then three. Now Viktor was dead, and Wolfe, and Erik lay at Petro's feet. Petro would feel only relief if it weren't for the old one looking at him intently, no doubt reading his thoughts, probing deeper, ready to take him as he had the others. Yes, Petro would die, and if he died what of Irena? Who would take care of her then?

That name again. Stephen paused, fighting the urge to finish the killing. There was more he needed to know.

"Come here, Petro," Stephen said, his voice kind, an arm extended as if they had known each other a long time.

Petro glanced down the road to the well-lit street a hundred yards away. Could he make it?

"Better to come here," Stephen coaxed.

"Why? So I can die too?"

"Come here and convince me that I should let you live."

Petro Sava wanted to believe the old one, wanted it enough that his hands shook with the desire to yield.

—Come,— Stephen said, a gentle order but nothing else. The man had to do this of his own free will.

Convinced that trust was the only thing that would save him, the man reached for Stephen's hand.

Stephen turned it so it rested palm up in his, one nail slicing across the soft tissue near the thumb. Blood welled in it. He raised it to his lips.

As Stephen had expected, the man's blood was hardly more than human. A large man, powerful as men go, but just a man with a mind far too easy for a creature such as Celac to control. With no way to resist, Petro Sava had been forced to join the group, most likely so that Celac would one day have another victim with the blood of his kind to feed on.

—Listen to me. You will stop this killing or you will die. Give me your word that this will be done.—

Petro faltered, wanting to promise, not certain he could keep it. Viktor had been that persuasive.

—Understand that if you give your word then break it, there will be no place you can hide from me and my kin. And your end will not be as quick or kind as these were.—

Petro felt it then, the terror building inside of him, the pain deep in his chest as if someone were squeezing the breath from his lungs, the blood from his heart.

"I swear!" Trembling then, Petro tried to pull away but Stephen only tightened his grip on the man's wrist.

—Tell me of the others like you.—

"Different cities. Countries. Here. Detroit. New York. Canada. In the homeland. I know just the little that Viktor told me."

—Did Viktor have family here?—

"No. Not here. He spoke of family, but never said where they lived."

—Your cousin said there were three left but only two would come. Who is the last he spoke of?—

"Please. She could not come. She is just child. No trouble to anyone. Has never even tasted blood. Never!"

But of course, Petro thought the answers he would not speak. In that moment, Stephen had a name, a place. He let go of Petro's hand and left him.

Alone, Petro paced, but could not go more than a few yards from the place where the bodies lay. Celac's was beyond his use, the old one had made certain of that. The other, the poor stupid cousin he'd had no part in killing, seemed to have been left as his gift. But try as he would, he could not bring himself to touch the body any more than he could leave that spot.

He could only pray that the old one returned before first light to help him hide the carnage. If not, when the police found him he would tell what he had done. He deserved no mercy, none at all. Alone, remorse flooded him. He broke down, fell to his knees, and cried.

From the shadows, Stephen watched the struggle, the last test the man need undergo, satisfied that even the orders he had not given directly would be followed.

In a second-floor bedroom some blocks away, Irena Sava woke for a moment. Her eyes fluttered as she rolled onto her side and, hugging her pillow tightly against her chest, fell into a deep, dreamless sleep. She was unaware that her half sister in the other bed slept too soundly or that a stranger sat beside her, his eyes huge in the darkness as he studied her.

He saw soft curly hair, thick enough for family but a pale shade of brown that would likely have russet tones in the afternoon sun. She had ivory skin dusted with freckles on the nose and cheeks. Her face bore little resemblance to the sharp Austra features. It was too round, too narrow at the forehead, lips too uneven—the top one thin, the bottom full, giving her a hint of a pout even in sleep. Though her eyes were shut, he glimpsed enough before he'd ordered her back to sleep to know that they were a warm, soft brown. A pretty girl, but not a beautiful one, except perhaps when she smiled.

He moved through her mind, deepening her slumber. When he was certain she would not wake, he pulled the quilt off of her. Her body beneath the thin sheet was lean, not from biology but from years of hunger, her arms and legs average but well-shaped, her waist small. No sign of any Austra length here. He ran a finger between her lips, over her teeth.

Human. Just human.

But then Viktor Celac had looked human as well.

He ran a hand under her thick brown curls, lifting them and exposing the back of her neck. He lowered his head, smelled the cloying hint of a drugstore scent.

That taste, that one tiny taste and Stephen learned something he would share only with Denys and Rachel, the sole remaining firstborn. It took years of effort for Patrick to ferret out this tiny piece of the puzzle but it explained so much that happened after.

In a dingy, half-heated flat in Chicago, he made an astonishing discovery. He found another Helen Wells. Thankfully, her cousin had told the truth. She had been born that way, not altered as Celac had been, and Celac had made certain she knew nothing of the killings. A good girl—or at least as good as these conditions would allow. But in this place, that could change and soon.

He considered the obvious course—take her with him now and let the rest of her childhood be spent among his own. He might have done so if she had been younger, but he would not add to the terrible legends already being spread. So his best course was to assure that the next few years were happier ones, then let her make an adult choice.

He wrapped the blanket around her, father to the child she still was. Then he paused, considered.

Softly, so softly that she moved from sleep to nearly awake with barely a stir, he tightened his grip on her mind. And she dreamed—or thought she dreamed—of lush mountains with jagged heights and buildings made of stone and sweeping panes of colored glass. She rolled onto her back and smiled and he saw that, yes, he'd been right. The smile did make her beautiful.

And her beauty made him long for her—for an exchange that would bind her to him.

Not yet, he thought, but . . .

Her eyelids fluttered and for a moment her eyes focused on his face before she fell back into his sleep again. But lightly, light enough that when he kissed her, she felt his lips soft on hers, a slight shift in the angle of her bed, the faint draft of a window opening and closing.

And Stephen? Most likely he relished his self-control with only a hint of regret. Thankfully, he had let two men live tonight, and both would be important. Perhaps it had been instinct not common sense that had dictated this. He hoped so.

Petro Sava paced as he noted the lightening eastern sky. When Stephen joined him, he all but collapsed, not sure if it was from fear or relief.

Stephen decided they could leave Erik's body for his family to claim. The injuries could have been caused by a hit-and-run or perhaps a fall from the tracks above. A mystery, but hardly an enduring one.

Celac's corpse was more of a concern. He'd been too clearly into the change; even the most simple forensics test would raise questions, especially given how he died.

"How did Celac hide his other victims?" Stephen asked.

"Ion's uncle has funeral parlor close by. I work there when they are busy. I know how to use furnace. If you help me get him there, we can burn him. We have done this before."

An hour later, Stephen stood in the dingy basement of the Ares Mortuary and fought the need for sleep as he watched Celac's body consumed by the flames. He did not feel the enduring sorrow of losing one of his own, nor any sense of victory. What had happened that night was too unsettling to his instincts as well as his conscience, and would remain so for years to come. Worse, there was the divide among his own; noticeable most in his children.

What would happen to me or to Laurie if we discovered coattail relations? Would we see these self-created hunters as a danger or as extensions of ourselves? If so, would we view tonight's killings as protection for the family, or as murder?

Stephen must have stayed there for some time, fighting the need to sleep, weighing what he would tell me. I only know what my brother and I could steal from his mind, and we hardly discovered all of it.

# CHAPTER 12

In spite of the pain he was in, Hunter stayed awake through the night, sitting close to the phone, ready to handle any emergency should his help be needed. We watched the midnight movie on TV, the flag flying as the anthem played, then we started in on board games. Just before eight that morning, Laurie returned and, seeing my disappointment that he was not my father, scooped me up.

"We would know if there was a problem, yes?" he said, imitating my father's accent, then laughed and carried me off to his bed. It was past dawn and I was exhausted. As soon as he lay beside me, I slept.

But when the front door opened I woke and ran down the hall. I'd expected my father to pick me up, to share all that had happened that night. Instead he only hugged me quickly and sent me back to bed. There was a weariness in his voice that, given the hour, I could well understand. But what I could not fathom was how carefully he guarded his thoughts. Curious, I left the bedroom door open then lay beside Laurie with my eyes shut, my ears on full alert, and my mind brushing against my father's.

He sensed my presence. —It is over. The beast is dead. Now go to sleep so I can speak to Hunter in private.—

I retreated from his thoughts and concentrated on Hunter's instead.

Weary but alert, Hunter had guessed a great deal from Stephen's expression, more from how Stephen had sent me away then deliberately waited to tell about the night until he had poured himself some Tarda water and settled into a nearby chair.

"How many?" Hunter asked.

"Two. The driver and one passenger."

"But not Konovic."

"It would have made things difficult for us. This is better." Stephen explained the source of Konovic's wealth and how he and the driver had both seen a connection between themselves and our family.

"Were they right?" Hunter asked, thinking of my mother.

"Enough that I could taste it. However, Celac was not content with that. He believed he was strong enough to become one of us through devouring his own."

Stephen explained what he knew about the Ukrainian's death, and what Celac had done to his own ally that same night.

"How many did they kill?"

"Celac spoke of dozens. Worse, the families of the victims thought we were doing the killing. Being more terrified of legends than the authorities . . ." He left the thought unfinished.

Hunter absorbed the information, answering his own questions almost as quickly as his mind could conceive them. When only one remained, Stephen gave a bit of Konovic's history, the encounter with Laurie's father in Bistriţa.

"We were content to be legends, Gregory. Something changed that." He brushed a finger over the scars on the back of Hunter's right hand. "I never asked what you and my brother did during those last years of the war. I need to ask you now."

We do not speak of the dead. Memory of them is sorrow enough. But Stephen had called on Hunter to share his memories. Laurie might not thank me, but I shook him awake, resting my hand on his lips when he started to speak.

I explained quickly, adding, —Stay with Hunter. Father thinks I'm asleep.—

—So you should be,— he replied but he squeezed my hand and held it through the next hour.

"In the beginning, Charles hid his nature when he could," Hunter explained. "But he was forced to fight and when he was losing, instinct took over and then he could not hide his speed or strength. When wounded, he could not hide his need. In the end, it almost seemed that he wanted to take a hit, to make them see exactly what they fought.

"I remember how we stumbled onto a combined German and Romanian patrol. We killed five before I took a shot in the shoulder and went down. They would have finished me off but Charles put down his weapon and ripped them apart. He killed ten that day and took as many bullets. The survivors carried the story home.

"At least there were a lot less locals willing to turn in the partisans after the whispers started. I doubt Charles expected that any of the stories would reach the west. I never did."

"Then anyone from that area might have seen Charles, yes?"

"And well beyond. We roamed all of Transylvania, a bit into Ukraine as well," Hunter replied, voice flat with too much emotion. The past was suddenly too vivid and he was hardly prepared.

"What about sex?" Stephen asked.

The question surprised Hunter. An image flashed through his mind, one I was too young to understand, the emotion that accompanied it full of grim humor. "It was war. Every day might be someone's last. That uncertainty makes even virgins passionate."

"How many?"

"Me? Ten, fifteen; and I was a monk compared to your brother."

"And him? How many?"

"Dozens over three years."

Privation had strengthened our blood in them and then a mating. I heard Laurie swear softly when he reached the likely conclusion.

Like it or not, our world would never be the same again.

Late that afternoon, Konovic was released from the hospital and went home expecting to find police at his apartment ready to arrest him for murder. But though there were men waiting there, they had only come to repair his window and were already at work with the building super hovering over them.

Anxiety had taken a worse toll on Konovic than the shooting, the loss of blood, the lack of sleep. He had imagined every footstep in the hospital corridor to be the police coming to question him about the body in his bedroom . . . and he could not think of any answer that would satisfy them, least of all the truth. Once home, he went directly into the bedroom and saw the blood on the sheets, on the floor, but the room otherwise untouched.

As he was leaving the room, Stephen walked through the still unsecured door.

For a moment he thought the visitor did not look like Laurence Austra, but quickly decided he'd been blinded by a sudden surge of fear. "I would invite you in," he said, finishing the thought with a shaky wave toward the workmen in the main room.

"In there will do," Stephen said and took such a quick step toward him that Konovic all but fell backward into his bedroom.

"Is Viktor . . . gone?" Konovic asked.

Stephen nodded.

"Will I need some explanation?"

"He is ashes."

Konovic's confusion was genuine. So he truly did not know it all. A relief to Stephen, who preferred not to leave Laurie and me anywhere in the vicinity of another of Celac's breed.

"And the woman?"

"If you follow my advice, she will keep silent, but you are not to harm her again. I have given my word on this to her and you will not disobey me. Now, Ion, we need to discuss your family. You have been thinking like a simple-minded kulak for far too long."

Stephen left for Canada two days later but did not go directly home. Instead, he stopped over for a week in Montreal, where he met with Denys and Rachel, the other firstborn, and shared what he had learned. Together they hunted and destroyed five half-breed killers in Quebec.

Then, in the next few months—aided by Petro Sava's sketchy knowledge, their own extensive files on odd occurrences, and Hunter's contacts—Rachel and Denys destroyed three other packs. All had been guilty of the same sort of murders as Viktor Celac. None of them were as far into the change as Celac had been but apparently on their way to it. I sometimes wonder what would have happened if we had not discovered their existence until a few years later.

We are unable to attack one another, could we have lifted a hand against them? And knowing how they treated their own . . . no, it is a thought too horrible to consider.

• • •

As for me, once I was alone with Laurie I had to face my fears and decided I much preferred to have others think of me as a child. Laurie did not push me, but instead offered to arrange music courses for me at the school where he taught.

"If I suggest it, they will not check your record too closely. Even if they do, many wealthy children are privately taught. Nothing odd in that."

And so I immersed myself in learning math through musical composition, English and history through a course on the lives of famous composers, piano and guitar and—in private, of course— the two-necked naizet my people love.

I also acquired my first true human friends and had my first freely given kiss from a girl who actually thought she might love me. Heady, marvelous experiences for a boy raised in solitude. And, of course, I walked the night streets with Laurie where I learned, in much the same way Patrick did in Chaves, how to feed and leave no trace.

But always there remained that uncertainty about myself, that feeling that I had somehow been tested and found to be lacking. I began picturing the Chicago map in my mind, those sections Laurie told me to avoid highlighted in brilliant red like the most important facts in some student's textbook.

One night when there were only a few remaining before I left for Canada, I found myself on the el, heading south. I was filled with resolve to know the truth about my nature and hardly confident about the outcome.

Three stops from the station where I intended to get out and walk and wait, a group of young men came into the car. They were all around fifteen, their skin various shades from white to brown. As for me, my clothes, my hair, the polite way I sat and tried not to make eye contact immediately branded me an easy mark.

I was soon surrounded. "Got any money?" the largest asked.

I had a five, but I wanted to keep at least a dollar of it to get home. Since I doubted they would give me change, I shook my head.

"Sure you do." He sat beside me, close enough that I tried to slide away. As I did, his hand closed over my wrist, pulling my arm behind my back.

"Sure you do, you little shit," he said and they all pressed a bit closer.

I had imagined my trial by fire as something gladiatorial, one on one, perhaps a weapon in my opponent's hand. But six on one, the battle raging in so public a place? So many questions for the police to ask the old woman pretending to be asleep at the opposite end of the car or the half-drunk group in the next car over coming back from a Cubs game.

So many dead.

No, I could not risk it. And they were just boys, vicious as any group of boys can be. I could not kill without good reason.

I looked at the boy holding my wrist and willed him to let me go, forcing the command just as the train pulled into a station. I waited, hoping someone would get on, but the place was deserted.

Just as the doors were about to close, I pushed two of the gang aside and retreated through the narrowing door, waiting in the dark, almost hoping that one would get out and follow.

They all stayed with the train, and I stayed where I was until a northbound el began rumbling into the station. I got on and went home.

Laurie was waiting up. He glanced at me and understood. But he never spoke of it.

When I returned to Canada in August, I brought Stephen a gift from Hunter. I don't know where Hunter found it, but it contained a reviewer's copy of Mario Puzo's book *The Godfather*. Stephen hadn't read far into it before he got the joke and began to laugh.

The following afternoon, while Patrick and I were exploring the acres of our new home some three hours north of Montreal, Patrick sensed a current in Stephen's mind, unfocused but strong. He paused midsentence, put his finger to my lips, and went to the source of it. Stephen had just awakened, his mind still half asleep, unguarded. As he lay beside our mother, a thought had come to him, a name I had all but forgotten.

Irena.

That was when we began our relentless pursuit of one little fact after another, until I could string together Stephen's part of that Chicago adventure. The rest of the story would be told to us a few years later, set down as it unfolded. Patrick will do that, for I have gone on long enough.

# PART 2

# IRENA

# CHAP†ER I3

## PATRICK

*Since my life has hardly been as interesting as Richard's has been, my brother entrusts me to tell the others' stories. And so I will step outside my self for a time and see the world through different sets of eyes. I will conjecture. I will imagine and fill in the blanks. Empathy is not hard to achieve when I have walked through so many minds already.*

*I suppose my brother is right to ask me to do this. He cannot be objective where Irena is concerned. I am not even certain I can be, but I will try to keep my own feelings at arm's length. Not so impossible for a creature so well trained to hide.*

It always seemed easier for Irena Sava to wake in the winter, to slip out of bed long before first light and take a leisurely bath before the rest of the crowded house woke and demanded their turn in the bathroom.

But that January dawn following Stephen's late-night visit seemed more frigid than most and Irena pulled her quilt tightly around her body. Shivering, she stared at the shadows on the ceiling, thrown through the narrow bedroom window from the street-light just outside. The drapes were open. Hadn't she shut them the night before? Frowning, she got up and, not wishing to wake her little sister, tiptoed out of the room and down the hall to the bathroom.

She felt a bit of sadness that morning, as if the coming dawn had forced her to abandon some marvelous dream. It would have been tempting to close her eyes and search for its thread but there would have been little point in doing so. She had at most a half hour before she'd have to wake and dress. With her mother working third shift at the factory, Irena had to rise early so she could be certain her younger siblings ate before they left for school.

It was an existence she accepted, nothing else. But then she had not cherished much in her life since she was seven years old and had left her village for a country that had yielded none of its promise. And so it was natural to assume that the happiness she felt meant that she had dreamed again of the home she had lost.

She slipped into the bathwater, so hot it made her gasp, and lifted her hair so that it lay over the rim of the huge claw-footed tub. Closing her eyes, she thought, as she did so often, of the sudden rush to leave Romania, of the dangerous trek across the border into Hungary, of how her stepfather left them to direct some border guards away from them and never returned. Of the constant battle to survive until finally the word that, yes, Uncle Ion had bought their passage to America.

She had been so young that she had thought of America as a village only a bit larger than her old one. A place with mountains and trees and farms with goats and feral kittens to coax out of the haystacks, and festivals where she could sing with the other children, earning special praise for the beauty of her voice.

But here the only trees were made of stone, their sharp-edged shadows blocking the sunlight. Here the only village was the ten-block area around their little flat, its six rooms holding Irena, her mother, her younger half sister, two smaller half brothers, and the two cousins recently arrived from Romania who slept on a roll-away bed in the living room.

And here she had no social life except for days at school where the teacher scolded her because she was not learning English as quickly as a girl with her intelligence should, and nights when she snuck away from her mother's watchful eyes and hung out with a crowd from her school in a dark deserted building. They smoked cigarettes and marijuana, drank sweet, strong wine and listened to rock music as loud as they dared, scattering whenever the one on guard noticed a squad car approaching.

She didn't like her peers but being with them was better than her crowded home, much better than school, and the pot made her feel happy for a little while. She thought she deserved the time. In less than three years, she would turn sixteen. Then she would have to leave school and go to work to help support the others or marry so her mother could have space for another source of income.

They'd been poor in the Old Country. They were poorer now.

Viktor Celac was often an extra mouth at their table, though to his credit he usually brought some marvelous take-out dish to share and took her brothers to the movies every few weeks. Her mother told Irena that he would make a good husband. Irena knew Viktor was only buttering her mother up but Irena did find him exciting with those intense gray eyes and the hints of secrets in his tone. But there was also a ruthlessness about him that made her wary. She confessed as much to her mother.

"It's because he is a man and you just a tiny girl," her mother replied. "But he has good job, good prospects with your uncle, Ion. If he still wants you when you are ready, be sensible and make a good match."

The thought of Viktor kissing her, touching her, made her shiver, and with more than just fear. Perhaps her mother was right and as she grew older she would come to desire him. And he would be good to her. Love, she thought, would be out of the question.

What she could not understand was the interest of a man of twenty-five for a girl half his age. To Irena's knowledge, until a month ago when he'd started coming by on a regular basis, Viktor had met her only once. Her family had just come to Chicago, and he had stopped by to talk with her mother about work that Ion had arranged for her to do.

Bored with conversation that did not concern her, Irena had wandered outside and stepped onto the sidewalk just as a boy on a bicycle was going past. He'd run into her and she'd fallen hard onto the dirty pavement, skinning her knee and forearm. Bruised and frightened, she'd shrieked for her mother.

It had likely not been a pretty sound, but even then her voice had range. Viktor was the one who reached her first; he picked her up and smoothed back her hair and told her she would be all right.

Perhaps it had been the pitch of her scream, or the scent of her blood, or perhaps he had already begun to find the taste of blood attractive. No matter the reason, he whispered to her that he had to suck the dirt out. He brushed off her knee and did just that, following with her arm. He probably swallowed quite a bit more than necessary, especially after he began to realize what she was.

A stupider man might have arranged to watch her and her siblings, then drug them all and drink. But to the credit of the now dead, Viktor was not stupid. And so he waited. And he died.

Irena, of course, knew none of this as she lay in the bath and thought first of Viktor, then her cousin Petro, whom her sister seemed to think was the man Irena should choose. But Irena looked on Petro as a brother, or the father she had never known. She reminded her sister that she could not marry a cousin in America and so did not give insult to Petro.

Had either man been in her dreams? She licked her lips and tried to remember but all that came to her were vague memories of buildings and mountains and something heavy resting on the edge of her bed. She thought of their older roll-away boarder, the one they called Uncle Toma, and how he brushed his thighs against her whenever he passed her in the hall. Had he come into her room last night? Had someone else?

She slipped lower in the water and felt something sting on the back of her neck as the warmth touched it. When she ran her fingers over the spot, she detected a slight swelling, a small scab. She rubbed a washcloth over it, held it up, and saw a tiny spot of blood.

The shard of a dream came back to her and she smiled and shook her head. Mother was right. She had let her head get filled with far too many stories if she thought for even a moment that a spider bite marked a visit from an old one.

She could hear someone stirring in the bedroom next door. Leaving the water in the tub to add more heat to the room, she dried off quickly and, wrapped in a towel, darted down the hall for her room.

A short time later, dressed for school, she got down on her knees and looked under the bed, checking for the spider that had bit her. She found one, but it was timid and thin and when she crushed it with her hand there was no blood in it. She would have gone looking for the guilty one, but she had no time.

Petro was waiting for her when she left school for the day. This was unexpected, since he usually worked evenings at his uncle's funeral home. He had seemed nervous in the last few weeks and in spite of the two jobs, always blamed money problems whenever she asked what was wrong. But something had apparently gone right for a change. She could see it in his huge smile as he slipped his hand over hers.

"I am going to work at a different place. Just one job," he said in Romanian.

"Speak English. Teachers said I need learn."

"To learn," he corrected then laughed. "I have new job. I start at Wyatt Construction tomorrow. Union card. Everything. Mr. Wyatt says that with extra hours, I'll get three times what I got before."

"But your . . . status. It is wrong."

"That will be handled as well. I have name of lawyer I must see."

"How did this happen?"

To Petro, that must have seemed the most marvelous thing of all. But he would not break his word and so he did not discover that Stephen had made certain he never could. Instead he invented a story about aiding a wealthy man after a car accident, the man's gratitude.

"Mr. Wyatt said that in summer, if your English is good, he will have job for you. Maybe you work after school next year, summer after. You will not need to stop school."

"How can he know my English is bad? Why would he care?"

Petro shrugged and took a turn to the right, away from home.

"Where are we going? I need to stop and see Marta and her sister," Irena said.

"We celebrate."

Irena reached into her bookbag for a cigarette. Before she could light it, Petro grabbed it away from her and tossed it and the rest of the pack into a trashcan. "What did you do? I paid good money for those," Irena yelled in Romanian, hitting his arm once with the side of her fist for emphasis.

"Taking care of you," he replied. "You waste money on stupid things."

The streets grew higher, the buildings taller, sharper, newer. Everyone seemed in such a hurry that Irena pressed close to Petro, fearful that the surging human tide would pull them apart.

"You will work near here?" she asked.

He waited another half block before answering then pointed at the shell of Stoddard Design's newest commission a block inland. "There," he said.

She looked up and up, finding the top in the dim winter light. "There is tree," she said.

"That is custom. It means the height is done. It will get no higher."

"High enough. You will work there?"

"Not at the beginning. When I am ready."

"And if you fall, who will take care of your sisters?"

"Insurance . . . it gives money to family if there is an accident. And I will buy the extra policy to be sure everyone will be rich."

"Not the same to your sisters as having big brother. Or me my good friend."

He thought her concern touching and told her so when they stopped for coffee and cake. After, they ate in silence. There was so much he wanted to say to her but could not. Finally, she finished the last of her coffee and stood. "We must go back. Viktor is coming for dinner."

He could not tell her that she was mistaken, and so he was content to walk her home. "Mother would want you to come too," she said.

He shook his head. He could keep the secret, but there was no way he could sit with her family while they waited and wondered where Viktor might have gone. He felt little but relief now, as if some terrible curse had been lifted from him.

Lifted from Irena, as well. The old one had made it clear that her life was important, too.

Certain that were she to speak of Petro's good fortune to her family, it would all dissolve, Irena said nothing about it at dinner. But after, having to tell someone, she slipped on her coat and went out into the cold. Crossing the street, she traveled down Rockwell Street to the little wooden house where Marta Saratov shared a single large room with her older sister, Marie, because the rest of the family had no room for them.

Irena rang the bell. When Marta opened the door, Irena stepped inside, heading down the hallway and into the large closet that had been reworked into a bedroom to give Marta a bit of privacy. There was only room for a single bed and a coatrack, so they sat on the patchwork quilt on the bed, hunched over to keep from hitting their heads on the shelf above it where Marta kept her clothes.

"Viktor never came to dinner," Irena said. "I thought it a good time to get away and see if your sister is all right."

Marta looked at her friend and her lower lip began to tremble though she did not cry. "I thought like you, that I would never see her again. I expected Ion to send her away. He didn't, though it was almost as bad."

"What did he do?" Irena asked, concern only making her friend break down completely.

"He . . . he . . ." She dissolved into tears, choked back to near silence. "I can . . . not say. I promised," she blurted and pressed her face against Irena's shoulder.

"You can tell me. I can keep secrets," Irena said.

And in a soft, broken voice that grew stronger as she spoke, Marta began.

Marta had just described how Viktor had shown up at the house the night before to ask Marie to come with him, when Irena looked up and saw Marie standing in the doorway, her face white except for the bruise on one cheek that even too much makeup could not hide.

"At least get the story right," Marie said then sat on the other side of Irena. "Viktor did not ask. He ordered. He always bosses everyone but you. Once we were outside, I thought to run and he grabbed my arm so hard I thought it would break." She showed Irena the bruise just above her right elbow. "I don't know how you can sit at the same table with him."

"We sit at different ends," Irena replied, thinking of the one time she had sat next to him and felt his hand sliding between her thighs when no one was looking and how weak his touch had made her feel.

But she doubted she would get so close to him again, after Marie went on, describing in a voice that seemed far too calm how Viktor told her she was only good for one thing with a face and body like hers. She described how Ion raped her. Later, she could recall going downstairs, the night guard who had driven her home.

Irena was shocked. To her, Viktor seemed coarse, but kind.

Now, considering Marie's words, she wondered if she'd known him at all. "That's it? What happened? Did Ion let you leave or did you escape? Tell me!" she demanded.

Though Marie was not the sort to cry, Irena expected her to do so now. But it was Marta who sobbed beside her, while Marie continued with an odd calm.

"When I got up this morning, my body ached from the beating Ion had given me. My legs were shaking when I went into the bathroom and pulled the chain for the light.

"I had expected to see the bruises but there were other marks that made no sense. I ran my fingers over them, and as I touched them I remembered something. Like a dream, but the marks were real. The marks made me remember."

"I don't understand," Irena said.

"I knew I was lucky to be alive. But that's because something wonderful happened." She described how she woke in Ion's bed and found an old one sitting beside her.

"Can you recall his face?" Irena asked.

"Only a little. Beautiful like the legends say. His eyes were dark, all black like a cat's at night."

"His body?"

"No." But she blushed.

"A name? Anything specific at all?"

"No . . . wait! I do remember something." She repeated Stephen's words back exactly as they had been spoken.

"It was a dream or one of Ion's tricks. An old one would have killed you. They always kill," Marta said.

"Perhaps Lev was mistaken about that. He learned it from his brother and now we know what a pig Ion is. Besides . . . besides, I remember one more thing. I . . ." Marie shook her head. "No! Lev was wrong and Ion is a lying pig." She all but spit the last word.

"But we should tell someone. Ion deserves to pay for what he did," Irena said.

"Who can we tell? We are illegals. The government would send us home."

"But you *want* to go home," Irena reminded her.

"I want to be smuggled back. If the government sends me home, I will be seen as a traitor. It would be the labor camp for me. Horrible places. Better here."

"Maybe the Old One on the Mountain would take you as a

bride since you are so passionate," Irena said and giggled, trying
to relieve the tension growing in the room.

"You don't believe me!"

"You had a dream."

Marie pulled her slacks partway down and showed the
scratches on her thigh.

"Ion did that," Irena said when she saw the scratch.

"And this." Though Marie blushed even redder than before,
she showed the mark on the top of one breast.

"Passion," Irena said with a great deal of certainty for someone who knew so little about it.

"And this." Marie lifted her thick, honey-colored hair and
showed the mark on the back of her neck, deep and clear and just
a tiny bit bruised at the edges.

"Can I . . . ?" Irena asked and held out her right hand to touch
it, feel the size, the shape. As she did, her left brushed the similar
mark on the back of her own neck.

Marta reached for a tissue, wiped her nose and the few remaining tears. "What is it?" she asked when she saw her friend's
perplexed expression.

"I believe your sister. Look at this," Irena said and turned sideways so that Marta could compare the marks and say that, yes,
they were nearly identical.

Irena explained the strange feeling she'd had when she woke
that morning, then asked, "Why would an old one do this to you
and me?"

"So we would know that Ion lies," Marie replied.

"And you can recall nothing else?" Marta asked her sister.

"One more thing only. The passion he spoke of was only in
my mind. Telling the story now, I am sure of it. The old one was
kind. He sent me home even after I . . . He sent me home."

"We must find him and ask him why he did this," Irena said.

Marie looked at her as if she had lost her mind. "What did you
say?"

"You said he was kind. If that is true, we can find him and ask
him why he did this."

"If he wanted us to know how to find him, he would have
told us."

"I am going to find him and ask him, whether he wishes it or
not," Irena said. Being a stubborn creature, even the next day's
news of Jules's horrible death, Erik's apparent accident, and the

disappearance of Wolfe and Viktor would not cause her to lose
that resolve.

To her, Ion had done it all.

When Richard and I learned how the girls met, our first thought
was that Stephen had been careless, or become a creature of too
much habit—natural after so many years of life. If we were to
question him, and we have not dared to do so, he would likely say
that he hoped they would know, compare, use gossip to undo
some of the damage Ion Konovic's lurid tales had caused.

And, of course, he would say that he wanted Irena not to fear
him when he visited her again. Or he might have been considering none of these things. Instinct sometimes handles matters on
its own.

If any of that had been Stephen's intent . . . conscious or otherwise . . . it worked far better than he would have anticipated.
From the evening the two women met and realized what had happened to them, Irena Sava became a creature driven by the need
to understand what she meant to my family.

And as it happened, the fates conspired to open doors to her
that she never could have broken down on her own.

# CHAPTER 14

Petro Sava received his legal residency and first good job through Stephen's intervention, but succeeded in keeping both through simple hard work. Within two years, he managed a crew at Wyatt and, on his own, he bought and repaired rundown houses in the Devon Avenue area.

Irena Sava and her family were his first tenants. The rent they paid was half again what their old place had cost but now they had a house not a flat. As they were soon charging their landlord board for the two rooms he used in the back and the meals they served him, they could easily afford it.

Irena's family flourished once their status changed. Irena's mother signed up for English classes, then marketed her language skills in Russian, Romanian, and German. She took a translator's job with an international firm that Ion had ties with.

The job was not the first time Ion had gone out of his way to help the family in those years since Stephen's visit. There had been so many of these that even Irena could see that he seemed to be a changed man. This actually made Irena less trusting of him. The change was an act, after all, and she could never forget that he was at his core a brute and probably a killer.

She was certain of that when, a few months after Viktor had disappeared, she finally asked Ion what had happened to him.

Ion shrugged. "Viktor was into so many bad things," he said. "Likely he had to disappear. Don't worry about him. I don't."

"Have you written his family to tell them he's missing?" she pressed. Not that he needed to, since her mother wrote them often, but it would have been the right thing for the employer to do.

"I'm sure he's done that himself. Don't worry about it. Now how is school coming?"

Yes, Ion was a cold man, but though she made it clear that she despised him, he kept up a cordial interest in her—always asking about school and what her plans for the future might be. Because of this, she decided that she had been singled out by Ion as well as the old ones.

This only made her more determined to one day meet the old one. And she pursued this goal with incredible logic.

When she was fifteen, she lied about her age and began volunteering to usher at the place where Lev had first noticed Laurie and my brother. But Laurie did not renew his box seats and stayed away. She did the same at another theater, then another. Three years after my father's visit, she spied Laurie at the Auditorium Theater and pointed him out to a fellow usher.

"I'm amazed that I can't recall that one's name," the older woman replied then grinned. "Well, I can see why you're so interested. Damned easy on the eyes, isn't he?"

"Almost too pretty to be a man," Irena replied as she watched him. He fit the description, but she could not be sure.

"Pretty? That's an odd way . . . Wait! That's it!"

"It?"

"The name. It's sometimes a woman's name. Laura . . . Laurie! Laurence Austra. I think he's related to the composer."

He was pretty, Irena admitted, almost delicate. But if he was an old one, it was a deceptive delicacy, likely no more real than the name he used. He seemed to sense her watching and turned and looked at her. And in that look from those dark eyes, she felt a stirring inside, a feeling that he was the one she sought and that no matter what she did in the next few moments—or the next few years—she would one day know him.

She felt at peace, oddly so since her heart was pounding. She took a step toward him, another, then decided that she could not meet him here in this crowded room. She turned and left the lobby for the dim light of the theater, her station near the stage.

She saw him enter as the lights were flashing; he took one of the box seats at the edge of the orchestra section. Saw an older man join him a few minutes later. Box six. Season seats.

By midnight, she had a second name to attach to the box, but it was not of a person, but of a place—the Chicago Conservatory of Music.

A week later, heart pounding as hard as it had the night she first spied my cousin, she went to the conservatory after school. She walked the halls for some time, looking in doorways, pretending to know where she was going, fascinated by the bits of music she heard: a woman's voice trilling up a scale, a chorus practicing a piece by Bach. There was an excitement to the place that thrilled her almost as much as the mission that had brought her there, and she felt a stab of disappointment when a sharp-eyed student guessed she did not belong and directed her to admissions.

The counselor spent nearly an hour with Irena then told her that she did not qualify yet. "We do not take beginners. If you have an interest in music, you must decide on an instrument and start taking lessons now."

St. Cecilia's, where her mother had sent her when she decided Irena was getting too wild, offered no music courses. And her family had no money for private lessons.

She scanned the list of possible courses, saw one for which she was sure she qualified. "You teach singing?" she asked.

"We cannot teach voice, but we train," the counselor corrected. "But it is not a regular part of our curriculum. This means there are only a few grants and no scholarships available."

It must have been the clothes that gave her poverty away, Irena thought. Or the accent. She frowned and, feeling out of place, looked away.

The counselor misinterpreted her expression. "Of course there is one other possibility. You could register at the college next door, arrange for a scholarship or some kind of aid, then come here and take the music courses as electives. The only part you would have to pay for would be the private voice lessons. In a year or two you would have the start of a good education even if you decided that there was no future for you in music."

"There is col . . . a college next door?"

"Just go out our front door and take a right. You'll find their entrance around the corner. They even offer a minor in Eastern European Studies if you have an interest there."

An interest! She had not expressed much interest in any of her studies before, but after a brief visit to the college admissions office, she decided she must try if only to get back into the conservatory. She went home with brochures from the college and the conservatory and spread them across her bed. In no particular order, she read one after another, scanning the conservatory brochure for a familiar name on the faculty and not finding it. Laurie's name had never been listed on the brochures, and he had left the conservatory the year before. That visit to the theater would be one of his last before he left Chicago.

With no way of knowing this, Irena plotted her first year at school, thankful she did not have to choose a major until later.

That night after dinner, she explained to her mother how she had visited the college. "I was only curious to go inside," she said. "But I could get in if I worked harder."

Her mother looked at the brochure Irena handed her. "You will have to go to summer school this year and next and I still don't think you will have enough to graduate."

"If I leave St. Cecilia's and go to public school, I could get a free tutor to help with math and writing. And it would save enough money that—"

"We sent you to St. Cecilia's for a reason," her mother said, the weariness in her tone making it clear that she thought her daughter's sudden interest in higher education was likely a lie. "We do not want you to turn out like Marie. Always in trouble and now gone, who knows where."

Irena knew exactly where Marie had gone, as did her mother, though the woman refused to accept Marie's choice to go back to Romania when there was so much more opportunity here. "Am I in trouble? Have I been in any trouble in the last two years? You pay for nothing at St. Cecilia's, not even a good education." She looked at Petro, who was pretending to read the *Tribune*. "Tell her!" she ordered. Aware that her temper threatened to get the best of her, she repeated more softly, "Tell her."

"She is right. My sisters go to public school. And they will go to college, too," Petro said in Irena's defense.

"College." Her mother shook her head and looked at the pamphlets, scanning the offerings. "What will you take?"

This was the moment Irena had dreaded, the answer she did not know just yet. But to say this would make her mother think that she was not serious, so she lied. "I want to teach little children," she said, hoping that would appeal to her mother's maternal instinct.

"Teaching is good. Good hours. Especially when you have children of your own." The woman glanced at Petro, seeking his opinion as if he were the man of their house, but he had folded his paper and gone into the living room to flip on the TV.

Irena wanted to go with him, but decided she needed to start her new, serious life immediately. She went into her bedroom—her own room now, no need to share—and did her homework carefully. Afterward she put on a record, a folk group her mother liked, and began to sing along. Soon her voice fell into the harmony, reaching high notes with natural ease. But these were only folk songs, not at all like opera. Though she found opera difficult to understand, when the season began, she would try to volunteer to usher for the performances so she could learn the classical pieces. Be prepared for the voice.

Petro heard her singing and smiled. As he listened, he might have thought of the infrequent phone calls, the melodic whisper of the old one reminding him to "take good care of Irena."

As if he could have done anything else. She was family after all.

# CHAPTER 15

## RICHARD

In 1975, when I was seventeen, I returned to Chicago to begin my university education—history and liberal arts at Roosevelt, with added classes in composition and classical piano at the conservatory. I moved back into the apartment everyone still thought of as Laurie's. Though I would share it with Denys, he was in Chaves when I arrived and not expected to return until after the New Year.

Not much had changed with the shift in occupant. Denys never seemed to mind whose furniture gave function to his dwellings nor who shared them as long as he was left in peace. The only things of his I found different were his bed and dresser and some clothes in the closet. I settled in to my old room, where Laurie's bedroom set had been moved, then took my first walk in years down the streets I had traveled so often with Laurie. As I did, I found myself thinking of what had happened there, then of Irena. Soon I was looking at every young woman close to my age that fit the image of her taken from my father's mind. Curious, I went home and looked up her name in the phone book. I saw twelve Sava listings, none of them with her given name.

I could have visited some of the family, gotten her address from a relative, but I had the same fatalistic feeling she did when she first saw Laurie—the time for our meeting would come.

During registration, I spoke with my counselor at the conservatory, a friend of Laurie's I'd met years before. I explained my desire to avoid preferential treatment and she let me enroll under the name Austin. I then chose an instructor who valued form over substance and found myself trying to unlearn the things Laurie had taught me and frequently tempted to reveal where I had learned them.

A few weeks into the term, the first grades came out. They were posted by course, and as I scanned the list looking up mine, I noticed the familiar name among the second-year students— SAVA, IRENA. I paged through the sheets, seeing her name on voice and piano courses. After a bit of inquiry, I learned she showed great talent and would be trying out for the Lyric Opera chorus that spring.

Knowing where I would likely find her, I began using the conservatory practice rooms instead of the piano Laurie had left for me. I did not get the same sound from the school's well-used strings, but my ears could adjust while I waited. Besides, the fantasy that Irena might come in, that she might hear me before she met me, made me stretch my limits a bit, though I tried to follow my conservative instructor's frequent reminders that music did not consist of "pounding on the keys."

It took some time before our paths crossed and in a most unexpected way. I was practicing when I heard a chorus singing down the hall: a few bars, then a stop; another few bars, another stop; and so on. Curious, I went to their practice room and saw that their accompanist—a novice volunteer—had picked up some sort of respiratory bug and had to keep pausing to reach for a tissue. He did not have the skill to catch up with the singers and so they were forced to stop with him. The situation might have been comical except the chorus itself looked so frustrated.

"Damn it, Ryan! Just shove some Kleenex up your nose," one of the tenors yelled to him.

Ryan responded with another sneeze.

They were practicing the choral pieces from *Così Fan Tutte,* an opera I knew well. I stepped forward.

"Let me," I said to the heavyset pianist. He looked at me with thanks, picked up his tissues, and went to sit in the back of the room while I took his place.

"You can play this piece?" that brash young tenor called.

I ran through the first bars once, double time to show off, and their volunteer conductor gave the group its cue.

While each voice was pleasant alone, together they had no unity. But apparently this was one of their first rehearsals. As I played, I concentrated on the separate voices, trying to pick out which had promise. As I did, I heard a soprano who would one day easily hit coloratura notes. I merged voice with face and saw Irena standing in the back row, her brow furrowed with concentration, her hands gripping the sheet music tightly. I admit that her face didn't look as beautiful as in my fantasies, but her intensity was arresting, so much so that I dropped three notes before my mistakes drew me back to the music.

We practiced for nearly two hours while the accompanist sat behind me perfecting the dying scene from *La Bohème,* but ready to resume his post if needed. When the group finished, he took the sheet music and went off with a girl from the chorus, I hoped home to sleep.

I watched Irena out of the corner of my eye as she packed her music into her bag and started off the risers. The thin girl I'd glimpsed outside the theater so many years before had filled out to a slightly plump hourglass, shapely enough that her waist would have seemed tiny even without the wide leather belt she wore with her black jeans and black knit top. The look was practical, likely inexpensive, and darkly artistic. Her hair was long, pulled back in a ponytail at the nape of her neck. I might have noticed more, but I was far too preoccupied with the first impression I wanted to make.

She passed by the piano just as I was getting up, giving me an opportunity to say, "You have a beautiful voice." I hoped she would understand it was the truth, not some idle compliment.

"And you did a good job," she replied with much the same thought behind it. Her spoken voice was rich, lower than I would have expected, giving hints of her range. She spoke English quickly and with precision, trying to mask the accent as best she could.

"Did you just start with the chorus?" I asked.

"Everyone just started, can't you tell?" she said and laughed. "Then our director got his turn with the flu. We are on our own until he comes back."

I walked with her and the others to the door, down the hall to the exit. By the time we reached it, we had all exchanged first names and I had volunteered to play for them the next afternoon.

As I left, I was aware of Irena watching me go. For a moment, she wondered about me. But at six foot three and with those broad shoulders, I seemed too large to her. And the hair not black enough or curled enough, the clothes too casual, and the accent, of course, not his.

I let out the breath I'd been holding as I'd absorbed that, a long sigh of relief.

I accompanied the chorus the next day and the next, saying a few words to Irena before and after each practice. Aware of her growing but still casual interest in me, I followed her lead to perfection. Three nights later, she agreed to take time away from her studies to have coffee.

She walked in front of me into the little cafe buried in the corner of one of the campus buildings and hung her frayed leather jacket—black like the rest of her wardrobe—over the back of her chair. Her sweater had a bit of powder along a part of the neckline and her long hair was loose with only the top pulled back and clipped. She dressed for utility, not vanity. That was clear from the lack of makeup, not even to hide the circles under her eyes from too little sleep. A universal condition among students. I shared it, but managed to show the effects far less.

When the coffee came, she insisted on paying for her own then inquired how I had come to Chicago.

I told her a bit about my private education, then the baroque group I'd joined in St. Michael, Quebec, how I'd decided to continue my music education in college, what else I was taking, the usual things.

"Will you play professionally?" she asked.

"I doubt it. It's just something I like to do," I replied, then asked the same question of her.

"I was not even interested in music when I walked into the conservatory." She smiled, then shook her head. "No matter. I came and found my true love."

Her eyes were bright, her voice animated, and her hands moving in time with her speech as she described her first courses at the conservatory, taken two years ago during the summer before she graduated. "I had a teacher, a young woman with incredible insight, who taught me to relax, to stand at ease and just sing. I had a good voice before, and I had always loved to use it. But when we were done with those few weeks, I knew I had talent."

"Opera?"

She nodded. "The stories are so beautiful. All that drama and costumes . . . and the music. I come from a country where people must hide what they feel. With opera I can reveal my soul."

"You said you didn't come here to learn music. Why did you?"

She laughed. "You will think it's silly."

"Silly? Why?"

She sipped her coffee, not looking at me. Her cheeks were flushed. "You will think I am a crazy woman."

I took her hand and gave her a subtle push and in the next hour a good part of the story I already knew came tumbling out. I listened, making only an occasional sympathetic comment to show her I did not think she had lost her mind. Though she never spoke Laurie's name, she knew it and I was thankful I had asked to be listed at school under an alias.

"What made you remember what he did?" I asked, curious how my father could have made such a mistake.

In response, she took my hand and guided my finger to the little scar at the nape of her neck. She then explained about Marie and the mark on her, then went on. "I was afraid that after it healed I would forget so I would not let it heal until it made this scar. I wanted it there, to remind me and as proof."

"So you thought you could meet him here, and spent those years studying hard enough to get a scholarship?"

"No scholarship. I studied, but . . ." She frowned and I sensed a painful memory. "My cousin Petro had a construction company. Last spring, one of his men came to work sick. The man was working on the second story, not far up, when he became dizzy. He decided to come down but lost his balance while he was moving from one safety belt to another. Petro was on the ground when this happened. He was always careful, but when he saw the man about to fall he ran and tried to catch him. It wasn't even twenty feet but the man landed against him and Petro went back against a pile of steel girders. He broke his neck." She paused, gripped my hand, and went on to describe Petro's days lingering in intensive care before the family finally let him go.

"He left enough insurance money to take care of his mother

and sisters, and my tuition as well. Petro always said he would
take care of his own, but I never thought that would include me."

As I said my words of sympathy, my thoughts turned to Viktor
Celac and what he and the others had done to their victims. Petro
must have been much changed in those last few years. I was glad
for him, and for her.

"My mother does not approve of the courses I am taking, but
the money is mine to spend as I wish and my teachers at the conservatory speak of a natural talent, as if I have not worked for
years to make it grow."

"Now you plan to audition for the Lyric?" I asked.

"I am going to try this winter. I doubt they will take me,
though. I am too young."

"Do you have an accompanist?"

"I thought I would find one after Christmas, when my knowledge of the pieces is better and I have the money to pay someone."

"Would you like one now?" I sensed her about to refuse, and I
added, "I'll do it for the experience. I can learn new pieces, and
how to pace myself with a singer. Besides, to help train a future
diva . . ."

When she laughed, I knew I had won.

We worked together the three afternoons a week she did not see
her teacher; it was all she was supposed to practice in the beginning, but I knew her teacher was wrong. Irena's voice was mature
enough to hit the highest notes with ease and I told her so when
we stopped for coffee after one practice.

"How can you be sure?" she asked.

"I have a good ear. And I've sat through a dozen operas. None
of the sopranos had as clear a voice as yours when you relax and
let the music flow through you."

"I've been to almost as many, and I can't hear that," she
replied.

"No one can hear their own voice as clearly as another can."

She leaned over the table and kissed me lightly on the lips. I
automatically pressed mine tightly together. Of course, she misunderstood. "I'm sorry," she said.

"You surprised me, that's all," I replied.

A witty comeback shot through her mind but she thought it
too forward to say. I wondered if she really meant it, and decided
not to wait too long to find out.

"I have two tickets for Thursday night's opera," I told her. "Would you go with me?"

"*Don Giovanni*'s opening night?"

I nodded.

She bit her lower lip and looked away, with much the same expression she'd had when refusing my first overtures for a date. "I can't. I'm too busy and I've seen it many times before."

Not the real reason. I sensed it and, breaking a vow I had made to myself about how our relationship would proceed, I gave her a small push.

"I have nothing formal to wear and I . . ."

"You told me you used to usher. Wear what you wore then. They're box seats. We won't have to see anyone. We can even leave just before it ends, if you wish."

Still that hesitation, so I added, "And after, I want to show you something you may not realize, something important about your voice."

"I really . . . oh, all right," she decided (completely on her own). There was far more enthusiasm in her thoughts than in her tone. I considered that enough.

# CHAPTER 16

She would not let me come and pick her up, so we met at a coffee shop near the theater. She arrived a bit late but I could see where she'd spent her time. She looked far from underdressed in a black sheath—a short clingy knit that showed off her legs and a low-cut neckline that drew my attention to her breasts. The heels were high; the nylons seamed. Since it was a warm winter night, she had chosen a deep green knit shawl rather than her usual worn leather coat. Home-crocheted, I was sure, but the skill of its maker made it look boutique-bought, and expensive.

She had curled her hair and her makeup was perfectly applied. I noticed for the first time how her wide-spaced eyes and full lips would give her a marvelous stage presence.

"Do I look so good?" she asked, smiling at my reaction.

"You've been hiding some talents," I replied.

"Not mine. I came down early, and walked through Carson's. Cosmetics is always doing free makeovers. I was so thankful that I bought the lipstick."

As she leaned forward and kissed my cheek, I caught the heady smell of roses and jasmine, beautiful as a French garden. I stored that knowledge away for a future gift. "We should go," I said and dropped a dollar on the table to pay for the tea I had nursed for the last hour.

Laurie had renewed his season tickets to the opera, as well as to the Chicago Symphony and ballet, assuming that, given my interest in music, I would use them with as much enthusiasm as I did the grand piano he'd left for me. I'd already let one event pass because I was too busy and would have likely ignored this one had I not met Irena.

I do not consider *Don Giovanni* to be one of Mozart's best. The humor seems flat, the ending overly didactic, and the destruction of the slovenly noble by a spirit rather than by those he had wronged completely alien to my nature. But that night, sitting with Irena's hand on top of mine, I felt entranced. As the soprano singing the role of Donna Anna began her first notes, I could feel Irena's growing excitement. She listened with a critical ear, hearing an occasional strain in the voice that a casual listener would miss.

"You see," I whispered and she gripped my hand to show she understood. I leaned closer to her and, as I inhaled the intoxicating scent of her perfume, the music grabbed us both and we were a part of it, soaring and falling with the notes.

We did not move at intermission, nor speak; each of us waiting for the other to begin. People milled on the floor below us, whispered in the boxes on either side of us. There were footsteps in the corridor, the tinkle of champagne glasses. I knew this, but I was aware only of her hand resting on mine, her fingertips brushing mine, her thoughts far from pure.

Had I somehow willed her that passion? I did not think so, and that was the most marvelous feeling of all.

We left just before the final bows. The night had grown colder and a soft rain fell. I hailed a cab and gave my address. I was assuming too much, perhaps, but she did not correct me.

As I paid the driver, she stood on the sidewalk, looking up at the building. "You live here?" she asked, clearly impressed.

"I live with my cousin," I replied. "He travels and I watch the place for him." I took her arm and pulled her under the winter canopy out of the chilly rain.

In the hour before I went to meet her, I had mentally walked through the apartment and building. The mailboxes were behind the downstairs desk. There were no names beside the buzzers that let late-night visitors in, no name on the apartment door, no mail lying about. There would be nothing to give my secret away until the moment I chose.

And it would have to be soon or whatever we did together would be a lie. I considered this on the elevator ride up, and sensed her reacting to my edginess with humor, as if it came from lack of experience.

We stepped from a warm, softly lit hall into a dark and chilly apartment. I turned up the heat, lit a fire, offered her a drink that she refused, tea that she accepted.

She followed me into the kitchen but did not stay there long. When I found her again, she had slipped off her shoes and was standing between the grand piano and the window, gripping the back of an armchair and looking out at the lake. I turned down the lights to enhance the view and moved behind her, my hands brushing her arms, my lips her shoulder. She pulled away from me. "Is this where you practice?" she asked.

"Yes."

"Play something for me."

I sat down, ran my hands across the keys. I might have chosen a romantic piece by Schubert or San Saens, but I wanted something I loved and regarded as a challenge. I considered and began to play.

"Armageddon" was a recent composition of Laurie's. He had played it for me at the last family gathering, then tossed me the sheet music as if he were delivering a simple exercise. I'd practiced it often since, trying to achieve that same fire and ice emotion he coaxed so easily from the strings. I was hardly his equal in skill, so I settled for a slower tempo, less drama to the crescendos. I played for twenty minutes, bowing my head when I had finished, as if accepting the accolades of a silent, unseen audience.

As I suspected, she knew opera but not classical music, at least not well enough to know that this piece had never been released to the public. But she was impressed, which of course I had intended. "You hide your talent too much, I think!" she said and hugged me.

"And you do the same though you do not know it."

She pushed away from me, pouting, half serious. "I do not! How?"

"I can show you. Go, stand there." I pointed to the spot to the right of the piano bench.

She did as I asked, listening with polite reluctance as I explained. "You are too concerned with hiding your accent and so you are always tense as you form words. It only shows when you are at the highest notes. But if you relaxed, worried less about the words and focused only on the purity of the music, your voice would expand into its true range."

She was about to disagree when I began playing the opening bars of "Der Hölle Rache," the famous aria from *The Magic Flute*. She knew it well, and always fell apart not on the high notes, but when the phrases had to rush to keep up with the music. "Sound the notes, but don't say the words," I said.

"The notes?"

But I played on, projecting the thought, —Calm . . . calm . . . —

She started, her voice rising higher and higher with the music, reaching the high F the song demands with relative ease.

"Ornament it," I whispered.

I sensed her doubt, tried to convey the relaxed confidence that she ought to feel without making my mental presence too obvious.

And heard in response a beautiful, perfectly modulated pair of notes ending with high A. Then . . .

Then she faltered. I held the sound on the piano, waiting. "Find the next note," I whispered.

The tension was growing in her again, constricting her throat, destroying any chance of reaching further. But the sound was in her, I could feel it echoing in her mind. If she felt it, I knew she could do it. If she heard it, I knew . . .

Without thinking, I sang B, then C, the sound high and pure. Simple for me . . . for any of my kind.

She stopped. Mouth still open, she gaped at me, her eyes wide. The first thought that came into her head was the most logical for a singer. And ludicrous.

"Not cut. Not illness. This is just my voice," I said.

She knew so many of the legends, but not this one. "The music I played before was written by my uncle," I explained.

"His name?" she asked, quick enough to guess the truth but needing to hear it.

—Laurence Austra.—

I'd gone too far. She shivered, backed away from me and toward the sofa and the fireplace, her bare feet feeling behind her for her shoes, her eyes on me all the while as if I might turn into a bat or a wolf and attack.

"I'm sorry. I won't tell anyone. But I have to go," she mumbled.

"You can't. It's freezing out there," I replied, then sensing her resolve rushed to the closet and took out a long wool coat that belonged to Denys.

I held it out to her. She snatched it from my hand, retreated toward the door. "I'm sorry. I have to go away and think," she said.

"Let me call you a cab. You can wait for it downstairs."

"No!" She pulled the door open and left me, closing it behind her with exaggerated softness.

After she'd fled, I sat on the sofa and stared into the flames until even the embers died. Hungry but with no inclination to hunt, I was about to leave anyway when the entry buzzer startled me. I went, hit the button that would open the door. The buzzer sounded again, longer, more insistent.

"What is it?" I asked her through the mike.

"Why did you wait until I was up there to tell me?" she asked.

"I wanted you to know me first. To come here because of who I am, not what I am," I replied.

"Why didn't you come after me?"

"Because that is not who I am." I waited a moment, then unlocked the outer door again.

The soft ding of the elevator was my first indication that I had given the right responses.

The coat was heavy with rain. I slipped it off her then went and found a towel for her hair and a blanket to wrap around the rest of her until I could stoke up the fire. She sat on the far end of the long sofa, body pressed against the arm, using the edge of the towel to dab away an unexpected tear. After the wood caught, I sat on the other side of the sofa. The two cushions between us seemed a fair distance for the moment.

"I'm sorry," she said without looking at me. "It happened too fast."

"Everything did. But you had to know. It would not have been right otherwise."

"Did you ever have a lover who did not know?"

"I've never had one who did." I did not add that Louise and those few weeks of sex that consisted mostly of foreplay comprised my entire human sexual experience.

"Was the rest of what you told me true?"

"All of it. I was the young one you saw at the theater that night."

Silence again. She broke it by stretching out her arm toward me, taking my hand. Her own was deathly cold and shook just a little. "It's late," I said. "If you need to call home, you—"

"No one is expecting me and I still don't want to go."

I brushed my fingers along the side of her wrist. Her pulse quickened. I was about to kiss her palm when she pulled her hand away. "Wait! There are questions I must ask." She paused then blurted out, "Did an old one kill Jules?"

"No," I replied.

"I knew it! I always did. It was Ion, wasn't it?"

"Viktor Celac."

"Viktor!"

I told as much of the truth as I dared. "Ion gave him the responsibility of keeping order but he did more than that. Anyone who opposed his authority was killed. He blamed the killing on us because he knew your community would believe the lie and not complain to the police. When Jules tried to tell us what was happening, Viktor murdered him."

"And what happened to Viktor?"

"He attacked me and my father killed him." No need to explain that a day separated the first act from the second.

"Attacked you? Why?"

"I tried to rescue Jules."

"And to think my mother would wait on Viktor like he was some prince visiting his peasants, always telling me what a great husband he would make. When Viktor disappeared, she was so upset that she even wrote his family to ask if they had heard from him. She still writes them every month to ask about him. I won't tell any of them that he is gone. They'd want the details. It's better they never know."

She stared into the fire for some time, then forced herself to lay her hand over mine, to move closer, to remember why she'd come home with me. She looked at my face, reminding herself that I was no different a person than I had been a few hours before. And she wondered if the stories she had heard about the passion the old ones could arouse in their lovers were also true.

I could not stop myself. My nature responded. I moved into her mind, and through it touched her body. She felt my power in a rush of warmth, a soft caress in all those places she longed to be touched. She wanted to feel my power, and I had waited so long to share my passion with a woman who would know what I was and come to me without fear.

She leaned her forehead against my shoulder and sighed. "Is that you doing these things to me?" she asked.

"Some of them. If I am moving too fast for you, I'm sorry."

"Don't apologize. I'm sure you know I like it." Frightened at her own daring, she stood and pulled me to my feet. Though her voice was almost playful, her heart was racing as she told me, "This room is too big. I keep expecting someone else to come in to fill it up. Show me where you sleep then show me what you do."

Where I sleep. What I do.

As I led her down the hall, I had to struggle to keep from laughing. It seemed we had grown up on the same movies.

I was proud of my room, the beauty of it. The master suite was on the south side of the apartment, with windows facing the lake and the city. Mine was the outside one on the north and I had that same magnificent view of the lake. Though I'd kept Laurie's Country French bedroom set, I'd added the wine-colored satin comforter on the four poster, the extra sets of paisley pillows. Everything neat as of that morning, except for the desk in the corner where the scattered sheets of my assignments lay ignored.

"Sleep and work," I said, lighting the pair of candles I'd put on the dresser earlier that evening. Their flames caught and flickered in the mirror, setting what I hoped would be the right mood.

I turned. She stood in the doorway, not indecisive about being there. Not frightened. Something else. "Is it true that we will not need to use any protection? Because if we need it, I brought some—"

"We don't need any," I said.

But she did not move. "And is it true that my blood in you will heighten our passion?"

"It is."

"But I already feel ready to explode."

"I can take care of that," I replied, drawing her close, kissing the side of her neck, that river of life inside her pounding against my lips.

"Then now," she whispered, tilting her head back, waiting.

I am not Christopher Lee and she was not my victim. I might

have said that but it would have broken the mood. So I kissed her
instead, my hands moving down her back, unzipping her dress.

"I want to feel it," she murmured. "When it happens I want to
feel you draw me in."

She could not have guessed the effect her words were having
on me; I, who had been so confident of my self-control. "I promise," I managed to mumble and pushed the dress off her shoulders.

"It comes off from the top," she said, stepping away so she
could slide the dress over her head and toss it on my desk chair. I
moved toward her but she held her hand out to stop me. A half-
slip and hose followed and she stood in front of me clad in lacy
black lingerie that, even had she not spoken of bringing protection, would have made it clear how she'd expected the evening
would end. As I watched, she turned full circle, then went and sat
on the edge of my bed, waiting for some sign from me on what I
wanted her to do.

I'd had only hurried moments with Louise—of unzipped blue
jeans and skirts pressed against my stomach, my senses alert for
any witness, my mind for any questions surfacing in her. All of
that had been no more than practice of the most elementary sort,
all leading to this.

—Take the rest off.—

She looked less startled than the first time I'd spoken to her
mind, even tried to relax as she stood and pushed the panties off
then arched her back to undo the hooks on the bra.

I knew the sum total of her sexual experience to be three times
mine, but her acting was flawless as she stretched out on the dark
satin as if she had been in men's beds many times before. I began
unbuttoning my shirt and walking toward her but she held out her
hand. "Show me everything," she ordered.

I did as she asked, undressing and turning full circle so she
could see the differences I'd hidden from her for so many weeks.
I felt silly and, being excited, far too exposed. I stayed out of her
mind while she looked at me, thankful that she did not ask me to
smile, more thankful still when she took my hand and pulled me
down to lie beside her.

"Less of some things. More of others. And enough where it
really counts." She stressed the last by running a hand up my
thigh and reaching between my legs, but not touching me. Not
fear; inexperience that she tried to hide.

I raised her hands above her head. Freeing her from thoughts of how she must act, I began kissing her body, feeling the fluttering of her nerves and the heat rising from her, hearing those low-pitched moans of pleasure.

"Please," she whispered and pulled her hands free. Drawing me close to her, she kissed me hard and deep, and gave a tiny cry of surprise when she felt my sharp rear teeth. She pulled away only long enough to look at me, to run her fingers over my mouth, my cheeks, my hair. She touched the pendant I wore, the family gift from my tenyears ceremony. "I know this legend. I should have guessed it all when I first saw this," she said then moved her face close to mine.

"Now," she ordered and before I could discover her intent she kissed me again, the side of her tongue pressing hard over the sharpness inside. A tiny cut, a bit of blood that hinted of more to come. As she had asked, I drew her in with one long kiss.

Before that moment, I had read her preferences through her thoughts. Now conscious directions were no longer needed. I felt what she felt, sent the feeling back, heightened and returned and heightened . . . male and female passion merged, enhanced. She wanted to know it all and I held nothing back.

No one above us, two inches of carpeting and a solid floor beneath. I did not try to muffle her cries, or even my own. We stopped only when we were exhausted. By then the sky had cleared and a three-quarter moon had risen, throwing silvery light against the smoky windows of my room. And yes, I was well fed.

"When we break up, you will have to dull the memory of tonight, you know. Otherwise . . ." Irena's voice trailed off, her laugh nervous and quick, her eyes bright.

I understood what she meant. If we stayed together, it would happen someday. I wondered when I'd find the courage to tell her we need never break up at all.

She cut her nine o'clock class on Friday morning. I did the same with my eleven. We managed our twos—her dress covered by a sweater she'd borrowed from me—but we met immediately after and took a taxi to the house she shared with her family.

Though I knew her house was empty, she made me wait in the cab while she went in and grabbed a few clothes and some books, coming out with them stuffed into a paper grocery bag.

After adding a second bag filled with things for her to eat, we went back to my apartment. Disciplined, we actually caught up

on our course work. She sang for me. I played for her. Then, with
Laurie's taped music providing the ambiance, I took her again on
the floor in front of the fireplace, later in the bed, later still on the
terrace, wrapped in blankets to keep out the winter cold.

Monday morning, passion spent, we put on our jeans and
sweaters and went back to our studies, our lives. By mutual
agreement, we hardly spoke during the week. By Wednesday I
could feel the craving beginning in me—that wanting of her. I did
not hunt Wednesday night, nor Thursday. By Friday at four, when
I met her in that same cafe, both of us were prepared to explode
from anticipation alone. We repeated the weekend before.

We went on that way for weeks, the tension in me almost un-
bearable by our Friday meetings, released over hours those Friday nights. Every time we were alone, I expected Irena to ask me
why an old one had visited her that night, but she never did.

And so everything seemed perfect, except for those moments
when my fingertips or my lips would brush across that little scar
on the back of her neck and I would feel as if I had stolen something not meant for me.

# CHAPTER 17

The weather grew colder. Christmas decorations appeared along State and Wabash Streets. I went into Carson's, asked what perfumes smelled like roses, and found the scent in a heart-shaped bottle fittingly called Joy.

I gave the perfume to her on the anniversary of our second month together, December 13, St. Lucy's Day. In one week, the family would gather in Chaves. For the first time in eight years, I would not attend.

I caught up on my schoolwork instead and, the day after Christmas, Irena moved in with me for the rest of the holiday break.

I thought we would be on vacation, spending time together, and in a way we were. But her stack of librettos, her books on the presentation of operas, and the long and boring term papers she had due on the history of music and an analysis of Byron took precedence over conversation, sleep, and even eating—hers and mine.

When we did speak, it was often about her audition. She'd worked with her voice coach to decide on the best pieces to accent her voice, language proficiency, and presentation. Though she would likely sing in the chorus if she were accepted, she

would also understudy one of the lead roles and would be expected to act it to perfection should the need arise. She had to
present her voice, and her poise, at their best.

Then there was her practice—an hour a day of scales, then a
run through one or two of the five pieces she had chosen. She had
seen three of the five operas and I the other two. I would show her
how the singers had stood in them, the gestures, even the ornamentation of the notes until Irena could absorb no more and went
back to her solitary practice.

Hungry, I would leave her then, stalking Lincoln Park, falling
in beside the occasional hiker or dog walker or lonely man looking for company. Conversation led to a quick stop in the shadows
then to a long night's hike through empty streets so that I would
keep out of Irena's way and simply let her be.

Once, I came home and found her still awake, sitting barefoot
and cross-legged in the center of the floor, Vanilla Fudge on the
stereo, a joint in her hand. She rarely smoked since it was bad for
her voice, so I knew she was trying to slow down, relax. I sat beside her and took a hit, then another, and lay back and laughed,
caught up in the sadly fleeting euphoria.

"What is it?" she asked.

"I was thinking we should just say fuck it to all this work, go
and grab Laurie and start a rock band. With Laurie's music, my
words, and you as lead singer, we'd be famous in a year."

"Infamous!" she giggled.

"And there would be rumors of the band members' shadowy
pasts, of late-night orgies in the lead singer's room, of odd ex-
changes of bodily fluids," I went on.

"My mother would have a heart attack!"

I started to laugh, and with difficulty managed to add, "My father would too!"

"Shortcuts," she mumbled. "You don't really mean it."

"Sometimes I wish I did," I replied, astonished at her sudden
shift in emotion over what was only a flight of fancy.

"Shortcuts," she repeated. She drew her knees close to her
chest, looked at me, and frowned. "Do you think I could ever settle for that?"

She was not by nature introspective, so I had little idea what
she meant. But I knew enough to rest a hand on her bare ankle
and say, "You don't need to. One day soon you will be the toast
of New York, London, Paris, Rome. And I will be your faithful

lackey, rubbing your feet when they hurt from too many re-hearsals. . . ." I did just that. "Kneading those sore muscles in your thighs. Opening your door."

She laughed as my lips brushed against the inside of her thigh, then stubbed out the joint and stretched out on the floor.

And for a time, she was there with me, mind as well as body. Later, as she lay beside me in bed, I felt dampness on my bare arm and realized she was crying. "What is it?" I asked.

"Do you really think I can do it? Be that person?"

"Why do you doubt it?"

But she was fighting her tears then, and did not answer. I held her close, using the bond to touch her mind as softly as I was able. She knew, and let it happen.

And I saw her—a thin child of about seven, going down the stairs from a tiny second-floor flat, clutching four dollars to give to the butcher dropping off their order. . . .

"You tell your mother she already owed twelve before this five," the man grumbles.

"I'm sorry. It's what she left me," Irena tells him, looking at him with her almost trusting child's eyes.

The man hesitates, then takes the money and sets the shopping bag down. "Poor kid," he says as she hugs him tightly around the waist. She carries the heavy bundle upstairs, sniffing back her tears because her mother is waiting on the landing and Irena has been ordered to lie. . . .

"When my mother got a job that paid a living wage, she took the bus over to the butcher's shop and paid the man every dollar she owed him. Now that she has a car, she shops at his store every week—loyal because he helped her. She's right but I won't go with her. I can't."

So it wasn't money she needed, but respect. A more worthy goal, but if her ambition ended in defeat, it would be that much harder to accept.

I didn't say anything, just held her close. With her stubborn-ness and talent there was no way she could fail. I told her so.

"But I get so tired sometimes," she admitted.

"You push too hard. You don't have to be perfect at every-thing."

"It isn't about perfection. I will never have this opportunity again. Nor will you. And lately it seems you've been wasting it."

An honest assessment. From the moment I'd met Irena, *she'd* been the center of my life, not the education I'd come here to receive.

I did not explain to her that my memory made my courses so easy that my grades had fallen only slightly over the last few weeks. But I did have a paper due soon on a subject I had chosen: "Charting the Future from the Last Great War." I should have been through the rough draft by now. I'd barely begun the research.

The following afternoon, Irena and I went to the city library . . . an incredible building with a rotunda covered in Tiffany glass tiles. The city boasted that the mosaic was as ornate as any to be found in Italy, a point I did not have the knowledge to dispute. We took a table upstairs where, for the next few hours, I absorbed fact upon fact, storing them as I always did, to sift and sort through later.

It was snowing when we left. I wanted to hail a cab but Irena felt like walking in spite of the weather. Though she hadn't eaten much since breakfast, she wanted to go straight back to the apartment. I insisted we stop at a casual place close to school that I had been told served some of the best Italian beef sandwiches in town.

I sipped my tea and watched her eat, noticing how after the first few bites her hunger kicked in. She'd been famished. She simply hadn't known it.

As we were leaving, we ran into another couple from the chorus, who were on their way to an impromptu holiday party at a campus-area bar famous for never checking IDs. "We need you. There's a piano," the girl said, grabbing my arm.

And almost tropical heat. And a crowd as thick as the cigarette smoke. We pushed through it to a somewhat emptier back room where Ryan was trying to play Christmas carols on an out-of-tune upright. I coaxed the right notes out of the unruly thing and soon everyone was drifting into rocky and uncharted harmonies. We switched to popular songs and Irena did a fair imitation of Marlene Dietrich in *The Blue Angel*.

We stayed until closing time, got home after three. Irena was cold and we both reeked of smoke. We took a shower together and went to bed. Later, I heard her cry out in her sleep. She'd done that a few times before, nightmares, I thought. I rolled over and rubbed her back until she quieted.

When I woke late in the morning, she was still beside me, curled up under the blankets. I kissed her shoulder, felt how warm she was, and brushed a hand over her forehead to verify my suspicions.

Two or three degrees above normal, maybe more. Hoping she'd be able to attend the New Year's party we'd been invited to that evening, I let her sleep, went to the coffee shop around the corner, and returned with hot cinnamon rolls and orange juice and one of those little tins of aspirin they display for sale under the glass countertop.

She was in the shower and came out a few minutes later, wrapped in her terry robe. "I thought the steam would help but my throat feels only a little better. I guess it's my turn to be sick," she said after she'd shuffled to the dining room table where I'd set a place for her.

—Don't talk. Let your voice rest,— I replied, reminding her of the advice her vocal instructor had given her early in the year when the campus bugs began making their rounds.

Though she looked miserable, she agreed. I did as she asked, started a large pot of water boiling on the stove and built a fire. We dug the TV out of the closet and watched whatever came on through the day while the steam-covered windows wept. She fell asleep on the sofa, and though she still felt hot, her breath was even and deep. Hungry, I left her for a little while.

When I returned, the air was thick and damp. Irena hadn't shifted position and her head was, if anything, hotter.

I didn't want to wake her, especially not to ask her how she felt, so I went into my bedroom, shut the door, and called my mother's human cousin, Carol Wells.

Carol asked for details, which I provided, concluded Irena had the flu, which I'd already guessed, and explained what the complications might be. She gave me the symptoms for pneumonia and bronchitis, and said I could only keep doing what I was already doing while we waited it out.

"How long?" I asked.

"A week, maybe more. With my brother it was always longer but he never had resistance to anything," she told me.

It had been one day, an eternity it seemed. I wondered if either of us would survive longer.

Three days later, Irena's fever spiked to 103 and there was an odor in the room that made me wonder if something had crawled under the bed and died. "You need to see a doctor now," I told her.

"No!" Even that single word made her cough. —No doctor.— She shook her head for emphasis. —I can't.—

—Can't?—

She pulled down the corner of her nightshirt, showing the mark I'd made on her shoulder. Old, almost healed. —No worse than those love bites so many students are always giggling about,— I countered.

—The other two are newer. Besides, I've never seen a doctor.—

—Never!— I thought of those immunizations the Canadian schools made me get. And I had been homeschooled. I asked about hers.

—In our neighborhood, the nurse would come to school and give us what we needed. My mother took care of us when we were sick. We didn't have money to spend on doctors or insurance.—

"Well, you need a doctor now and I have the money. Pay me back when you're famous." I would have taken her anywhere, but what she said was valid. I called the offices of Stoddard Design in Chicago and explained the situation to Alex Savatier, a friend of Laurie's whom I knew well. As I expected, he provided a name.

"How much does he know?"

"Know? Nothing. Guess? Likely quite a bit since he's been treating me for years and long since stopped asking about my suddenly remarkable good health. Make sure you tell the office that you're Laurie's cousin, that should get you in right away."

Two hours later, we arrived at the doctor's, Irena wrapped in Denys's coat (the warmest thing we had to put her in), one of my hats, and a scarf wrapped around her mouth and neck.

Irena wanted me to go into the examining room with her, but the nurse made me wait outside. —I'll be in there anyway,— I told her and went back to my chair, thankful the office was empty. I had little experience being around the sick, and wished to keep it that way.

Though the doctor noticed the marks on her, he did not comment on them as he listened to her breathing and heart, and stuck a stick down her throat to get a tissue sample. When he'd finished, he asked her to get dressed and meet him outside.

I cornered him in the hallway. "How is she?" I asked.

"Give her a minute to come out and I'll talk to both of you at once," he said.

The diagnosis was no worse than what we'd already thought.

But he added that she appeared to have a strep infection in her throat and needed to take it easy even after she felt better.

"How long?" Irena whispered.

"At least another week away from school. I'll give you a written excuse and a prescription for one of the newer antibiotics. I also want you to start taking a vitamin with iron. You college girls are always pushing too hard and eating too little. No wonder half of you are borderline anemic."

She looked at me with fever-bright eyes, squeezed my hand. I explained about the audition.

"I wouldn't try to sing with a throat so raw," the doctor said, speaking to her. "If the infection decides to settle in the larynx it could do permanent damage. I'll call you in a day or two when the tests come back. In the meantime, shhhh."

She wiped tears from her eyes as she slipped on her coat. "The auditions are only twice a year. Isn't there anything else we can do?" I asked for her.

"Alex might know that better than I do," he told me.

As soon as we left the office, Irena brushed my arm to get my attention and asked the question I'd been dreading. —What did he mean by that last comment?—

—I'll explain later,— I said, making her wait in the lobby while I went outside to hail a cab. On the way home, I stopped at a pharmacy to get the prescription filled while she waited in the cab. I gave her a pill as soon as we stepped into the apartment.

A half hour later, with her back in pajamas and lying on the sofa wrapped in a blanket, I sat close to her on the floor. "This requires a bit of recent history," I said and explained how my father had shared his blood with the uncle for whom I had been named. "The bond when I share your blood is tight. When it is shared both ways it is all the tighter. My father and Richard needed it that way." I briefly explained why, and the unexpected outcome.

—The legends say the exchange guarantees a horrible death,— Irena said.

"True. But until my uncle Richard lived years after he was supposed to have died, we did not understand the benefits such a sharing creates.

"Because she loves him, Elizabeth shared her blood with Paul Stoddard. He's in his sixties. He looks and acts twenty years younger. Ann did the same with her lover. And Rachel with hers. As to Laurie, he and Alex grew up together. When Alex started feeling his age, Laurie gave him that gift. Alex's doctor noticed his improved health. Maybe the doctor guesses more than he lets on. I'm sure that's why he said what he did."

—You speak only of men.—

"There was a woman, and recently." I told her about Laurie and Kathleen and the outcome of what they'd done. "It's been thirty years and he still grieves for her. So much for the myth that the old ones cannot love," I said.

She shut her eyes and considered what I told her, her thoughts sad. "So what you said our first night will no longer be true?" she asked after a while.

"Shhhh . . . exactly. You could have a child."

—No, no children until I am much older. After we do this, we will just have to be careful like every other couple I know.—

"*If* we do this. We may not need to. You may feel better tomorrow."

I prayed she would. I did not want to tell her the thing that was so obvious to me—once we understood the gift our blood imparted, we did it for people we cherished. Young though I was, I understood that my love for her, deep as it seemed now, could prove fleeting.

There was also the troublesome matter of who Irena could one day be. I did not want to risk awakening things in her best left sleeping for another few years.

If I'd dared, I would have called my mother, asked her how it had been for her in those weeks after my father shared himself and began the change. But I knew she'd made a choice to join the family, and she had done so well after their sharings had begun. A comforting thought since Irena, too, deserved a choice.

I sat holding Irena's hand until she drifted off to sleep. I was hardly hungry but sitting there listening to her breathe, praying for some sign that the drug was working and she was improving would have driven me insane. I moved the phone within easy reach of her, left a note on the floor beside her, went out for a while.

It had snowed again, covering already icy streets with a wet slush. I slogged north on Sheridan, determined to put some distance between me and sickness and decisions I felt too young to make on my own.

There had been an excitement to these walks not so long ago, but the hunt seemed empty now. I did not want anyone for a quick moment's use but the alternative seemed too much a betrayal.

I'd just decided to settle for anyone, to take and be done with it, when I noticed a slim young woman crossing the street in front of me, dragged along by a small dog that seemed to be walking her. The woman was young, foolishly stylish in her short leather coat and over-the-knee dress boots that gave no traction on the ice. The dog, a small spaniel, seemed better suited to the weather in a quilted chintz coat with a thin lace trim along the edge and his name embroidered across the top. "Can I pet Roger?" I asked, crouching down before she answered. Wild beast that he was, Roger licked the snow from my face.

"I can't have pets in my apartment," I explained.

"That's so sad," she replied, as I scratched behind the dog's ears. I had a sudden glimpse of the cabin, of the wolf that had watched me when I made my first kill. No, a dog like this would hardly last long in Dawson.

"Doesn't he get cold?" I asked.

The woman laughed. "Never as soon as I do. I was just taking him home."

"If you're going south on Kendall, can I walk him for a little bit?" I asked.

She looked at me, not because she was wary but because she wanted to size me up and to try to figure out how, in the next few blocks, she might find out if I were seeing anyone and, if I were not, how to suggest that I take her number without seeming too forward.

We walked to her door. I said I would wait until she got in safely, then followed her in when she offered a cup of tea. So far as I could discern, I had not pushed her at all, not even for that last. A dangerous world, the dating scene.

Some minutes later, I left her stretched out on her bed, her soggy shoes on the mat beside the door. In the morning, she would remember me standing outside to see her safely in. The rest would be no more than a marvelous dream. We are all so creative that way.

I heard the music when I was still a few buildings away, *The Magic Flute* played for all the city to hear. I looked up at the terrace but could see nothing from that angle but the strings of white lights. Quickly, I went inside and up the elevator.

One of my floor's other tenants was pacing outside my apartment, uncertain what to do. "I pounded but no one answered," he told me. Seeing my concern as I rushed to unlock the door, he added, "And with you so young we always thought we'd have to worry about rock music."

I assured him that I'd handle everything and went inside, locking the door behind me.

I turned down the volume. "Irena!" I called.

"Don't do that. Please don't," she whispered. I followed her voice from the dimly lit apartment through the open terrace doors.

She sat on one of the iron deck chairs, wearing nothing but a nightshirt, her bare feet brushing the snow. "Irena, you shouldn't be out here," I said. I touched her and found that only her hands were cold, the rest of her far hotter than she'd been when I left her.

She giggled. "If I am going to die, I want to do it beneath the stars listening to the angels sing." Her voice was softer than a whisper so that even I had to strain to hear.

"You're not going to die," I said. I scooped her up and carried her inside.

I placed her on the sofa, and looked at her with growing alarm. Her fingertips were blue, her lips as well, and in spite of the fever her face had lost all color. I reached for the phone. She guessed my intent. "No ambulance," she muttered. "Please, no hospital."

It was pneumonia, most likely. The complication Carol said would be the most dangerous. Only hours ago, the doctor had not seen it coming, nor had I, and the antibiotic had done nothing. With sudden clarity, I understood that the sharing she'd asked for might be to allow her not to sing, but to live.

No one in my family would let this woman die. And I was the one who believed I loved her?

"All right. No hospital yet. We'll try something else first," I said and took off my jacket, rolled up the cuff of my shirt.

This should have been done in a moment of well-planned passion, not with all the speed of an emergency transfusion. Wondering if she would share my disappointment, I concentrated instead on how much I cared for her and admired her talent, her ambition. I bit my wrist, then held it to her lips, brushing back her damp hair as she drank.

And I could feel everything she felt—the pain in her chest, the struggle to breathe, the fevered delirium. Not pleasant, especially to someone who had never been even the slightest bit ill.

And my father had done that with his victims?

Realizing that I must not be comprehending the full potential of this sharing, I dulled the pain I felt, slowed the labored breathing I shared, quieted my thoughts.

Her body also responded.

"I feel better," she whispered. This time I did not try to silence her. Instead, knowing that what she felt was not real, I went into the kitchen and poured her some water, brought her another of the pills.

"They're not working," she said and tried to push my hands away.

"I can only make you stronger. This is what will make you well." I watched as she swallowed it and managed a weak smile. I put the glass on the end table and lay on the floor beside her, holding her hand.

"Give me a dream, Dickie. Show me your home."

Only my family called me by that name, and rarely in the last few years. Not a coincidence that she used it, I was sure, and I wondered how close Irena and I would become.

I shut down all thoughts of what my father had learned about her and concentrated instead on Chaves, the village, the houses.

—I've seen that before,— she told me, a hint of a question in her thoughts, shut off as quickly as it had formed. —Show me something new.—

For the next hour, I shared scenes from my life until she drifted off into a healing sleep filled with dreams of her own.

I woke soon after she did the next morning and listened as she drew in a breath—a deep one. There was only a little pain, and though her eyes were still too bright she said she felt better than she had in days. By the next afternoon, she could practice her scales again, and I sat at my desk, hunched over five years of postwar reports I had ordered from Chaves, sifting through the dry and depressing facts about the future of this world. Occasionally I would pause in my work to listen to her sing, a nightingale piercing all that darkness. A beautiful sound, all the more welcome since I had not heard her voice in so many days.

Then I would return to my work, wondering if the future could be so bleak. What if the men we employed to create these projections of the world's wars and famines, ecological disasters, and man-made plagues were only responding to what they knew we expected to hear?

Not likely, since only one or two of the many projections each year did not come true. But in spite of the knowledge, the world constantly surprised us. In the days when barbarism was the norm, our strength protected us. We'd numbered more than fifty then. Now we are twenty-eight, only six of us women. My mother is our hope. And Irena.

By the next afternoon, Irena ran through her scales, stopping a few notes below the top of her range with no hint of straining. I went to the piano and began the famous aria from *The Magic Flute*. She hit that high C, went two notes further. She had never gone that high before. Perhaps the rest had done her voice some good, or perhaps it was the strength I'd given her. No matter; when the piece was over, she fell onto the bench beside me, wrapped her arms around my neck, and kissed me with the passion I had been missing for too many days.

"We should go out and find you something more nourishing than crackers and canned soup," I said.

"We should make love first. Then go out. Then come back and make love for the rest of the night." She began unbuttoning my shirt.

"Irena!" I exclaimed in mock horror.

"You did it. You must have done it. I have never felt so hungry for you," she said as she reached for her purse, digging out the condoms we hadn't needed two months ago.

Hungry? Yes, I understood exactly what she meant.

I was as aroused as she was and as soon as our clothes lay in a heap on the floor, I sat down on the piano bench and pulled her onto me so that we both faced the keyboard. She leaned forward, hands splayed across the keys while I touched her—mind and body—as she chose.

Later, only somewhat sated, she twisted around to face me, her legs dangling over the back of the piano bench, the backs of her knees locked against the edge of its seat.

—Now draw me in,— she ordered. As I happily obeyed, I felt

her hand brush against my neck, reaching for the pendant I wore. I was dimly aware of her lifting it, using the tip of the teardrop to cut my neck. I should have stopped her but I wanted to feel first-hand that passion my parents felt. I let her do it, felt the bond between us tighten as she pressed her lips to the wound.

She started to move above me, but I gripped her hips, held her immobile with only my mind touching her. I grew in her. She tightened around me. Suddenly she pushed away from me, arching her back against my arms.

I began to move then, slowly, slowly, letting the feeling extend for as long as we both could stand it.

When it was over, I ordered enough takeout for a small party, more than enough to see her through the next four days.

On the Sunday night before classes resumed, we decided to go out for dinner. As she was putting on her makeup, Irena stepped back from the mirror and turned to me. "I think were I to dye my hair black now, I could pass as your cousin," she said.

I grinned. "Not with those lips and teeth," I whispered and kissed her.

When we came home from the restaurant, Irena did not pack her things. Without either of us speaking, we both knew it would be impossible to separate for so many days.

There is a legend among our kind that says to share blood with a lover creates a slave. And so it did. I belonged to her; completely, totally. I suspected she knew it. I hardly cared.

# CHAP+ER 18

Two weeks before the audition, Irena had the five pieces she'd chosen committed to memory and her presentation was impressive. But one thing troubled me: her voice was stronger than any of her traditional choices would reveal. I knew something that would—a piece by Laurie ideally suited to her. But I was loath to suggest it, until I learned that the initial competition for the sixteen openings would include more than five hundred, and that if she were chosen she would be one of the youngest ever picked for the chorus.

More importantly, John Saille, music director for the conservatory's performances and one of Laurie's closest friends from the school, would be sitting in on the preliminary round. My presence as an accompanist would likely assure that the aria would be requested, perhaps as a second or third selection.

"I want you to hear something," I said to Irena that evening. I put on a tape of the opening aria that Laurie had recorded in the apartment.

The opera is called *Romania-Pace*. Laurie has invented a story to explain the subject, but the truth is far darker, and much more barbaric.

In those months during the war when Laurie was a captive of a madman, he'd been kept at a Gestapo headquarters in the shadow of the Old One's keep. There he had been forced to interrogate prisoners. He lied about the major things, told the truth about the minor ones, and when he was done the prisoners were left with him to be devoured. Had he refused to kill them, they would have died far more painfully, so he took what was given but stored their lives inside him. And in those long hours when he was alone, he composed music in his mind. *Romania-Pace* was a memorial to those he had killed.

It is publically thought to be the last composition of Laurence Austra, smuggled out of Romania where he died a captive of the Nazis during the war. In truth, it took Laurie ten years to find the strength to tap those memories and set them to music.

The opera focuses on Natalya, a woman imprisoned and sentenced to die by the Gestapo. Her crime was loving a partisan who was aiding the communists. She in turn is desired by a Nazi officer who tries to get her to betray her lover in order to live. She refuses. In spite of this, the German officer helps her escape. As they flee, he is killed by the partisans, who are themselves hunted down. Her lover is shot and Natalya is recaptured. The story of her life is told to the audience in flashbacks on the night before her death.

Because of its context it has been embraced by both communists and pacifists. As a result, it has been staged only once, sung in the Romanian in which it was written, in Bucharest. Ironically its opening night was in tribute to the despot Nicolae Ceauşescu, who is particularly fond of it.

The aria begins with a cry of anguish. Opening on the G in the second octave above middle C, the soprano's voice is supposed to start at that note, sustain it, then fall over an octave in one smooth decline. As with so many of the Austra pieces, the work is modified at the high end. A solo violin plays the high notes until they fall comfortably within the singer's natural range, usually ten or so notes lower. Then the singer's voice melds with the strings and takes command of the declension a few notes below that. No trained singer has ever hit that first note. But on the tape I played for Irena, an untrained one did, and with no accompaniment until the actual aria.

Irena had been lying on the sofa when I'd put the piece on.

Hearing that opening, she sat up, eyes huge with amazement, and looked at me standing across the room at the reel-to-reel player. "Who is that?" she asked.

"Laurie is singing his own work," I replied.

She listened through to the end of the aria, then asked me to rewind the tape to the beginning and play it again. This time she listened to the entire first act.

The opera spoke of her country's anguish in her own language. With her history, I did not have to touch her mind to know how much this music meant to her.

When it was over, she wiped tears from her eyes and took a deep breath. "It would be a mistake. It's never been staged," she said.

I told her what I knew about one of the judges, adding, "He's the old man you saw with Laurie that night at the theater. He will ask for it."

"It would be cheating."

"Cheating would be if I sang the note for you."

"But I can't sing it either and I don't have the violin to open the music."

"You don't need the violin. Listen." I played the first few notes on the piano, one tone falling smoothly into the next as my current instructor had taught me until I fell into that impossible E that ended her range and sang it. "And you don't need to learn another language, either," I added.

She decided to add it, to present six pieces for consideration instead of the usual five.

The day before the audition, she practiced for an hour in the morning, and only the scales. "If I don't have it now, I never will, and I want to rest my voice," she said. She projected calm, but I knew that inside she was boiling.

We went out that night, dining at a well-vented restaurant, then home. She lay on her stomach on the bed while I rubbed her back, kneading the muscles along the spine. They were tight, but not nearly as tense as I would have expected given how hard she'd been working for that quarter hour's judgment tomorrow.

She rolled over, pulled me down on top of her. "You'll have to help me if I'm going to get any sleep tonight," she said, her fingers already reaching for the pendant I wore, the sharp tip.

What had been a means of healing her had rapidly shifted into something more. I wondered sometimes if what we did would hasten her change but the times she had taken blood from me had seemed only to make her voice a bit stronger, her mind more easily linked with mine, and sex far more passionate than I had ever expected something so already perfect could be.

And she was not so young anymore. My mother had been younger when she'd changed. I concentrated on this fact, not on how different their situations were, or that my mother had entered our world with her eyes fully open. I had made a vow I intended to keep. Irena would know the whole truth soon enough.

The auditions ran for two weeks, four singers every hour. Irena's was at two on the fourth day; a good spot, we thought, though I wondered how the judges could keep one voice separate from another.

She'd bought a new outfit to wear to the audition, a black knit dress with calf-length skirt that, while modest, showed off her curves just enough to make the judges see how appealing she would look in costume. The shoes had a slight heel, not enough to throw her off balance but only to give a bit of added height. Her makeup was as carefully chosen—to accent the slight hollows in her cheeks, the wide-spaced eyes, the full lips.

On the day of her audition, she was ready by noon then ran scales for half an hour before I called for a cab. As we waited those last few minutes, she had me sit at the piano, play the opening note for *Romania-Pace,* then sing it for her.

She smiled, shook her head. "Never," she whispered.

"If you hear it in your mind . . . ," I said, repeating what her teacher had told her often enough.

The cabbie buzzed. She jumped backward, then gripped my hand and did not let go until the moment she walked before me onto that stage where the spotlights were waiting, brilliant as her voice.

She had debated for hours what she should choose for her first piece. Any soprano with half an ounce of confidence would be trying to hit the money notes in "Queen of the Night." That made her think she should pick something else. I disagreed.

"No one else will hit that high C. You'll guarantee a space with the first piece alone," I told her.

So that was how we would begin.

She took one final breath, drew in the calm I projected, and raised her head. My signal. I started to play.

She was nervous, but that faded as soon as she began to sing. What followed was as perfect as any practice we had done, and as her voice began the oddly playful rising of one note to the next, as her hands began to flirt with the empty seats and the judges in the back, I sensed their interest. When she began the ornamentation from F to G then the quick rise of A, B, C, I knew that never had operatic vengeance been so beautifully portrayed. She'd made that first cut.

She was breathing hard when she finished, more from fright than exertion. The panel gave her a moment to catch her breath, whispering together in the dark. Saille's voice called from the back. "The Austra piece, Miss Sava. And please, feel free to act the part."

I had never seen it staged, nor had the judges, so Irena had free rein to interpret the part purely on the words and emotion of the song.

With both arms raised, crossed at the wrists above her head simulating what might have been a position for torture, she looked up at the stage lights above her, the notes forming in her mind as I played them slowly down. G. F. E.

I felt the E form in her mind, heard it begin in her throat, cut off before it became audible. Wisely, I thought.

D was a stretch, a big one, but possible. She declined.

She joined me at C, the soft tone growing in her until it had all the intensity Laurie had wanted to see in it.

Fingers spread, her arms moved slowly to her sides, falling as her voice fell until she began to sing of the lover she had lost, in a minor chord she had said reminded her of the folk music of her old village. In that aria, fear shifts to sorrow then to determination to die as bravely as her lover had died—a tribute to his courage and an acknowledgment of her own.

As the aria reached its courageous concluding lines, she stood with her right fist raised in defiance. When it ended, she fell to her knees, touched her forehead to the stage, the fist over her heart, the other arm outstretched with fingers spread to press against the light-warmed wood.

John Saille's voice broke a long silence. "Please join us, Miss Sava," he said. "And bring your accompanist with you."

I sensed her disappointment. They had not asked for a third piece.

—That's because you're in! Saille's all but turning cartwheels!— I told her as I gathered my sheet music and followed her off the stage.

When we were out of sight of the judges, she turned and kissed me hard then took my hand and led me down the side aisle. I saw Saille standing at the end of it, waving toward the lobby door. As we followed him out, another nervous singer began to sing.

"Incredible!" he told Irena, hugging her as if he had been her teacher not her judge. "Laurence once told me how his uncle had wanted that opera to open. You did it that way, but perhaps you spoke to Laurence directly about it?" He looked past her to me.

Irena shook her head. "I am Romanian. That was how the piece spoke to me."

"And I've heard my cousin play the music many times," I said. "But he never said anything about the staging to me either."

"So he did not tell you that it is going to be performed in Romania again?" Saille asked me.

"I've not spoken to him in weeks," I replied.

"As part of a cultural exchange, the New England Regional Opera Company will be touring Romania. The director has been asked by the Romanian government to do *Romania-Pace.*" He took Irena's hand. "It's a new company, a small one, and this is a huge undertaking for them. Unfortunately, with the tour itself little over a month away the only singer in the company who could come close to doing justice to the Natalya role broke two ribs in an auto accident and now that the season has started, they can't find a suitable replacement. I was asked to watch for someone with talent like yours. Given what I saw on that stage today, I believe they will break the rules and take a beginner in the main role."

I looked at Irena, expecting to see her trying to hold back a whoop of joy. But she seemed more concerned than interested. Saille caught that as well, and continued, "There's not much prestige in the company, which is why they would take on a tour like this. But there's good young talent signed on. You could learn a great deal from all of them. And, I suspect, get a great deal more notice than in a larger company."

As she considered this, I felt the fear rising in her. "And if I chose to remain here?" she asked.

Saille didn't seem surprised by the question. "My dear, the second audition will likely be a formality. But for your first year or two, you could only pray for the chance to step into a lead role when a critic was in the audience."

"It is the security that concerns me," she said and pressed her lips together, considering.

"I understand," Saille said. "And you don't need to make a decision now. But I would like you to come over to the conservatory so that I can tape you singing that piece and send it to the company's director. If he is interested—and he'd be a fool not to be—you can discuss any concerns you have with him directly."

She sang as beautifully at the conservatory as she had at the audition. When she finished, Saille hugged her even harder than he had before. "If you can sing this well now, imagine what your voice will sound like when you are thirty-five or forty and it is fully mature. I am witnessing the birth of a legend."

At forty! Belatedly, I began to understand that the profession Irena had chosen was both public and geared to those who were much older than she could ever appear to be if she joined my family.

And if she waited to change until she was fifty or older, we might be able to restore her youth but there would be no children.

Her smile was genuine as she slowly pushed away from Saille's embrace, but I noticed something else, something so familiar to me. Her hands had fallen to cover his wrists, her fingers pressing against the pulse points. She looked past him to me, her eyes promising passion and fulfillment—hers and mine.

But passion was far from her mind on our twilight walk home. "This is all happening too fast. It will bring bad luck," she told me then went on to list all the logical reasons why she should not go. I felt the temptation to simply agree with her, but I could not. I reminded her that the semester had just begun, that the money she would earn would likely more than offset the tuition she would lose, and that for the sake of her career she could not ignore such an opportunity.

"I can't go alone. Will you come with me?" she asked.

"I'll try to, if they will let me," I replied, but I could already sense doubts nagging at me, telling me that it would not be in her interest or mine for me to go with her. "But even if you go alone, you'll only be abroad for about two weeks, and away from Chicago for five total. While you're in New England, I can fly up to see you if you can get some time off from rehearsals every now and then."

She gripped my hand more tightly. "They may not even want me and I may not accept even if they do," she said.

By then we were nearly home. I waited until we were inside to ask the real reason why.

"Damn it, Richard! I come from that place!" she retorted, temper rising. "If I go back, I may not be allowed to leave. I am not like you. I cannot simply run for the nearest border. And even if I were sure I would be safe, I am to sing for that monster?"

"Irena, whatever Ceaușescu thinks is irrelevant. You wouldn't be singing it for him. And the American government must be involved in this exchange. Tell your concerns to them."

A valid argument, I thought, but still she frowned. "Very well, I will talk to the company if they call. But it is all happening too fast. Bad luck."

I hugged her, then recalled, somewhat belatedly, that we ought to be celebrating. While she changed, I went into the kitchen and found the split of champagne I'd hidden in the refrigerator, the small box of Fannie May chocolates I'd placed far back on the top shelf of the cupboard. I set both of them on the dining table, along with a pair of crystal glasses.

She came out of the bedroom wearing my blue silk pajama top with the sleeves rolled up. She smelled of Joy and I thought that perhaps she shared the need to lighten the mood.

"What is this?" she asked, grinning.

"What you deserve," I said and popped open the champagne. I poured her a glass, and a bit for myself, enough that I could hold up my glass and say, "To Irena and the best sort of luck, the luck she earned."

"I will have to drink to myself. There is no one else here," she said and we drained our glasses together. I poured her another, which she drank nearly as quickly before holding out her glass for the rest.

"I shall drink enough to get us both drunk. We have both earned it," she said and laughed, the first time in days that I had heard her sound so relaxed or so happy.

She reached for my hand, pulled me close so she could kiss

the back of it, her lips pressed against the skin for a moment. "I am beginning to understand what you mean when you say you are hungry for me," she whispered.

She meant it flirtatiously, but I felt the truth behind the words. She did hunger for me, for more than what my body and mind could give her. And I loved her, and wanted to give. More than that, the drive for this sharing was strong in both of us.

Later, as I lay tight within her, my lips against her shoulder, hers against my neck, I felt a moment of dread, of hope. She would be leaving soon.

But that was not the time for such a thought, not when she was moving so exquisitely around me. I pushed it deep into my mind, then pulled her head back and kissed her, tasting myself.

That was one of the last peaceful hours we shared.

# CHAP+ER 19

Saille called early the next morning with a suggestion on a local agent. Irena met with the man and decided to use him for these negotiations, and possibly more later.

Two days later, with barely enough notice for her to catch a flight, she was off to New Haven for another audition in front of the New England Regional Opera Company's general and artistic directors and the chorus master.

That evening, they and the two men who would be playing the major male roles had dinner at one of the main backer's homes. They discussed the classes she had taken, even the plays she had appeared in during her last two years in high school. The director asked her to sing again, using the pieces from her audition.

Travel home took up most of the next day and she arrived back in Chicago after three. Always thrifty, she took the el from the airport to the Loop before catching a taxi for the apartment, arriving there a bit before I did. When I came in, I found her sitting cross-legged on the floor, the phone in front of her. Her agent had to repeat the offer three times because she couldn't believe what he'd said.

The company would pay her tuition for the semester missed, a generous stipend for the month's rehearsal time, three times that for the weeks of the tour, plus full coverage of all her expenses. And yes, though the request was an odd one, she would be al- lowed to take me on tour to assist in her rehearsals. I would also be paid.

I guessed that Saille had told them who I was and that was why they allowed it. This meant that there would be interviews and cameras focused on me as well as her, and eyes that would look at me. Given the legends of the country, some would guess the truth.

I did not think of any of that, or even how I would manage to refuse to go. I only tried to look pleased as I asked, "And what did they say about security?"

"The artistic director, Mr. Korval—did I tell you that he has a Russian father?—Korval said that he has done similar tours twice before and there has never been trouble. He said I must remem- ber never to insult our hosts. When asked, I should only say that I left Romania with my parents when I was very young but that I still remember it well and hope to see some of my family while I am there."

"That is diplomacy, not security."

"He said if I wish to be secure, I should always stay with the group."

"How many cities?" I asked.

"Five in twelve days." She pulled out a map to show me the places they would be visiting. Bucharest was first. Then the com- pany would go northeast to Iasi, then west to Baia Mare and down through the center to Sibiu, then further west to Timisoara. From there they would return to Bucharest, then home.

The journey from Baia Mare to Sibiu would take her through the shadow of the Old One's keep, in the area where Hunter and Charles had fought during the war. "These cities are dangerous for me," I told her, and explained why.

"I never guessed what you were. They won't either," she replied, her tone light as if my concern was groundless.

But as I looked down at the dots on the map, I felt a chill roll through me, unfamiliar and grim. And I know that though she might swear she would not leave without me, I would not go there. This might have been logic, or possibly instinct, but as I thought of her there alone, I realized I did not much like it.

While I finished the last of a report I had due the next day, she was on the phone, discussing the matter with the college then sharing the good news with friends from school, inviting them to the Friday night celebration I'd agreed to host.

During a lull between calls, I put down my pen, turned to her, and asked, "Are you ever going to tell your family about this?"

"Just before I leave. I can't trust my sister to keep the secret and there is no use worrying everyone else until I have to. I only wish I could tell them why I am going to feel so safe."

For Friday evening's celebration, Irena put a donations bowl near the front door, but most of the guests took one look at the apartment and its decor and held on to their precious bills. Some brought a gift, most something to add to the food table.

As for me, I sat in the corner close to the half-open terrace door, sipping a glass of ice water and sharing a joint with anyone who cared to join me, all the while making sure that a hot ash didn't fall and burn the carpet, or that someone didn't get too drunk or stoned and try walking the terrace rail. I moved from the spot only occasionally, mostly to turn the stereo down.

Tonight, I played the role of party prig, but I'd told Irena to relax and let me handle those annoying details.

I watched her greet the guests, laugh at their compliments, play the guest of honor to perfection. She had a vitality to her that I'd never noticed before and I wished that I could take her into the back room for an hour or so. I brushed her mind to share the thought and saw her turn, blush just a little, and smile.

She sang the opening aria from *Romania-Pace,* and after, with me, a duet from the same opera that she'd been practicing. One of the other girls from the chorus, with a rich mezzo voice, sang the "Ave Maria," which started what seemed like an endless hour of carols, no one much caring that they were several weeks too late. We pushed the last guests out into the hall a bit after two.

She leaned against the closed door. "Shall we find that back room now?" she asked, her tone seductive.

I grabbed her around the hips, lifted her over my shoulder, and was about to carry her off when I heard a faint knock at the door.

I turned to open it. "Put me down," Irena whispered, and laughed.

—Silence, wench,— I replied and spanked her once, playfully, then looked through the peephole.

Then I did set her down, her humor shifting with mine as she caught the concern on my face. I pulled open the door and stepped into the hall to greet the building's night guard, who was holding a special delivery envelope.

Thinking it concerned her tour, Irena began to follow me. But the man handed it to me instead. "With the crowd up here, I thought I should sign for it and bring it up myself when the air cleared," he said.

"Thank you," Irena called from inside.

"I hope we weren't too loud," I added.

"Respectably so. 'Bout time you two let loose a little." He winked once and headed back to the elevators.

Once the door was shut, I opened the package and pulled out a pair of airline tickets for a direct flight to Montreal and a note that said only, *I will be waiting for you and Irena outside of the Dorval baggage claim at three. It is time we met. Stephen.*

I handed her all of it and walked past her into the living room.

"Damn him! How dare he just assume!" she said after she'd read it.

"You can ask him that this afternoon," I said and began picking up the plastic cups scattered around the living room.

"No! I am not being ordered around like a child! You can just tell him that for me. . . ."

I was hardly listening. Instead I was piecing together a likely scenario to explain the note. John Saille must have called Laurie and told him about Irena. Laurie had called my parents to share the good news and given her name, and now . . .

Well, I had dreaded telling them. Now, it seemed, a good part of that burden had been taken from me.

". . . And he could have added some polite words for me, like 'please' or 'looking forward to meeting you' or something civilized. . . ."

The tone of that letter was, of course, not directed at her, but I was hard-pressed to explain any of that as I listened to her tirade.

"Irena, stop!" I finally said. I brushed my hand across the back of her neck to that round scar at the hairline. "The day you told me about the old one's visit, you said you wanted to meet him. Now you have your chance."

"Your father!"

"With everything you've told me, and what I've told you, how could you not have known?"

She straddled the arm of the sofa, still gripping the note, saying nothing as she considered the logic of what I'd just said, too confused to even form a conclusion she wanted to keep to herself.

"Irena, I have told you a few things about myself and Laurie but outside of mentioning my brother, I have said next to nothing about the rest of my family, nor have you asked. Thinking on that now, don't you find it odd?"

"You did that to me! Why—"

I cut in before her temper got the best of us again. "He did. And now he sends a note like this, all but ordering us to meet him. He may have a reason. Given that you will be traveling to a place that we both think is dangerous, we ought to go see what he wants."

She considered this, a bit more calmly. I sensed her agreement before she spoke and was thankful. I had not wanted to force her will. "When is our return flight?" she asked.

"Tuesday afternoon."

"I have to leave for rehearsals Saturday."

"Then before you leave, I want to show you my home."

She nodded, went into the kitchen, brought out the trashcan, and began filling it with the empty cups. An hour later, we dumped the leftovers into a second bag and threw everything down the garbage chute in the hallway.

With enough accomplished to keep the cleaning lady from giving notice, I took her hand. "Are you tired?" I asked.

"You're the one who will be tired, getting up so early," she answered, brushing her middle finger down the center of my palm.

In the bedroom, she paused as we undressed to ask one more question. "Richard, will they mind that you and I are lovers?"

Mind? "No," I replied, wanting to laugh.

"Good. Because if we only have this week before I go to rehearsals, we cannot be apart."

We slipped off the rest of our clothes. I got to bed ahead of her, the sheet pulled back, waiting. She lit a candle on my dresser, turned toward me. —Touch me, Richard,— she said.

I obliged, feeding her passion as she walked toward me.

Later, as she reached for that pendant, I wanted to take her wrist, pull it away. But it made no difference. If we had made a mistake in doing this, Stephen would know everything anyway. One more night would make no difference.

# CHAPTER 20

Thirteen hours after we'd received the tickets, I picked up the single large suitcase we'd shared and carried it out to the pickup drive at Dorval Airport in Montreal. I wasn't sure which of us was more nervous though Irena showed it more.

A girl who normally put on the first clean thing she found in the closet had dressed with all the care she'd taken before the audition—the russet sweater I'd bought her for Christmas over a pair of new black jeans and suede boots. On the way from the gate she stopped in the ladies' room to put on more lipstick, a bit more powder.

It was snowing, huge flakes that coated the pavement, swirling under the canopy, catching in our hair. It slowed the traffic, so that we waited a half hour in the cold. I told Irena to go inside, but she was too nervous to wait alone. So she paced, eyes fixed on the arriving cars, watching. When I saw the Jeep and pointed it out to her, she moved close to me, gripping my hand.

I tried to stay calm, to project the feeling. For reasons difficult to explain to her, I found both impossible. But as the Jeep pulled up, I saw the familiar face through the smoky windshield and relaxed. I'd gotten a two-hour reprieve.

"Hello, Richard! And hello, Irena!" Patrick called as he got out of the car.

Irena stared at him, confused. He had the looks, but there was no way to hide that eagerness of youth. And the clothes, bell bottoms and a tie-dye shirt, not exactly what she'd expected. "This is your . . . Stephen?" she asked, staring at him and speaking to me.

Patrick laughed. "My brother," I explained.

She looked from Patrick to me, noting the marked difference in our height and weight and coloring, and asked, "Aren't you twins?"

"Fraternal," Patrick supplied. "Strange term, isn't it? Stranger yet when it's applied to girls." He stowed the suitcase in the back and the three of us climbed into the front seat, me in the center so she could take in the sights.

"I thought you would be in New York," I said.

"I got summoned, too. Came up yesterday."

—And the mood?— I questioned privately.

—A lot less tense once Father broke down my defenses. I accepted the inevitable. I told him everything. You can't plead ignorance, Dickie boy, so don't even try. He knows we've been spying.—

"Shame we'll miss seeing most of the city on the way out. Maybe you'll see some of it before you go back," Patrick said to Irena.

"Tuesday, most likely," I added.

She caught the tension in my voice, looked from me to my brother. "What have you two been talking about?" she asked.

"Sexual exploits," Patrick replied. "He lost the wager. I've had way more lovers in the last six months than he has. But I may have to let him win based on the quality of his choice."

—Shut up,— I ordered.

"Irena, he just told me to—"

"Shut up. I know." She patted my hand. "It's all right. He lies beautifully."

"And she's a wit besides. Score one more point for you, Dickie boy."

"Are those the sort of lines you used on all those women in New York?" Irena asked.

"Only three. Then Georgie came down to Julliard."

"Georgie! You remember, Irena. I told you we were the

baroque group together. How is he?" I asked, stressing the pronoun slightly.

"As always. There is music, there is me, and there is the church. Fortunately, he has not been attending church much as of late. Something has gotten into him."

I glanced at Irena, saw that she was blushing.

Patrick noticed that too. "It's not the gender that's important, Irena, it's the passion. And his guilt adds a little spice to the meal."

—Shut up— I repeated and began to point out some of the sights as we left the city and headed north toward Saint-Jérôme, and Saint-Michel beyond.

The hills were covered in white, the trees coated by the storm. A few hardy skiers were still on the slopes, but most had moved into the lodges to sit in bars and wait out the weather. I pointed out some of the more popular slopes, saw that she had little interest. "You live here?" she asked.

"Some sixty miles further up," I said.

"But it's so empty."

"We like our privacy."

"Since we moved to Chicago, I've never left the city until a week ago except for one quick trip up to the Dells in Wisconsin."

"With your family?" Patrick asked her.

"A class trip. We sold candy door-to-door to pay for it. We stayed in a hotel with a swimming pool and went down the river on the boats with the silly name . . . ducks, I think they're called."

"Did you like it?" I asked, thinking her nature should have reveled in any bit of wilderness.

"I thought it would be a terrible place to be lost, but not as bad as this."

It was getting dark. Patrick increased our speed but the drive still took twice as long as in good weather. The lights were on at the split log house my father had purchased that summer after our tenyears, drawing attention to the wide front porch and the south-facing bay windows glowing in brilliant shades of cobalt and green and ruby.

We got out. Irena looked at the house then away from it, taking in the hills, the isolation. "I can picture you here," she said to me, following me inside.

The house held its usual scent of oranges and cloves, those pomanders Stephen loves. Added to it was the smell of chocolate and some sort of stew. My mother had cooked, a skill she still practiced when friends came to visit.

Helen was dressed casually in jeans and a red sweater that added some needed color to her face. When she saw us come in, she dropped a towel on the kitchen counter and stepped into the hallway to hug me, then Irena. "Welcome," she said and, catching Irena's confusion, added, "I'm Helen, Richard's mother."

Irena stared at her blue eyes, the straight blond hair. "You said you were their mother?" she asked, wondering if she had heard the words correctly.

Patrick had come in just in time to hear that remark. —Really kept her in the dark, didn't you, Dickie boy?— he commented.

"I'll explain that all later," Helen said, then stepped out of the doorway to make room for my father to join them. Useless in the kitchen, he had been able to dress more formally in a deep blue peasant shirt with a collar he had embroidered himself, and a pair of snug-fitting jeans. Yes, he looks young, almost as young as my brother and me, and he can act the part when he wishes. Not that night. Instead, he looked at her with all the wisdom and power that his age and lineage had conferred, pausing a moment before holding out his hand.

Irena hesitated, heart pounding, then took it and forced herself to defy the old legends and look directly into his eyes. I felt the charge between them, sensed him brush her mind. She frowned. "I remember you now," she whispered, looking from him to me.

"Of course you do," he replied. "I'll tell you why I made that visit after I speak for a time with my son. Come back to the kitchen. We can talk more at the table, yes?"

There was cocoa for the women, tea for the men, and a small pot of dumplings cooking on the stove. We sat for a while, my parents asking both of us about school. Gradually, Irena began to relax, enough that my father said, "While you and Helen eat, I will have a few words alone with my son."

Patrick started to follow us down the hall but Stephen glanced back at him—a quick, sharp warning, then took me into the living room and shut the French doors behind us.

I watched through the glass as Patrick started back to the kitchen. Halfway there, he turned and went upstairs—banished by both his parents.

I sat in a caramel leather wing chair, fingering the hobnails on the edge of its arms and settling in as best I could. My father straddled the high roll arm of the leather sectional across from me.

"I am aware that you know how important she is to us. So tell it all to me, exactly as it happened," he said.

And I did. Holding nothing back from our meeting to the present moment, not even my doubts as I made the first exchange that I believe saved her life, the temptation that had prompted the second, and all the ones which followed.

"How many times have you shared blood with her?" he asked.

"Six. The final one last night."

"And what changes have you seen in her?"

"Her voice seems stronger. There is more passion in her singing, which could be a reflection of her life. The bond between us is stronger. Otherwise, nothing seems different."

"She's never asked to join you when you hunt? To taste?"

"Never. She's never even asked what I do."

"But she demands the sharings?"

"She asks and I give. I'm sorry, but sex . . . but passion is so much better if the blood flows both ways."

"There is that." I caught the humor in his thoughts. He paused, then asked, "So of course, if she craves life, she has yours to share and may not even realize those unfamiliar needs."

"She has mine," I admitted.

"And how does she view us?"

"I don't think it's a matter of 'us' " I said after I'd considered the question. "I work so hard to fit in that she sees my facade and does not fully understand what lies beneath it.

"Then there is you. You are her legend. I am merely her lover."

The questions stopped as he considered my words, no doubt thinking of how he would approach her in a few minutes. This gave me time to add something that needed to be said. "I'm sorry for what I did. I should have called you when I first met her."

"What did you think I would do when you told me?"

"I thought you would tell me to leave her . . . and I could not do that. But I should have called, especially when she was so ill. There were things I should have asked," I said.

"No matter. You were right to assume that any of us would have done the same. As to what followed, you should have asked my advice. But you are both young, and passion is hard to resist, yes?"

A most rhetorical question. "Have I done any harm to her?" I asked.

"Harm? I doubt there is any. Helen and I were together for longer and she did much more than taste and still she could have turned her back on our life. No, not any harm. And, Richard, I cannot think of a more ideal person to introduce Irena to our family."

At the least I had expected anger. I looked at him, astonished.

"No, I am not angry, because I used up two months' supply of anger on your brother last night. I am sure he will delight in sharing every painful detail if only so you can experience your portion of it. But I doubt he will ever spy on me again.

"As to the things you did not tell her, you believed those were mine to tell. If she asks, that is how I will explain it to her."

I followed his gaze through the doors and down the hall to where Irena sat at the kitchen table, chin resting on her hand. Whatever she and my mother discussed relaxed her. I could only hope that my mother had prepared her a bit for the revelations that were to come.

He walked to the door, paused with his hand on the knob, then turned. "One last question. Her music, how much does it mean to her?"

"Everything," I said.

"And she has talent?"

"Exceptional talent."

I sensed his concern. I shared it. If Laurie had not been born one of us, and had known of the limitations we must impose on ourselves, I doubt he would have chosen our life.

"Ask her to sing and you'll know this is not just love speaking," I added.

He stared past me into the fire, thinking of our family, of her, and of me. "She will have questions, many of them, in the next few days. When she asks them, answer honestly but don't try to push her into knowledge. Let her come to you."

"I've noticed that trait in her since our first night together. But there won't be much time for questions in the next few weeks. Unless I go with her to Romania. She wants me to."

"And you?"

"Bucharest and Iasi, yes. The cities to the west . . ." I struggled to find the right words to express my feelings, though of course I didn't have to.

"You are right. It would not be wise."

I wanted to ask about the difference between instinct and logic, but he looked down the hallway to the kitchen. "Helen says they've finished. Let's go and see how Irena is faring," he said and pushed open the doors.

The dishes had been washed and put away and Irena and my mother were sitting at the kitchen table drinking tea, sharing a plate of homemade bread and jam. Though my mother rarely ate the foods she'd loved before her change, I'd seen her take an occasional chocolate or pastry at a school social, beer or wine at the summer picnic, even dinner out with friends. But she rarely cooked unless there were others to enjoy it.

"In the last hour I've learned so much about you that I never knew," Irena said as I entered the room. She looked past me at my father, and found the painted roses at the bottom of her china teacup suddenly fascinating.

"It's all right. There's nothing to be afraid of," Stephen said.

She looked at him, fear shifting to fury. "You call what happened that night nothing! You came into my bedroom while I slept! You fed on me! You—"

I wanted to laugh. I'd mentioned her awe of him, but I'd never warned my father about that Sava temper. He acted as if he'd expected it, though, letting the tirade run its course before motioning toward the hallway.

"Now let me explain everything. Come."

She glanced at me, trying to size up how my meeting had gone, before she followed him down the hall. But she did not ask if I could join them, nor did she invite me to ask. I thought of how Lev Konovic had put a bullet in his head rather than face my cousin. Irena had been raised on those same distorted tales. Yet she faced her legend alone. I thought her remarkably brave.

Helen poured me a cup of tea. "Tell me more about school," she said, drawing my attention away from that room. As a result, what I learned of their conversation, I learned later—freely given by both of them.

Irena followed Stephen into the living room, watched him shut the doors, took the chair he suggested, the one close to the fire. Alone with him, her anger retreated until only the fear remained. She had her hands folded in her lap, her eyes fixed on them.

"Irena," Stephen said softly, "look at me."

She did as he asked, not because he'd ordered her to, but because it would have been rude to admit how afraid she was. She knew there was no reason for it but the stories her family had been told. She knew most of them were lies; still . . .

". . . It's hard to forget them, yes?"

"Yes," she whispered, and glanced at him as he sat on the floor, back against the sofa, long legs stretched toward the flames.

"But you know there is no reason to be afraid if only because it is most improper for a host to devour an invited guest." He bowed his head and smiled, a habit most people interpret as shyness. He is hardly that.

Irena unclasped her hands and rested them on the arms of the chair. She took a deep breath. "Sometimes fear doesn't need a reason. I'll try to ignore it," she said.

Though I can project calm, my father can positively radiate it when the need is great enough. And it was. Later, Irena told me how she felt that calm grow inside her, quieting her thoughts, stealing her fear. Slowly, they settled in, and he began to speak.

As he had when he first revealed his nature to my mother, he spoke of our history, then asked for hers, something I had not tried to do except to inquire about her immediate family in Chicago. I had been afraid to seem too interested while he had to know.

Like Konovic, her relatives had come from the Ukraine where privation had killed her mother's parents and siblings. She knew little of her father except that he had been the only surviving son in his own family. She could provide maternal family names back four generations except for her maternal grandfather.

"My mother was conceived just after the famine. There were bandits in the hills, living off what they could steal in wealth or food. They discovered my grandmother and her two brothers walking alone. They killed the men and carried her off.

"Two weeks later, she wandered into the village, half dazed and starving. She had been beaten, her clothes were torn, and she clutched a blanket around her bare arms. She could remember nothing but she must have been raped, since she was pregnant. She was seventeen. She died giving birth. Her parents raised her baby—my mother."

"Where was their village?" Stephen asked.

"In the far south of Ukraine. Near Khust. We moved later, as did most of the family, across the border into Sighet."

Stephen considered this. Khust was not so far from the Old One's keep. Had the woman been raped by a man or had she fled the men, taking refuge in the mountain pass where no man dared to go? Had she met Charles or the Old One? Someone like Viktor? Impossible to know.

"Does your mother look like the rest of her family?" he asked.

"I can't remember them well but she is darker, I think. Her hair and eyes are brown like mine rather than the blue of her relations."

"Darker than yours?"

"Yes, but nowhere near as dark as Richard's, let alone yours."

"And your father?"

"I don't know. He disappeared before I was born and we had no photographs. The family swears she was married to him, but I wonder if that was a lie for my sake. My mother married and had three more children—my younger sister and twin brothers. My stepfather was killed during our escape."

As Stephen considered what to ask next, Irena countered with a question of her own: "Am I like Helen? Can I be changed?" When he didn't answer immediately, she persisted. "That is the reason for all this interest in me, isn't it?"

"It is."

"And my mother? My sister and twin brothers?"

"Your half sister cannot. Likely your brothers cannot either. Your mother? I do not know but I doubt it."

"But how did you know about me?"

"Because Viktor told me your name before he died." He explained the reason for the killings that Viktor and his pack had done, adding the near outcome.

"I had to be sure you were not like him and so I came to you that night. Thankfully, you are not. Instead you are like my Helen."

"Why kill anyone? Why kill Viktor when he could have fathered more like me?"

"We can father our own children, Irena. We do not need the help of monsters. But there is something else about us you do not know. We cannot kill each other. We can barely conceive of harming each other. When Viktor told me what he had done . . .

no, rather when he boasted of what he had done to his own relations, I knew he could only be a threat to us."

"But you would have tried to change me because of the children I would give you?"

"Yes." He let the implications of that one word settle into her mind before he supplied the grim facts about our numbers, concluding with the obvious. "Our children are precious. My chosen must have explained that to you."

"Helen? She did." Hesitating a moment, Irena blurted out, "Did you change her for the children she would give you?"

A question so direct she flushed once she'd asked it, but he answered it with the same honesty. "I would have done it for that alone but only after she made the choice. I would not have forced her decision even when I already knew she was the better part of my soul and always would be."

"Did Richard tell you of our . . ."

"Sharings? He did."

"Should we have done that?"

He held out his hand. Understanding, she took it, but looked away. She felt the charge when his lips touched the side of it. Then a brief pain, the drawing in. No more, it seemed, but there was a moment of forgetfulness. He had sealed her lips, so carefully she never knew. No matter what the future, our secret would always be safe with her.

He kissed the back of her hand. Let it go.

"Our blood is changing you," he said. "Just as the hints of it that Viktor stole from his family had been changing him. Until you know for certain that this change is what you want, you should not drink from my son."

"Did you think I would meet Richard? Is that why you allowed him to go to Chicago for school?"

"Allowed him? No, I did not know he knew of you when he chose to go there but I am pleased that he went. I told my sons they needed to discover a passion in life. Patrick has his in our firm. Richard found his in you."

"In me?"

"In your talent and how he helped you develop it. He had considered teaching before. I believe that he's sure of it now. I am hoping to hear you sing before you leave."

Not the conversation she had expected, she thought. She wondered why he hadn't questioned her on her thoughts for her future, to try to get some notion of what she might decide. But he only glanced at her and shook his head. "Coming here is a beginning. Nothing more."

# CHAP╋ER 21

Throughout their conversation, I had glanced often at the closed living room doors. When they opened, it took every bit of resolve to stay where I was, and not go to her and reveal every bit of anxiety—and, I admit, possessiveness—I felt.

But she seemed calmer than she'd been since we'd received my father's telegram, actually joking with him as we all settled into the living room.

Patrick joined us a bit later. He'd changed out of the jeans and sweater into tight-fitting black knits. His feet were bare. "It's stopped snowing. Care to join me?" he asked, the question directed at no one in particular.

"Where are you going?" Irena asked.

"Hunting." He sighed with all the drama of a hack actor. "Though the pickings here will not be nearly as ferocious as the rats in Central Park."

"You're joking again, right?"

"Of course," he replied, shaking his head no. My parents glanced at each other, at Patrick. Minutes later the big house was empty except for Irena and me.

"You could have gone if you wanted to," Irena said. "I'm too tired to stay awake much longer anyway."

They'd left to give us privacy, but I didn't tell her that. Instead, I said, "I may later. But now let's go upstairs while the others are gone."

I stopped in the guest bedroom to get an extra blanket and pillow then took her to my room. In harmony with its rustic location, it had a platform bed, closet, dresser, and mirror frame all in golden maple. The outside wall was natural log, the inside walls and floors whitewashed pine. As soon as I'd moved in, I'd pushed the bed close to the French doors that led to a deck that ran across the back of house. From that spot, in the northeast room, I had a magnificent view of the land and sky. Even with the light on, I could see that the storm had ended and the Arctic front had come through. The stars were brilliant in the frigid sky.

Remembering something she had told me in the car, I wrapped the blanket around her and flipped off the lights, then led her through the doors and onto the open deck.

—Look up,— I told her and she pushed back the blanket and did.

The moon had not yet risen and the cloudless sky was black, filled with stars so bright the universe revealed its depth. She must have seen stars like this when she was young but, city raised, not since. I felt her awe at the brilliance of them. She let go of my hand, tilted her head back to take in all the sky.

Suddenly dizzy, she gripped the rail. I stepped closer to her and she leaned against me. "You live in a beautiful place in Chicago, Richard, but this place suits you better, I think."

"It should. When I'm around people, I have to be constantly on guard to stand right, move slowly—"

"Stay out of people's minds?"

I laughed. "That's easier for me than for most of the others. But there's nothing I fear in this wilderness. We live in places like this so we can remember what we are."

"Tomorrow night, I want you to take me for a hike. It is so beautiful here and I ought to try to understand more of what I could become," she replied, a comment I found hopeful.

I wrapped the blanket around both of us and began pointing out constellations, planets, and stars. We were both cold when we went inside. Just before I joined her in bed, I took off the pendant I wore and dropped it on the dresser. I didn't have to say why. We both understood. The double bed was narrower than we were used to, the room colder. We fell asleep wrapped in each other's arms.

I was dozing when she moved away from me. The moon had risen, coloring the room with silver. I watched as Irena walked across the bare floor, cracked open the porch door, and stepped outside. At first it seemed she simply wanted to see it alone, then I noticed she was staring down at the lawn and the trees beyond it. Thinking she'd spotted a deer or one of Mother's pets, my mind joined with hers, seeing what she saw.

My father stood at the edge of the lawn, looking back at the trees, waiting for the others to catch up. At home in the black-and-white landscape of the night, body still tensed from running, dark hair blown by the wind, he looked leaner, more savage. And she thought, as she likely could not help but think, how the meeting he had planned would have unfolded. How he would have approached her. How he would have touched her. What he would have done.

I wondered that myself as I lay there, pretending to be asleep. Did he know he was being watched? Curious, I tried to touch his mind. As I did, he sensed my intrusion, knew for the first time that she was there, turned and looked up at her.

He did not acknowledge her in any way except for that long look. Then Helen, thinking she had caught him unaware, ran up behind him, knocking him forward into the snow. I heard her laughter. His. Her cry of mock fear as he twisted around, pinned her beneath him, and stole a kiss of victory.

Irena retreated, shutting the door and coming back to bed, pressing her body against mine. I rolled over to face her. She was cold and I pulled her close and drew the blanket over both of us.

Irena had gone downstairs by the time I woke late in the morning. I discovered her settled into the kitchen, where she had made coffee and toast and was sitting at the table looking through a photo album Helen had left out for her.

We do not have photos taken once we become adults, but children grow and change and my parents were as doting as any when it came to burning through film and sending copies to relations. Though they were careful to make sure the shots they kept showed nothing out of the ordinary about us, there were pictures of us sitting on the porch stairs in Dawson, sledding in the snow, a few from our tenyears ceremony in Chaves. The last had been taken four years ago, and was of the classical quintet my music teacher had organized. I'd deliberately looked away from the camera, so my face was in profile and a bit out of focus.

"Georgie?" Irena asked, pointing to him staring straight at the camera, glasses reflecting the flash, an expression on his thin face not unlike a deer trapped by headlights. I nodded.

"And Louise?" She pointed to a pretty girl seated in the front. I corrected her, pointing out the slightly plump and mousy-looking girl in the back row, wondering how much my mother had told her.

The next dozen pages were empty. "Go to the back of the book," I said.

She did and saw full-page photos of church windows. The first half dozen were traditional, meticulously detailed New Testament scenes painted in the medieval manner. Later, the glass itself became more prominent until in the final four pages there was no painting done at all. Second to last was the window from the rectory at St. John's, the one my father created in the summer he changed my mother. The last was even more abstract—the hand of God moving over the waters, separating day from night. Denys had mixed the tones and crafted that window. My mother had designed it. I explained the history of both.

"So she has not given up art?"

"Not at all. But she has given up being known as an artist. You'd have to ask her if that was a sacrifice."

Irena did ask Helen that later in the day when the two of them were driving alone down to Sainte-Marguerite for a bit of shopping and a late lunch.

"What have I given up?" Helen looked at her and smiled. In spite of the sunglasses that shielded her eyes from the winter glare, Irena knew the smile was genuine. "It does not seem anything at all. When I met Stephen, I was nineteen and in a wheelchair. I had my art and I was in a hurry to make a name for myself so people would remember me after I died. Now my priorities have shifted. I don't need personal fame. And these years of hiding in the small wilderness towns mean nothing. I am not losing time, as mortals do. I have an unlimited amout of it to spare. Besides, you've met my children and Stephen. Do you think I have sacrificed anything?"

Irena thought of the scene she had witnessed the previous night, the way my parents, together twenty years, looked at each other, the way Stephen had looked at her when he explained what Helen meant to him. "No, and if you did, you'd never know," she replied after a while.

"You're right. Every choice negates other possibilities. And once made, mine wasn't a decision that could be undone."

"Few important ones can," Irena commented and stared out the window at the drifts of snow, the skiers on a distant slope. Any one of them could become distracted, hit a rock, lose control. Any one of them could be dead in minutes.

"We are going to lunch," Irena resumed after a long thoughtful pause, "and last night we had dinner but later you were hunting. I don't even know what Richard does, but I would guess it isn't the same for you. This probably is the time to ask what it is that . . ."

Helen looked at her. ". . . that we do? You never asked my son?"

"I was afraid. Since he would know my thoughts, if it disgusted me, that would hurt him and . . . I couldn't do that. It seems easier, somehow, asking this of you."

"We approach it from the same perspective, yes?"

"You're reading my thoughts before I think them."

"Guessing, actually. I would have asked the same had there been anyone in the family like me. Do you want to experience both sides of it?"

"Experience?"

"The best way to know. It was how I learned." Helen slid her hand across the seat and rested it on top of Irena's.

Irena looked out the window, the brilliant white of the sun on the snow reminding her of the spotlight on that stage in Chicago, the way she had sung, the triumph she felt when she had finished.

Then suddenly, as if a dream had descended and covered her, she is there on the stage, her voice rising and rising, impossible notes, alien sounds, and Saille clapping from the back of the empty theater. I kiss her, run a finger down the side of her neck, and . . .

A wind, bitter cold, blows against her face. . . .

She squinted from the sun then looked around her. She and Helen stood beside the car, staring out at the valley and frozen lake below. Irena's hand rested on the snow-covered brick wall and as she lifted it, she saw a drop of blood on the snow. Her finger had a cut on it, a quarter inch, no bigger than the mark she would make on my shoulder at night. Just a taste.

"And now you are . . . ?" Helen asked.

"Astonished! Even though I was expecting it, I never knew."

"If you were truly my victim, you would forget everything about me as well and perhaps even the vision I imparted. Next time you will be the hunter."

Irena hoped that could wait at least until after lunch. Helen, aware of why she felt that way, changed the subject, telling her about the long weeks of wonder as her body had mended then grown strong.

The restaurant they went to was French, elegant in spite of the rustic walls and plank floor of the century-old building. They sat at a booth against the front windows, the high seat backs giving them a bit of welcome privacy, since Irena had dozens of questions she wanted to ask.

The waiter hovered, asked Helen about the drive, the state of the slopes further up. As usual, Helen was dressed modestly in the red cashmere turtleneck, loose jeans, and boots. She wore no other makeup than a touch of blush on the cheeks and a bit of lipstick for color, no perfume. There was nothing to draw any attention to herself, yet the waiter had his hand on her shoulder as he suggested a wine, came back moments after he had poured it to check on its quality, later yet to inquire if the escargot lived up to his recommendation.

"You must come here often," Irena commented.

"A few times, but he's new. He won't bother us anymore, though, so you can ask away."

Irena did, with the most obvious question first.

"We think it is the life contained in it, not the blood itself that nourishes, so a little bit is enough," Helen replied. "We cannot just walk into the butcher's shop down the road, say we are addicted to coq au vin, and expect to live on the quarts of blood the shop would provide. My family needs life to survive. So do I, just not as often."

"And it doesn't harm the ones who give?"

"No. But it makes them hungry." Helen sipped her wine, and looked at the single slice of bread left from the small loaf the waiter had brought with their escargot. "Your appetite brings up something else as well. People change food into energy. We skip a large part of that process and steal the energy directly. The life."

"I understand. But why is your blood beneficial to us?"

"We don't know any more about that than you do. It came as a surprise to us all."

The conversation drifted for a while, then Irena asked the obvious, "Will you have more children?"

"Yes. I'm thirty-eight. I've put off having more for Stephen's sake. Now even he agrees that I can't wait much longer. I'll likely conceive soon—this summer—so that they will be born next spring when the roads are at their best. Fortunately, the nearest hospital is much closer now than when we lived in Dawson."

"Was that delivery so dangerous?"

"I doubt my labor was any worse than it would have been for any woman carrying twins. But in the last month before they were born I could feel them draining my life. Fortunately, I had more than one way to sustain myself. It will likely be the same with the next pair. The food in our kitchen is not there just for guests. Every meal I eat makes Stephen a bit calmer about what will be, of course, my choice."

"You have that much control?"

"Over when I conceive? Yes. There are no accidents in my family. Like the decision to become one of them, the matter rests in my soul. And my heart."

They dropped that discussion after the waiter brought their food: stuffed pheasant with cherry sauce for Irena, sole baked in puffed pastry for Helen. Helen ate half her meal and asked for a box to take it home. "You can have the rest for dinner, if you wish," she told Irena then ordered them both sweet crepes for dessert.

By the time they'd finished, the restaurant was all but empty. The maitre'd had disappeared into the kitchen, and the waiter that had shown such interest in Helen was the only one still on duty. When Helen signaled for the check, he started over immediately, bill in hand. Helen reached into her handbag, pulled out a tissue.

"Now," she said to Irena.

Irena felt her perspective on the room shift, as it sometimes did when I was sharing a private observation with her. She looked up at the waiter as he placed the check on the table and said he hoped the meal had been memorable. Then, instead of leaving, he stood at the end of the table, staring at Helen, who smiled up at him and rested her hand on his arm.

Suddenly the attraction the young man felt for Helen exploded into a fantasy, sharp as reality in his mind. Caught up in the thought of kissing her, he was unaware of Helen raising his wrist to her lips, the quick painless cut of a sharp rear incisor, the explosion of life in both women as Helen drew him in.

It ended as quickly as it began. He barely noticed as Helen pressed the tissue against the tiny cut, holding it there a moment before handing him the money for the bill and tip. He remained motionless and staring out the window, even after the women left the restaurant and Helen released him.

They were pulling out of the lot when Helen said, "So now you've felt both sides but there is one thing you must understand. That need for blood is the least important aspect of what we are."

Later, on their way home after an hour's worth of shopping the local craft and specialty shops, Irena asked one more question: How was the change done? Helen spent the entire drive home providing the answer.

# CHAPTER 22

Irena and my mother returned to the house with cheese and two bottles of wine, a thick merlot and a sweet sauternes. They opened the red as soon as they got home and sat drinking in the kitchen, giggling together like best friends.

I knew Irena liked Helen, but I was not sure if the warmth my mother conveyed was totally genuine. I might have asked the question privately but I really did not want to know the truth, unless the truth was as I saw it.

Later, we all settled in the living room. I played some of the pieces I'd recently mastered, then accompanied Irena. She sang the two pieces she'd used for her audition, then another from Laurie's opera. We'd practiced some of the other pieces but Stephen knew them as well and soon they were doing the duet between Natalya and Johann, the young Nazi officer, while I provided the music. I watched his hand resting on her arm as he mentally provided cues for the occasional phrasing she had not completely mastered.

"Do you remember any Romanian folk songs?" he asked when they'd finished and Irena had returned to sit beside me on the sofa.

She nodded, eyes bright. "I will always love them," she said.

With me on the piano, Patrick and Helen on drums, Stephen on guitar, and he and Irena providing vocals, things became impromptu strange. And beautiful. And wild. I could feel in the lyrics the life she missed, as did he even after so many centuries away from it. I noticed that Stephen had set aside his guitar and moved to straddle the arm of the sofa, his hand on her shoulder. Visions of the country he knew so well seemed to radiate from both of them so that for a time we were all there.

"Now your turn," Helen said, bringing Stephen the naizet they kept in the corner. I had played it only once for Irena, admitting beforehand that I had no skill for it. Not understanding how it should be played, she had still been awed. I almost prayed he'd say no, though I knew exactly why he could not.

It looks like some odd, gourd-shaped wooden sculpture, until it is unlocked, revealing two stringed instruments shaped much like lutes. The two pieces can be played separately, something Patrick and I often did when we were younger. But Stephen locks them together, the joined center sitting on his crossed legs, the two necks facing in opposite directions, each hand alternating between fingering the strings and strumming them.

The songs composed for it alternate between slower sections played on one or the other of the two halves and incredibly quick sections played on both sides together. Helen says the shifting tempos of the songs remind her of the Hungarian dance, the czardas.

As Stephen began testing the strings, Helen rested a hand on his shoulder. "Take Irena hunting, love. Show her the scenes you shared with me," she suggested.

"Please!" Irena said. Still stunned by the detail of his visions of the country she had left, she was more than ready to explore.

He nodded and moved closer to her so that his shoulder was resting against her knee, strengthening the bond as he began to play.

The music began slowly, one side playing then the other. And the vast and empty plains of the land that would one day be called the Ukraine expanded in her mind. I saw her eyes shut, felt her breathing quicken as she moved through the vision he created of that long, wild run across the plains. I shared it, but I chose to share it through her. And so I knew that, as the music quickened, she felt the muscles in his shoulder moving, hard and quick as his hands alternated from frets to strings. And she could not help but be aware that he was the instrument, the one who had lived the scene and created this music, this ordered vision. When he beat his bare feet against the sounding board then began to sing, I felt her pulse quicken, her hand move to his shoulder, fingering the soft silk collar of his shirt, brushing against the flesh beneath it. Her eyes were closed, her lips slightly parted. Had he stopped the playing then, had he leaned over and kissed her, she would have kissed him back. Like any prey, he had her while I . . .

Someone nudged me hard in the ribs. I looked and saw Patrick walking softly toward the door, motioning me to follow. I did, shutting the doors behind us, following him down the hallway to the kitchen then through the back door and into the growing darkness beyond. Even there, I could hear the music and the beat of his feet, feel the pounding of her heart.

"Damn it! The bastard is seducing her!" I whispered, hitting my fist against the cement block foundation of the porch. I knew it was irrational, but I could not help the feeling.

Patrick surprised me, pulling me close, all but pinning my arms to my sides, his lips brushing against my cheek, his breath tickling my ear, reinforcing the words he whispered, "It's a collective seduction, Richard. A family welcome. Let it happen. It has to sometime."

"Let me go, damn it!" I shook him off me. "She's just met him."

"Then I'd say he's doing his job remarkably well." He brushed the snow off the top step with his shirtsleeve, clearing a space wide enough for both of us to sit.

Now that I wasn't compelled to feel what she felt, some of the fight drained out of me. I sat down beside him, brushed my hand over the snow, then rested it on my forehead, an old trick my parents used for cooling us off when our tempers ran too hot. "You're right. But it can't change how I feel about what he's doing."

"Every year during shutdown, Helen goes off for a night alone with Denys. The first time, Stephen was furious at his own jealousy. But of course Helen came back. It will be the same with Irena and you."

"Even when it's him?"

"Especially him. He has what he wants already, and I don't think Helen is one to tolerate a harem. Besides, one of these days if all goes as we hope, you will have to explain to your lady love precisely who will father her children. Better she has a few fantasies aimed in his direction when you bring up his name."

In spite of how I felt, I had to nudge him back just a little. "I won't be bringing up your name?" I asked.

"Hell no! I lost all those illusions when he ripped through me on Friday night. That was the most painful part of the entire experience."

We returned to the others bearing glasses of water for ourselves and Stephen, the bottle of wine for the women; our excuse for leaving should Irena ask.

The song's tempo had begun to slow, ending with the lone slow beating of Stephen's foot against the sounding board. I saw him reach for Irena's hand. She didn't move as he raised it to his lips, brushed a kiss across the back of it. I couldn't help myself. I felt sick inside . . . and if jealousy is the measure of love, then love be damned as well. But when Irena opened her eyes, she looked straight toward me, then at the darkened windows.

"You promised me a walk tonight," she said, taking my hand and pulling me down beside her. I could feel the heat rising from her. He may have lit that fire, but he had directed it back to me.

I looked down at him. He glanced up, one brow rising slightly, the hint of a smile on his lips. I didn't thank him, nor apologize, though in truth, I never should have expected him to do anything else.

The night was still and cold and Irena and I walked for an hour beneath the shimmering sky, the subtle shades of a curtain aurora beginning to heat on the northern horizon. When I felt her grow cold, we started back.

I stopped at the edge of the lawn. I'd heard a familiar sound, thought of something I needed to share.

I gave a soft howl. Concentrating on the pack I'd sensed nearby, I took her hand and waited.

They came from between the trees, four graceful gray shapes barely distinguishable from the snow or the frost-coated trees. As they neared us, Irena moved closer to me.

—My mother's pets,— I told her and rested my hand on the largest one, the leader, whom Helen called Gandolph.

—Can I touch him?—

—He knows you're with me. But move slowly or he'll run.—

She did as I directed, laying a bare hand on his back, feeling the coarse coat, the softer winter fur beneath.

The other three kept their distance, moving to the edge of the trees, stopping there. As the last joined them, they turned and disappeared.

When we returned to the house, Patrick and Stephen were absorbed in a game of chess in the living room; Helen was stretched out on the sofa reading a novel. None of them did more than glance up when we said good night. A calculated indifference; in a family that reads minds almost as easily as words on paper, disinterest puts guests at ease.

As I had done the night before, I placed my pendant on the dresser before I joined Irena in bed. Though I missed the intimate perfection of that double bond, the lack seemed to trouble her more. Her hand brushed the back of my neck, seeking the chain, the glass, its sharp tip. When she lay beside me some time later, her muscles were taut, her fingers rolling the hem of the sheet.

"I should just tell everyone yes and be done with it," she said, frustration sharpening her whisper.

"It's barely more than a habit. Once you're on tour, you'll be too busy to even think about it."

"With you in bed beside me, I am not to think about it?"

One more reason why I should not go, I thought, though I did not say it. I guessed that she would make that decision for me, sparing me an explanation of still another of our limitations, one that would likely cause her to worry needlessly.

She rolled over, her back to me. I touched her shoulder, felt the tension there. I would have massaged it away but I knew she did not want me to. So I lay where I was, with that gulf of inches between us, until her breathing slowed to sleep's pace. When I was sure she would not wake, my mind sought Patrick's. As I'd guessed, he was outside waiting for me. I slipped out of bed and onto the porch, and from there dropped to the ground below. The snow hit my bare skin and I shuddered from the sudden shock of the cold.

I paused at the edge of the tree line. Moving my mind through the wilderness, I entered the woods following the path Patrick had taken.

When I joined him, we had a wordless greeting, a sharing of emotions far deeper than speech could convey. Then he ran, me pursuing, a game we never tired of. When I caught him, the force of my leap sent us both sprawling facedown in the snow, laughing at the cold of it, the emptiness of the night. Laughing at what we were.

We roamed until nearly dawn, and returned the way we left. I climbed the end post of the back porch and swung my legs over the rail, stepping back so Patrick could do the same. He'd reached his room at the far end of the house before I stepped into mine.

I'd intended to go straight to the bathroom and take a shower, if only to warm my body before I put it anywhere close to Irena's. But when I glanced at my bed, I saw that it was empty.

"—Irena—" I called, my voice a whisper, my mind nearly as quiet. She was not in the room or in the hallway. Not in the bathroom.

—Irena!—

I expected her reply, got my mother's instead. —Come downstairs,— Helen ordered.

I did as she asked, saw Irena in the dark hallway shuffling toward my parents' room. The flannel shirt I had given her to wear over her nightgown was unbuttoned, the front of the gown as well. Afraid I would startle her, I called to her mind again, more softly this time. When she did not respond, I ordered her to stop. She did, rising on her tiptoes, as if trying to will herself forward. Before she could move, Helen came out of the room and took her by the shoulders. I expected Irena to wake then, expected the thrashing or the cry of fear from some nightmare from her past. But the sleep seemed unnaturally deep, almost trancelike in its hold on her. Helen guided her to me and I carried her to the living room and laid her on the sofa. Helen got a spare blanket from the hall closet and covered her.

"I'll stay. Go and get your father," Helen said.

An odd request. Even at dawn, when we sleep our deepest, we can wake one another with a thought. Wondering at her reason, I entered their room and stopped. My father lay facedown on the bed, one hand gripping the edge of his pillow so tightly the hem on the case had ripped. I realized, as my mother must have, that what was happening in this house was far more serious than sleepwalking.

"Stephen," I called softly, adding, —Father?—

No response. I moved beside him, rested a hand on his shoulder, spoke louder. "Father!"

His body jerked and he opened his eyes so quickly I jumped backward. His eyes were full-black, as if he had been dreaming of a hunt; though of course, we do not dream. "It's Irena," I said, and as I spoke her name, I heard her calling me, her voice filled with surprise and justified confusion.

I suspected it was no greater than my father's. He shook his head as if trying to clear it. Calmer then, he stared at me, catching snips of thoughts rushing through my mind. "Is she all right?" he asked, sounding unsure of himself. From the puzzled way he looked at me, I guessed he didn't have that feeling often.

"She was in a trance, in the hallway outside. You were calling her," I said.

"It did not seem that way. It seemed . . . she was calling me."

He got out of bed a bit slower than I would have expected. As he tied his robe, I picked up a pair of his jeans and slipped them on.

"She wanted you. You responded," I said.

"I would know," he retorted, as if my conclusion challenged him.

Perhaps it did. I wondered then how deep the subconscious would be in a creature centuries old, decided to ask Patrick his opinion on it. He'd likely come up with some equation beginning with "directly proportional to." I pushed the notion out of my mind as I zipped the jeans halfway—as far as they would go—and returned to Irena.

When Irena saw me, she managed a smile. "They tell me I was sleepwalking. But I have never—" She stopped speaking when she saw Stephen enter the room, looking at him as she had looked at me the night I sang that high note for her.

Her expression was mirrored by my father's. "Someone should stay with her," he said.

"I will," Helen said.

I was in no position to argue. Had I been left alone with Irena, my eyes would have shut within minutes. She could have roamed where she would and I would not have noticed.

After we left the women and Stephen shut the doors behind us, he held my arm a moment. "I'm sorry," he said. "She must have called to me, but it could have been to any of us. I was merely the one who responded. As long as she is here, someone will have to watch her, or what happened tonight will happen again. If she wanted the change, I would be honored to act as third and assist you. But I don't think she does, at least not yet."

"And the two of us?"

He shook his head. "You hardly need my answer."

I returned to my room, filled with remorse. I should have taken her to the hospital that night the illness peaked. I should have forced her to forget what I had done for her. I should have consulted my father. Should have . . .

I was exhausted and asleep before my list of mistakes grew too long.

Much later that morning, I was buttoning my shirt when Irena joined me and held me close. "I've left good-byes for everyone through your mother. She said we should take the Jeep and go. Please, I want to stay but I can't face anyone."

"You didn't do anything wrong, Irena," I told her.

"I know. It's just that I don't want to disappoint anybody." She held me tighter. "I'm sorry, Dickie. Your father said our meeting was merely a beginning, but it doesn't feel that way inside me. I need to get away from here if I want to think about this rationally."

Rationally! As if the choice would come from her mind instead of her soul.

We packed quickly and drove away from the house, my dark glasses barely compensating for the dazzling brilliance of the sun on the snow.

# CHAP+ER 23

When I left for Chicago, one of my father's parting gifts had been a credit card to be used for emergencies. I hadn't used it before, but was thankful I had it when we reached Montreal with barely one hundred dollars between us.

No matter what happened later, I wanted this night to be memorable so I found the place the older girls in Saint-Michel often mentioned, a small hotel on Saint-Denis just a bit south of Sherbrooke. Little more than the width of a storefront at the street, the hotel widened and extended nearly to the street behind, its rooms looking onto a narrow courtyard garden that must have been beautiful in the summer, considering the winter elegance of the spotlights aimed at its bare trees and the statues in its corners.

We dropped our bags on the white iron bed in our room and went out to explore the city. Though I had been here often, it had always been for a specific social event, never just to take in the sights. And so I looked at it as she did as we wandered streets I had never seen, both of us trying to fall into the small adventure of a new place and forget the odd night that had brought us here.

On the walk down to Vieux-Port, we followed the scent of baking bread into one of the city's patisseries. My tea tasted better for the aroma of the breads I could not eat and the sight of

Irena happily absorbed in devouring a hot croissant and slice of local brie followed by a tiny marzipan-stuffed napoleon. Whatever uneasiness she had felt that morning lifted with distance from the house, making me wonder again if it had been caused by her need or by my father's.

But we didn't speak of that, hardly spoke at all as we wandered in and out of little galleries where hopeful artists, trying to look disinterested in peddling their work, were desperate for a sale. We wandered through the Place-de'Armes, then took a long solo tour through Notre-Dame Basilica. We stopped in a corner where, beneath a window nearly equal to the ones my own create, I whispered to her the legends about its building that my father had told me years before.

By then it was growing dark and we headed away from the St. Lawrence, stopping at a turn-of-the-century house resurrected as a restaurant. Expensive, but she would be the only one dining.

"You and your mother are both trying to fatten me up," she said as she studied the menu before deciding on trout stuffed with lobster mousse. When I asked only for tea, the waiter looked down his nose at me. I explained in French that I had a touch of the stomach flu but could not let my American guest miss an opportunity to eat at the best restaurant in Montreal. Perhaps he had some mint tea he could bring for me, oui?

Perhaps it was more than mint, some exotic aphrodesiac. Perhaps it was simply the sharing of Irena's sensations as she savored the unfamiliar melange of spice in her meal. But then, I love watching even strangers eat, wondering what sort of things they like and why, reveling in observing one of the few things I cannot do.

Irena noticed my interest, amused as she always was. "If it is true that we all have lived before, you must have been a chef in an earlier life, considering how well you cook in this one," she told me and laughed.

The sound was hollow at its core, her gaiety—and mine— nervous and forced. Night had fallen and we both wanted more than sex.

We stopped often on the walk to our hotel, my mind set on finding her the perfect gift to take on tour. I discovered it in a little clothing shop on Saint-Urban, a tie-dyed wool jacket and beret. "You need something to brighten all that black," I said and put the hat on her.

She tucked her hair behind one ear, angled the beret as a French girl would, and draped the jacket over her shoulders.

"You look marvelous in blue and yellow and pink and orange and . . ."

"Purple," Irena supplied, puckering her lips as she said the word, kissing me quickly, urgently. I paid the cashier and we left and made a straight line for our hotel, the waiting tub, the white iron bed.

I thought that perhaps ardor alone would keep her mind off what we could not do and for a time it did. But when the moment came that I drew her in and she felt my mind so strong in hers, her own need responded.

It seemed far more demanding than the night before, a craving so strong that I could barely touch her mind. Had she asked me, I would have refused. Had she begged . . . I would have given in. But she did neither. Instead, she managed to enjoy what we did, and well enough that her passion was genuine at the end, though hardly the feeling we had shared before.

But after, she lay with clenched fists, eyes bright with unshed tears. "I'm beginning to understand what Viktor did," she mumbled.

"You can't mean that."

She rolled up on an elbow, rested a hand on my chest. "I understand but I would never do it. Viktor would have been dangerous even without that craving inside him."

She was quiet for a while, then asked, "What will happen to my voice?"

I laughed and hugged her. "Irena, that was always you. All I did was show you what you could do."

"Really?"

"Last night, did you ever hear my mother sing?"

"Terrible?"

"Not terrible. Good enough for a church choir. Not our equal, certainly not yours. No, Irena, your voice is yours to keep. And if that bit of us in you helped you achieve that range, it was there before I met you."

The words made her feel better, but hardly relaxed. I thought of what had happened the night before and realized I would have to sleep with one eye open, more likely not at all. I felt her trying to find peace, forcing herself to the edge of sleep before the need rose and demanded its satisfaction. A few times, she began to slide the covers back slowly, wondering if she could reach the dresser without waking me, if she could return with that sharp piece of glass, wound me, drink. It was as if we were addicts. I'd had my fix, denied her hers, and the injustice gnawed at her.

Finally, I moved close behind her, wrapped an arm around her waist, and held her, her back pressed against my chest. "I love you," I murmured. The first time I had ever said it. She did not reply.

—Sleep,— I ordered, and for a time the calm engulfed us both until the growing dawn pulled me into a deep and heedless slumber.

When I woke later, I was alone. At first I thought that Irena had gone downstairs for breakfast then noticed that the pendant had been moved to the bedside table. Our suitcase was open, her clothes missing from it. I picked up a note laid next to the TV, already guessing what it said.

> *Dearest, I am not telling you good-bye, but I need to get away from you for a while, to sort out everything I've learned. I am glad you decided to wait to drop the rest of the semester because I've decided to go on the tour without you and am too much a coward to look at you and tell you this. We need a separation. Perhaps you are right and my work will make this craving easier to bear. We should see the future more clearly by the time I return. I hope so. I love you, too, Irena.*
>
> *P.S. I will pay you back when I am the rich woman you assure me I will one day be.*

I crumpled the note, threw it in the wastebasket. A moment later, I fished it out and smoothed and folded the paper carefully. As I slipped it into my wallet, I saw that she'd taken nearly all my travel money, which explained the postscript.

She'd likely caught an earlier flight and when I got home her clothes would be gone. I respected her decision, enough that I packed my own things, settled the bill downstairs, and took the Jeep back to Saint-Michel.

Helen was sitting on the porch when I drove up. She came

down to the driveway to meet me. "She left," she said, not quite a question.

I nodded. I did not want to share my misery but it was too strong to be contained. Helen pulled me close to her, and I rested my head on her shoulder, wishing I were capable of tears.

"She's flying to Connecticut on Saturday. I want to stay here until she's gone," I said.

"Stay as long as you wish. School can wait." Her hands rubbed my shoulders and stroked my hair as if pain could be stolen with a mother's touch.

It couldn't. I thought of Irena in that terrible country alone and I phoned her. No answer at the apartment so I called the lobby desk and learned that she had already dropped off her key.

I tried calling her at home but got no answer until the next evening. "My mother sometimes turns the ringer off when she is trying to sleep in the morning and forgets to put it back on. I just noticed it a little while ago," Irena explained.

"Does she know where you're going yet?"

"I told her. I thought she would be worried but she was so excited." Irena explained how her mother had invited all their friends over earlier that evening to celebrate, and how they all said they would write relations and tell them to go and hear her sing. "And I have not told my mother that Marie is living in Sibiu. I have written her and hope we can meet as well."

Her excitement was infectious and for a few minutes I almost forgot how frightened she had been about the tour only days ago. "Just remember to stay with your group."

"I know. I know. I will."

"And call me after you get to New Haven. And while you're in rehearsals. And from Romania. At least every few days to tell me how it's going. And my father tells me that Romanian hotel rooms are bugged. The phones, too. So if you call from there be careful of what you say. But promise you'll call anyway."

She laughed then her voice fell to a whisper. "You don't have to make me promise. I meant what I wrote. I do love you. Whatever happens, that won't change. I won't let it."

I felt better—and worse—at the same time. And long after we had both hung up, I sat with my hand on the receiver, wondering if I should call her and tell her not to go.

But she would not have listened if I had. The contracts were signed, the arrangements made. Her career would be ended if she backed out now. A few hours after she flew to Connecticut, I was on a plane bound for O'Hare, the empty apartment, and school.

I fell back into my studies with directed intensity, making up the week of work I had missed in a few days. I continued to help with the chorus as well. A couple of the girls in the group, sensing a breakup, began to flirt. I ignored them. To take up with any of them would have been too much a betrayal of Irena, and too complicating when she returned. Instead, I hunted every night, long solitary walks that ended in quick feedings, the victims of my anger barely distracted.

I began to wonder what it would be like to take them aware, as I had taken her. To savor their fear as I had savored her passion. An odd, strange thought, unlike me, beneath me. "I was raised to be kind," my father often told me, but I hardly felt kind to anyone in those next few weeks.

Irena arrived in New Haven five days after she left Montreal. She took with her four changes of clothes, a good dress and shoes she had bought for the tour, the russet sweater and bottle of Joy that I had given her, along with a half dozen bottles of perfume to give as gifts. She wore the hat and scarf that I had bought her in Montreal, the tip of the scarf a bit damp from the tears she had shed on the two-hour flight.

Not tears of fear exactly. Not even sorrow at having left me. It was more the excitement of the journey, what would lie at the end of it—its consequences for her life. At such times, Irena always cries.

She called me three nights after she arrived there, and after a few awkward comments about the weather, we relaxed.

She spoke of their rehearsals and how it had become her added duty to correct everyone's pronunciation during them, which hardly endeared her to the cast.

"I tell them that this is the native language of the place we will be touring and that our audiences deserve to hear us sing it properly and not sound like a bunch of hissing snakes," she told me. "And I am glad to coach them, especially Mr. Korval. The more he speaks to the press, the less the spotlight will be on me."

I pictured her the spokesperson for the company, always in the limelight. The thought unsettled me more than I liked to admit. "Are you and Korval the only ones who know the language?" I asked.

"There are also two men and a woman from the State Department, though I do not think the woman speaks Romanian so well. They will be touring with us. While on tour, the woman and I will be sharing a double room and the other two leads will each get an agent as a roommate. I like the idea of having someone from our government close by. They have made it clear that we must not speak to any native Romanians at all without permission from our translators, who will of course be part of Ceaușescu's securitate. So I will not get to see my family or my mother's friends unless they are with me. I have been told that any meeting will likely be strained and swift, but safe if it is public."

Somewhat reassured by that, I asked about the staging.

She explained that they practiced in a restored theater about the size of most of the halls they would be performing in. Because the sets were simple ones, each city on the tour would build a set of its own to the company's specifications so that all the company needed to take with them were the costumes and props.

"And your singing, how is that?" I asked.

"They all love me. They are in complete awe." She laughed. "Is that what you wanted to hear?"

"It's true, isn't it?"

"Musically, yes. But my acting is terrible. I just hope I don't make a fool out of myself in Bucharest and start to cry in front of that despot. Though from the rumors that fly through the company, I would prefer to spit in his face."

"I hear from Hunter that Ceaușescu loathes artistic performances. Maybe he'll be asleep by the second act."

"Good. But still I just wish . . . I wish you had some way of bottling that calm you project and sending me a case of it."

"You'll be fine . . . more than fine. You'll be a marvel."

The night before she left the country, she called me to say good-bye. Well aware of the Romanian reputation of bugged telephone lines, we created a simple system she could use if she could not speak freely; another to alert me that she felt in real danger. Hunter had told me we had our own contacts in that country and that she would be safe. But as we spoke, I could feel her slipping farther away from me, heading toward her destiny and, it seemed, mine.

# CHAPTER 24

## PATRICK

*Let us leave Dickie boy to his misery—not that he didn't have good reason to be miserable. The story does not belong to him for a time, but to those who love him. It is an adventure my father would have relished when he was young. Knowing his history as well as I do, he's had more than his share of them, even in my lifetime.*

Irena's flight to Europe began with a commuter flight to JFK followed by a two-hour wait between connections. She had mentioned to my brother that some of the families of company members would be meeting the New Haven flight. My brother mentioned the flight time to me. He did not ask me to go but I went anyway, waiting with the others for the plane to land, flirting with a girl about my own age who clutched a bouquet of roses she intended to give her sister who was in the chorus.

I was just thinking that I might lure that luscious young creature into the nearest phone booth, when Irena's prop plane pulled up to the gate. She walked up the stairs and into the terminal not expecting anyone to meet her. When she saw me, I felt her shock until she realized that I was alone.

"What a surprise!" she said, awkward until she decided to give in to the impulse and hug me. I paid close attention to that because I knew my brother would be sure to ask about her feelings then. But sadly, it was just a hug—no attraction, no sense of need.

Since Air France would serve lunch and dinner on the plane, we settled into an airport bar for drinks. And though I had heard it already from Richard, I listened as she described the rehearsals, how incredibly the music touched her. "I am afraid I will cry during that opening aria," she said. "Not the best way to hit those notes."

"Then cry as you finish. Let the audience see the tears on your face. You'll be their darling and you'll have a good fifteen minutes of applause in which to compose yourself before you have to sing again."

"Pig!" she replied, though she was smiling as she said it.

"And a damned good pig! But seriously, Irena, did you really want me to commiserate with you or give you something to smile about later? No, don't bother to answer. I already know what you're going to say."

She looked down at her drink, frowned, and said nothing.

"Dickie thinks you're euphoric about this but you're petrified, aren't you?"

"I've never sung alone before an audience," she admitted. "How can I know how I'll react?"

"Would you like a guarantee?" I asked.

She had already decided yes, though she had not answered. I moved behind her and put my hands on her shoulders. A few women in the bar were watching me, nothing odd about that. To them it would have seemed as if I were kneading her shoulders, rubbing out the tension. One of the women close to us smiled at me. I smiled back as I lowered my lips to the nape of Irena's neck.

Yes, I drank, because I was curious. But I used the bond to give her what she wanted. The calm would last at least a few days, long enough to get her through opening night and that state reception with the despot and his sow of a wife. Then she would be on her own though she would not know it.

When I saw her off at the Air France gate, she hugged me hard. "Tell Richard I'll call after that first performance," she said.

I watched her go, the taste of her still on my lips. Much like Mother, she seemed, and that same sense of destiny that frightened my brother rolled through me like a sudden chill.

Twelve hours later, when the Air France flight landed at Otopeni Airport in Bucharest, Irena had her nose pressed to the glass trying to see something of the city. But there was only darkness broken by the lights of the landing strip that outlined antiaircraft guns installed along the edges of the field.

The company was met on the plane by two members of the securitate, Ceauşescu's internal police, a man and woman who eyed them all as if they were spies rather than invited guests. The woman, Katharine, must have been alerted to Irena's status, because she stayed close to her on the frigid bus ride from the airport to the Athenee Palace Hotel, making patriotic comments on the comfort of the public housing they passed. Deciding it was better to appear ignorant than dangerous, Irena replied in halting Romanian and often asked the woman to speak more slowly.

The Athenee Palace had a faded glory, the white marble pillars in the lobby discolored at their base from the sooty air blowing in through the front doors. When they entered, Irena saw a pair of women in miniskirts and go-go boots sitting on couches near the door. The women looked up, hopeful and hungry, until they noticed the austere dress of the translators, guessed what they really were, and looked away.

The entire company was whisked past the reception desk to the elevators, which took them to the top floor. The room Irena would share with Monica Harris, the liaison from the State Department, had threadbare carpeting of an indeterminate dark color, wallpaper that might have been cream some hundreds of cigarettes before, and a little balcony that looked across the plaza to the Athenaeum concert hall where they would perform. When Irena tried to go outside, she found the balcony doors were locked.

With her roommate off for a further briefing with Ceauşescu's police, Irena inspected the room. The blankets were thick, the mattress worn but comfortable. There were towels and washcloths in the bathroom, a used bar of soap, and a half roll of toilet paper. Her mother had told her to expect none but perhaps things were worse in the northwestern part of the country where the government distrusted the heavy population of immigrants as if, like the Basque in Spain, they might try for independence.

Though the well-scrubbed porcelain tub looked inviting, the trickle of water from its faucet was brackish and barely luke-warm. Irena settled for a sponge bath, then, because the room was cold, slipped between the covers. She'd just settled in to bed to read when she heard a knock on the door.

No peephole, so she attached the chain and opened the door a few inches, enough to see a young man standing there, holding a pillow and a bottle of wine. He wore jeans and a sweater and she was about to shut the door on him when he asked, "Is everything well?"

She answered in halting Romanian. "There is no hot water and the room is cold."

"I will see what can be done." He punctuated that with a shrug and handed her the bottle. "This is gift. Enjoy."

"Wait here," she said and went to get him a tip. But even after she gave it to him, he stood there as if he expected her to invite him in for a drink. She thanked him and shut the door slowly, leaving on the chain until she heard a key in the lock, Monica returning.

Monica Harris was hardly the sort of stone-faced bureaucrat Irena had expected. Soon after they met, the woman had explained to Irena that she had studied languages in college and that she had been chosen for this assignment, her first in the Eastern Block, based on her skill in speaking both Hungarian and Romanian. Until this trip Monica had never been east of London and she approached her assignment with a breathless excitement usually seen in someone far younger than her thirty or so years.

When Irena told Monica of her encounter with the bellhop, the woman reacted with a mixture of humor and alarm. "They say there are many prostitutes working the hotel. Perhaps not all are women?"

"I didn't think I looked so hard up," Irena said, grinning as she studied the label on the wine. It was a sweet muscat from Baia Mare, a town near the one where she'd been raised. The label appeared homemade, loosely glued. "Should we open it?" Irena asked.

Monica shook her head. "It might not agree with us and we have so much work tomorrow." She held her hand over her stomach, pantomiming her real concern. Irena doubted someone would deliberately try to poison her, but her illness would mean the understudy would sing her role and the company—and the United States by association—would look bad.

Morning came. Irena woke because she'd become hot under the three blankets she'd piled on for warmth. Heat flowed from the registers. The water trickling from the bathroom faucets was hot as well. Apparently her comment the night before had been noted.

It was snowing, but even that could not lift the gloom outside, oppressive and heavy as the slush the company waded through on their short walk to the Athenaeum. The hall was magnificently overdone, almost rococo in its well-maintained splendor, and had been heated only enough to keep the pipes from freezing. Most of the set had already been built, enough that the company could get a feel for the slight changes. But when it came time for a re-hearsal, the company's singers were shivering so much they could barely sing.

"Get us some heat," Korval demanded.

The well-dressed little man who had let them in shrugged, mumbled something to himself, and barked an order to the back of the hall. A moment later, every stage light went on, a blinding display of light that quickly made the stage area comfortable enough for work.

The Romanians knew the Austra score well and Korval had sent them a tape of the music the company had used for re-hearsals so that the pace would be the same. And it was, perfectly so. The sets, too, were done with incredible skill, a realism that Irena found astonishing. When the group took a break from re-hearsal, the little man, the theater manager he told her, took her backstage to show her the greenroom and her dressing room.

"I apologize for the cold," he said. "We do not have your . . . luxuries."

"But you've prepared everything so beautifully," Irena replied.

He waited until they were in the hallway to answer. "We work together, make statement," he said and flashed a conspiratorial smile that revealed teeth yellowed by nicotine and neglect.

They went through one complete rehearsal again that day, a dress rehearsal the following morning, then a long afternoon of rest.

Irena's nervousness faded as the hours passed, so that she was one of the few in the company who actually managed enough of a nap that afternoon to look refreshed when they met in the hotel restaurant at five for a light meal. The main one would come after the performance, at the reception the government would host.

As she sat in the dressing room, sipping bottled water while the final touches were done to her makeup, a deep calm descended on her—my suggestion and her own great resolve. When the lights came up onstage, revealing her in chains in that too realistic prison cell, she did not look at the box seats where the dignitaries would be seated, but at the audience on the floor—silent, rapt, waiting.

As the solo violin began its slow smooth fall, her voice caught that impossibly high note and fell with it, the long sad scream that mirrored the agony of the people to whom she sang.

For a moment after the aria ended, the audience was as silent as Irena. Then, when the tenor who played the Nazi lieutenant stepped onto the stage and held out his hand to help her rise, scattered clapping lit a fuse that ignited the audience.

Irena looked up, dazed at the applause. As she did, the audience caught the tears on her cheeks and the applause grew louder. Stomping feet and whistles came from somewhere in the back. "Acknowledge it, you idiot, or they'll never stop," the tenor whispered to her, though not unkindly. She bowed her head, once, and the orchestra resumed play.

The rest of the performance was met by a charged silence from the audience, held-back emotions that exploded only at the end when Natalya sang her final aria—one of triumph not despair.

To convey the feeling he'd wanted at the end, Laurie had abandoned operatic tradition and had his heroine die offstage. The drama ended with soldiers leading her from the cell. Not even the sound of bullets marred the triumph of that incredible piece. Instead, the orchestra and chorus began a symphonic movement incorporating bits of melody from the Gypsies, the Romanians, the Saxons, the Hungarians, and the Jews and melded them into a magnificent finale that continued as music only when the chorus took its bows. It stopped completely only when no one could have heard the music any longer . . . after the male leads made space in the center for Irena to receive her just praise.

Flashbulbs reflected the tears on her cheeks, the cameras' film

the smile of innocent triumph as she bent down to pick up a rose
that someone had tossed onto the stage. "Our Natalya" the state-
run papers would proclaim her the next day. But that night Irena
knew none of it, only that the audience had loved her and she had
earned it.

The familiar strains of Romanian folk tunes flowed from the
open salon doors of the Athenee Plaza and mingled with laughter
and voices. Irena smelled expensive perfume and Turkish cigarettes. As she stepped through the door, the talking stopped and
Irena's face reddened as every face turned in her direction. The
males looked at her with almost predatory interest and she was
glad she had taken Monica's advice and worn the long dress skirt
and silver cardigan rather than something more revealing.

Seeing her, Korval come over and held out his arm. "We
might as well get it over with," he whispered. "I don't know what
he thought of the opera but his wife was most impressed, which
is a good thing. Come."

With Korval pulling her forward, Irena had no choice but to
walk or be dragged into the adjacent lounge.

The Ceauşescus were seated in the center of a large group at a
low mahogany table close to the stage. Though the buffet in the
main salon offered an incredible array of local dishes, the president had only a plate of peasant bread, feta cheese, tomatoes, and
onions in front of him. Later Irena would learn this was his favorite dessert, no doubt a holdover from the days when cheese
and tomatoes would have been luxuries in his life. Elena had
nothing at all in front of her but a large glass of champagne, the
rest of the bottle of Cordon Rouge chilling in a bucket to her
right. When she saw Irena approaching, she looked up and
smiled. "Pour her a glass of champagne," she ordered the woman
sitting beside her.

The woman rushed to obey, but she was drunk and poured too
quickly so that the foam overflowed onto Irena's hand as she held
out the glass that had been given her.

"I hear you are Romanian," Ceauşescu began in English, before there was any formal introduction.

"Yes. My family is from Sighet."

"You were very young when they left."

She hesitated before replying to what did not seem like a
question. "So young that I barely remember the journey."

"Are you happy to be home?"

"I am not home yet."

"What, you do not like Bucharest?" Elena Ceauşescu asked, her voice shrill, as if this were a personal insult.

"I was . . . I was afraid I would not sing well in front of the rulers of my homeland," she answered. "I am pleased you liked my singing but I am looking forward to the two northern performances on the tour. Some of my cousins may even come to hear me in Baia Mare."

"If you give Andrei Oprea"—Elena motioned to a dark-haired man of about thirty near the end of their table—"a list of their names, we can assure it."

Irena glanced at Korval but got no hint from him on how to respond. "I have only a few that I remember."

"Nonsense, child. We can arrange anything. Tell him the names you remember and where they might be found. No one should miss a chance to see their kin."

Andrei Oprea stood, smoothed the front of his black suit jacket, and moved beside her. He took her hand and kissed the back of it with only a hint of exaggeration. When he looked up at her face, he winked at her. His eyes were warm and brown, large and slightly slanted, the lashes long, almost feminine. His mouth was thin-lipped but expressive. He was probably a killer with women, and though he clearly knew it, his expression was so good-natured that he seemed almost an innocent in this company. But there was nothing innocent in the cunning of his words. "Our esteemed . . . how do you say in America?—first lady? . . . is always right about these matters," he said. "But perhaps you would reward us with a song . . . something more traditional?"

"No!" Ceauşescu barked. "Sing American. Something from the American movies."

"Our president loves American movies," Andrei Oprea whispered.

"What are you saying to her, Andrei? Tell us?" Elena demanded, her voice even shriller than before, making Irena begin to wonder how much champagne the woman had consumed.

"I suggested 'Goldfinger.' "

"I don't know all the words," Irena replied.

"Just hum the ones you don't know. Even your humming will sound beautiful," Elena countered. "Take the woman to the stage and introduce her, Andrei. I know they can play that."

When they were some distance from the table, Andrei leaned close to her and whispered, "See, I rescued you. Now thank me." His English was as good as hers, though a bit slurred, and his breath reeked of brandy and peppermints.

"Thank you?"

"Give me names."

"Why do they want them?"

"It is their way of being gracious. If they help you, you are thankful. They feel good and think you are in their debt and so they trust you and everyone is cheerful. It is best that they always feel cheerful," he said softly in his excellent English.

She sang the song Ceauşescu had requested, another from *My Fair Lady,* then one of her favorite childhood songs, a ballad from the Maramures region where she'd been raised. The president clapped after the first, Elena after the last. On the second, they both looked bored.

The band took a break and Irena left the stage. Korval was on the opposite side of the room with a pair of elegantly dressed older women, steno books open, taking notes. American press or Romanian, it made no difference. Irena didn't want to talk to any of them. Monica was nowhere in sight, but Andrei Oprea was waiting.

"When the music begins, will you dance with me?" he asked.

"I'm not sure you're even up to standing. Perhaps you should eat something. I know I should."

Taking the hint, he walked with her to the buffet. Even by American standards it was lavish. Black Romanian caviar served in white porcelain dishes, a pork stew with potato dumplings and stuffed cabbage, and, of course, feta and onions and dark peasant bread. There were no dining sets, only sofas lined up along low mahogany cocktail tables. As she and Oprea sat side by side and ate, Irena looked across the table at a woman whose dress was cut so low that her breasts all but popped out of it every time she reached down for another cracker and caviar. The men sitting on either side of her seemed to take great delight in watching that. Most men would, Irena admitted, but not so openly.

When the band began to play, Oprea stood and took her arm. "I am ready and you promised," he said.

He was passably good on the waltzes, as terrible on the quick-moving folk dances as she was, but at least he had alcohol to blame. "I should retire," Irena said after a while. "I've had a long day."

"I will go with you."

She pulled away from his grasp. "What did you say?"

"It is my experience that a great triumph should be followed by a great fuck. You had a great triumph this evening and I am said to be the greatest fuck in Romania. Perhaps you would like to . . ."

Irena felt the heat rising to her cheeks again, but the double meaning of his words made her laugh. "And to think I took you for a diplomat!" she responded with mock surprise.

"My uncle tells me that's what diplomats are, my Irena. Experts at fucking. In my own case, I am working hard to become the minister of foreign affairs."

"Then perhaps I need to speak to the *current* minister." Irena laughed, surprised that the humor wasn't forced. Though still wary, she found his overt lust refreshing. It took her mind off her real concern of how to leave the salon without saying good night to her hosts.

"I will escort you to your room. Perhaps on the way I can convince you to change your mind. . . ."

Irena started to walk away from him but he grabbed her wrist and continued. ". . . Or not; but if I go out with you it will look like we are sneaking off together and so you need not say good night to anyone, not even your hosts. Then maybe you will be thankful and have breakfast with me. I think you would find the meeting useful."

She turned. "Useful?" she asked, her voice suddenly cold.

"Excuse me . . . my English is sometimes not so good. I meant educational. I can tell you about the cities you will visit."

"All right. When?"

"Eight. Come down to the lobby. Wear a coat. We will go outside. There is a good cafe close by."

Irena glanced around the room and found Monica backed into a corner by an older man. Walking over to them with Oprea following behind, she pulled Monica aside. "I'd like to retire," she whispered. "And Mr. Oprea would like to go with me." She shook her head slowly as she said the last.

Monica understood the message. "Then leave. I'll be a few steps behind you."

Oprea took Irena's hand, kissed the back of it, and walked with her out of the room. As they left, she felt him rub the soft flesh between her ring and middle finger, a hint of what he might do if she let him. But he did not repeat his suggestion, only kissed her on the cheek outside her door and held her close a moment. "We watch you," he whispered to her. "We keep you safe."

Once in her room, Irena glanced at the corners, the heat vent, the television that got nothing but a state-run station. She decided the television offered the best view of the room. When she took off her sweater, she draped it over the front of the controls and speaker.

When Monica asked how her evening had gone, Irena wanted to talk about Andrei but decided that someone might be listening, so commented instead, "The Ceauşescus were kinder than I'd expected. I will have to tell my family how interesting it was to meet them."

"And that young man you acquired is certainly handsome," Monica added, winking to show she understood the meaning of the conversation.

Irena smiled. "Not only that. He told me he was the greatest fuck in Romania."

Monica laughed. "All men say things like that. Only half are lying."

# CHAPTER 25

Monica accompanied Irena downstairs the next morning. After seeing that Oprea had come alone, she followed at a discreet distance as he and Irena walked to a cafe down the street. She entered alone just after them, took a table close to the door, and opened a paperback she'd brought with her. Irena glanced at Monica, noticed her attention was on Oprea, and relaxed.

There were no menus, only a short bill of fare posted on a chipped green chalkboard over the counter. The tile floor was well scrubbed but there were cracks in the heavy traffic areas, cracks in the plaster walls as well. "Do not order sausage," Oprea said as a young man came over to take their order. He asked Oprea for both their orders. Andrei asked for fried eggs, polenta, and jam then motioned to Irena, who requested the same.

Irena had to admit that Andrei looked much better after a night's sleep. His eyes seemed even more beautiful now that the whites were not bloodshot, and there was a bit more color in his cheeks. The quick recovery made her wonder if he'd really been as drunk as he'd seemed the night before. If not, it had been a good act. She said as much as they waited for their order.

"Not good act. Weak constitution. It does not take much to turn me into a fool. Of course I cannot refuse the hand that holds the glass out to me when it belongs to my boss. At least not need-ing too much means I get over the effects quickly. Leaving with you was as good for me as it was for you."

Irena laughed. Monica looked up from the book. Oprea no-ticed her and shrugged. "So you brought your chaperon, I see."

"Escort. Our State Department suggested it."

"If we really wanted you, she would not stop us, any more than a single securitate escort could stop someone in your coun-try. But you are a singer, not a rocket scientist, and what is the point of an international incident over music?" He grinned to soften the remark, showing even white teeth.

"You're right. But it makes everyone feel better."

"Is someone assigned to every person in your group?"

"It is a group and I am supposed to stay with them. But you were kind last night so I thought I would meet you. But I don't want to give you any ideas, not when I'm seeing someone al-ready."

Oprea scowled. "You are too serious. I did not want to 'see' you. Only last night once, to celebrate. I would not want to come between you and your man."

"You couldn't. We are to be married."

She had said this only to discourage him, and so his reply shocked her. "Interesting. I understood his family only married kin."

"What! What did you say?"

Oprea had spoken without thinking and his accent thickened as he rushed to cover his mistake. "Richard Austra. His name was on the original guest list. With same phone number as you. And your director said he was . . . was relative of the composer. The opera and its history makes Laurence Austra our treasure, so of course we know of his history also."

She knew she should remain calm, find out how much they knew, but her temper got the better of her. "This isn't right, this spying!"

He beat his palm flat on the table. "This is not spying! Do you think your State Department would just let *us* roam around *your* country without a checkup?"

"And from what I've seen, you'd deserve one." Irena picked up her bag, stood, and grabbed her coat.

"Wait! I have not talked about the cities yet."

"I'll discover the cities on my own." Irena walked away from him, her legs a bit unsteady.

Monica caught the exchange, laid a bill on the table to cover the coffee she'd ordered, and met Irena at the door. "You just sat down. What could be wrong?" she asked.

"They know I am seeing someone. They know his name. About his family. What kind of a place is this?" Irena's voice had grown loud enough that the few patrons in the restaurant could hear her, though most pretended not to.

"Communist . . . so keep your voice down!" Monica replied in a harsh whisper. "Let's go."

They'd no sooner gotten to their room when the bellboy came up, carrying Irena's breakfast in a paper sack, along with a bunch of flowers. He handed both to her without any explanation, then declined the tip, saying that he'd already been paid.

"Damn it and damn that man! I'll sit in this room until we leave," Irena moaned, flopping back on the hard mattress.

"Which must be at noon today to get us into Iasi by nightfall. Most of the company is across the street viewing the art collection in the Royal Palace. We could meet up with them until eleven, when you need to meet with Korval and the other leads for some state-run interview."

Irena's cue to be nervous again. "Then let's go. But I need to make a phone call first."

"Pick up the phone and dial the operator."

"Long distance."

"It's in your contract. And the outgoing lines are the same everywhere, so remember . . ." Her voice trailed off, a quick reminder Irena did not need.

She called Richard, as she had promised. While she packed the few articles of clothing she'd taken out of her suitcases, she told him how well the performance had gone, the reception after. She laughed about Oprea's unintentional boast, then added, "Did you know they had us all investigated? Even you. He thinks the Austras always marry their cousins or something like that. Isn't that an odd thing for him to say, dearest?"

That "dearest" was their code for a comment she could not make as bluntly as she would like, though she had been blunt enough. "We have done that a few times," Richard admitted. "Maybe it's enough to give us a reputation for it."

"Did the tour make the papers there?"

"Just a short mention of it in the *New York Times*. Gregory will check the Boston papers. Any information on the opera will be in the Sunday art sections. I'll let you know next time you call. Perhaps after the next performance. Still Iasi?"

"No schedule changes. We're going by train this afternoon. We'll have two quick rehearsals tomorrow, then most of Monday free before an early evening performance."

"Any chance to play the tourist?"

"Not so far. But there will be free time in Iasi and Sibiu and two days there before we leave for the final performance in Timisoara. But I may run out of suitcase space before I get a chance to buy anything. I have admirers." She told him about the wine and how the securitate had no idea who had left it.

"What sort?"

She lifted the bottle off the nightstand. "Local. The label isn't even stuck on very well." She'd begun to wrap it in a sweater to keep the bottle from breaking when she noticed that one corner of the label was coming off. "There's a message on the back," she said and sat down on the edge of the bed, peeling the label carefully away from the glass. "It's written in Romanian. I don't read the language well, but sounding it out I think it says 'Archangel Michael protects you.' I wonder what it means?"

"Probably some local superstition. Guardian angel of singers or some such."

"I'll ask one of our translators if I think of it."

After the call ended, Irena finished packing then left her suitcase closed but unlatched with the sleeve of one sweater hanging out. She thought this would be a way to see later if her bag had been searched but when the group returned all the company's luggage had been carried down to the lobby. Monica went up to check the room while Irena went into the salon with Korval and Phillip Lane, who played her partisan lover. She expected a number of questions, but no one asked her anything except to order politely that she smile for photographs. She wondered if it was eastern chauvinism or if her outburst earlier had been noted. If it had, so much the better. At least she would be left alone.

The bus arrived precisely at noon but Monica still hadn't returned. Irena saved her a seat near the front then grew worried as the driver stowed their luggage and shut the cargo doors. She would have asked him to wait but he left the door open, a cold draft swirling around everyone's feet until Monica got on with a man close behind her. It was Oprea.

"He's been assigned to the group," Monica said, taking the empty seat beside Irena before the Romanian could claim it.

"Wonderful," Irena mumbled, watching as Oprea took a seat further back. Irena ignored him as they drove to the station, and during the first half of the long rail journey across Moldavia.

Their private car had been added at the end of the train, well away from the fumes of the engine. The seats were hard, the car drafty but not dangerously so, and there were blankets for those who wanted them. The company had a private bathroom at the front of the car. Irena got up to stretch her legs and use it then stopped outside its door to look through the little window into the car in front of them. It was as crowded as a Chicago train during rush hour, its seats taken by parents with children in dark-colored coats piled atop them like shopping bags.

The bathroom for that car was at its rear, just past the glass Irena peered through. A group of young men had claimed the hallway outside it and were sitting sideways shooting dice and passing a bottle around. A bronze-skinned gypsy woman leading a small child by the hand tried to get past them to use the toilet. They made way grudgingly, one of them running his hand up the inside of the woman's thigh. The woman pretended not to notice but, spying Irena watching her, shrugged; the gesture less defeated than resigned. The bathroom had no door, and Irena was surprised to see the men look away, offering a bit of privacy.

Irena did the same, turning her attention to the view beyond the side window—the fir trees covering the rolling hills, the fields with their blanket of early spring snow. It should have been beautiful, but like Bucharest everything seemed covered with a layer of dirt beneath the sooty twilight sky. She was aware of a reflection, a face growing larger in the glass—Andrei Oprea coming up behind her. "Even the countryside is dirty," she told him.

"This is how America started. And England. Out of the ugliness comes empires. It will be the same for us someday." He spoke those words with pride.

Irena wondered at his naivete. "I pray it will be so, for their sake," she replied, motioning toward the adjoining car.

She pushed past him and took her seat. He did not speak to her for the rest of the six-hour ride.

The train pulled into Iasi in early evening. Once again, a private bus waited to take them to the hotel.

As they assembled on the platform, Oprea took charge of the group. "The drive will take only a few minutes. Would anyone like to walk to the hotel instead?" he asked.

When a handful of the company took him up on the offer, Irena decided to go along. They stopped at the city square, where Andrei gave a brief history of the oldest town in Romania. He dramatized his words well as he described how the city had repelled invasions by Turks and Greeks in the sixth and seventh centuries; protected Queen Marie ("the only member of the royal family worthy of protection") during World War II; and how it remained the intellectual heart of Romania. The religious heart, as well, she decided as he went on to describe the Byzantine churches within walking distance of their hotel. But in spite of the drama and the beauty he promised that they would see during the bus tour on Monday, the city had the same sad pall as Bucharest, as if its soul was dying, and it was a sentient creature and knew this.

Their hotel was on edge of the central square. The Traian, designed by Eiffel some years before he built the tower in Paris, possessed a garish sort of elegance the faded Athenee had lost at least a decade before. Students waited in the lobby to greet the company with open enthusiasm, crowding around Irena and asking her to autograph the review that had appeared in the morning paper. The questions thrown at her were wearing, and she retreated to her room after a few minutes, wishing that Richard were there.

The company's rooms were on the second floor; they were large, and even more garish than the red-carpeted lobby. Their purple-papered walls, red upholstered furniture, and white empire beds and armoires made them seem less part of a hotel than a geriatric Frenchman's idea of an upscale bordello. But at least the rooms were well heated and the bathwater was clear and hot. While Monica went for still another briefing with the local securitate, Irena banished the chill of the train ride with a long soak, made festive with the scented bubble bath she had brought from home.

After, alone, she sat close to the window and, with lights off, watched the city beneath her.

It was a university town, the main campus close enough that the streets that Saturday night had a good share of students—friends in groups, lovers walking arm in arm. She watched them laughing, saw a quick passionate kiss and without warning, she began to cry. She never knew what caused that sudden rush of tears but thought it may have been the moment when she realized that her life was moving in a new direction and Richard would not be a part of it much longer. She may have been mourning the loss of his love—or, given the ideas the room must have brought to mind, his passion. Or the loss of centuries. Or of eternity. Or all of it. But, of course, her tears would make no difference in the end.

Monica arrived as Irena was pulling the box of tissues out of her luggage. "Are you all right?" she asked when she noticed Irena's red eyes.

"Almost that time of month. I get emotional . . . more emotional, that is, since I'm always a bit on edge," she replied.

"And that awful train ride! Did you bring everything you need? Aspirin?"

"Enough for the entire company."

"Korval is buying drinks for everyone at the bar downstairs. He all but ordered me to bring you but if you're not up to it . . ."

Irena had been thinking of opening the bottle she'd been given. But a crowd would be better, take her mind off everything.

"Any officials?" Irena asked.

"Just university students. The translators have spoken with them and given the okay for a little bit of socializing."

"Then I'd like to come," she replied. Most of the company was so much older than she. Here was a chance to socialize with Romanians her own age, to get their feelings on the changes in their life, if they dared to speak of politics at all.

She splashed some cold water on her face and added a bit of powder, then pulled on her black jeans and a black knit shirt, which she covered with an embroidered wool vest she'd purchased from a street vendor outside the Royal Palace.

The hotel bar was so dark she had no idea what color the walls might be. A Beatles album played painfully loud, providing music for the handful of couples on the dance floor. The mirror behind the bar was cloudy from smoke and the room reeked of it and every ashtray was overflowing with butts. Someone handed her a shot of plum brandy so fiery that it made sweat bead on her forehead. A beer chaser followed and she settled near the entrance with Monica, Korval, Phillip Lane, and Brian Essex, who played the role of a Nazi officer to perfection. As she finished her first beer, one of the group milling at a respectable distance from the company offered to buy her a drink if she danced with him.

"You are a student?" she asked slowly in Romanian.

"Yes. And I like opera. My name is Mihai," he replied. "Now we dance?"

She nodded and he pulled her onto the floor, holding both her hands as he began what seemed like a jitterbug step. She tried to follow suit until both of them were laughing. The song shifted to a slow number and he pulled her tight against him, his hands pressing her pelvis against him. "No more," she said, pushing away. "Beer."

"Beer! Yes, come," Mihai yelled and took her to the far end of the bar, well away from the others in the company but close to where the male translator—a dour-faced man whose name Irena never discovered—sat nursing a Coke.

"You like this country?" Mihai asked.

"Very much. I was born here."

"I know. But papers say you left a long time ago."

"I remember it, though. Are you coming to the opera on Monday?"

"I get off work to come. The government gave away many tickets so that students can go. They are generous that way. But then, *Romania-Pace* is our story. For Iasi."

"It is?"

"What did you think the story was about?" he asked, clearly perplexed.

She began to wonder. "That . . . bravery can overcome anything," she finally replied, a difficult concept to explain in the simple words her feigned ignorance forced her to use.

"You have it all wrong. It is how Communism won over Fascism because of comrades willing to be martyrs to their cause."

Irena forced back laughter. She had never heard such obvious propaganda before.

"But you cannot understand these things," Mihai went on. "You are from America, a place bombs have not touched. Not like here. Especially not like Iasi."

"Why Iasi?" she asked.

"Because the Iron Guard began here . . . the Legion of Archangel Saint Michael."

"Of what?" she asked.

"Of Archangel Michael. You are Romanian. You do not know the story of the fascist Codreanu? A lunatic." He made the words of his explanation deliberately simple. "The Iron Guard killed Jews. Intellectuals. Anyone who disagreed with them. Even the Nazis said they went too far. I think that is why there are so many churches still in Iasi. Even atheists feel the need for atonement."

"Why Archangel Michael?" she asked, thinking of the message on the wine label.

"Codreanu said an icon of the Archangel Michael spoke to him, demanding he create the Legion to rid Romania of inferiors." Mihai went on, but Irena was hardly listening. No government official sent that wine, not with that message. But then who?

Mistaking her silence for disbelief, Mihai grew defensive. "You do not believe me? There are books. Written here and in the west. You should read about your country."

"You're right. I should. I will."

The music started to play again, but Irena did not feel like dancing. Eventually Mihai got the hint and moved down the bar to sit beside one of the younger girls from the chorus, a petite redhead who had smiled at him.

Irena waved to Monica and they met at the lobby door. "What do you know about the Legion of Archangel Saint Michael . . . the Iron Guard?" she asked the woman.

"I recall something. They were fascists. Why do you ask?"

"Come with me. I need to show you something upstairs," Irena said. On their way across the lobby, she noticed Oprea talking to the receptionist.

"Hello!" he called to them. "You are leaving? You do not like our party?"

"I was just . . ." She hesitated. If her phone at the Athenee had been bugged, they knew about the wine already. Now she had to tell the truth about it immediately to keep any hint of suspicion from her actions. "I was just going to show Monica something I discovered about the bottle of wine. Come and I will show you as well."

If Oprea knew about any of this, he pretended surprise well. And concern. He sat on the edge of her bed, staring intently at the label he still held close to the bedside lamp as if he could read more into the message than was already clear. "This is not a good thing," he mumbled. "Why did you not speak of it right away?"

"I thought it was just some local superstition. I did not know about the Iron Guard until tonight."

"You would not have been born yet so why would you? And it was a Hungarian thing. A Saxon thing. After years of struggle, there are still fanatics in the northwestern part of the country."

"I come from there," she told him.

He looked up at her. "Still, it makes no sense unless they think of you as one of their own."

"I have some Hungarian relatives. I don't know about their politics."

"Your mother? Her . . . maiden name . . . is?" Oprea asked, his English uncertain.

"Andrassi. But the tie is further back. We stayed with a distant cousin in Budapest after we left Romania. Tripolski, I think the name was."

"All they have to know is that you are Hungarian. Is enough if they wish it to be." He frowned.

She waited for him to request the names of her family, but he never did. "May I have these?" he asked instead, holding out the bottle and label. "I will, of course, get you more."

"Take it. I don't need anything else."

"No, no. I get you something better."

Just as she was ready to go to bed, she heard an argument in the hall, cracked open the door, and saw three girls from the chorus being moved out of their room across the hall. Andrei and their translators were moving in. When he saw her in her nightgown, Andrei grinned and studied what little he could see.

As she started to close the door, he called to her to wait then brought her a bottle of Romanian Murfatlar. "Best in Romania. Take home for your sweetheart. And when you call him, you can tell him that you are in good hands."

The acting in Irena's second performance suffered from her occasional preoccupation with things unrelated to music but her voice was still magnificent. That evening, still flushed from the adulation, she called Richard, who read her a pair of reviews. One, in *Variety,* called her "a promising young American soprano whose sweet song is melting the Eastern Bloc." The other, from the

*Chicago Tribune,* not only gave a long review of the opera and her performance, but added her high school graduation photo, a picture of her in the conservatory chorus taken only months before, and short quotes from Saille and two of Irena's teachers at the conservatory attesting to her talent.

"Would you say the trip has been worth it?" Richard asked after he'd read the reviews to her.

"I think so. I did have one scare, though." She told him about the message on the wine label and how the Romanians were responding, even the comment Andrei said she must pass along to him.

"It's good they take every little thing seriously, so there is no reason to worry."

"How can I be worried, dearest, when the greatest fuck in Romania is camped right across the hall keeping such a careful eye on me?"

"Now how can I not? Call me Thursday, tell me how the performance in Baia Mare went and that everything is all right."

# CHAPTER 26

During their long walking tours of the museums and churches of Iasi, Irena had purchased a pair of English language books on Romanian history. She spent some of the hours of the train ride to Baia Mare reading one. Andrei noticed the book and crouched beside her seat. "Is good you learn about your country," he said. "I cannot believe your parents told you nothing. It . . . it takes away a part of who you are."

His words touched her. She slid sideways so he could sit down. "You must know we left the country illegally," she said.

"We know everything." A smile softened the comment.

"My stepfather was shot and killed by the border guards. I think that is why my mother does not speak of the past."

"He was not your real father?" Andrei asked, surprised.

"So much for your knowing everything."

"You are right. What was your real father's name?"

"I don't know. He left her before I was born. My mother never spoke his name. I took my stepfather's name after they married."

"An odd woman."

Irena stared out the window at the rolling hills, the jagged mountains beyond them. Wild country. Beautiful. Filled with secrets.

"I am sorry," Andrei added.

"Don't be. I am thinking that you are right and wondering why I never realized that about her before."

He started to leave, and she touched his arm. "Stay, please. I want to ask you about something else I learned from my reading. Why do we perform in Baia Mare instead of Cluj-Napoca? Cluj is a bigger city, and closer to the area where Laurie . . . Laurence Austra acquired much of the folk melodies he used. It would seem natural to perform there."

Andrei glanced over his shoulder, noticed the translators sitting near the back, well out of earshot. Even so, he moved his face closer to hers. "I will tell you truth," he said softly. "The city is Hungarian. The Ceauşescus do not like the Hungarians. They say they cause trouble and this opera is one the Hungarians consider theirs . . . you understand the trouble this could cause?"

"And you said no one would make a fuss over opera."

"Over singer. But opera is more. It has consequences. Like Wagner."

"Where are you from?"

"Timisoara. I will see my kin when we go there."

"Where did you learn English?"

"In America. At Columbia."

"Recently?"

"I am not so young. It was the early sixties. My uncle was high in the party and my family close tied and so I was allowed to go. But I did not get a degree. My father said two years of . . . decadence? . . . was enough and ordered me home. I finished school in Timisoara."

"You might have stayed in America."

"And to stay, I had to do what? Ask for asylum? Then I could never come home. I love my home."

His words made her long to see her family here, but she did not dare to give him names. "So now you know why I can tell you so little of my family," she said.

"We'll do our best to find them for you. Good for east-west relations and our Natalya." He grinned again, an expression that said he hoped she might yet agree to that belated celebration.

Two nights later, as Irena sat in the greenroom waiting to go on, Andrei brought two visitors to see her. The man and his wife looked ancient, with their black coats, sun-leathered skin, and deep-set Slavic eyes. The woman played nervously with the tip of her dark print scarf but the man hugged Irena tightly, holding her at arm's length so he could see her face. "Yes, you look like your grandmother, your mother's mother," he said, speaking slowly in Romanian. "She was my cousin so I am your old cousin, Radu Tripolski. A Hungarian name but we are two generations in Romania. This is my second wife, Olga. We are pleased to meet you after so many years."

"Does no one eat in America?" the old woman asked in a loud voice.

"Eat?" For a moment Irena was confused then laughed. "No. No, not thin. This is makeup. For my part. You will understand when you see the opera."

"I heard the music once before. In Bucharest. I was invited by my party to the great reception for Ceauşescu," Radu explained, looking sideways toward Andrei as he said this.

"Then you will know if I am as good as that Natalya," Irena replied, this in English, which Andrei translated for her.

"We hear you are better," Olga told her, pinching her arm as if still convinced it would only be skin and bone beneath the rags.

"Is more of my family here?"

"Only us, because the government found us and made arrangements for us to come. Maybe you will see closer family in Sibiu. More of them live there."

Irena understood most of the words but moved closer to Andrei and waited for him to finish the translation before she told him, "Thank you for bringing them." She looked at her old cousin. "I did not know who I should tell the government to look for. My mother does not talk of the past."

"That was because of your father. Always at war with someone. No one liked him," the old man told her.

"I don't even know his name," she said in slow Romanian.

"Mihai . . . Mihai Celac."

The shock of that name must have shown on her face and she was thankful Andrei was standing beside her and could not see her expression. But Olga did. "You know that name," she said.

"I know a Celac. Is it a common name?" Irena asked, hoping to learn that it was like Smith or Jones in America.

"A big family, most live near Cluj and Turda but the name itself is not so common."

"Do you know a Viktor Celac?"

"The old man. I hear he died many years ago."

"Not an old man. He would be forty or so now. He went to America when he was young."

"The old man's grandson was named Viktor," Olga told her husband.

"Would I have been closely related to any of them?"

This was more than Radu could calculate. He shook his head, shrugged. "Cousins, maybe," Olga said for him. And Irena's mother never spoke of it. Irena wondered if her comments about Petro and their connection had made her mother so secretive about Viktor. But even that motive made little sense if their tie was distant.

Radu continued on, listing more family names for Andrei. Irena ceased to care. Here was another mystery about her mother. When she returned home, they would have much to discuss. She was collecting her thoughts, trying to decide how to ask the old couple about the history of her kin, when Korval came to remind her that she had only a few more minutes before she would be needed onstage.

No time to consider anything, then, except the music. She hoped to see the old couple again at the evening reception but they left with the rest of the audience.

The following morning, as always, Irena called Richard in Chicago. The press had apparently stopped their coverage of the tour after Bucharest, but her agent had phoned and said two larger companies were interested in auditioning her as well as the Skylight Opera Company in Milwaukee. And the *Chicago Tribune* wanted to do a story on her as soon as she returned.

"So you will be famous soon," Richard concluded.

"The trip has been about more than fame. I've been meeting family." She told him about Radu and Olga. "And they told me something I had never known, dearest. My father's name was Celac. Isn't that a coincidence?"

"Truly. So you would have married a cousin."

"Radu said distant but he did not know how distant. Maybe I will learn more soon. Radu is party. He gave names to Andrei— people he says are related to me. Perhaps he lied and they will all be friends of his, though, and how would anyone know the difference?" She laughed. "Thanks to my mother, certainly not me."

"That reminds me. My mother called. She asked how you were."

"Tell her I'm fine. Just a bit starry-eyed. I think of her often and am looking forward to seeing her soon."

Mentioning his mother meant that Richard was concerned. Had Irena replied instead, "Send her my love," it would have told Richard that she was frightened and believed she needed help.

A simple code, and hard to break when it would only be used for a handful of phone calls.

About the time the Irena began the train ride to Sibiu, Georgie and I flew into Midway Airport. Georgie is terrified of flying. It had taken much convincing, two stiff drinks, and a subtle mental push to get him on an airplane, but he managed the trip better than I'd expected. And he had a good reason for going. Someone with the Chicago Symphony had heard him play at a Julliard recital and spoken so highly of his skill that now he had a meeting with Georg Solti himself. Fear of flying would never have kept him from that audition, even if he had not had me to help him board.

I dropped Georgie off at Symphony Hall and went on to see Richard. My timing could not have been more dismally perfect. For the next two hours, I heard my brother dissect every nuance of that last conversation with Irena in excruciating detail.

"If you're so concerned, call Hunter," I told him.

"She's only in the country for three more days; what could he do in that amount of time anyway?"

"He could send some of our Romanian staff to the performance. As some of the country's only western investors, they could pull some strings, get backstage and keep an eye on her. It's something." I held out the phone to him, all but demanding he make that call.

Fortunately for my sanity, Hunter was around to talk to my brother. Richard explained about the message she'd received, the securitate reaction.

"If the Romanians know about it, there's not much we could do to make her any more secure. She'll be fine," Hunter told him.

"But she doesn't feel fine. Is there any way of having some of the staff get over for the performance?"

"They're already planning to go. Some will see her in Sibiu, a few more in Timisoara. They'll be at the receptions after each performance. It should be enough to put her at ease."

Probably not enough for her, since she was in the thick of the problem, but it did calm my brother down. After Georgie returned, flushed from an impressive audition that might mark the beginning of his professional career, Richard asked the night clerk to pick up any incoming calls at the front desk so the three of us could go out.

We went to the theater, then to a gay bar off Lincoln that made Georgie so uncomfortable we had to leave. We ended at a coffeehouse. There were groups of single women all around us, many of whom noticed us and began to flirt. Though I knew my brother was famished and almost painfully in need of a good night of passion, he paid no attention to any of them, until eventually I noticed him glancing often at a woman at a nearby table. She was dressed all in black and wore a peace button on the lapel of her jacket and her russet hair tied back in a style that did nothing to flatter her round face. He was drawn to the girl because she looked like *her,* of course—but the reason be damned.

I caught her eye, rested my hand briefly on top of Georgie's to make my position clear, and motioned for her to come and join us.

Then there were four of us and a heated few hours of seditious conversation ending with Georgie and me in Denys's bed and my brother and Margaret, that intense young poli sci major, in his room. It was hardly a family moment, though it was likely as close to one as Georgie would ever get or I would dare to have with a stranger. I drew in my brother's passion and hers, shared it with Georgie, and sent ours back. Walls are no obstacle with the familial bond so tight. I pulled away from Georgie and lay on my back beside him, both of us listening to the sounds coming from my brother's room, a song nowhere near as pretty as Irena's likely would have been, but filled with passion nonetheless.

Poor girl had the night of her life but never had a clue as to why, and later only a vague memory of a major indiscretion she would never mention to the fearless leader of the campus SDS she'd been dating. She blamed the gaps in her memory, as well as her actions, on the wine and pot we'd shared before retiring.

As for my brother, he was trying not to smile as he left to see the girl home well after midnight. But by late the next morning, when he got up and saw us packing our bags, the euphoria had fled.

"I hope you don't mind, but I'd just as soon not go and see the two of you off. It's a long trip out and back and Irena will be calling. I don't want to miss her."

We had an awkward silence as we waited for the taxi to arrive. When the front desk rang us up, Richard hugged Georgie and me and waved as the elevator closed. Even so, it was clear that he was relieved to see us go. I glanced at Georgie, raised my eyebrows, and shrugged.

"Feeling guilty, is he?" Georgie asked.

"Pathetically."

"With so much guilt, it's a wonder you didn't try to seduce him."

"We outgrew that years ago," I replied—too quickly; I saw the shocked expression on his face. He'd been joking and I'd answered honestly. "Siblings fool around," I said, more than a little defensively. But I could feel the bond I'd forged with him breaking, and wondered about the future of his soul after I left him.

# CHAPTER 27

Though a bit flustered, Irena finished the opening aria on the stage in Sibiu and, as always, the applause stunned her. There seemed to be even more of it than usual and, following the advice she had been given at the evening in Bucharest, she stopped at the side of the stage as the lights went down to acknowledge their praise. As she did, she saw a young woman step through the crowd and wave. Even with the light half blinding her, Irena recognized Marie.

Seeing the one face she had hoped to see, Irena bent down to take the rose Marie held out to her, palming the note the woman passed along with the flower.

Her dressing room had a vase to keep the flowers fresh. Irena put the rose in the water then sank into a corner seat and grabbed a tissue to dab at her eyes. She held it in front of the note as she read: *If you can get away, meet me at eight tomorrow morning on the corner to the south of the hotel. We'll go someplace private and catch up on old times. So many changes for both of us! I am so proud of you! Marie.*

Irena had no idea if the news of the tour had alerted her friend or if Marie had gotten Irena's last letter, mailed just before she'd left for New England. No matter. They would meet, alone if she could manage it, but she also wanted her friend to be with her to celebrate that night.

With little time left, she sat in a chair while Katie, the company's makeup artist, applied a bit more color to her cheeks and lips, combed out her tangled hair, and unzipped the back of her tattered dress. Irena stepped out of it and slipped on a print skirt and a peasant shirt with an embroidered vest attached, turning so Katie could zip it up. Then, with a lavender scarf covering her hair, she was off to woo her partisan lover and meet the Nazi who would destroy them both and himself.

She found Andrei waiting outside the door, decided it was fate. "Did you see the woman who gave me the rose?" she asked him.

"The pretty one? How could I not?"

Irena laughed. "She was my closest friend when I was young. We have tried to keep in touch since we were separated. If she could come to the reception, I would be thankful. So would she, I think."

He understood. "I will try. Then perhaps you will tell her good things about me."

"You need someone else to do that?"

He had a beautiful laugh. "Sometimes it helps a little."

As she walked toward the stage entrance, she saw Andrei heading toward the theater door. Mindful of everything Korval and the State Department had advised her, she would not meet Marie without Andrei coming along. But if he met Marie tonight and saw them together, he would be more likely to give them the privacy she wanted.

Through the rest of the performance, Irena tried to see if Andrei was right about the applause. It was different but only because the audience applauded everyone's solos with enthusiasm as if it would be impolite to give any one singer special praise.

When it ended, Andrei was waiting for her in the wings. "I found her. She will come, she said. Now you should hurry. Get there before the room gets too crowded, so you can talk."

Usually the reception was held in a room at their hotel, but tonight the hotel restaurant had closed early to accommodate the private party. Like the rooms upstairs, the restaurant was spotless: the mirrors and brass on the bar well polished, the carpets worn but clean, the tables covered with linen. When Irena arrived, there were only a few people in the room, most of them local extras and stagehands who had not taken the time to change. A band was setting up in the corner, not rock, Irena noted with relief. Until they were ready to begin, a record player with passable speakers played a piece by Strauss; a waltz, which seemed fitting in a city that looked like a postcard from Bavaria.

She scanned the room, saw Marie in the back sitting at the bar beside Andrei, and went to join them. When she saw Irena, Marie met her halfway, gripping her shoulders, kissing her on the cheek. "I am nervous. He is party. I do not want to be near him," she whispered.

"I couldn't wait. And I need him to translate unless we speak English," Irena said quickly in Romanian.

English, of course, was not an option and not just because Marie's skill had never been good when she lived in Chicago. Revealing that she knew the language might make the authorities curious as to where she had learned it.

Marie understood, enough that when Irena introduced them formally, she was speaking to her friend through Andrei. They took a quiet table close to the bar. While the room grew crowded and the orchestra began to play the first soft live classical music Irena had heard in Romania outside of the opera halls, Marie told of the changes in her life, her move to Sibiu.

"And you have kept contact all these years?" Andrei asked.

"I would send her postcards when I was young," Irena said. "She would send me letters that my mother would help me translate. Then Marie moved and I had no address for a long time. I'm glad she got in touch with me before the tour left."

"I came to Sibiu looking for a good life," Marie told him.

Andrei smiled at her. "And did you find it?"

"Nothing is ever really good. But this is better." She looked at Irena as she said this.

"Then I am glad you moved . . . here," Irena said.

"And I am so proud of you!" Marie replied. The women looked at each other a moment, then hugged. Andrei retreated to the bar to get them each another drink.

"Tomorrow we can talk more. I've met someone. I want to tell you all about him," Marie whispered.

"I'll try but I will have to bring *him* with me. And someone from the State Department."

"You can't just get away?"

"I can't."

"Then I suppose I should butter him up so he leaves us alone if we ask him to."

Andrei rejoined them, balancing a beer for himself and two glasses of wine. "I have been telling her all sorts of things about you," Irena said to him.

"Good things?"

"As good as my pathetic Romanian will allow."

Marie smiled at Andrei as she took a glass.

"Then perhaps she will dance with me?" he asked Marie.

Marie sipped the wine then set her glass down, and the pair moved onto the dance floor. Throughout their long conversation, Irena had been aware of Monica watching her from the far end of the room. Once she was alone, the woman came over and joined her. "An old friend?" she asked.

Irena nodded. "I've known her forever."

"They make a nice couple."

Irena had to admit that they did, which surprised her. But she supposed that Marie was right. If she played up to Andrei, he might relax a few of the rules tomorrow.

And Marie played the flirt to perfection, laughing as they tried the more complicated ballroom dances, letting him hold her close on the waltzes. They danced close, whispering until the band took a break.

Soon after, Marie decided she had to go. Andrei left the restaurant with her. Curious, Irena waited a couple of minutes then followed them into the lobby and found Andrei standing alone.

"I bought her a taxi fare so she gets home safe. Perhaps she will give me her number tomorrow and I can call her. Are you going upstairs?"

"In a bit. I'm going inside to wait for Monica."

"How much do you know of Marie's life here?" The question was asked quickly as if to catch her off guard.

"Only a little," she replied carefully.

"I think she puts up a false front. She has much pride. I will buy you both breakfast tomorrow."

"And I'll pay you back later."

"No. Not necessary. I am reimbursed for any entertaining. I might as well spend the state's money on a pair of pretty women."

She kissed his cheek. "Thank you," she told him and went back inside, aware as she left that he watched her go.

The previous night's weather had been balmy, damp with melting snow. Looking out the polished windows of her room, Irena saw that snow was falling, heavy even by Chicago standards. The flakes were small, beating against the window. She put her palm to the glass, felt the cold.

It was cold in the room, too. She pulled a pair of tights and loose jeans from her suitcase and a knit shirt to go under her sweater. Monica had not stirred. Deciding to let her sleep until the last minute, Irena went into the bathroom to dress.

At 7:45, the portable alarm went off. Monica moaned and sat up, hit the off button, then immediately flopped back on the bed. "I feel hung over on two glasses of wine. How the hell do they make that stuff?"

"Andrei will be going with us. Since that first night, he's been almost polite. We'll be okay if you want to sleep a little longer."

"Are you eating here?"

"I don't think so."

Monica sat up, lowered her feet over the side of the bed, and groaned. "Then I've got to go with you. That's my job, the same sort as Andrei's."

While Monica was in the bathroom, Irena went through her funds. She had only one more city on the tour and a hefty paycheck waiting for her when she got home. Andrei could likely arrange a currency exchange for her if she ran out before they left. With that in mind, she pocketed nearly all her remaining Romanian lei, intending to give it to Marie for a wedding gift, if a wedding was in her plans, or for her family here or for whatever other excuse Irena might be able to invent to allow Marie to take it with her pride intact.

Perhaps she should simply say it was a gift from the old ones. And how would that go over?

Smiling at the thought, she put on her boots and the bright coat and hat Richard had bought her in Montreal. A gust of wind shook the window. Irena added a wool scarf.

The phone rang. Andrei telling her that he and Marie were waiting downstairs.

"Are you almost ready?" Irenà called to Monica through the closed bathroom door.

The toilet flushed. Not the first time. Monica opened the door. Her face looked pale, her eyes watery. "The best damn meal I've had on this whole trip and I swear it poisoned me," she moaned. "Willie will have to go in my place." She phoned him then suggested that Irena call downstairs and tell them she'd be late.

Irena did. Marie took the phone from the desk clerk, listening while Irena explained the delay.

"I don't have much time. I go to work at eleven," Marie told her.

"Could we just eat here?" Irena asked.

"There are better places close by. Come down and we can talk while we wait. Andrei is very nice." Her voice grew louder as she said the last, no doubt wanting him to hear.

Irena checked on Monica, then took the elevator to the lobby. Marie was waiting in the same print dress and coat she had worn the night before. Her best clothes or had she not gone home last night? Irena wondered.

But Andrei did not look like someone who had made a new conquest. Instead, he checked his watch. "I have a meeting of my own at eleven," he said when he noticed Irena watching him.

"Can we go outside?" Marie asked him. "Just outside the door where you can see us."

"It looks so cold!" Irena said.

"Not cold. Beautiful." She took Irena's arm, led her toward the lobby door. "I want to get away from him," she whispered. "My man is waiting outside. I want you to meet him."

"He could come in."

"Not if Andrei is nearby. He is nervous about party. Even more nervous than I am."

Irena held her breath as they stepped into the swirling snow. The world seemed to end in the middle of the street. Things closer seemed muted and colorless, like an overexposed black-and-white photograph. As they stepped to the right of the lobby doors, Irena looked over her shoulder, expecting to see Andrei following. But the doors remained shut.

"Where is your friend?" Irena said, loud enough to be heard over the wind.

"There!" Marie pointed to a large dark automobile parked at

the corner. "Come and meet him before Andrei wises up!" she said and ran toward the car.

Irena looked over her shoulder at the doors, wishing that Andrei or someone would come out. No one did. She looked forward at Marie, standing by the driver's half-open door, her arms around a man's neck. "This is Irena," she said, pointing toward her. "She is being careful."

The man stood, waved at her. Irena, squinting as the snow blew in her face, could only see that he was young and dark-haired. Marie walked around the car, got in, and rolled down the window. "There!" Marie said. "Now do you feel safe?"

Smiling, uncertain, Irena walked forward, intending to move close enough to see him clearly and say a quick hello. But once she was a few feet from the car, its rear door opened. A man reached out and tried to grab her wrist. Her skin was wet and slippery and she jerked away from him. Backing away, she turned to run and saw Andrei coming up behind her.

"Thank God!" she called to him. "They are trying . . ."

She never finished. He slipped in the snow and fell into her, the force of his impact pushing her back toward the car. Someone grabbed her from behind, yanking her into the backseat. There was a quick, barked order from the man who had her, a gun pointed at Andrei. The man got into the car beside her and shut the door.

"How dare you!" Irena yelled, feet kicking at nothing but the back of the passenger's seat.

"I am so sorry, Irena," Marie said. Something pricked Irena's arm and the gray day faded to black.

# C H A P T E R  2 8

Irena regained consciousness briefly when the truck carrying her out of Sibiu hit a bump in the road. The drugs kept her groggy, enough that she did not yet understand that she'd been kidnapped or that she was bound hand and foot. The blanket she'd been wrapped in barely kept out the cold draft blowing through the covered truck bed. Her shivers drained what energy she possessed and she slept again through the rest of the drive.

She woke when someone pulled her from the truck. Through half-open eyes she saw mountains rising around her, green shadows against the brilliance of a cloudless sky. She tried to call out, realized she was gagged, but loosely as if someone had taken care to be sure she did not choke. She might have made some soft sounds but decided not to try. Instead, she inhaled as deeply as she could; air fresh and dry and smelling of spruce and pine. The scent calmed her and made her think of her village, her old home.

The path the men used sloped downward at a steep angle to a house half buried. The snow-covered roof, the dark brown outer walls, and the trees close around it would make it difficult to notice. She turned her head, trying to see if there was a road nearby but the rutted path wound down too steeply. The man holding her feet kicked open a door. They carried her through a small room and into a smaller one and dropped her on a bed in a corner, her face to the inside wall. They left her for a few minutes then returned and dumped someone else in with her, shut and locked the door. The room went black. Irena stifled a cry.

She tried to get loose, managed only to push the gag onto her chin, then slide it down to her neck. Nearby, she heard her fellow prisoner moving on a second cot. She recalled enough of how she'd been taken to whisper, "Andrei?"

"Ah-ah."

"Can you get the gag off?"

"Ah." More struggles. "Better," he replied.

"Where are we?"

"I don't know. High in the mountains. Maybe—" He stopped speaking when they heard voices outside.

She listened, terrified at first. But when no one came for them, she relaxed and tried to understand what they were saying. "Isn't some of that Hungarian?" she asked Andrei.

"Yes. I think we have found your admirers, my Natalya," he replied. "I am sorry. I did not take such good care of you."

"It was my fault."

"But I still did not do my job."

"Did Marie have sex with you?"

"Yes. But that is good. We were taped so my people will at least know what she looks like."

"Taped?"

"We tape everyone."

"It doesn't bother you?"

"It used to. But it has worked in my favor. Elena Ceaușescu is said to be particularly fond of watching me perform."

"So if you and I had—had—"

"Yes. And we would have kept the tape. Someday, if you become famous and have any political influence at all, having it might be useful. I was supposed to make a pass but I liked you, so I was deliberately not—how you say?—persuasive."

She considered that, decided she ought to be thankful. "Do you think they are going to kill us?"

"Not you or you would be dead already. But they may have taken me to make it look like a defection. Now they have no further use for me, so perhaps I become history. What I do not understand is their interest in you."

Irena could guess, which made her shiver all the harder. "Slide over here if you can. We can untie each other," she suggested.

He did. With difficulty, she managed to get his hands untied. He was doing the same for hers when the door burst open and two men came to take him. Andrei fought, but without being able to stand there was little he could do. One of their captors kicked him hard in the side and they dragged him away.

By then, Irena's bonds were loose enough that she managed to untie herself. She went to the door, found it unlocked, and slowly pushed it open.

The room was about a dozen feet square, with peeling paint on the walls, a dirty wood floor, and an open beam ceiling. She saw a small window in the door and another window beside it, both covered with boards so only a small bit of light leaked in from outside. She glimpsed a door on the same wall as the one leading to her cell but it was closed and locked. The outer room had bare wood for walls and floor and held only a cast-iron stove in one corner, a huge wooden cupboard, and an old wooden table and four chairs. The table was empty except for a pair of votive candles, their tiny flames barely penetrating the darkness.

Andrei had been placed in one of the chairs but he was far from subdued. The two men who had brought them here stood behind him, holding him down. A third man, about Richard's size, stood in front of him, pacing as he spoke to Andrei, who responded with threats of his own.

"Enough!" the man bellowed. "Take him outside before you kill him. We don't need the smell of death in so small a space."

"Wait! Please!" Irena called.

The man who had given the order turned to her. She saw deep-set eyes, the rest of his face in shadows. "Yes?" he asked, not sounding surprised to see her.

She thought quickly and, all pretext of not knowing the language gone, made her best argument, "He told me he is a favorite of Elena Ceaușescu's. If you kill him, you will only make the government all the more determined to find you."

"What would you have us do?"

"Send him back, with a warning."

"To tell them where we are."

"He doesn't know that any more than I do. How could we know when we were locked in the dark and unconscious most of the way?"

The man moved closer to her, close enough that she could smell the sweat on his clothes though in the dim light she could not see his face clearly. He rested his hands on her shoulders. "If I give his life to you as a gift, what will you give in return?" he asked.

She shut her eyes, took another deep breath. "Me," she whispered.

"You know what I want?" he asked.

"Ransom," she said quickly, hoping. "But I am not rich. Not even famous."

He brushed a finger down the side of her neck. "What I want is more valuable than money. You know that," he replied, his voice deliberately seductive, his touch so much like her memory of Viktor's that she was not certain if he meant sex or blood, or something more. She refused to answer him.

"But this is no bargain. I have you already," he said.

Tears rolled down her cheeks. She hated the weakness they revealed, hated how he used his thumbs to wipe them away, then tasted the salt of them. "Very well. If you value him so much that you would cry for him, I give his life to you as a gift. No strings, as the Americans say." He turned his back on her and faced the others. "Take him back. Dump him a few miles outside of Sibiu. Make sure his superiors know he put up a good fight."

"I don't want him hurt," Irena protested, her voice rising. She fought back her temper; there was no place for it here. If it didn't enrage her captors, they would likely find it amusing.

But it was Andrei who laughed. "He's doing me a favor, Irena. If they don't leave me bloody, my superiors will think we are in collusion. The result would be worse for me than any fleeting pain these bastards could inflict."

The men pulled him to his feet and wrapped a rag over his eyes. "Wait, please," Irena said and moved close enough to Andrei to kiss him on the cheek. "Call my fiancé. Tell him that I'm all right," she said in English.

"If I can . . . no, I promise," he replied.

She watched them drag Andrei away. They left the outside door open. The man who'd been asking the questions shut and locked it, took a seat at the table, and motioned for her to sit across from him. She stayed where she was, studying him in the dim candlelight. Thirty, perhaps a bit older. He had a jagged scar running from his temple down one cheek, its end barely hidden by a few days' growth of beard. His dark hair was shoulder length and slightly curled and his arms revealed the muscles of someone used to heavy labor. When he looked at her, she saw his eyes were the same light gray as Celac's had been, the hunger in them like that of some pale wolf.

"Come. Sit. There are things we must discuss," he said.

She shook her head, pulled in another deep breath and tried to sound forceful. "Before we discuss anything, I need a bathroom unless you want me to ruin the only clothes I have. I also need something to eat."

He actually laughed, as if her needs were as insignificant as those of a puppy. "You do, do you? Very well, we have the short discussion then. It is good you were concerned about your fiancé at home. But let me make it clear. I am Michael Codreanu Celac and you, Irena Sava, are my bride."

For a moment, she was speechless, and remained so while he handed her a candle and pushed her back into that little room. "There is a bucket in the corner by the bed that you can use," he told her and closed and locked the door.

She waited until she was sure he would not come back before unbuckling her belt. Later, she sat on the side of the cot. Alone, with only the candlelight for comfort, she gave in to the despair she felt. Her body shook and she began to cry. As the tears fell, she thought of the character she had played, of all the horrors that had inspired that opera. And she vowed then that for as long as it took, she would continue to play the Natalya role. With enough practice, she might even become truly brave.

She lay on the cot, almost composed, until she heard the lock click. She could not stop the pounding of her heart then, nor how she jumped when the door opened.

He'd changed his shirt, smoothed back his hair, washed and shaved. The effect made him seem almost civilized. She saw past him through the doorway that food had been laid out on the table. He'd started a fire in the stove and there was a large pot of water heating on top of it.

"Come. Sit. See, I listen to you. It is not much, but we are in the mountains and it is all we have."

She followed him to the table and sat. There was a small plate of sausage and cheese and a box of some sort of crackers, a bottle, and two small glasses like the ones with grape jelly in them that her mother bought in Chicago. She took a piece of the sausage and put it on the bread. The meat seemed too salty, the crackers so stale that one crumbled when she tried to pick it up. She put it down, tried a piece of cheese instead. It had a well-aged sharpness that stuck in her throat. She coughed and he poured her something from the bottle. Brandy, harsh as the drink she'd had at the tavern in Iasi, but she swallowed it, thankful for the warmth and the relaxation she hoped it would bring.

"Eat more," Celac ordered.

"I am not as hungry as I thought," she replied.

"No, you just prefer better."

"This is not food I am used to."

"Acquire an appetite, you are going to need it," he said as he picked up the knife. He held it for a moment, until her expression said she understood what he meant, then sliced her off another piece of cheese, handing it across the table on the tip of the blade. In the candlelight, she noticed that he was missing the tip of his little finger and that there were burns on the back of his hand, his fingertips, and his forearm. The burns did not look accidental. From their shapes, she guessed they had been put there deliberately.

Her hands trembled as she reached for the food. She thought he'd find that amusing, but instead he looked concerned. He poured her another glass of the alcohol. "Drink it," he ordered.

"I don't want to be drunk," she replied, surprised to find her temper rising. "Whatever you do, I'll have my eyes wide open."

"Then just one more, please." He spoke the words a bit more gently and, reluctantly, she held out her glass. For the first time since she'd gotten here, he did something more than scowl at her. His brief smile softened his features, but there was something predatory about it, an expression she knew well.

"How are you related to Viktor?" she asked.

"That troublemaker? He was my cousin."

"Have you heard from him?"

That scowl returned. "Don't pretend. You know he is dead. He was wanted here and not just for his politics. He thought he could go to America and escape his fate. But an old one found him anyway and killed him."

As she finished the brandy, he picked up the knife and the bottle, got up, and moved behind her. "Another," he said, one hand on her shoulder as he filled her glass again.

She set it on the table, pushed it away. His hand tightened then released before the grip caused real pain. He ran his finger across the nape of her neck until he felt that little scar. "Is this the spot where an old one fed on you?" he asked.

No use lying. She nodded. He pulled the knit shirt off her shoulder, saw the bruise there. "And this is where your lover fed?"

"Go to hell!" she told him, and tried to spin around, to fight, but his right arm circled her shoulders so tightly that she could barely breathe. He pushed her head down and sideways. She felt his breath against her flesh, then a quick stab of pain below it, the heat of her own blood dripping down her chest.

"It would have been better if you were drunk," he said and pressed his lips to the wound.

This was rape, as certainly as if he had ripped off her clothes and penetrated her, and though she tried to struggle, she could barely move let alone resist. He drank until her vision grew cloudy, her face damp with the onset of shock. But her heart still beat, pounding with the fear that, bride or no, he might not stop.

"Please. You are killing me," she gasped when his grip on her chest momentarily slackened.

"You are only feeling the drugs from before. I am not killing you. I am a doctor. I know how much I can take."

When he finished, he forced more brandy into her then picked her up and laid her on the narrow cot. He stretched out beside her, covered them both with the blanket. With his head resting against her back, one hand on her chest above her heart, they slept.

# CHAPTER 29

## RICHARD

When Irena didn't call at her usual time, nor any other time the day after the performance, I phoned Hunter. The calm I can project to others had become impossible to achieve in myself but at least I managed to keep my voice even as we spoke. "Something has to be wrong," I said.

"Phone the opera company in New Haven. I'll see what I can find out on this end and get back to you in a few hours."

I was the one who discovered that an understudy with a bad case of stage fright had sung the Natalya role in Timisoara. Hunter supplied the reason. "The State Department is keeping this quiet but they believe that Irena has defected," he told me.

"She wouldn't do that!"

"She took all her Romanian currency with her. And her passport. She was seen getting into a car with a representative of the Communist Party."

"I told her to take her passport with her everywhere. A precaution."

"And her mother told authorities that she was always homesick and had once commented that with the money she made on this tour, she could live like royalty in the town where she'd been born."

"That's a lie!"

"So why did she say it?"

"I'll talk to the woman," I said.

I had occasionally spoken with Marina Sava on the phone, but Irena had been adamant that we never meet. Although Irena hadn't realized what I was until I told her, she was convinced her mother would know and never even gave the woman my real name in case she might have heard rumors about it. "And besides, it would be awkward no matter what. She doesn't approve of my spending the night with anyone who does not speak fluent Romanian," she'd explained.

I'd laughed and made her teach me enough to converse in it when I called their house, but Irena never suggested a meeting.

After I got off the phone with Hunter my first thought was to call Marina Sava and ask if I could visit. But that would only give her a chance to refuse. I knew her work schedule, though, and I was waiting on her front porch when she arrived home Monday evening. The neighborhood was good, but far from perfect and a stranger on a porch in the drizzly twilight did cause a brief surge of fear.

"I'm Richard Austin. I've come about Irena," I called before I started toward her.

She looked; resigned, as if she'd been expecting me. "Come in," she said.

I studied her while she took off her hat and coat. Her hair was the same soft shade as Irena's, worn shorter and streaked with gray at the temples. Her face had the same soft curves, the full lips. Only her eyes were different—smaller, deeper set. As she looked at me, I sensed suspicion tinged with anger, not unusual since I was the man who had been living with her daughter. But what was odd was the hint of triumph I sensed in her, as if Irena's disappearance had been not only expected, but welcomed.

She took me into a living room painted a soft shade of cream with tiny flowers stenciled along the edge of the wall just below the ceiling. The carpeting was new, the deep green fabric of the provincial sofa and chairs worn in spots. Crocheted doilies covered the arms and back, giving the decor an Old Country feel. Plump pillows with handmade lace on the edges rested at the cor-

ners of it and on the two chairs. Old photos covered one wall;
Irena's sepia-toned ancestors.

Marina Sava did not ask me to sit down so I waited a bit then
sat anyway, fingering the lace edge of one cushion while she remained standing near the outside door. "I've been questioned
about her disappearance," I began, "and was told you believed
she would defect. But I know she was terrified of being forced to
stay. I'm sure she said the same to you."

Her feeling of triumph increased, flowing through her reply.
"She met someone. Was struck by love or however you want to
put it. It isn't the first time she's done something so foolish, is it?"

I might have argued about Irena's brilliant future, or pointed
out how long I'd had to work to get her to even have coffee with
me. But I didn't have to. My mind was already brushing the
woman's and I knew she was lying.

I sat silently for a moment, apparently considering what she'd
said while making certain that we were alone in the house.

We were. "Please sit down," I ordered.

Like Irena, she had an explosive temper and I had just ignited it. "What! What did you say! I did not invite you in for a
conversation. I did it only to hear you say you were sorry for
pushing her off to that place. Since you haven't you should go
now before—"

A lie. A vicious one. She wanted to hurt me. —Sit down and
shut up!— I ordered and gave her a mental push so strong it must
have felt like a slap. I was furious and this was the only pain I
trusted myself to give.

Her eyes widened. She sat, held by my mind. I took her hand,
felt her pulse pounding, quickened by fear. "I was never certain
until now," she said. "But you cannot have her, Old One. We
brought her here to protect her. Now she has returned to her own
and you will never find her."

I began to sense what she had done, probably with a single letter. Irena had been meant for Viktor. When he disappeared, there
was Petro. Not as pure in the bloodline but better than an out-
sider. With Petro gone, there was only the family at home. Now
Irena had conveniently returned to them.

"If there had been no tour, would you have suggested a Romanian visit and taken her there yourself?"

Marina Sava pressed her lips tightly together and refused to
even think the answer. I pushed, not lightly, and saw her wince.

"Someone would have come here for her. Now that is not necessary. You saw to it," she said.

"Do you know what the ones here did to their own?" I asked.

She knew a good part of it, though she did not answer me vocally.

I thought of Irena in the hands of creatures like Viktor Celac and I felt the fury rising in me, the tension in my arms and back. But whatever this woman was, she was also Irena's mother. I searched for calm, but my eyes betrayed me. The woman looked at me, smiled.

"I saw my husband shot. I watched my village starve. Nothing you do can equal what has already been done to me and my own," she said.

She might as well have held out her arms and welcomed death. The difficult things I had done in my short life seemed insignificant compared to getting to my feet, moving behind her, and taking just enough to forge the bond that would give me the names of the ones who had taken Irena, a place where she might be found. But the woman knew so little, only one name. Michael Celac. I wiped most of her memory of this visit; difficult since all I wanted to do was wrap my hands around her neck and snap it.

I left her lying on the sofa with my words her only true memory. —Tell the ones who took her that I will find her. And if she has been harmed in any way, there will be nothing left of them for their kin to devour.—

The phone was ringing when I opened my door, Hunter calling with some hopeful news. Though the Romanians were publicly calling Irena's disappearance a defection, the securitate agent assigned to protect her had been dumped north of Sibiu, so badly beaten he was taken to the hospital. Though the official story of her defection had not changed, privately the incident was now viewed as an abduction by Hungarian dissidents. "Not that the Romanians would ever admit they can't control their own citizens, especially to the west," he told me.

I reminded Hunter of the message on the wine label. Not that I needed to as it was uppermost in his mind.

"The message was a sham to steer off the communists," he said. "Now there's likely some poor dissidents in Wallachia being tortured so they'll confess to something they didn't do."

"Is there a way for one of us to get in?"

"Stephen or Denys could walk through Otopeni Airport naked. No one else can get into Romania without at least the pretense of papers."

"I have a passport. And an invitation from their government. Would that be enough?"

"Probably. But once you're there you'll be on your own, without the protection of the firm or even the family name to rely on. Our relationship with the Romanians works so well because they think AustraGlass exports Tarda water to resell. If they guess what you are, they might realize how much their little spring means to the family. A dangerous position to put them in."

He was right. There isn't any of us who doesn't have a few bottles on hand to appease our hunger when hunting is not an option. I'd been living on it since Irena had been taken.

After I hung up the phone, I considered the matter from every angle and called my father.

As I told him what I'd learned from Marina Sava, I grew more anxious. "I have to do something," I concluded. "I know it's a risk, but I have to find her before they devour her."

"Devour her? If Viktor Celac knew what she was and let her live, Michael Celac will too. They want her for the child she can give the strongest of them, or if they are unaware of that possibility, then for the blood that might force a change in one of them. No, Richard, killing their golden goose is the last thing they plan to do."

For a moment, I understood how my father had been raised, though I could only appreciate the insight later. "You said that to make me feel better?" I asked.

"The fact that her life is not in danger does not? At least now you understand that rushing to the rescue without being prepared will not serve anyone's needs, yes?"

"I know," I admitted, though I still wanted to do just that.

"We trade with the Romanians. We can apply pressure. Now that we have a name to give them, they'll find her," he said. "Now promise me you won't do anything without phoning me first."

"Easy to do, under the circumstances."

I didn't actually make a promise and he knew it. I considered how Laurie had been my age when he'd broken every rule for his Kathleen and paid such a terrible price. I considered Patrick's need for Georgie and I had enough detachment to wonder if this urge to rush headlong into something more meaningful than lust affected everyone in my family at my age. One day I would have to ask my father if he'd ever done anything so foolish as what I contemplated and what the outcome had been in that barbaric age.

I stored the thought for some future time, read over the invitation I had been sent by the Romanian government, then dug my suitcase from beneath the boxes of books I'd stored in the closet. I was about to phone a travel agent and book a ticket, when my father called again.

"There is something you can do. Go to Ion's tomorrow night at ten. He will have information for us. For the family's sake, don't hide from him. Reveal every bit of what you are."

Not hide?

In all my years, I had never consciously done that. Other than relaxing a bit at the family gatherings or at home, the concealment had become so natural I had little idea how to act.

Perhaps my father had suggested this to keep my mind off Irena for at least a little while. If so, it worked.

Nearly everything I own is oversized—the jeans, the sweaters, the flannel shirts all designed to conceal differences, not reveal them. But Denys is thinner than I am, enough that the black wool sweater from his closet fit me tightly across the chest and arms; its deep V-neck revealing the glass pendant I was never without. I slipped on a pair of his dress pants, the knit snug enough on me to show the length of my legs.

I took the cream Irena used to keep her hair smooth on windy winter days, smeared some on my hands and ran it through my hair. The strands darkened to nearly pure black and fell into the loose curls she says are too pretty for a man. I dug in the box on the dresser and pulled out the emerald ring Laurie had given me before I'd come back to Chicago; I slipped it on.

I studied myself in the full-length mirror on the back of my bedroom door. The tight clothes seemed effeminate, deceitfully so. And though I felt like a cub trying to imitate a wolf, I suspected I would be the only one aware of how young I actually was.

I had the night to get through and another day besides. I had not hunted since Irena had been taken and I was hungry. I decided to test this new look, slipped on a black leather trenchcoat, and left the apartment. I walked west toward Lincoln, well aware of how passersby glanced my way, then looked again, trapped by the magnetism I did not try to hide. Tonight, I was my father's son, reveling in my nature. It brought an odd and heady feeling.

Not the park tonight. Given my current state, I wanted some-place more intimate. With that in mind, I headed west toward Lincoln. I didn't have a specific destination in mind. I would let my instincts decide.

As I walked, my mind moved through the places I passed. Smoke-filled neighborhood bars with the same clientele for de-cades. Ethnic bars. Hippie and college spots. A damnably loud disco club. The gay bar I'd been to with Patrick and Georgie just days before.

I stopped on the street outside of it, moved my face close to the dark tinted glass. My reflection startled me—the neon light reflected on my dark hair, in my eyes. My father's face. I looked past my reflection to the space inside. Two dozen people, no more. Singles at the bar, groups at the tables.

I'd liked the place when I'd been here before. The privacy pa-trons allowed each other. The quiet booths in dark corners where hands or lips might touch, exploring the future or dangerous fan-tasies that would never be fulfilled. Some patrons were predators, others willing prey, others nervous and guilty like the men in the park. I'd rarely spoken to any of those I used beyond a quick greeting, a quicker thievery. I could have that here . . . and much more. Knowing finally why I had stopped at this place, I drew in a long breath of the cold night air and went inside.

The bartender asked for my I.D. I handed over my student pass, which was accurate, but he read a different date and let me order that imported beer I wouldn't drink. As I waited, I scanned the bar. I did not have to worry about catching someone's eye— the singles were all watching me from the moment I stepped in.

I spotted someone in his early thirties who was staring at me, trying to place me. A conquest from the park. It had been sum-mer, I recalled, as I waved and walked past disappointment to where he sat, waiting.

"I can't remember but I'm sure we've met," he said.

A question I did not answer. "No matter." I made that dismiss-ing motion with my hand and rested it close to his. "Beer?" I asked, sliding mine over to him.

"You don't like it?"

"I don't drink." I wanted to grin, that perfect movie sort of moment just before the mayhem begins.

But he was the one who showed his teeth. After all, he thought he understood. If I'd given him a chance he would have started talking, giving me his name and age (which I knew), his relationships (married), his occupation, what he thought of his job, all those little things that make humans feel connected. I knew it all and didn't care about any of it. "Let's take a table," I suggested, pointing to one some distance from the bar.

The patrons on either side of us barely glanced up as we took a seat at a small booth with a U-shaped seat. I slid around so I was next to him, one hand on the table, the other resting on his thigh.

"I don't come here very often," he said, a fleeting nervous smile as punctuation.

"I've only been here once before."

"Are you waiting for someone?"

"No." My hand moved upward. He caught his breath.

"We could go somewhere."

I shook my head and kissed him, my lips tight together. I thought of Irena, of drawing her in. Things reserved for her.

This place was safe from my guilt. That was why I had come here.

"Lord," the man whispered, leaning close to me as my lips brushed his cheek, my hand already exploring the back of his neck.

Fearful the passion I'd ignited in him would draw attention, I willed him to silence. As I drank, his body shuddered. "Lord," he said again, mouthing the word. Almost soundless. So obedient.

"I'm sorry," he said when I let him speak.

"Don't be." I slid out of the booth, reached for my jacket.

"Will you be coming back here?" he asked.

"I could." After another visit to Konovic, I'd likely need it. "Tomorrow night? Same time?" I suggested.

"That's good." The blood had moved us closer. I saw children, something important at school that he could not quite remember. I sensed the depth of his guilt, an emotion my brother seems to adore.

"Is the next day better? A bit earlier. Six?" Happy hour.

I felt his relief. "I don't come here often," he repeated.

"Neither of us belong here," I responded and he looked up at me, eyes too moist, grateful for the lie.

I left him with my beer; walked out into the cold. I had been right to come here. I felt so much closer to Irena then, as if I could reach out a hand and she would take it. And one day I would. And she would. No matter what our future might bring, I would not let her be taken from me without a fight.

# CHAPTER 30

As I walked to Konovic's apartment the next evening, a chilly rain began to fall, well in keeping with my mood. Though I was a half hour early, I went in. The front desk was gone, replaced with a locked front door and buzzers. I was about to press the button for Konovic's apartment, when a girl came out, smiling as she let me pass, forgetting my face a moment later.

The hallway outside Konovic's apartment was empty, the residents of the other apartments on the floor out or nearly silent. I heard the soft drone of a distant TV, smelled a steak cooking. Nothing else. As I approached Konovic's door, I saw that it wasn't latched. I touched it and it swung open.

I'd begun to think it odd of Konovic to be so careless when I caught the scent of blood, sharper than I was used to, similar to our own. My mind rushed through the space. Konovic. Two men with him, if that's what they could still be called.

I sensed our kinship, thought of my brief and terrifying encounter with Viktor Celac, and froze. Mindful of what might be coming up behind me, I shrugged off my fear, stepped inside, closed the door, and bolted it. Two on one. I could handle that if I could act at all. I made my way down the hall, careful to make no sound.

Konovic sat in one of his dining chairs, facing the dark windows. He was shirtless, his hands resting on the chair arms. He seemed unbound at first, but I spied the tape that held his wrists. One of his attackers sat behind him, bent over so his mouth pressed against Konovic's neck. I saw the handle of a revolver sticking out of the waistband of the man's pants. A second man crouched at Konovic's right, lips pressed to his arm. The cut there was deep and blood dripped from the wound to the floor. Konovic's pulse raced from the blood loss. Soon he would be in shock.

Here was the moment I'd been praying for—and dreading— for years. Gladiatorial, yes. Possibly too well matched. I considered a quick attack but with Konovic so weak, even a man with ordinary strength might have the time to snap his neck. So I settled for stealth instead.

One step toward them. Another. Another. The crouching man saw me and I moved, not attacking either one of them but instead jerking chair and victim out of their reach. The chair fell sideways and skidded across the hardwood floor to stop close to the inside wall. With Konovic pulled away from immediate death, I moved between the men and their prey.

"Still hungry?" I asked. I might have grinned to answer the obvious question, but the larger man had guessed what I was from staring at my hands, tensed and ready to destroy. I heard Konovic's forced breaths and knew I had to start and end this fight soon, preferably with one of them alive and able to answer questions, but I felt frozen, uncertain I could strike the first blow.

The larger of the two, and the weaker one mentally, rushed me from the side and my instincts reacted as they would to any other attack. I was faster, much faster than I ever thought I could be. The logical part of me actually seemed to be looking on, watching a defense I could barely control. My leg lifted; I kicked hard, sending the man flying in the direction of Konovic. As I did, his partner attacked from behind, pushing my legs out from under me. I went down hard, rolled onto hands and feet. He'd been about to jump me, but saw my speed and backed off, one hand reaching behind him for the gun.

I shook my head. A warning he obeyed, motioning instead for his partner to get up and move in. They meant to take me as they had Ion, to disable then devour. The rage I felt rose then, unfamiliar and welcome. My lips parted and pulled back, revealing the long rear fangs. I snarled—a sound I had not made since I was much smaller, taking on creatures three times my size, my eyes now as dark as those Canadian woods.

Konovic groaned, distracting me, and the smaller of my opponents rushed from my left, retreating at the last moment while his partner hit me from the right. I swung my free arm. It connected with the larger man's chest. I felt something break, smelled blood, heard his moan, then nothing. Not dead, but dying too fast to question. A firstborn can touch a dying mind. Impossible for me and so I had to take the smaller one alive and able to answer my questions.

That thought took only an instant but as I swung to attack, the man was on me, the knife I'd missed gouging at my eyes. It did damage, enough that I was blinded for a moment. The pain mixed with the scent of my own blood, both sharpening my other senses.

But lack of vision made me slow, enough that he got away from me and, desperate, went for his gun. His revolver clicked. I felt the explosion hit my chest, heard the window shatter behind me as a second bullet went through it. Another hit me. Another. Had I been human, I would have been dead. As it was, though I shrieked from the pain, my heart barely skipped a beat. No time for questions now. I would not have the focus and the police were likely on their way. I lashed out, sending the gun flying, and was on him, my vision clearing quickly enough to see the surprise and terror on his face as he watched me heal.

—Don't assume too strong a kinship,— I told him, slashing at his arm and chest. He pushed away and tried to run but I was faster. I grabbed his wounded arm, intending to pin him and take him from behind. But my hands were slippery with his blood and he broke free again, rushing toward the hallway and the bolted door. As he did, I spied an envelope on the floor near the spot where Ion lay. I scooped it up, opened it, and scanned the list while my opponent struggled to break through the outer door. Before he thought to scream for help, I pulled him back and fed on him, enough to draw some strength from his life into me, nothing more. With his use to me over, I kicked him out what was left of the window.

With that distraction ended, I could turn my attention to their captive. I made no effort to undo Ion's bonds. Instead, I lifted his head into my lap and told him that help was on its way.

—Who were those men?— I asked.

"Men?" I was astonished he could even mouth the word, then he shocked me more with an actual reply. "Like Viktor." I caught a thought, only half formed and tinged with grim humor. —New ones. Impatient.—

New to this country or to the change I sensed in both of them?

"Don't go yet—" he whispered, even the thought cut off as he passed into shock.

I stood and studied the room. I knew little of forensics, but the bullets were still in me. Those wounds had barely bled so I guessed that only a tiny bit of the blood coating the walls and floor belonged to me. I shoved the knife my attacker had used into my pocket. I thought that if I could get a pitcher of water, something to dilute . . .

There were people in the hallway. Police soon to follow. I glanced through the broken window glass, saw the body on the ground below me. No one had spied it yet, so if anyone saw me fall, they would assume that body was mine. I hoped so as I followed the dead man down.

Staying in the shadows behind the iron fence that ran the front of the building, I scaled the gate that led to the back and the alley. Distracted by pain, covered with my victims' blood, I kept to the shadows as I made my way home. I went in through the parking level, wary as the elevator took me up. I'd stopped bleeding long ago but the bullets were still in me. The one in my shoulder wasn't too painful; the two in my chest were. At a pace just short of running, I got into the apartment and bolted the door. And realized I was not alone. I was weary but if I had to, I—

"Hey, Dickie boy! I've come—"

Then he saw me and rushed forward, backing off when he realized that what he had sensed was only physical pain. I hadn't been this happy to see my brother in years.

I staggered into the bathroom, looked at myself in the mirror. My hair was caked with blood, the dark shirt black and sticky from it. I stripped everything off and threw it all into the bathtub. I got out the bullet in my shoulder and the one in my lung myself, then lay on the tile floor, biting my lips to keep from screaming as Patrick dug through my flesh to find the one embedded close to my spine.

"I don't recommend getting shot," I told him once he was through and we were both washing off the gore in the shower.

"No need to remind me. I saw our father take that hit in Cleve-

land. It's lucky we don't dream, eh?" He left me with the vision
of my father's shattered face as the water ran down my body,
warm as blood.

While I finished in the bathroom, Patrick had heated water for
tea and burned the ruined clothing in the fireplace. I'd been right
about the contents of that envelope. Inside it was a carefully
printed list of names and Romanian towns. On the last sheet,
written in a quick scrawl, were initials and a place: *A.I. North,
Castelul (Tr.)*.

"There are to damned many castles to choose from," Patrick
said as we consulted the Romanian map in my atlas.

"And going there would take take money. According to
Hunter the country runs on bribes."

"What's on your credit card?"

"Three hundred."

"How about cash? I brought seven thousand with me give or
take a hundred." Patrick grinned and answered the question before I asked it: "Poker. I'm a whiz at it."

"And a cheat."

"Only when a life is at stake."

"You didn't have to—"

"My life, you fool, not hers. It's over between Georgie and
me. I've taken a month's leave from school. Family emergency, I
told them, as if with my grades I have to justify anything. I've
come to give you moral support, or if you wish, I'll go and bring
your diva home."

"You'd do that for me?" I asked, astounded.

"For me. I feel like killing someone. Maybe I'll get lucky over
there."

I didn't refuse his offer, though I intended to; instead I asked
him what had happened.

He plopped down on the couch. Exaggerating only slightly, or
so it seemed, he gave me a brief account of the near constant battles he'd had with Georgie since he'd made that offhand remark
as they were leaving here.

"You should never have lied to him for so long," I said.

"Dickie boy, he can't even deal with being gay."

I wanted to ask how Patrick had managed to hide his nature
from someone he lived with, but I knew. The mental challenge
would have been exhausting. My brother must have loved it.

Patrick followed my thoughts, pushed them away. "In the end, the guilt was killing him and I was starting to feed on it. Finally, he said that if I didn't move out, he'd quit Julliard, go home, and be a farmer and I'd have the ruination of his career on my conscience. His timing was perfect. So here I am, cash in hand, ready to take on an enemy that can be killed."

I was almost sorry to disappoint him. "I let her go there alone. I want to be the one to get her back," I told him.

"I thought you couldn't."

"Something has changed, or maybe my resolve is just stronger."

"It's not a matter of resolve. You either can or you can't. Which is it?"

"I can."

"How will you get past the airport guards?"

"Well, I'll try the polite approach first. My fiancée is missing. I couldn't let her defect without at least a good-bye. And it's such a pretty country, I might just stay myself. *Ştiaţi că aunt român, domnule?*"

Patrick laughed. "Third-generation Romanian? So we are. Long, long generations."

We settled into the living room, turned on the nightly news. Reporters showed footage of Konovic's building, the broken window, interviews with neighbors, a comment from a police officer on the body they'd found inside. They reported a resident, Ion Konovic, had been bound and bled nearly to death. The camera panned to the place outside where a second body had been discovered some time after the police arrived. The reporter dubbed it a "vampire" attack and said the smaller man had likely been so delusional that as the police closed in, he actually seemed to think he could fly away. He added that the victim was Romanian, and could not hide his smirk at the joke.

As I'd hoped, Konovic had survived the last few hours. He was still unconscious, the victim of a concussion most likely caused by the force of my rescue. But he was stable, his prognosis guarded. I had no doubt that he'd survive. He comes from hearty stock.

"Maybe you should wait to go until after Konovic wakes up. Then you can talk to him first," Patrick suggested. I didn't agree.

"Weird news travels fast. I've probably got less than a day before you-know-who catches wind of it and orders me to stay home."

"Would you?"

"No."

He sighed, that drama again. "All right. You go and I'll stay here. Roam the city. Watch the apartment. Answer the phone for you." His voice deepened with the last few words to a near perfect imitation of my own. "Stephen can't read minds over the phone line. He'll never guess. And you can call me every day or two once you get there so I can tell you if Hunter has learned anything new."

"I'll call."

I left the next morning on Pan Am. First class, but then Patrick cheats at cards so I could afford it.

# CHAPTER 31

Five mornings after Irena's abduction, I arrived in Bucharest. I presented my Canadian passport, my visa, the official letter inviting me to the country, and a copy of the news story about Irena's disappearance that had run in the *Chicago Tribune*.

It was enough to get me bumped from one worthless and annoying customs officer to an older, larger one with more clout. He led me through the narrow halls of the airport, past throngs of Western businessmen in well-tailored suits, almost every one of them carrying a cigarette. I shuffled along behind him, fingering the money belt beneath my oversized shirt and wondering how much of it I would need to get outside and find a breath of what passed for pure air in this city.

The official led me into a little room, closed and locked the door behind us, then lit a cigarette of his own. I gave my story again. "This is strange story. Take off clothes," he said in heavily accented English.

"Please! My fiancée is missing and I don't have much time to catch the last flight to Sibiu."

"Clothes first."

Which would expose the money belt; and worse, the length of

my arms. I touched his mind. He was supposed to be looking for
drugs or contraband, but what he mostly wanted to do was look at
me. He would take a nice, long look, during which he would
likely decide I was very suspicious and begin a full cavity search.
I'd likely have no choice but to rip him apart. Not an unobtrusive
arrival, so I turned, met his eyes, and trapped him. I took his
hand, rested it on my cheek. "I'll do whatever you wish," I said,
my voice filled with promise.

Somewhere in the middle of his fantasy, I ordered him to sit
and undo the buckle on his belt. I hoped it would be enough to
convince him that what he thought we had done had actually occurred. Five minutes later, he unlocked the door and waved me
past the guards outside. Not certain that my mental image of the
last few minutes would survive his comrades' scrutiny, I did not
try to make the Sibiu flight. Instead, I thumbed a ride outside the
airport and headed into Bucharest.

The student who picked me up seemed astonished that I was
from America and that I spoke Romanian. Guarded at first, he relaxed after I told him a shortened version of why I had come,
enough to refer me not to one of the major hotels, where the securitate might be looking for me, but to a friend who could put
me up.

"But I need to leave Bucharest tonight," I told him.

"No. No nighttime driving is allowed. You would attract too
much attention."

His friend turned out to be a pretty, red-haired girl, about my
age, who had a cozy one-bedroom apartment and had recently
lost her job. I suspect what I paid for that one night covered her
month's rent but since it was against the law to speak to foreign-
ers let alone harbor one I did not begrudge her that. She also told
me she knew someone who had a car I could use—for a hefty fee,
of course—or the car and its owner as driver and guide for
slightly more.

Her acquaintance, a young man named Teodor, came by an
hour later. The car was a stripped-down Dacia that he'd purchased after it had been in a nasty accident. He'd pounded it back
into some semblance of drivability, possibly with his fists, given
the thickness of its steel. I hired him as guide and driver, but only
after he agreed that, if the car coughed its last on some desolate
mountain road, I could remind him that it was his problem not

mine and take off on foot. We struck a quick bargain and he left with a small advance. I guessed how he would spend it and told him to pick me up at ten the next morning.

With travel plans out of the way, my hostess (who called herself Doina, like the music, rather than her given name, Elena, because she would not have any tie at all with "those Ceauşescu pigs who are ripping down our city") fixed us both a cup of tea. We talked for an hour about our countries. As it grew late the room became colder. She explained that everyone had been asked to conserve fuel that winter. Her landlord, an ardent party member, turned off the gas each night at ten. Since she had only that one bed, she suggested we do our part to thaw east-west relations.

But all I did was hold her, tell her a bit about why I had come, then ask questions about the country until she told me to shut up and go to sleep.

In the morning, she was justly famished but insisted on sharing her breakfast—an unappetizing mix of polenta and eggs—with me. I played the usual game of push-it-around-the-plate then passed it over to her, insisting I would get carsick if I ate too much. She gladly consumed it all. While she did, I asked if she had a telephone and if it was tapped. She looked so alarmed at the question that I decided to phone Patrick later, so Doina would not be endangered by our conversation.

So far the adventure had proven to be so easy that I felt almost giddy. I decided that, once I left the communist stronghold of Bucharest, everything would go even more my way. As Teodor and I got into his car, Doina waved good-bye from her second-floor window. I flashed her a peace sign and we were off.

I had decided that I did not need to see any of Konovic's contacts in Bucharest and asked Teodor to take me straight to Sibiu, some two hundred kilometers northwest of the capital as the crow flies. Unfortunately, the roads were not built for crows and the mountain curves doubled the distance. Teodor was also worried about the state of his auto so that, in spite of his reassurances to me, we kept to the crowded, and slow, roads. During the first half of the journey, we had to stop twice so he could disconnect the fuel line and blow back to the gas tank to clear the filter. "I don't have the money to keep it full and the tank rotted," he explained.

We reached the village of Arefu at nightfall. Teodor refused to drive on, citing the icy mountain roads ahead. "Besides, this is a pretty place. You are in too much of a hurry. You must see things on the way," he told me.

We settled into a tavern, where over a couple of beers, I explained what had brought me here. He nodded, as if everything made sense. "We get you to Sibiu tomorrow then find her," he said.

"Actually, it isn't Sibiu I need to get to," I replied. "It is a place called Castelul. That means 'the castle,' doesn't it?"

"There is Castle Dracula."

I stifled the urge to laugh. "I don't think that is the castle I need. It may be the name of a village."

"I don't know of any village by that name, but I am from Moldavia and have not come to these parts often. You could ask the woman who is serving us."

"No. I have someone else I can ask when we get to Sibiu." I thought of Patrick, waiting for my call, and asked our server about using a phone.

"No phone," she said. "Go up to the castle. At the dam, they have a shelter and phone for tourists who come there and get stuck."

By that she meant the Castle of the Arges, the one northwest of Arefu that Teodor had called Castle Dracula. Calling from there made sense, really, if I kept my comments vague and perhaps in Latin. If the powers that be were listening in, I doubted they could translate before I was long gone and I didn't intend to say anything incriminating anyway.

"I guess I may have to play the tourist tomorrow," I told Teodor.

"Good. You will like the place," he told me, only half listening. His eyes were scanning the room, looking for a likely person from whom we could rent a room.

Teodor turned out to be a savvy negotiator who talked some poor old fellow into taking half what he'd wanted and giving us breakfast in the morning besides. But when we entered his house on the edge of town and I smelled the scent of thousands of cigars smoked over decades, I decided to sleep in the car.

Both men argued when I told them what I intended to do, but I refused to give in so Teodor handed me a spare key. The old man provided a blanket and a pillow and told me to be sure to cover up well, especially if I heard someone walking by, since what I was doing was illegal. He added that he would be happy to let me in if the winter cold made me change my mind later.

The temperature had fallen to about twenty. I'd spent many a peaceful night camped in the snow wearing far less than I was at that moment. At least out there I'd be able to breathe. I'd also decided that if I were asleep in the back, I could manage to avoid having to deal with both breakfast and an early rising. I'd simply mumble something to my solicitious driver about waking me when we reached our destination.

I settled into the backseat, staying put and presumably asleep until long after the lights winked out; then I changed into the knit pants and shirt I'd brought with me. Dressed for a hunt, I got out of the car, locked my bags and money in the trunk, and headed north and west. Yes, I would play the tourist, but in the way that I preferred.

The keep that had sheltered my family for so many centuries was little more than a night's hard run from Arefu. My father had been raised there. My grandfather, the Old One, was still there and would likely always be. Like all my kind, I felt no urgency to go out of my way to meet him. It would happen in time, perhaps as a refuge for Irena and me after I found her or years from now on a less hurried visit.

No, it was the forest itself that called to me. Hundreds of years ago, when this country was more openly barbaric, my father might have hunted in the very woods I walked in now—lynx or wolves or even men. I felt a need to see this country as he might have seen it, in darkness and alone.

The moon had not yet risen but the stars overhead were dim, pollution and the damp haze rising from the valley robbing them of their winter beauty. The woods were thick with fir and beech, beautifully scented even in winter. Near the valley, they had been much cleared for farming but as I climbed, the trees became denser, older. There were a few wolves in the area, some bear and deer. Not many, no doubt because of poaching when times were lean and men became desperate.

My mind moved away from me, focusing on the life around me, finding a young deer that might require some effort to catch and subdue. I fell forward, hands flat on the soft, scented earth. I ran until my heart pounded, sprang and captured, and fed then let it go.

After, with an entire luscious night ahead of me, I wandered through the woods. The moon rose, and I saw the outline of the Impaler's keep on a nearby hilltop.

I've seen all the old vampire movies, of course. My father loves them and I loved the stories he would tell—and show—us afterwards. I saw him face down Vlad Dracul so many centuries ago. I knew what the man really looked like, the rage that could cross his face, the intelligence and cunning lurking in those fierce emerald eyes. Did he change into something else at death? Vampires are only legends, I believe, though the keep-born disagree. But my father also told me that when he walks through a place where many have died he can feel their essence through the blood that has merged with the earth.

The Castle of the Arges was such a place. Dracula had ordered his enemies, the boyers, to build it. Men and women and their children worked the rest of their short, sad lives creating a small and sorry edifice that did nothing to protect Dracula or his wife from the Turks. What better place to discover the truth of my father's words?

Ignoring the hundreds of steep stairs, I chose the steeper mountainside climb instead. I reached the top just before moonrise, sat on the ruined walls, and looked over the Arges Valley below, the mountains rising to the west.

A beautiful view. I lay back, face to the stars, and shut my eyes.

Nothing but the whistle of wind in the pines, melodic as pan-pipes. The call of some night bird, harsh as an infant's scream. The deep throbbing in the earth beneath me, as if the dead were struggling to wake, to rise, to seek their vengeance. That last must have been fancy, not real, but my senses had never betrayed me before and so I could not be sure.

I stood on the edge of a ruined outer wall, looked down at the valley and the Arges River below. This was where the Impaler's wife had stood in the last moment before she jumped to her death. Had the souls of their dead slaves caused their oppressors' victory? Did all the dead and their dreams of vengeance cause the sorrow that now afflicted what should have been this rich and peaceful land?

Then the moon rose. I saw oceans of mist rolling through the valley below my feet, and for a moment, viewing such beauty, I could understand why the Old One chose to remain in this land.

I stood there for some time, lost in thought, then took the

stairs down, found the shelter near the dam, the telephone. My brother would be asleep, no doubt with one eye open. I picked up the receiver, waited for a dial tone. A woman's voice asked where I wished to call. I gave the city, the number. After what seemed like an hour's wait, she came back on the line. "Who are you?" she asked.

"A relation. He'll know the voice."

From the way I spoke she must have sensed I was no local. "Call back in daytime," she said.

The line went dead again. Not sure if hers was the only human contact I would have in the next few minutes, I disappeared into the trees and made straight for Arefu to become human again.

# C H A P †E R  3 2

Later that morning, everything went much as I'd hoped. After a few minutes of final negotiation, I snuggled deep in the blanket I'd just purchased and slept, not waking until we arrived in Sibiu a bit before noon.

I'd decided that whoever had taken Irena would not risk taking her far, and so decided to center my search there. Not being certain of the state I might find her in, I asked Teodor if he would stay in Sibiu with me for at least a few days in case I had need of his car again.

The contacts Konovic had given me were clustered together on the south end of town. Teodor found us a pair of rooms in a private house in the area. They were clean and had their own entrance—a far better arrangement than the night before. I gave him some money to get something to eat then went calling.

The first name on the list was that of a young man who had disappeared only days earlier. The second was out of town though the neighbors had no idea where he might have gone. I'd begun to wonder if Irena's abductors were one step ahead of me until I found another, Oleh Halas, at home. He was a dark-haired man with a middle-aged spread and a long face and large nose that made him look rather horselike. He'd just gotten off work, still covered with factory dust and none too pleased about being disturbed. Nonetheless, Konovic's name opened his door. He invited me into a stifling kitchen and offered me a seat at his already crowded dinner table and some of the stew they were eating, which I declined.

"This is Richard. He is a friend of Cousin Ion's," he told his wife.

"Ion!" The woman beamed at me, happy for the novelty of a guest. Because the discretion of children is always suspect and a foreign visitor could bring the securitate calling, I followed my host's lead and did not speak of the reason for the visit until dinner was over. Then, on some unspoken cue, his wife retreated with her brood of four, leaving us alone.

"Wait! Mikel, go and get your uncle," Oleh called to his oldest son, a boy of about eight who rushed to obey.

The second man arrived a few minutes later. He was older and a bit better dressed and said he worked as an accountant for a government agency. He introduced himself as Sandor Usenko, a name I recognized as another of Ion's Sibiu contacts. Sandor took a seat at the table while Oleh shut the kitchen doors. From elsewhere in the house, I heard an infant cry, the youngest children arguing.

The men knew something of why I had come, and added that all Sibiu had heard of the singer's abduction. No matter what the official line, everyone believed she had been taken by extremists. The men added that she had been lured into a trap by a woman though they did not have a name.

I could guess it, but I would not ask about Marie yet. Instead, I asked about Michael Celac.

Oleh thought of ways to lie. Sandor was frank. "We know the name. Some saw him as a hero, some as a troublemaker who brought problems for us all. But why do you ask about him? He was taken away by the government months ago. He is likely dead now."

I let them believe that and listened while they gave all sorts of possibilities, then another lead.

"The party member who was taken away with her is still in the hospital. We hear that he will be released soon."

"Could I go and see him?"

"Better to wait until he is released."

I thought of Irena, shook my head. "Tell me where he is and I will go and see him myself."

The confidence with which I spoke those words made Sandor look at me sharply, trying to guess for a moment how old I was, or how rich. Then he noticed my eyes, the shape of my face, the hair. I pushed the questions from his mind. Asked him one of my own.

"His name is Andrei Oprea," Sandor replied.

"I know of him," I said, thinking of the title he'd given himself.

"He is on the third floor. All private rooms are on that floor and he is party so . . ." Sandor shrugged as if to add, What did anyone expect?

"When we are ill, we get no private rooms. Often we do not even have our own beds," Oleh added by way of explanation.

"There will be people watching that room. Cameras. You must be careful," Sandor went on. He looked at the door nervously, all but begging me to go.

"I need to ask some other things. First, what do you know about the Legion of Archangel Michael?"

Both men were astonished at the question. Neither had heard that name for many years. "Fascists. During the war," Sandor said.

"Partisans," Oleh corrected.

"Oleh is half right," Sandor added. "You cannot just look at the atrocities, you must consider the why of some acts."

Spoken like a good Nazi, I thought. I touched his mind and was surprised to find no hint of rancor there. Sandor had merely stated what he thought was a fact.

"Today the Legion would be anticommunist, maybe even in favor of restoring the monarchy, though who knows if there is still a monarch to restore," Oleh said.

"Do you know of such a group active in this area?"

Oleh shook his head. "Just the whispers of the discontented. Those are everywhere."

He told the truth as he knew it. "Have you ever heard of a place called Castelul?" I asked.

Neither answered. Neither knew. "But there is a legend," Sandor said after a while then recited it: "When Romania is purified by the plagues and the blood, the god will return to the castle and the king will bring peace to the land."

I had heard a similar quote from Rachel a few years back. She thought it had a family connection, and I had argued it was only the story of poor people looking for hope. "So it is not a place, then?"

Oleh looked at me, watching my reaction as he replied, "There are many castles, but only two close by. One is the ruins on the Arges, the other is the Old One's keep."

I did not pretend ignorance, only said that I was sure that those were not the ones. Then I asked about Marie Saratov.

"That *curvă!*" Oleh shook his head, a hint of disgust in his thoughts, more in the way he had all but spit the insult. "You can find that one at the downtown hotels. The ones for party members or the foreign bigwigs with money."

So she had made good use of her passionate nature. "Could you suggest which ones would be most likely?" I asked.

"Try the Imparatul. You'll find her sitting in the lobby with the other whores."

"Whatever you want from her you will have to pay well for," Sandor added.

She was the one who would pay, I thought as I left them. I considered my next move as I walked toward the place I'd rented. I decided on Andrei first, and headed toward the hospital.

Dark and squat, the hospital spread its ugliness over half a city block. Not wanting to enter through the lobby, I walked around it. I saw a flight of stairs going up to the roof but it was too exposed to use in daylight. There was also a cargo bay in the back. A truck had backed in, so the door was open.

The truck had left a narrow space along the driver's side, one that forced me to move sideways between the truck and wall. The area was empty but I could hear men just inside, arguing over a payment for the shipment.

The driver was irate. He had been put off three times in the past month and his boss was losing patience. The hospital order-lies admitted their accountant was a lazy bastard who had no business going home two hours early but "that was life, come back tomorrow."

The driver was nearly ready to explode on his own. I gave a subtle push and he did. "This is for the lazy bastard," he said and swung at the nearest man, who was too slow to get out of the way.

By the time I passed them, the fight was in full swing, so to speak. No one noticed me.

The supply closet was just inside the loading dock. I grabbed a gown that might have been for a patient or a doctor or even a nurse, slipped it on, and stepped into an inside hall.

The space was well scrubbed and badly repaired. There were spots where the recent white paint had worn off, revealing under-layers of beige, green, and dusty rose. Fluorescent fixtures in the ceiling lit the space but a number were flickering or out. The hall was also crowded with patients lying on wheeled carts, visitors standing beside them. The impression was one of a sudden disaster, though it was likely only a normal afternoon here.

Whatever I was wearing had nothing to do with patients. Most were lying in beds in the corridor in street clothes. One had on nothing at all but a thin sheet and shivered from the cold. I hoped this ward was what passed for an emergency room in this small building.

An old woman, a visitor sitting beside an old man lying on one of the beds, grabbed my arm. "Doctor, stop please."

Doctor? So I had gotten a bit lofty in my choice of attire.

"Doctor, please, can you get him something for pain?" she begged.

I wanted to run from her sorrow, from the pain I sensed in both of them, but I forced myself to touch his forehead, his body. Something was eating his insides. Cancer most likely. There was little life left in him and I doubted he had long to live.

"What did the others tell you?" I asked.

"Nothing. They say nothing." But she knew.

"Take him home," I said. "Let him say his good-byes to his family."

"There is just me." Her eyes filled with tears.

"I'll see what I can do," I told her, and ordered the man to sleep. It would not last long but at least he'd get a few minutes of respite.

I passed a nurse as I walked to the end of the hall. She looked at me, did not know my face, and was about to ask who I was when I silenced the question, pointed to the old couple I'd passed. "The man needs something for pain," I said.

"I will get it when I am able." Her reply was accompanied by that expression I'd seen throughout the country, and the resigned shrug that implied, What can we do?

I passed an alcove where a crowd waited for a single elevator, opted for the stairs at the end of the hallway, and took them three at a time. Not surprisingly, the third-floor door was locked. Sensing no alarm or anyone inside to sound one, I applied a slow and steady pressure and the frame cracked.

This hallway was brighter, wider, with large private rooms along its east side. I heard voices from an office near the elevator, nothing else.

I stayed where I was for a moment, my mind taking in the space. There were eight rooms on this floor, only three occupied. One held an old woman who had been there some time. Another a young boy with a broken leg. The third a man in great pain and, judging from his confused mental state, well drugged. This was my man. Though I wasn't clear how much I could learn from him, I had to try.

His room was large and airy, painted a pale shade of green with a dark wood trim. A pair of framed photographs on the wall showed happy, prosperous farmers. Even party members got their share of propaganda. The room was the antithesis of everything I'd seen in the crowded hallway below. Not surprising. There is that gap between rich and poor everywhere and my father told me it always seems most pronounced in places that proclaim complete equality.

Oprea's face was a mess—bruises on the left side of his forehead and cheek, the left eye swollen shut. His right arm was in a cast, and an IV ran into the back of that same hand. I could see a bit of gauze and tape showing through a missing button in his pajamas. Cracked ribs perhaps? Or something worse? All told, he looked thin and weak and incapable of his reputation. I wondered how much of it was really true.

A folded newspaper had been placed on the bed beside his free hand. I was surprised anyone would bother since I doubted he had the ability to absorb much at the moment.

I pulled a chair close to his bed, the noise waking him from a half sleep. "How are you feeling?" I asked, a greeting similar to the opening line of every doctor-patient scene I'd ever viewed on television.

He looked at me some time, those long-lashed eyes fighting to focus. "You're too young to be a doctor. Are you one of them?" he asked.

I shook my head, astonished that he'd managed this much logic.

His voice grew soft. He considered my accent. "The fiancé?"

So now I was getting married? I wondered if Mother would host the bridal shower and which of my relations might attend. I moved closer to him. "Yes," I said.

"Why the disguise?"

"I don't know whom to trust but Irena spoke well of you. Your government says she defected but she wouldn't have done that."

He shut his eyes as if he'd fallen back asleep but I saw his finger move, motioning me forward. I moved close, close enough to hear him whisper, "No."

Point noted. Even party members could expect their conversations to be recorded. Especially party members, if the leaders had any intelligence at all.

"That is what we believe to be true," he said in voice loud enough for the mike to pick up.

I wanted to ask him to help me find her, but I wasn't sure how to begin. He took the lead. "I need to use the toilet," he said. "I think I'm going to be sick. Help me."

He sat up. I helped him swing his feet over the side of the bed. I looked away while he disconnected the IV tube, leaving the needle in the back of his hand. "You'll need to hold me. I'm not so weak but I'm dizzy. It's the morphine."

"But your chest."

"Bruises. Another fall would only make them worse."

I helped him into the bathroom. "Shut the door," he said and turned on the water in the sink, splashed it over his face, then left it running. For someone so drugged, his mind seemed surprisingly clear. "I get out tomorrow morning. I'm not sure, but I think I can take you to her," he whispered.

"Why didn't you just tell the local police where to look?"

He took my hand, resting my palm against his, looking at the back of my hand then at my face. "The ones who have her would kill her before they would give her up and then they would kill themselves. The people in charge here would not think that such a waste. I disagree, especially since the girl is so beautiful. I assume you would like her saved."

I nodded, lips tight together.

"I have to know who my ally is," he said, insistent but vague.

"You already do," I replied, thinking that, sadly, my words were the truth. I'd find out how much he knew, but not here or now.

He knew enough to back off. "I get out of here tomorrow

morning." He whispered an address where I might find him sometime after noon.

I helped him back to bed. He was about to ask me to reconnect the IV line then saw the expression on my face and decided otherwise. I left him struggling with the line and made my way downstairs and out the front door. On the way, I encountered only one person who looked closely enough at me to form a question but I caught his intent before he could ask it, and silenced him.

There was something too odd in that hospital meeting, the drugs and the strange lucidity of their recipient. It was enough to send me to the Imperatul that evening in search of Marie Saratov.

# CHAPTER 33

The Imperatul must have been glorious once. Traces of its past could be seen in the arches in the lobby, the plaster pattern on the ceiling, the deep colors in the unworn corners of the carpeting. But like so much of this country, it had fallen into disrepair, the bulbless ceiling fixtures attesting to the odd shortages that turned honest men into petty criminals.

I saw the group of women I looked for in one of the darker corners. Of course, they had seen me as soon as I walked through the lobby doors. One glanced in the direction of the front desk, noticed the clerk pretending to look the other way, and walked over to me. The skirt, a full foot above her knees, revealed long and shapely legs, marred only by an old scar and a run in her hose. Her heels were leather, worn but polished, the dress a western pop-art sort of style. I suspected she would be expensive, not that I was buying anything but information.

She rested a hand on my shoulder, moved close enough that I could smell perfume and peppermints. "Are you staying here tonight?" Before I could answer, she added, "I have champagne. I would be happy to share."

I walked her back toward her group, waiting until my voice

would reach the others before replying. "Just looking . . . for someone. Her name is Marie."

"Her real name? She probably isn't using it here."

I had a vague notion of what Marie looked like, courtesy of my father's memory, but the way I had obtained it and the number of years that had passed would have made identification difficult.

"A friend had a most fulfilling night with her some years ago. He said I had to try to find her."

The girl laughed. "Some years ago? You want an old woman?"

The others looked at me with similar amusement. All but one of the older girls, who backed slowly toward the lobby doors. I focused on her—the blue eyes and thick hair, the round face—that shared memory. "There you are!" I called merrily, walking toward her, taking her arm. "We need to go somewhere private," I whispered. "Somewhere more comfortable."

She tried to pull away but I had a tight grip on her arm and a tighter one on her mind.

"Please. Not outside. I have access to a room here."

I shook my head and she all but fell against me, her heart in double time, her breathing quick. In her current state, the best I could do was keep her docile and distract the other women as I all but pulled her out the lobby doors and down an icy flagstone walk of Republic Square.

"Please. Let me walk in front of you. I will go wherever you wish, but we must not walk together."

Which would give her a chance to run, not that she'd escape, but we might attract too much attention. "You stay with me," I said. "I won't hurt you, I promise. I only want to talk to you."

The square was empty, the streets clear of all but a few cars—all new and dark and undoubtedly belonging to party members. One slowed down as it passed us. My mind was on Marie, not on the driver, who was likely only checking out my purchase. I couldn't blame him. Though she was thinner than my shared memory recalled, she was still beautiful.

Marie looked at the driver, all but begging him to stop. I pulled her closer to me, rested my arm over her shoulder, planted a kiss on her neck.

"Just talk. I'll even pay you for the time," I whispered again as we walked under the dark archway of a side street I'd passed on my way to the hotel.

As in so many cities, the streets and buildings of Sibiu's old section had been erected before automobiles had claimed the roads. This one had likely been a footpath in the past. No wider than a Chicago alley, the soffits of its tiled roofs overhung the roadway, almost covering it completely. Beneath them was a single-lane one-way street with narrow sidewalks wedged between the curb and buildings.

"Keep going," I said to Marie, steering her into the darkness, pushing her ahead of me since it was impossible for us to walk side by side any longer.

We'd gone only a few yards when a car turned into the road at the far end of the block and came toward us. Marie gave a startled cry and leaned against me. I thought the car belonged to the police and had started to lead her back the way we'd come when it gained speed. The window rolled down. I saw the barrel of a gun. I recalled my father's advice to always protect my back and stayed where I was, intending to dodge the bullet at the last moment rather than be hit from behind.

When the barrel pointed at us, I started to push Marie down. As I did, she broke free and ran. My attention was on her when I heard the explosions, felt the bullets enter my shoulder and leg. The car lurched forward, its rear door opening so Marie could jump inside. Distracted by the sudden pain, I waited too long to trap the driver. I'd lost her. And them.

Bucharest suddenly seemed so much friendlier.

Teodor was snoring when I returned to our rooms. He smelled of cigarettes, brandy, and garlic. At least he'd had a good night. I slipped off the clothes I'd stolen, washed the blood off my face and hair, and went to bed. When I woke late in the morning, Teodor had gone in search of breakfast. I left him a note saying I'd taken the car and, dressed in the best clothes I'd brought, I drove to my meeting with Andrei Oprea.

I parked some distance from the address he'd given me, one not far from the hospital he'd left that morning. He'd moved into the ground floor of an old house of dark-colored brick with a tile roof. Once it may have been a mansion; now it held a number of small apartments.

I had been expecting a trap, or police outside the door, or at least an armed guard in the foyer. But when I studied the space, I saw that there was no one in the building but him. He let me in quickly, locking the door behind us, then showed me into a first-floor study. Books lined the walls. There was a typewriter on a desk, electric and new, and a telephone.

Oprea motioned me into a chair covered in worn brown leather then took a similar one across the desk from me. His face looked less swollen than the day before, enough that I could glimpse the looks that had given him his reputation. He rested his broken arm on the desktop. In spite of his medication, the fingers sticking out of the cast twitched from pain.

"I thought I might have difficulty finding some privacy for us but my comrades are aiding the local police in investigating a shooting. Do you know anything about that, Old One?"

I felt the slightest hint of fear in him, as if he were uncertain how I would react to his knowledge. I only shrugged, the universal sign for maybe. "You said you could find Irena?" I prompted.

"I can get us closer." He spread a topographical map on the desk and explained why the kidnappers had changed their mind, how they had beaten him half to death before they drove him back to Sibiu. "I was only unconscious for a little while. When I woke, I saw a little crack in the cover along the passenger's side. Sometimes I could see a shaft of sun on the inside of the truck, sometimes the truck would turn and it would move. It was afternoon so we were heading mostly south and west. There were a lot of turns and we were traveling downhill. She is in the mountains."

A good observation under the circumstances. "Any idea of how long they drove?"

"That is the hard part. Two hours, maybe three, and that is after I regained consciousness. I was not awake at the beginning and judging distance on mountain roads is tricky."

He was still on drugs and had to focus his thoughts carefully but he seemed to be telling the truth.

"What will you do when we find her?"

"My uncle has an important role in the government but family ties will only get me so far. Better to do something heroic. America will be grateful when I bring Irena back. The Ceauşescus will be happy. My future will be secure. Perhaps they will even let me travel again. I would like that. I would like to go back to America."

Again, he was telling the truth but not all of it.

"How much do you know about me?" I asked, my mind prodding his, now, insistent enough that he would feel the pressure.

He waved his good hand, as if motioning me out. "Your real name is Richard Austra. You were born in Canada some twenty years ago. Your firm, that is, your family, trades with us and has for as long as anyone can remember. We appreciate your buying that water since we otherwise have no use for it. But we have, on occasion, called on your executives to do our country favors. With the exception of the war years when they were wisely neutral, they have always been helpful. We have no reason to assume they will not continue to be so in the future.

"That is the official file much condensed. My opinion? When I had a particularly boring job monitoring the foreign firms that trade with us, I made it a hobby to piece together all the facts we know about your family. I believe you are descended from the Old One. I have kept the knowledge to myself because it is prudent to do so. I trust you will be grateful for that."

"And Irena Sava?"

"I believe she is somehow related to the ones that took her. That is all I know."

Now he was lying. He knew much more. "And what would you want done to the kidnappers?"

"I am sure my government would prefer them chopped into tiny pieces and fed to the wolves, but I cannot. I feel—"

He felt the tie of blood. "You're one of them, aren't you." Not a question. He knew the answer, and so did I.

"Let us say that I am a distant cousin through my mother's blood, and I do not want them killed. Promise me that." His voice was even, his eyes looking directly into mine all but challenging me to find the lie.

"If you've made a hobby of studying us, then you know our limits. But I can promise to do my best to let them live but only if Irena has not been harmed."

"I said I could get us closer. It may be a long search after that."

"I can help with that."

His eyes widened, showing real emotion for the first time. "You know something?"

"We can discuss that when we are on our way. Now give me your hand."

"What did you say?"

"You know what I said. I need to know what I am dealing with. It is better you let this happen."

His hand shook a little as he held it out. Good. I tasted and noted the familiar nuance of family. Not as strong as in Irena, but there. I let his hand go, gave his mind a push.

"Take more if you wish," he said, all but holding the small cut to my lips.

Satisfied that I could control him if need be, I let him go. He looked dazed for a moment, an expression I knew well, then rallied and said, "I had hoped I was right about you. I did not want to go back there alone."

This should have made me feel better, but something gnawed at my mind. I wanted to use his phone, not for Patrick, but for my father. But when I considered doing that, something stopped me. I knew what Stephen would say: stay where I was and wait for him. But if I did, Irena would be lost to us; and as for me . . . ?

We have odd minds, restricted from logic at a time when logic matters most. Yet instincts were always correct and mine said waiting would be deadly. I had come this far, I had to go on.

"Can we leave now?" I asked.

"I'm ready."

"Is your phone clean?"

He smiled at the term. "I don't know. I like to think so."

"I need to call New York."

He made the connection for me, handed me the phone. It was nearly midnight there, a fine time to reach my brother, but no one answered. I asked the operator to try the building's front desk, where I left a quick message saying everything was going exactly as I hoped.

"Your brother says it is imperative that you do nothing until you call him," the clerk said.

"I will. Tell him I am visiting our friend Andrei and I will call from his house tomorrow. Same time."

I hung up. Oprea was at the front door, the lace curtain cracked back. He gripped the map he'd shown me earlier. "I think we should leave now and by the back way," he said.

"Party?"

"I don't think so. I think you were followed here."

The gnawing increased. A vague premonition became clearer and nastier. "Let's get the hell out of here," I said.

Before we left, Oprea returned to his desk to grab a revolver, some ammunition, and a knife. For someone who did not want to kill and probably was not capable of it, given his injuries, he intended to travel well armed.

At the beginning of the ride he told me some of his history. His mother had been born in Sibiu to a woman of Hungarian descent. His father had been a hero of the revolution and an intimate of Ceauşescu's. That had given Andrei privilege, until he made a blunder that allowed the Transylvanian Hungarians to smuggle anti-Ceauşescu writings to the west, creating a diplomatic uproar. With his loyalties suddenly suspect, he was not given positions of trust or permission to travel abroad.

"I came home of my own free will, and now I cannot leave," he complained.

"Your chance will come, Comrade Oprea," I replied.

"Andrei, please. I told you, first names are better." I detected a bit of distaste for his family name, even more for that title.

Comrade Andrei: not much of communist, really. Poor soul.

I drove with my eyes on the road ahead and a good part of my mind on the way we had come. When I was certain we were not being followed, I relaxed and pulled over at a spot that gave a good view of the road we'd been on. Though it was cold, we got out of the car and spread the map on the hood. "You said you have a lead on where she is?" he asked.

"A name. Castelul in Transylvania. There were letters after it. A. I."

"The castle?" He paused to consider, then pointed to a small dot on the map. "There is a place called the Citadel in Sebes and the Citadel in Alba Iulia, which is sometimes called the Castle of Martyrs. Those initials are often used, a shorthand for the city. I was taken to the wilderness, and high in the mountains, but there is much wilderness near both towns, particularly the last. How did you discover this?"

"I have my own sources."

"So you do. Well, Alba Iulia is a good place to begin. There are many small towns nearby, so people miss nothing and that is a good thing. If anyone will talk to us."

I knew I could get the information, but we never got so far. When we stopped for gas in Sebes, the station attendant recalled a truck that had come by twice and did not belong to anyone who lived there. And yes, on its first trip it had been heading north toward our main destination.

We continued on but never reached the second city. About ten kilometers past Sebes, we passed an uneven dirt road that curved hard to the right just before it reached the intersection but was obviously banked in the wrong direction.

Andrei asked me to stop and back up. "A hunch only but I think I was on this road."

We turned and drove nearly an hour before reaching another, narrower road that wound upward into the foothills of the Transylvanian Alps. No one had come that way for some time, and snow had drifted over the ruts. I didn't think the little car would go very far before we got stuck but I doubted I would need it much longer.

"This is it," Andrei said.

He drove past the road to a wider spot, half covered with trees. I got out of the car and walked uphill for a time, barely aware of Andrei close behind. My mind was so focused on the road ahead that it was Andrei who noticed the landmark. "Look!" he said, pointing to the crest of the hill where a handful of rocky outcroppings gave the illusion of a castle wall, a tower beyond.

"Quiet," I whispered, then stepped into the shade of a beech tree and leaned against its trunk. My mind moved away from me, up the snow-covered mountainside to a little cabin, half buried under earth and rocks. There were only two people inside. One was Irena, the other most likely the man who had taken her. I considered touching his mind or hers, decided against it. He might be strong enough to feel the touch. She might give my presence away. Better for them both to be surprised.

Eight days after Irena was kidnapped, I had come to take her home.

PART 3

MICHAEL

# CHAPTER 34

## PATRICK

After so many days in the company of Michael Celac, Irena had discovered three definite things about him. He had no vices she could use against him. He was completely ruthless. Last, and most dangerous, after he provided her with some of his history, she no longer believed him insane.

The night after she'd been taken, she'd sat at the small wood table in her dirty clothes, a blanket around her shoulders to keep out the chill. Her stomach felt queasy from the blood loss but after a shot of brandy to steady it, she realized she was more famished than weak.

He'd made some sort of stew, low on meat but the potatoes and parsnips filled her. He poured her another brandy. She didn't fight that. After a day alone with his silence for company, she needed it.

Over the meal, he told her that he'd been born at the end of the war, the product of rape, his mother had told the village, though privately the family knew she had been seduced. The one who had slept with her ("As if they ever slept!") had first saved her from a pair of German brutes. When he was younger, Michael thought that she was hiding his father's identity. By the time he was ten he'd begun to understand that his mother was not being evasive. She honestly did not know the man's name.

His grandfather gave the first real information, saying the man who had sired him was a hero. "He might have told me more," Michael said bitterly. "He might have explained enough so I could understand the tricks my mind liked to play. He might have given some hint to explain those cravings that seemed even more senseless."

"For blood?" Irena had whispered.

"And more! Every little cut that did not heal made me furious. This scar on my cheek is an insult. I look in the mirror and see in it a reminder of what I should be. As for the gift the old ones' blood is said to impart, that was a curse as well. My gift was my mind. Growing up in a village filled with peasants who blew horns during eclipses to keep ghosts from stealing the milk of their cattle, I became most careful of how hard to prod my friends. But I did have friends. I knew exactly what to do to be ingratiating."

"And you became a doctor?"

"I have a good memory. I do well on tests. It seemed natural to pursue a profession that would make my differences easier to hide.

"This area needed someone to run the local clinic. They sent me to school in Timisoara. There I began to see the problems of my country clearly. I got involved in politics. When I heard of the hardships in this part of the country, caused by our dictator's hatred of the ethic Hungarians, I became pro-western. A serious mistake.

"There were ten in my group. Eight were arrested and sentenced to work on the canal near Constanţa. In a year, everyone but me was dead. The work and the beatings killed them. I only felt stronger from them, as if I were finally being born.

"With no one to worry about but myself, I escaped. I came here because I know this country, who to trust and who to kill if I must."

"Why did you come back at all? You could have gone to the west and publicized what was going on."

"Left the country, yes, but not my conscience. Besides, I believed I had a sweetheart here, a cousin I was to marry, and she had her family. Ana never would have left them." He rested his forehead on his palm and rubbed it as if the motion could erase her memory.

"Where is she now?" Irena asked.

"Gone. She left work one evening in the company of her brother and my sister and and they never came home. I was still in the camp then, and everyone thought the government had taken them to question because of me. But they never came back. So we know it was the Old One on the mountain who took them. And so they vanished as if they had never lived at all."

"Was Ana . . . like you?" Irena asked.

"Yes. But she never believed in any of this and so . . ."

"She would not let you taste?"

"I did once, but she did not like it. There was an attraction, though. A strong one between us. Even stronger than the one I feel for you."

An attraction. Irena considered this and how she had felt about Viktor. Perhaps she did not feel the same for Michael because she had already met the old ones, the purebloods. There had certainly been attraction there, so much attraction that she had run from it.

"Word spread back to my own that I had escaped. Now I am a hero to some of them. To those who know the truth about me, I am more than that. They help me and we wait. I need only survive until I claim what is rightfully mine," Michael continued.

"To be one of them? The old ones?"

"I am one of them." —All I lack is the promise of years.—

Until that moment, Irena had not realized how strong his mind was. True, the words seemed no more than a whisper in her mind, but someone with a scar on his face had conveyed them.

"And when I am changed, I will use my blood to change others and we will fight."

"I don't understand. You mean you would rule this country?" She could not keep the amazement out of her voice.

"Rule this country? No. There are others better suited to rule. I wish only vengeance on the ones who have taken our children. When we are strong enough, we will bring down the Lord of the Mountain and his kin; their blood will make us strong. No one will stand in our way. Then yes, one of us will rule."

"You would bring down your father's kin," she reminded him.

"If he cared, he would have come for me. No, Irena, the old

ones use us and they leave us and when they think we are a threat, they destroy us, and do not care. In time, the one you love would have done the same to you."

Irena had heard enough. She pulled the blanket higher on her shoulders and hunched over her food. Since she had become his captive he had stayed close to her, a steadying hand when she stood too fast, fingers touching hers when he handed her the bread. She wondered when he would try to consummate what he saw as their marriage and how she could stop him when he did. Perhaps if she managed to grab his knife . . .

"My gift is my mind. What is yours?" he asked.

Pulled from vague thoughts of self-defense, it took a moment for Irena to focus and reply. "It has to be my voice."

"Ah, yes, our little Natalya." He poured her another brandy, and one for himself.

After another, he got up and walked around the table, taking her hand and pulling her to her feet. This was it, she thought, and wondered if there would be any way she could simply relax, perhaps pretend he was someone else. Or pretend that she cared just a little for him.

It was what she should have done, but her soul would not allow it. "Let me go!" she screamed. She kicked and hit only air.

With one arm wrapped around her chest, hand gripping her hair, he pulled her into the darkness of her cell and threw her facedown on the bed as if she were a child being punished. She was still fighting when he pulled her sweater off her shoulder, ripped the gauze from her wound, reopened it, and pressed his lips to her skin.

He did not drink so much that night. She felt relief . . . and fear. Had he shown restraint only because he wanted something more?

"Go to sleep," he murmured. "I am no brute. Perhaps your blood will be enough to change me. If not, I will not take you until I need to."

He'd said something important with that, but her mind was past focusing. She moved close against him. Stealing his warmth, she slept.

When she woke again it was to darkness broken only by a flickering candle on the table in the corner. The door was shut and when she tried it, she found it locked.

But he had left things for her. The candle to give comfort, the end of a loaf of bread, the brandy, some water and some cheese, and a copy of a Bucharest newspaper with a large story on her "defection." It was the first she'd read of that official line, and as she held the paper close to the light to make out the words, she grew furious. How could they print such a lie! The story came with no evidence. Had Andrei really been allowed to leave or was he dead? She could only hope that Michael had kept his word and that the authorities were quietly looking for her.

With little else to do to pass the hours, she read the rest of the paper, every upbeat piece of obvious propaganda, every distorted shred of international news. Garbage, all of it! Good only to start another fire in the stove.

If that was why he had left it for her, it had worked. Alone in that little room, she began to see Romania through his eyes. She wondered what it must have been like to grow up with that mental power, to live with it in a labor camp, to watch—to feel!—close friends die. Had they known what he was? Had they told him to feed on them after they died? To use their blood to make him strong? Cannibalism was a taboo, a strong one in every civilized culture, but it was what she would have wanted anyone to do, even Michael; anyone who had a chance to live.

It was the moment when she saw her ties with the old ones clearly, and found herself thankful for them. The candle went out. There wasn't another. To pass the time, she practiced her scales then sang Natalya's first aria. Near the end of it, she sensed someone else's pleasure and guessed her jailor had returned. She continued anyway, deliberately trying to be as perfect as she could, to give him some guilt for the future he wanted to steal from her.

He waited until the song ended then opened the door. Seeing the darkness, he looked apologetic. "I did not think it would take so long," he said and pointed through the open outer door to where a deer lay dead in the snow. "I thought some meat would be good for us. With the weather so cold, we can freeze what we don't eat in the snow and not have to worry about catching another for a while."

He went outside, leaving the door open. For a moment she wondered how he had caught the animal, then decided he could not be that fast yet. She came outside, saw the animal's broken leg, the cut throat. Snared, then a quick kill.

"Go inside and start a fire," he told her, an order but a gentle one.

There were split logs beside the door. Heavy ones. She considered using them as a weapon and decided against it. She would have to beat him to death. Even if she'd hated him, she didn't think she had the stomach for that.

He made venison steaks in a cast-iron fry pan, salt and pepper and some of the brandy the only spices. She ate it thankfully, watching him all the while, looking for some sign of what he would want from her that night.

Very little, it seemed. A taste, no more, taken at the table instead of the bed as if he did not trust himself. Then he built up the fire and locked her in her room. She heard him pacing the floor in the main room and sensed his vague disappointment as she forced herself to sleep. Later she heard him leave the cottage but did not get up to follow.

She woke as he joined her in the narrow bed and shivered from the cold. Light leaked around the closed door, coming in from the outer room. "What time is it?" she asked him.

"Ten, maybe later. There is a bitter wind today and the house cannot hold its heat. Better we sleep until it is dark and I can start a fire."

So he worried. That meant someone must be looking for him. Or her. The thought gave her hope as he pulled her closer to him. "I keep you warm," he said.

She didn't resist because he was right, and because she did not see him as a complete brute, she asked, "Wouldn't you be better off with a willing woman? One who loves you and shares your cause?"

"My cause?" He held her tighter and she could almost sense him seeking the words that would explain. "My cause is nothing compared to what I am. There are few like us, Irena. We belong together."

She wanted to laugh, to tell him he was insane, but he was right. The attraction he spoke of was real. If she had never left this country and they had met, she doubted she would lying here unwillingly.

The next day a storm blew huge drifts against the front of the house. With the air so filled with snow, he risked a small fire in the stove, and brought in chunks of snow to melt in their largest kettle.

When he had a full pot of water, he went to the cupboard and took out a little bar of scented soap, the sort tourists lift from plush hotels, a towel, and a toothbrush. He handed them to her and started for the door.

"Wait!" she called. "Do you have anything I can put on so I can wash my clothes?"

"In the cupboard," he said and went outside, shutting the door quickly behind him to keep in the heat.

She pulled out a pair of his jeans, a thick sweater, some wool socks. She stripped and washed quickly then put the clothes on and rinsed out her underclothes, laying them across the back of a chair close to the fire. She wondered if he had gone off somewhere, hoped that everything might dry before he came back.

It was the first time she'd been alone since she'd come here and she used the time well, checking out the cabinet for something she might use as a weapon, pulling at the heavy padlock on the door beside the cupboard. When it did not open, she sat in the chair close to the stove and waited.

The door banged inward, pulled from Michael's grip by a wind so cold it stole all heat from the room. Michael's hair was white from the snow and he looked half frozen. Irena forced herself not to feel pity. If he'd survived a labor camp, he could survive an hour in the storm.

He walked past her to the cupboard and took out the brandy, swallowed from the bottle, and passed it to her. She shivered as she drank but felt a bit warmer from its heat. "Get into bed if you're cold," he told her, his voice oddly remote.

Instead, she stood where she was, watching him as he took off his sweater, then the two layers beneath it, and began to wash. There were scars crisscrossing his back. She felt a sudden stab of pity and retreated to her room to lay damp and shivering beneath the blanket.

He came into the room some time later. He was shirtless, carrying the bottle and a candle. He set the candle down and handed the bottle to her. He watched her face while she drank then took it away and put it beside the candle. His eyes were steady, cold, determined. And she knew.

She retreated to the corner of the bed, pulling her knees close to her chest, wrapping her arms around them, looking away. Could she pretend? she wondered.

His hand closed around her ankles, jerking her body straight and pulling off the pants that were sizes too large for her. As he took off his own, she made a quick dash for the door. Not quick enough; he caught her hair, an arm, flung her back onto the bed. Her head hit the wall. For a moment, she lay stunned. Then he was on her, the weight of his body pressing her down.

If he'd taken her right away, she would have been helpless, but he wanted something more from her, some response. As his hands moved under the sweater, caressing her breasts, she bit him hard on the shoulder. He pulled away, briefly freeing her hands to claw at his face, his shoulders. She hoped he would have new scars, her insults. He caught her arms at the wrists, raising them above her head. His knees forced her legs apart.

Irena stopped struggling when she felt him inside her. It seemed pointless then, a better insult to simply lay passive.

Her chest was sticky with his blood. More from instinct than logic, she raised her head, licked his flesh, drank from one of the deeper cuts, drew him in. It heightened nothing between them. There was no passion to touch. She only sensed a brief rush of happiness in him, when he thought that she might actually be yielding, then disappointment when he realized what she was doing. But he let it happen. Like and like.

One quick, final thrust and it was over. He pulled away, got up, tossed her the clothes. She put them on and turned her back to him, too numb to cry. She didn't move when he lay beside her and planted a kiss on the back of her neck.

"Thank you," he whispered.

For what? she wondered, but did not speak.

"I would have thought less of you if you hadn't fought."

As if his opinion mattered. But then he was in charge so perhaps his was the only one that did.

He took her again in the morning. Again that night and the next. There was a desperation in his rapes, as if he sensed that their time together was running out and he had to take advantage of every moment.

Irena knew he wanted her to conceive, thought it would bind her to him. If he got his wish, it would be fleeting victory. She might have told him that, but sensed it would be the wrong words to say if she ever hoped to see freedom again.

# CHAPTER 35

## RICHARD

There was a frigid wind blowing in our faces as we made that final uphill trek. The hour-long climb drained most of Andrei's strength. I was impatient but the man had been through days of pain and I could hardly blame him for being human. Under the circumstances, he seemed a good sport, so much so that I was the one who made the stops when it seemed he was in danger of passing out from exertion in the thin mountain air.

We halted just after we had the house in sight. It was cut into the earth like our cabin in Dawson but deeper so it seemed more cave than house.

"An old place," Andrei whispered. "Under the snow, the roof is probably thatch so it would be impossible for anyone to see the house until he was nearly beside it. It was done for safety. Even a century ago my people worried about the Turks."

I barely heard the words, my mind already moving through the space inside that low sheltered roof.

There were three rooms. Two were in use. The third held only a cot and was locked and empty. The man and Irena were at the table, his back to the door. Again, I did not dare to touch either mind. "Try to keep up," I whispered to Andrei and ran toward it.

Andrei did his best and was only a few yards behind me when I kicked in the door.

Irene gave a startled cry. "It's—" It took a moment for her eyes to adjust to the sudden burst of light then she began to run to me.

"Go to Andrei," I said to her and she looked past me and saw him coming inside. When he held out his arms she ran into them and began to cry.

Michael Celac got to his feet slowly and turned to face me. He knew exactly what I was and had no fear. I tried to touch his mind, felt him thrust me out.

"Stand very still," he said, his voice soft and calm.

"What!" I wanted to laugh. He would order me?

"Turn around," he said.

I would have ignored him but Irena gave a strangled cry. I glanced behind me and saw Andrei had his bad arm wrapped around her chest, a gun pressed under her chin.

"He will kill her if you don't do exactly as I order you."

That wouldn't be so easy, not if he laid a hand on me. But he seemed to understand that. "Be assured that I don't want any of us to die. Just stand still," he said, his voice low and soothing. "I am going to move up behind you for a little while. I need to touch you, for just a moment."

Later I had much time to meditate on what my father would have done. I assume that his mind would have trapped Andrei's and Andrei would have aimed the weapon at Michael. Some seconds later, Michael would be dead and Andrei helpless, and all Stephen would have to do would be to enjoy his feast, and take Irena home.

Unfortunately, I did not have his mental strength or the experience of years of such dilemmas to draw on and only thought of this response later. Instead my instincts were sleeping, their lack of warning telling me that I would survive. I looked at Irena, her eyes huge with fear, her body shaking, and I knew that for her sake, and my family's sake . . . I would do as he asked. My chance would come; likely soon.

Michael rested his fingers on the nape of my neck then moved them slowly down my vertebrae, touches that made me shiver. When they stopped, his mind opened to me—a sharing that he, not I, had willed. I saw his intent a moment too late and my body exploded in pain. I heard Irena scream as I went numb and my legs gave way. For one impossible moment, I even imagined I might be dead.

Michael caught me as I fell and laid me on my stomach. I struggled to speak, to breathe as I choked on my own blood. Then for a time, the pain retreated into blissful oblivion and I felt nothing at all.

When I woke, I was lying on my belly on a cot in a little room, my face turned toward the door. My body felt absent, my neck and head throbbing. I could breathe, could swallow. But when I tried to move, spasms of pain rolled through my skull. My nerves, cut off from the orders of my brain, convulsed, until the entire cot shook. I moved out of my body, looked down at myself. At my useless legs, my useless arms. At the knife stuck sideways through the back of my neck, the short length of rope that acted as a collar to hold it there. The cut had been made low enough that I could breathe and swallow, high enough that I could move only my head. And as long as that knife remained where it was I would not heal. He had me. But not quite certain of this, he'd also wrapped a rope around my chest and arms and fastened it to the metal frame of the cot I lay on.

He'd wagered his life on the logic of some old folktale. I felt a bit of admiration for his faith and courage, even more for Andrei who'd had to hide his thoughts for all those hours, knowing that if I'd guessed the truth he would have died. The drugs had likely helped him and Michael had probably coached him in how to pull it off. When I got free of this mess, I'd be sure to tell them both what a good con it had been sometime before I granted their last gasped wishes and killed them.

But I had more important things to do than dream of vengeance. My mind, the only thing that still worked as it should, moved through the space to the room beside mine where Irena lay on her side facing the wall, awake and crying as quietly as she was able. Michael was asleep and I decided it was safe to touch his mind.

That was how I learned some of his history, his plans for Irena, his short-term plans for me. A smart man. My admiration only grew when, even in sleep, he caught my presence inside him and woke.

—Don't worry,— he told me. —I fed from you after I tied you down. I'll take more later.—

I asked about the effect.

—Yes, it did make my mind stronger. My body? I don't know. I think so.—

I was impressed and told him so. I heard him laugh through the wall, watched him run his hand underneath Irena's clothes, cup one palm against her breast, another over her sex. I watched him play with her until her body betrayed her. Watched him kiss the back of her neck. Roll her over. Enter her. Feed.

I shared Irena's frozen calm, her pity, but I could do nothing for her but wait.

When Michael returned to sleep, I brushed Irena's mind and told her that I was as comfortable as the situation allowed.

—I'm sorry. It's all my fault,— she told me, the emotions inside her so intense that even her thoughts seemed wooden.

—No, Irena. It's his.—

She asked my advice. I gave it. —When it seems right to do so, tell him the truth about why you left me. Try to find some affection inside yourself that you can transfer to him.—

She couldn't. After she told me her account of the last few days, I could hardly blame her for only wanting him dead.

I spent the rest of that night considering the ways I could help her perfect that vengeance when I was finally free.

# CHAP+ER 36

Michael left Irena's side in the morning. Though she was sleeping, he locked her door before he came to me.

Since I'd retreated from Irena's mind the day before, I had not touched her or him. Instead, I'd simply taken my mind somewhere else. Sometimes I slept, a merciful state. Sometimes I lost myself in memories. Pulled to reality by Michael's sudden presence, I was not surprised to find myself holding on to the shred of the Canadian woods, hopeful that the aurora heating overhead was the reality and this little room some kind of nightmare.

The nightmare won. Michael made that all too clear when he rested his hand on the back of my head. I kept my eyes shut but it made no difference. He was in my mind, and his presence felt much stronger.

He used a knife and the cut on my back was deep. As he pressed his lips to the wound, my nerves short-signaled and my body began to shake. The motion jarred the knife in me. I bit back a scream as the pain returned as sharp as the day before. I tasted my blood in my mouth. I caught his hint of amusement over this until the trained side of him realized that the shaking was only reflex, not fear.

He drank until the well filled in. He made another cut, fed, and

watched. Long after he'd stopped drinking, he continued making
shallower cuts, as fascinated as he was furious at my body's
power. I wondered if he knew how much energy my body had to
expend to heal and if he thought it one more way to torture me.

I tried to retreat into memories but he straddled my back, sat
down hard. He ran his fingers through my hair, down the side of
my face. Touching the legend.

"After I change, do you know what I am going to do to you?"
he asked.

I had a pretty good idea, but this was hardly the time to display too much intelligence or any power.

He rested his fingers on either side of the knife, pushed down
with a tiny bit of pressure, enough that my heart pounded in spite
of my willed calm. "That," he whispered, his breath warm against
the side of my face. "All the way through. Legends say you cannot comprehend your own death, Old One. I doubt that is true for
you here and now. Consider this my gift to you, a sense of what it
is like to be cursed by the promise of death."

He left and locked my door. I heard him go into the next room
and say some words to Irena, her mumbled reply.

I licked my blood from my lips. I was hungry, and not likely
to see a meal for some time. Worse, I was thirsty and my body
would soon start making demands. I wasn't sure how my knowl-
edgeable jailor would react and hoped that Irena had some control over him.

I heard their voices in the outer room, triumph in his and tension in hers. I smelled coffee. Deciding to conserve my sanity as
best I could, I shut my eyes and took my mind back to Chicago
and that first snowy night that Irena let me draw her in.

It was nightfall when Michael returned to me again, carrying a
kerosene lamp. This time, when I looked beyond him, I could see
Irena in the doorway with her hands tied behind her back. Knowing what would happen if she somehow pulled out that blade in
my neck, he'd been wise to take the precaution.

"There! You see. He is as he was. No change. Now, are you
satisfied?" he asked her.

She looked at me. I conveyed what I needed, the thirst strong
enough that I saw her wince, look away so that I only felt her
pity.

He crouched beside me, one hand on my back to steady him.

The knife he carried slipped into the flesh on my shoulder. This time I felt pressure, though still no pain. I heard Irena gasp, stifle a cry. Rage boiled inside me. I think my finger twitched. I hoped he didn't notice.

He didn't. He was too busy reveling in the taste of my blood.

"What will you do when he has nothing left to give and you are still the pig you are now?" Irena asked with contempt.

He ignored her but her words did plant a bit of doubt in him. I told her as much.

"They need water, even more than we do. Have you given him any? And they need blood to live. How can he give his to you if he gets nothing in return?"

If I'd had the ability to do so, I would have crossed my fingers. As it was, I thought of the comfort God gave my mother and I prayed.

"I will not give him that power over me."

"Then let him take from me."

Whatever impact her words had made vanished in his surge of jealousy. He stood, running the side of the blade in his hand along the edge of the one in my neck. Surprised by the pain, I shrieked. Irena lifted her shoulders as if to cover her ears and tried to turn away but Michael held her by the back of the neck, forcing her to look at me.

"Taking! What about all the taking they have done? Now it's my turn."

Knowing I could not help but see, he kissed her. She seemed to yield then bit his lower lip. He pushed her away and back-handed her hard enough that she slammed against the door frame and fell, blood welling on her cut lip. A lesser woman would have been frightened into silence. Not my Irena.

"Taking! They know nothing about any taking! That one has never even been to this country. What can he be guilty of?"

"Shut up, Irena," Michael warned, his voice low and furious.

She stayed where she was, on the floor, helpless except for that magnificent fury. "I will not," she retorted. "I see how you use your power! Do you know how your cousin Viktor used his? He killed his own people then he ate their flesh to take their blood. When an old one killed him, he destroyed a monster and freed us all. When they kill you, they will have done the same."

I felt Michael's surprise at her revelation before his anger took charge of him again. "Don't push me, Irena."

"Or what? Will you devour me too?"

He walked toward her, his hands curled into fists. "Stop defending your lover," he growled.

"My lover? You stupid fool!" She all but screamed the words up at him. "You think your mind is so strong when you don't even know why I came to Romania alone! I left this one when he would not share his blood with me any longer. I don't give a damn about him except that once you take everything he has to give there will be nothing left over for me or your child!"

Her words gave Michael so much hope that he didn't question them. Instead, he rested a hand on my back, the steady pressure quieting the spasms in my muscles. "This is true?" he asked her.

"You ask if it is true?" She laughed and wiped the blood from her cut lip onto the shoulder of her sweater. "A powerful mind like yours should know. Touch mine. See if I have lied."

He hesitated. I suspected he did just that because a moment later, a bit more calm, he asked, "What do you want me to do?"

"I need his blood as much as you do, and more of it so that if we have a child it will be strong. He needs to feed so that he has life to give."

"I need to consider this."

She looked at me, her pity sharper than any knife and far more painful. "While you think about it, at least give him some water. He'll be dangerous if he gets too desperate."

I'd been contemplating the advantages of desperate, but comfort was likely the best I could hope for here.

"He'll last awhile longer," Michael said then dragged her into the outer room and shut the door. I wanted to follow him with my mind, push him a bit, but I didn't dare. Instead I waited.

Some time later, he returned with a cup of water.

After he checked the ropes holding the blade in my flesh, he knelt beside the cot and held the cup to my lips. I drank it all. I could have used more but decided not to ask. He pulled out his knife, cut, and drank, then pulled Irena on her knees beside him. "Go on," he ordered, pushing her face toward the wound in my back.

—You'll force your change, Irena,— I reminded her.

—Changing myself is the only thing I can think to do.— She drank, taking far more than he had.

"And you thought *I* was going to kill him," Michael grumbled when he saw how much she took.

She raised her head. Licked her lips. "If we give some back, he'll be all right," she countered.

In response, he pulled up his sleeve.

"Not you," she said. "If he takes from you he will have too much control over you. Let it be me."

He'd known that; she'd guessed he knew it and had passed his final test. He pulled up her sleeve, made a cut on her upper arm, pressed the wound to my lips. His expression warned me that I had better not hurt her. I found his logic incredible. As to her . . . I tried to convey only thanks and confidence and love and a promise that we would both survive.

"Enough?" Michael asked after a moment.

She ignored him. As I drew her in, I recalled our nights, that passion, far better than any old memory. Knowing what she attempted, I took far more than would have been wise at any other time.

"Enough," Michael ordered when her lips pressed against my back again. But it wasn't bleeding any longer and so she looked at him.

"I need this for our child," she said.

I sensed the depth of the love in her. So did he. She had tapped her feelings for me and transferred them to some tiny ball of cells that might or might not exist in her yet. I felt the pressure against my shoulder again, the knife, her lips.

—You'd change your future for me, Irena?— I asked her.

—I don't know. Hopefully I need only drink enough to become stronger and quicker than he is.—

Michael had a genetic head start. I did not tell her that, only agreed that her plan might work. I wanted to leave her with some hope while I came up with a better idea.

Michael pulled her away from me and out the door. By the time he'd locked it, my shoulder had healed. I studied the two of them in bed in the room beside mine. Shared the lust he thought was love. Shared the loathing she thought was bravery. I saw no sign of any added strength in her, but she seemed to feel that there was.

—Find just a little passion for him, Irena. Enough to give him hope,— I suggested.

I sensed she was about to cry. Not sure what else to do, I touched her mind. I calmed her, then aroused her. She knew. She let me. Acting was all we had.

And it worked. Michael had never met a woman who stood up to him as Irena had. That moment when she finally choked back a cry of passion filled him with joy that ended as soon as he glimpsed the tears in her eyes, that longing for me. She rolled over and, her back to him, shut her eyes.

She slept for a time, then woke in the center of the night and called to me. —When I get away, I should know where we are,— she told me.

She was right. I had her shut her eyes, then caught her mind, moving us both away from the cottage; not down the mountain, but above it.

As we rose, the forest gave way to windswept peaks topped with scrub trees and snow. I saw a trio of rivers below and compared their curves to the Romanian maps I had memorized. The Mureş, the Crişul Alb, the Crişul Repede. I saw that we were northwest of Sibiu, perhaps eighty kilometers from the Old One's keep, and nearly the same distance to the town of Cluf.

She asked where she should go, whom she should trust. I thought of Oprea and how he had betrayed her then tricked me so easily. No, the government here was suspect. I could think of only one place she could go.

—Travel north on the road that runs east of this peak, then take the fork that leads into Cluf and stop some twenty kilometers down. Look to your right and up. You cannot see the top of that peak until you are almost on it, but the Old One's keep is there.—

—You've been to it?—

—Only in my mind, Irena, but I know the way. All my family does. If we get separated, I will meet you there.—

—And the road that goes to it?—

Road? I showed her the narrow trail that curved up and up, an impossible climb for all but the very strong. But she was strong to begin with and the Austra blood had made her all the stronger. If the weather was friendly. If she got that far. If she made the climb. If the Old One saw her as one of his own . . . and how could he not? . . . then, yes, there would be a refuge for her there. And if I were still bound there would be a rescue, too.

I imagined Michael coming face-to-face with the creature he hated most and what his last thoughts might be. Imagination can be so comforting sometimes.

When I was alone again, I considered what my father might

do and decided some risk was in order. My mind moved out of the room, the cottage, soaring away in a widening circle. No people lived in this desolate area but there were deer and fox and, just waking from a long winter's sleep, a famished brown bear and her two small cubs.

There was blood on the back of my shirt, blood on the rope that held the knife in place, blood in my hair. And there was a bloody bandage on Irena's shoulder. The scent might draw the mother bear close enough for me to catch her mind. I had experience with hunting bear, none with controlling them. The rope around the knife also troubled me. A swipe from a powerful paw would only cut that blade deeper into my neck.

On the other hand, my instincts were quiet. Only logic prevented me from calling that she-bear to the cottage door. I would wait another day then decide.

# CHAPTER 37

## PATRICK

Given how tired Richard seemed when I hugged him good-bye at O'Hare, I doubted he'd wake before London. I felt the same way so I bought a *Sun-Times* to keep me occupied until I got home. The "vampire attack" made front page, of course, with the news that Konovic was awake and stable.

I waited the better part of a day then called the hospital and asked if he could see visitors yet. They connected me to his phone.

"I thought I might come and see you, if you're free," I said, trying out my brother's voice on someone unsuspecting.

He understood. "I've been talking to the police all day, but what can an old man remember? Come over. I'll tell the nurses that you're expected," he said.

He was sitting up in bed when I arrived, wearing a black cotton robe and red pajamas beneath them. His neck and arm were bandaged and he had an ice bag balanced on the pillow near his right temple.

He did not look surprised to see me rather than Richard, but I doubted he remembered much of the night before. "Anybody outside?" he asked when he saw me.

"No."

"Good. I want to thank you . . . for coming to see me today, of course."

"Of course. Glad to."

"Bastards would've sucked me dry. Police think they were actually crazy enough to start fighting with each other. They were certainly on something when they came in. The police aren't sure what it is they found in their blood."

"It must have been some psychedelic. News reports say one actually thought he was a bat." I made a flapping movement with my hands.

Konovic started to laugh, thought better of it when he felt the pain. "Show me what happened to them, if you can," he said.

He deserved it. I touched his arm. Passed on the scene Richard had shown me as if I had been there. I wasn't surprised when Konovic smiled. "You know my history?"

"I do."

"So you'll understand that all the time they were feeding on me, I was thinking it was not so different from how I'd survived when I was a boy. Great irony if I died that way."

"Do you think about your past?" I asked.

"Often. More now since the other one made me recall the details. Remembering took some of the anger away. I don't know why, but it did. Don't tell him that, though. He's a pain in the ass and doesn't deserve to know."

His secret was safe with me. "I got the list of places from one of them. Was it the right one?"

"I think so, but there's more. They knew all about you. I didn't tell them, but they knew. They were supposed to give me that location and town. Once I wrote it down, they jumped me, figuring if I was dead you'd never know. Now, over there, they'll be expecting one of you to come for her. You get my meaning, I assume?"

I did. Richard would be walking into a trap.

We talked for a few more minutes until the phone rang. I knew who it was the moment I heard that distinctive voice coming from the receiver. I pressed the side of my index finger against my lips and waved good-bye.

Outside, it had begun to sleet, driving the early evening rush hour crowds off the streets. I recalled something my brother had said about an appointment at the bar I'd taken him to. I had the night, no one to answer to. A delicious sense of destiny rolled through me as I walked toward Lincoln and my prey.

When Richard did not call the next day, or the next, I found myself thinking too often of Ion's warning. When I missed his one call, I swallowed my pride and most of my sense of self-preservation and phoned my father.

Yes, he was furious, but I expected he would tell me to simply wait as I had been doing for some word from him. When he told me to be ready to leave for Romania the next day, I asked if he was concerned for my mother's sake.

"Not entirely. Consider this, Patrick. The ones who made certain Ion received that information had no idea which of us would go to get Irena. They think they are up to facing even a firstborn. We are both right to be worried, yes?"

That chilling thought stayed with me on the flight to London, and during the day we spent there while quick arrangements were made for our visit to Romania. Then we were off, in one of the Austra planes, wearing the cloak of wealth, secure in the protection of a firstborn's power.

When we arrived, he and I and Hunter walked through swirling snow on the tarmac of Otopeni Airport in Bucharest. I carried my passport, Stephen a letter of welcome from the Romanian government, Hunter a loaded Glock automatic in a holster beneath his jacket. There was likely another handgun and ammunition for both in his luggage. Traveling with Stephen, we weren't concerned about being searched.

Stephen and I were formally dressed, in perfectly tailored silk suits and overcoats. Dark glasses hid the blackness of my father's eyes and a bit of his apparent youth. Hunter also wore a suit, though he looked out of place in it and was constantly fiddling with his tie. Even that worked in our favor, as the wealthy often have bodyguards travel with them in countries where kidnappings were a threat.

Stephen looked the part he played, that of a wealthy western businessman heading for trade meetings in Bucharest and Sibiu. He explained that he'd brought along an associate and his nephew who wanted to see some of the country. Since we had come for a meeting with the minister of foreign trade, we walked through customs, Stephen brushing aside the few short, polite questions with a languid wave of his hand.

In a call to Bucharest made only hours before we left London, my father had explained that our firm wished to increase shipments of Tarda water and purchase some special silica that is used to create a deep teal shade in glass. He would also begin talks with the Romanian government for the purpose of setting up a glass house as an investment in the Eastern Bloc. The possibility of investment gave us more leverage than if we had come merely to buy.

That evening, the government's liaison to our group, accompanied by his wife and two pretty girls who seemed too forward to be his nieces, took my father and me to a performance of the Romanian National Philharmonic, then to a reception at a private bar. Drinks, and a great deal of champagne, were on the house. It seemed a celebration, though I was never sure exactly what we celebrated. I held the glass as if I were sipping it, pouring bits of it into my charming escort's glass whenever she wasn't looking.

Stephen seemed at home here, politely meeting the party elite who had come to call. Everyone seemed drunk beyond our mental control, but in marvelous good humor. Word of the gathering got out and the room grew crowded. Each new addition coming through the doors drew Stephen's brief attention.

I knew who he hoped to see, watched with him. A bit after midnight, our quarry arrived.

Prime Minister Georghe Oprea did not look like a politician. Tall and thin and wearing an ill-fitting pin-striped suit and a pair of gold-rimmed glasses, he seemed more like one of my well-tenured professors.

We waited until he'd gotten a drink, said a few words to friends. Then Stephen touched my arm. —Come,— he said.

I followed him across the room to meet the man. Oprea joined us in a quiet corner and inquired how things were in America. After a quarter hour of news, Stephen scanned the room, then moved closer to the prime minister.

"Is there someone here from the securitate?" he asked.

"No one would spy on us," Oprea answered.

"No, you misunderstand. I mean someone who can join us for a few minutes of conversation somewhere much more private?"

Oprea scanned the room and focused on a man difficult to ignore. "There! General Luchien," he said, pointing to the huge man making his way to the bar. He was built like an Olympic wrestler, huge but with only a bit of fat. I doubted there were many men in this room that his hands could not snap in two.

"Is he devoted to his family?" Stephen asked.

"As much as I am to mine."

"Then, please, have him join us."

Some minutes later, the four of us retired to a private room off the back of the bar. It was time to inform the right people of what they already knew.

Stephen explained that my brother was engaged to marry Irena after she returned from the tour. When she disappeared, the young man was certain she'd been kidnapped though the rest of the family was inclined to believe the government's story that she had defected. Convinced otherwise and forbidden to take action, he had used his visa to get into the country and had also disappeared.

"We are happy you've explained this to us," Luchien said in a bass voice perfectly suited to his size. "We were aware that Richard Austra had entered our country. Though his means were not quite legal, I am sure rules can be stretched under the circumstances."

Stephen's palms were pressed together, index fingers against his lips as if he were weighing how to explain a delicate matter. He looked at Luchien as he went on. "The circumstances are the problem, General. You see, we have been contacted and asked to deposit a ransom of two million dollars in a numbered Swiss account if we wish to see my nephew or the young woman again. So it seems that she did not defect, as your government has reported, and now the ones who took her also have him."

Luchien bit back a retort. His muscles tensed.

"You must understand my firm's position," Stephen continued. "One of our family is missing along with Miss Sava. And now this demand for money. We have reason to believe that the persons holding them intend to use the ransom to finance a civil war. I cannot allow our firm to become involved in that, however unwillingly, nor can we invest in a country whose government is unable to control its own people."

Luchien's face was taut with fury at the insult, his huge paws curled into fists. But he wisely stayed silent.

"It would seem that our local police have not completely understood this matter, General. Please look into it first thing tomorrow," the prime minister said, his voice soothing. He turned his attention back to us. "And I will personally speak with my nephew to see if he can recall anything else that will be of importance."

"Was he the one taken with Irena?" I asked.

"And beaten. He is lucky to be alive," Luchien commented.

"I would like to thank him personally for how he tried to help her."

"I understand," Oprea said. "Perhaps he could visit you at your hotel tomorrow afternoon after he speaks with me? Luchien, have someone arrange both meetings, please."

The general pushed his bulky body out of his chair. Before he could leave, Stephen looked up at him and said, "The champagne has been good, but would you stay for a glass of Chivas, a toast for success in all these complicated matters?"

As Luchien went off to find a bottle and glasses, Stephen touched the prime minister's hand. The man's face went slack, the eyes behind his glasses unfocused. He stayed that way until Luchien came back with a bottle and four shot glasses. Stephen poured full glasses for the men, a third of that for himself, a symbolic sip for me.

"To our triumphs," Stephen said, raising his glass.

We drained our glasses. A few minutes later, we were out in the cold clear air. I drew in a few deep breaths to settle my stomach as we waited for the car and driver. It was the prime minister's Mercedes.

Inside we found an open bottle of Cordon Rouge and two glasses. "Elena Ceauşescu's favorite drink. Thoughtful of her," Stephen commented loudly enough for the driver to hear.

The car drove through the dark and empty streets, swift and smooth with baroque music filling the space.

# CHAPTER 38

The Romanian government had provided us with a third-floor suite at the Intercontinental. Three bedrooms and a great room with a well-stocked bar, all compliments of the communists for their bourgeois guests. When we opened the door, I saw that Hunter had rearranged the furniture so that the sofa now faced the door. He was lying on it with the Glock on the table beside him, a second one hidden between him and the sofa back so that, if he were disturbed and could not reach one, he would have the other. Sound asleep when we were in the hallway, he was sitting up, gun on his knees by the time the door opened.

He laid the weapon down, stood, and stretched. "Did you have a good night?" he asked, his voice hoarse from the sudden waking.

Stephen handed him the champagne. "I've brought you a present. We've both had more than enough," he said; adding, —Patrick and I are going out.—

—I flew all this way just to sleep?—

—Andrei Oprea lives in Herăstrău. Three miles on foot. Better you sleep.—

"Well, I might as well get my share of the bubbly before it

goes flat," Hunter said aloud. He clinked the bottle against one of the glasses then touched the side of his index finger to his forehead in a casual salute. His signal.

—I spoke to the staff then cased the place. Mikes in this room are in the base of the phone and the heat vent and a camera in the outlet in the corner by the window. They had a good view until I redecorated. Cameras and mikes in all the bedrooms: mikes in the phones, cameras in the vents above the closet and aimed at the beds.— He beat his middle finger against the other palm and grinned. —I've been told there are dead spots in front of the closets and in Stephen's room at the windows. It's your best exit anyway.—

—Are they using . . . night vision, is it called?— I asked.

—My sources say no.—

—Are they watching or recording?— Stephen asked, as always concerned about any of the family being photographed.

—I believe just watching, but I can't be sure. I suggest you change clothes near the closet and try not to face the damned thing.—

—Why not just find whoever is recording and make them turn it off?— I asked.

—Someone else might come and turn it back on. Better to just be careful. If we slip, I'll have the tapes erased before we leave,— Stephen replied.

I went to change out of the suit. Stephen switched clothes in the main room, making small talk with Hunter while he did.

He noted the prime minister's concern as well as Luchien's patriotism. "I've no doubt they'll find that pair of idiots and our negotiations can proceed," he said.

"Are you certain building here is for the best?" Hunter asked.

"Better here than with the damned Hungarians. No telling who will be in power in Budapest in a year or two." There was no love lost between Romania and Hungary, expecially since the revolution in the fifties, and Stephen played to it.

A few minutes later, I slipped along the closet wall in Stephen's room and over to the window. Dressed in black, padding around in the darkness, we looked like a pair of well-heeled cat burglars, a most apt analogy.

Stephen's window opened onto the side of the building. Safer than going down the front but we'd have to push off to avoid landing in the bushes directly beneath us. The jump back up looked possible, but barely, and there was a narrow ledge between the first and second floors, a handhold if it were needed.

I might have scanned the space below myself, but Stephen's mind is stronger. I waited until he motioned me out, landed on hands and feet, then moved out of his way.

Keeping to the quiet side streets, we ran silently through the night, stepping into the shadows from time to time to avoid being seen from an occasional passing car. Only the wild dogs of the city noticed us and though they barked they did not dare approach us.

We'd just reached the open land to the east of the sports complex and the chain of lakes that separated the city proper from the northern suburbs when I noticed a woman standing in the shadows beneath the lime trees that lined the boulevard, her black coat and scarf billowing in the wind.

When she saw us, she did not look incredulous at the sight of our bodies, long and lean and low to the ground as we ran. Instead, she raised one pale hand and waved a slow, knowing greeting.

Catherine? I wondered. I wanted to get close enough to her to see who or what she was, but she drew the shadows close around her and vanished into the darkness. I wanted to call to my father to stop but he was far ahead of me and I had to fight to catch up.

Herăstrău was known for plush apartments for party members and, more importantly, foreign diplomats—a mix perfect for espionage. The streets were shaded by beech trees and every building had its own garden space. The neighborhood might have been pretty in the summer but in the frozen dark it seemed only as bleak and empty as the rest of the city.

Andrei Oprea's rooms were on the main floor in the rear of an old stone building. They were entered through a little porch with a decorative metal railing. Though it was well after midnight, Andrei was not alone. Given his injuries, I was surprised; more so when I realized his partner was a man.

—Someone with the German embassy,— Stephen told me. We leaned against the wall beneath Andrei's bedroom window, close enough to it that I could hear the men's muffled voices, the occasional squeak of a bedspring. I looked at Stephen, saw the hint of a smile on his lips, gone when he shut his eyes.

"Oook, my head," the German moaned an instant later. The

springs complained as he rolled off the bed. I knew his pain well. Though I'd never received that strong a mental slap, I sympathized.

"What! What is it?" Andrei asked.

"A damned migraine! I've never had one come on so fast. I feel like my skull is about to explode."

"Should I call a doctor?"

"No . . . no, they would wonder what I was doing here. I'll go upstairs. If a few aspirin don't tame it, I'll call for one myself."

"There are morphine tablets in the kitchen. Swallow one now and take another with you for later."

The German asked if Andrei needed them. From the way they spoke to each other, I guessed they'd been meeting for some time.

—Cameras?— I asked.

—I'd assume so.—

I wanted to question more, but Stephen held up his hand, pressed the other against the bricks below the window, his concentration intense.

Though his doctor had ordered Andrei to avoid cigarettes until his ribs healed, he suddenly decided that he needed some fresh air and a smoke. He put on a flannel robe and slippers and, in spite of the cold and the pain that walking still caused his bruised ribs, picked up his cigarettes and shuffled onto the back porch. He lit one and, leaning on the metal rail on our side, exhaled smoke into the night.

He thought he heard something move on the side of the building. Curious, he looked our way, straight into Stephen's eyes. Stephen had the man even before he felt his first surge of fear.

—You know why we are here, yes?—

No answer. In spite of the morphine he still took, Andrei's heart was racing.

—Answer me!—

Andrei tried to speak and could not.

—Think the words, fool!—

—Yes!— He nodded, too. That much motion was allowed him.

—Come and join us, Andrei.—

Andrei did not want to move, but he had no choice. He shuffled down the stairs and into the shadows and, as directed, leaned against the wall. His lips were pressed together, his pretty eyes looking from Stephen to me and back again, his body trembling with pain and cold and fear. Irena had not done the man justice in her description of him. Under different circumstances, I would have found him a perfect conquest. Now, with my father ripping through his defenses to expose his guilt, all I wanted to do was devour him.

My fingers traced the artery from his breastbone to the hinge of his jaw, stopping where the pulse was strongest. —Where are my brother and Irena Sava?— I asked.

—The ones who took her beat the hell out of me. I was blind-folded. I never saw!—

Stephen's hand slipped under Andrei's robe, palm pressed tight against the bare skin just below his taped ribs. —You know,—Stephen insisted. He moved his mouth close to Andrei's ear so he could whisper, "You helped take him."

Andrei barely thought the words, but we caught them. —Michael went too far with this.—

"So Michael has," Stephen whispered as his mind brushed against the man's, an invasion too insistent to refuse.

—An idiot!— Andrei replied, responding to the spark of anger that Stephen had ignited. —He's gone too far!—

—Your cigarette, Andrei,— I said to him. He raised it to his lips, inhaled. As the tip flared, I grinned, felt the fear rising stronger, my soul reacting to it. I took the cigarette from his hand and dropped it in the snow.

—What did Michael do, Andrei?— I asked.

Andrei fought us, managing to avoid an answer until Stephen broke him completely and laid bare the details of how they'd trapped my brother and what Michael planned to do with him. I sensed the rage building in my father, the only outward sign of it in how his hand inched upward beneath the tape supporting the cracked ribs until his fingers were over Andrei's heart. We were all aware of it, Andrei, who knew the damage an old one could do, most of all.

—And they are still there?— Stephen asked, the pressure of his hand increasing. Andrei would have tried to push him away but he could not move.

"They were this morning. Our own check on them," he whispered and shut his eyes. Tears rolled from the edges of them and down the sides of his face. "Please," he said, not sure what he was begging for.

I wanted to be the one to drink in the last bit of his life and passion. And yet, I hoped for some better outcome. —You are party. You can have everything you want here. Why would you risk it all?— I asked, hoping for an answer that would make vengeance uncomplicated.

—What do I have? You've seen the pigs that run this country. My uncle was a good man once, now he lets the others make me their state whore. When we are strong, no one will be able to harm us. Then I will happily castrate the ones who have ruined my life.—

—If you knew what we were, why didn't you come to us and ask for help?— I continued.

—You know why,— Stephen told me, grip tightening.

—No, it is not that ancient pact that keeps us away. Let me answer, please,— Andrei begged, fighting for another few minutes of life. Stephen decreased the pressure, enough that the man could speak, though only in a whisper. "If Michael changed, he could change another and another. We would have done it already if you'd left us the strong ones from among our children."

—We do not take them!— I retorted. I saw him wince from my anger. Stephen would have made him cry.

"Where do you think we take them?" Stephen asked.

"To the mountaintop. To the grave. We don't know. Some are young. Some almost adults. I know names. This is not a rumor."

"And Irena?"

"We knew what she was soon after she was born. Grandchild of an old one, well matched to Michael who is a son. We sent her away to protect her. Now she is with her own."

"If everything you believe is true, why would we allow her to return here?" I asked.

"I . . ." He spoke too loud. Stephen silenced him. —I don't know. That makes no sense, I admit that.—

—We can't kill them all,— I said privately to my father.

Stephen looked from me to Andrei.

"Please," I whispered.

—Very well,— Stephen said, resignation in the answer. He gripped Andrei's chin, forcing the man to look at him.

—I give you a gift of time, Andrei. You will help us find my son. Then it will be his choice if you live or die. If he is merciful, we may even help you discover where your own have been taken.—

—How can I help you? We cannot even be seen together. Everyone will be suspicious.—

—Of me?—

—They know nothing about you and so they suspect everything.— His words were as bitter as his thoughts.

Their faces were only inches apart, Andrei still staring into
Stephen's dark eyes. They stood that way, still and silent, as
Stephen's hand moved up Andrei's chest, the side of his neck.
One long finger traced the line of Andrei's jaw, the gesture inti-
mate, knowing.

—Then it is time we provide them with a most unexpected
discovery about me. You do not wish to be the state whore, Andrei? Very well, tomorrow you will become mine. Attend that
meeting prepared to make a powerful conquest, and no one will
question our being together. Instead, they will thank you.—

Stephen never took his eyes off Andrei's as he raised the
man's wrist to his lips and bit (harder than needed, but the man
deserved the pain). He took far more than a taste, enough that
Andrei would feel the loss, then moved aside so I could do the
same. As I drank, I felt Andrei shiver with weakness and fear,
heard Stephen's words flow into Andrei's mind, a dangerous
punishment:

—You will remember this meeting, Andrei. But if you try to
inform anyone of it, you will feel such pain that the torture another could inflict would be nothing by comparison. Try too often, and you will not be able to think at all. Remember that. If
you wish to test what I have done, go inside and try to speak of
our meeting to those cameras aimed at your bed.—

Andrei shook his head, too quickly it seemed.

We left him standing in the cold. Pausing in the shadows, we
waited until he shuffled to the porch and stopped to have another
cigarette. He needed three matches to get it lit.

I did not feel sorry for him, not even the next day when, in the
company of his uncle and the general, we met with him again in
our suite and offered our thanks for everything he had done for
Irena. Stephen touched his arm and inquired about his health. A
natural thing to do since Andrei's eyes were red from lack of
sleep, his speech slurred from the extra morphine he'd taken simply to get out of bed.

I had a vision of him then, fallen to his knees on the soft carpet in his bedroom, the exposed hand beneath the broken arm flat
on the floor for balance, the other pressed to his forehead. His
lips were tight together because if he were to open them he would

scream in pain and someone would come to inquire what was wrong. Inquiries might lead to suspicions, then to interrogation, even with his family connections.

As Stephen asked about Andrei's abduction, his dark eyes were fixed on the man as if he were prey. Even when the topic switched to our potential investment in the Banat, Stephen's attention seemed to drift in the direction of his handsome guest. It was Prime Minister Oprea, not one of us, who suggested that Andrei would be the perfect guide for our tour of the Banat region the following day.

When it was time for everyone to go, Stephen rested a hand on Andrei's and looked at the prime minister. "We will be leaving early tomorrow and I'm sure the city will have its usual traffic snarl in the morning. Perhaps your nephew might show us some sights after this meeting, then stay with us tonight?"

Andrei looked ready to faint from fear, but he'd learned his lesson well and agreed. At the other end of the table Andrei's uncle and General Luchien misunderstood his reaction and exchanged a quick, knowing glance. It seemed that young Andrei had made a powerful conquest. Of course, someone had.

# CHAPTER 39

## RICHARD

A winter storm and a sudden blast of northerly air drove the mother bear back into the shelter of her den. I did not try to override the maternal instinct that had her wrapped tightly around her cubs to keep them warm. Instead, I interpreted the storm as a sign and waited, all the time trying to conceive of a different and less risky means of escape.

The following day was frigid and clear, which meant no fire. When Michael came to me later, he was wearing a black wool coat over his clothes for extra warmth. Irena followed, looking deceptively festive in the tie-dyed jacket and hat I had bought for her in Montreal. As before, her hands were tied behind her back.

Michael drank first then pulled Irena down to kneel beside him. His grip on her shoulder was hard enough that she winced. He'd become stronger, and so suddenly that he didn't even realize that he had hurt her.

The cut he made for her was lower and deeper, his mind filled with regret that I could not feel any pain. It seemed that the predatory aspect of my nature that had considered all the terrible ways for him to die was a part of him now. He'd been fantasizing about my end in much the same way I did his, and his ideas were just as terrible.

I sensed that he was close to the change, close enough that soon he would not need my blood any longer. I had to act. I got Irena's attention, told her about the bear.

—You can control that?— Damn it! Did she have to sound so doubtful?

—You saw me with the wolves. I can do this.— A false bravado. Given my circumstances, I didn't feel strong and my reservations passed to her with the rest.

—You said the wolves were your mother's pets. I won't help you. It's too dangerous.—

Dangerous. Michael with his hands on that blade was dangerous. The bear would be merely annoying.

That gave me a sudden, much safer, idea. —I will use the bear to distract Michael. While he is dealing with it, you can untie the rope and pull out the knife.—

—Michael will have your door locked.—

—Not if I call the bear to us later, after dinner, while you and he are in here.—

—My hands will be tied then.—

—My teeth are sharp.—

The timing would have to be perfect. I sensed her fear, justifiable since she would be in no position to defend herself against Michael or the beast.

—He's right on the edge of change, Irena. When that happens, he won't need me.—

—I'll need you. I'll make that clear to him.—

—Then you'll have him for the blood. Please, Irena!—

I assured her then assured her again. I could do this. It would work. When Michael was outside using the last bit of twilight to cut wood for the fire, Irena pulled the bandage off the wound on her shoulder and dropped it on the other side of the snowdrift just outside the door—one more lure to bring the beast to our den.

Not that I needed her cooperation. Michael had dug up the frozen deer carcass and hacked off pieces for stew, leaving the snow speckled with scraps of frozen meat. I called to the animal, drew its attention to the cottage, and waited while it studied the space and sniffed the air and finally fell for the lure.

The sow's skin, stretched by the autumn gorging and loosened by the winter's fast, sagged and shook as she lumbered down the hill in pursuit of food. She was over twice Michael's weight and like me and mine she had the advantage of teeth and claws. Michael, kneeling by the stove and feeding the crackling fire, did not hear the bear digging up the frozen meat. Irena did and retreated to the bedroom and shut the door. —What will you do if she gets full and starts to leave?— she asked.

Irena was right. The door to my room was locked, but that bear needed to come in now while it was still hungry. I sent it a vision of a table full of nuts and berries and honey and every other delicacy I'd ever seen Canadian grizzlies all but swoon over. And every last bit of it was waiting behind the locked door of my room.

The scent of the onions Michael had begun to fry added a touch of reality to my mental lure. Drawn forward, the bear broke down the door and pushed her bulky body through.

Michael whirled and dove for the knife he had left on the table. He almost had it when one swipe of a huge paw sent him flying against the hot stove, the knife skittering across the floor. Michael yelped with pain and rolled away from the blaze, keeping low to the ground.

I called to the hungry creature, feeding her more visions of glorious, glorious food inside my room. Obedient, the beast butted her shoulder against my door, hard enough that I heard the frame crack. She hit it again and the door crashed inward. Michael, whether guessing what I intended or concerned that he would lose the key to his immortality, grabbed his knife, pushed himself to his feet, and went after the beast.

She turned, swiping at him again. I heard him bellow with anger and pain, backing away from the door. She followed.

—Irena!— I all but screamed, forcing her out of the fear-induced paralysis that had taken hold of her.

Irena darted around the cupboard and ran to me. Trying not to cause me pain, she began to undo the knot on the rope. She'd managed to loosen it a bit when Michael realized what she was up to and came after her.

—Pull it out, Irena. Don't worry about untying the rest of it.—

She reached for the handle, but as her fingers brushed it, Michael pulled her away from me and flung her toward the door where the bear was on all fours trying to wedge itself through the narrow opening.

Irena rolled sideways, pressed herself flat against the wall behind what was left of the broken door, and waited, frozen with fear. I doubted I would be able to pry her from that spot to help me again until the danger to her would be too great.

Michael looked from me to the beast to Irena. Not certain what part of the crisis to handle first, he decided the best course was to minimize distraction. He grabbed Irena and threw her over the bear. When Irena landed on the beast's back, it reared on its hind feet and snarled. Irena rolled off and landed hard in the outer room, dazed and far too frightened to try to fight her way back to me.

—Run, Irena!— I told her. —I will meet you on that mountaintop!—

She hesitated, too worried about me to go, too frightened to come and help.

—Nothing can happen to me. Now, damn you, run!—

She might have asked why, if nothing could happen to me, she had to run anywhere, but she was wise enough not to argue with my lack of logic. Instead, she grabbed her hat off the floor and scrambled down the hill as fast as she could move. She slipped in the deep snow, rolled, caught herself, and went on. Michael, trapped inside my cell by the brute, had no way to stop her.

As for me, my rescuer came when called, one huge paw raking my back. The swipe loosened the knife, enough that I had some feeling in my shoulders, more in my feet. I wiggled my fingers, made a fist. In a moment I could move my shoulders as well. I shrugged them back against the edge of the blade. It moved a few centimeters out of my spine.

Michael saw this and started for me. I knew what he intended and had no way to stop him except with the bear. Fortunately, the beast's fury at being denied her meal matched my desperation. Bellowing, she slashed at Michael's leg, brushing him away from me. I smelled his blood. I felt a bit of triumph; however indirectly, I had caused the pain.

But it was my blood the creature wanted. Mine, and she would not share her kill. I'd convinced her of that in the last few moments and so she was on me. Her claws raked over my back, breaking the rope that held me to the cot, shredding my shirt and the flesh beneath. I felt a glorious agony, bit back a scream.

Michael laughed with relief and backed toward the door and through it. Blood from the slash on his leg coated his pants and he could barely walk, but he thought himself still in charge. "So the predator is about to be eaten," he called to me. "Such a fitting end."

I heard him banging around in the outer room. No fool, I knew what he intended and had no way to stop him.

Some feeling had returned to my back, enough that I could feel the searing passage of the animal's claws. Her tongue licked the wounds, her teeth tore at them when they started to close. Enraged, she swiped at me, rolling me off the cot and onto the floor to expose the softer flesh of my belly. The fall jarred the knife and the wound in my neck began bleeding. I felt her rake me again, the pressure of the cut deep and blessedly painful. She licked at the cuts, nose digging in the deepest one, trying to get a hold to rip my flesh.

I smelled smoke. Michael's idea and not a bad one, I thought. The bear turned away from me and looked toward the doorway where Michael had shoveled the burning wood from the fire. If I did not act quickly, predator and predator would be roasted. I took the most dangerous course, forced the bear's attention back to me. I was the one who had lured it away from its den and its cubs and brought it to this deadly place. Enraged, it swiped at me again, harder this time. Hard enough that my body rolled sideways and the knife fell free. I ordered one final swipe, the force of it thrusting me hard under the metal-framed cot.

I had no more need of my savage savior. Once released from my mental hold, the bear became frantic to escape and return to her children. I am not sure how I found the control, but out of gratitude for what she had done for me and a desire to be rid of her before she did any more damage, I calmed her enough to show her the way. She made it through the main room and outside just as the timbers in the front of the house started to burn.

My stomach was ripped open, the flesh of my back in shreds. The air was so thick with smoke that even near the floor I could hardly breathe. So I waited, praying that the flames would not reach me before my body gave me means of escape. I recalled Catherine's visit, the only time I had felt the full pain of flames, a pain Father says is the worst kind of all.

I had survived that without a scar. I would survive this.

Some minutes later, I could move my legs and my arms but the flames had spread to the broken door and were dancing across the ceiling of my room. Cinders rained down on the mattress above me and the bedding began to smoke. I was blistered and a bit dizzy from lack of blood, but whole.

More searing moments passed before I rolled out from underneath the metal frame of the cot. My hair was singed. My stomach still bled but I could move. Could stand. Could run!

Keeping low to the ground, I made for the splintered doorway and quickly surveyed what remained of the outside room. Half the ceiling had caved in; the walls were on fire. The outer doorway had vanished, replaced by a boiling patch of smoke.

Squinting to keep my eyes clear, I ran for the smoke, not at the speed I'd achieve later, but quickly enough. My clothes were on fire by the time I reached clear air. I rolled in the snow to put them out then lay looking up at the magnificence of the stars.

And I drew a breath into my scorched lungs and laughed with a deep and incredible happiness that sprang from the core of what I am. *"Szekorny!"* I called to the world and laughed again. True, I had not lived many years, but in all of them I had never felt so alive.

As the euphoria faded, the need that came from so many wounds made its demands. My mind spiraled outward, seeking life. I sensed the bear and her cubs, but I was not so desperate that I would devour my savior or her children. I went further, but the one I sought had moved out of my range. I thought it a pity that Michael hadn't waited to be sure the fire finished me. I expected that he would pursue Irena. If so, I would find him soon enough.

In the meantime there were deer in these woods. Too weary to hunt and with a need for life and a healing sleep hard upon me, I pushed myself to my feet and called to the first course of what I hoped would be my feast.

# CHAPTER 40

## PATRICK

By the time Irena paused to catch her breath and turn to see if anyone was following her, thick smoke was rising from the mountaintop. Her first thought was to return to help Richard, but she realized that by the time she climbed back up the battle would be over. Given his position when she left, it was understandable that she would brush away her tears, say a prayer for his survival, and go on with only a slim hope that he would meet her at the Old One's keep.

When she reached the narrow dirt road at the bottom of the hill, she hesitated. Her destination lay to the left, in the wilder part of the Bihor Range. Taking a right would lead to the main road. There might be cars she could thumb a ride with or houses where she could find shelter. But that would also be the first place Michael would look for her.

The sun had set and the air was growing colder. The tears on Irena's face cooled as she looked into the wind and shivered. Survival was more important than speed now. Winter forced her decision. She headed for the main road and help.

When she reached it, she walked to the right, the opposite direction from the way Michael would likely assume she went. She kept to the bushes along the side of the road until after dark, then began walking toward what would have been oncoming traffic had there been any cars on that road at all.

She'd gone nearly two miles before she saw headlights, high enough that they had to belong to a truck. Mumbling a quick prayer for luck, she stuck out her thumb. She could not make out details of the truck in the dark but the engine coughed as it pulled to a stop beside her and she saw the rust covering the bumpers, the front one held up with a rope. She doubted that any party member would dare to be seen in it.

The passenger door creaked as it opened, revealing a lined face she could barely see in the dark. "Come," the driver called. "The heater does not work but it will be warmer than standing out there."

She took the old man's hand because he offered it. She was thankful she had when the high step into the cab proved to be too much for her. Until that moment she had not realized how exhausted she'd become.

The worn fabric seats were topped with embroidered slipcovers and there were matching covers on the door handles and steering wheel as well. She saw a bottle on the passenger floor half filled with cigarette butts. Studying the driver, she realized he was more weathered than old, most likely a farmer, she thought.

"My name is Olha. And you?" he asked.

"Irena."

"Where are you going?" Olha asked as he coaxed the engine into gear.

She thought before she spoke, recalling a town beyond where she needed to be. "To Nucet," she replied.

"You won't get there tonight."

"I know."

"I can drop you at the crossroads where I turn off or you can come into Teius with me. Then you'll be sure you won't freeze before morning. Tomorrow you can go on."

"I . . . I have no money to pay for a room."

"What?" He looked at her for so long she was sure they would run off the road. "You aren't from this area," he concluded aloud. The question he'd been too polite to ask was why a stranger had been standing back there in the dark, alone.

Not that he didn't expect some sort of answer. She thought of how she must look even in the dim dashboard lights and made up a story that was almost true. "I was with someone. We were hiking but when it was time to go back he got demanding. He hurt me. I got out of his car, threw his keys in the ditch, and ran."

He pulled a flashlight from between the seat and shone it in her face. He saw the bruises. Her tears. "He did that to you?" he asked, voice rising in fury.

She nodded, raised a hand to brush back her hair. As she did, Olha saw the rope burns on her wrists. "And that, too?" he asked.

"He tried to tie me up."

"I should drive you into Aiud. You should go and tell this to the police and they will catch him."

Spoken like a man who had daughters. She tried to think of an excuse but none made any sense. As they reached a curve in the road, she saw Michael standing in the center of it, his pants bloody. She slid down in her seat. "Drive by, please," she whispered, her voice breaking. If he was alive, Richard had to be dead.

Olha shifted up a gear. Passed him by. "You hurt his leg like that?" he asked.

"He attacked me. I defended myself. When I kicked him away, he fell on his own knife."

"Well, you had good reason."

"He deserves to be arrested. But I think I punished him enough. And this way my . . . my reputation will be intact."

"Perhaps you punished him too much? Maybe I should go back and pick him up before he turns to ice?"

"No! Please! I could not sit so close to him."

His sympathy returned. He patted her hand. After what she'd been through, she had to fight the urge to pull away. "Someone else will likely drive by," Olha said.

Which only meant that, wherever Irena slept that night, it would not be soundly.

Fortunately Teius proved to be a larger town than she'd expected. As they drove through down the narrow main street, Irena saw houses on either side of her, so close to the road that there was no sidewalk and barely a space between them. Olha turned onto a narrow brick-paved alley and pulled up behind a tiny house. Stucco and exposed bricks caught the lights as he parked.

"I should not allow this without taking you to the police first. But I will not put you through so many questions when you are so cold and tired. Come inside and I will make you some tea." They walked to the house and he opened the door and stepped back so she could enter his kitchen first.

The room was what she'd expected, given the state of his car. The linoleum floor was worn through by the sink and door, the wood beneath it darkened and splintered. The thick green curtains on the windows were brightly embroidered along the edges but gray with dust. "Someone does good work," Irena said, pointing to the needlework.

"My wife made them," Olha said. "She died last year. Something in her brain burst." He started water heating on the electric stove then laid out a tea ball, a canning jar of tea, and a cup and saucer.

"When the water boils, make tea for yourself." He buttoned up his coat.

"You're going out?" Irena asked.

"Just to my son's. Nearby. He will want to know that I am all right. I was late, you see."

He went out the back way. She watched him walk down the alley then went and stood by the stove, welcoming the warmth as she waited for the water to boil.

She'd just finished her first cup and was about to pour another when the door opened. The man who came in with Olha was huge, with the same dark hair as Michael, the same gray eyes. She screamed when she saw him, jumped to her feet and backed away, holding the pot of scalding water in front of her like a weapon.

"It's all right, little one," the man said as if speaking to a small, frightened child. "I am a policeman. No one will hurt you anymore."

She wanted to run but there was no fight left in her. Wisely, the policeman did not try to touch her. Instead he sat at the table while Olha fixed them all tea. They did not speak of how she had come here, but as they drank it Irena noticed how both men stared at the rope burns on her wrists, their expressions sympathetic. She did not repeat what she had told Olha but instead told the truth.

"Did the man who took you have a scar on his face? A missing fingertip?"

- Irena nodded. "He said his name was Michael Celac."

The policeman seemed satisfied. He waited until she had finished her tea, then stood. "You come with me. I have a place you can sleep tonight."

"But Michael Celac, the man who . . . who attacked me, is getting away!" she explained.

"He is wounded. He won't get far in the dark. We'll find him at first light. Now come." He wrapped the blanket tightly around her and with an arm over her shoulder began leading her away.

Outside, she saw that a few of the neighborhood men had gathered to find out why the policeman had come to Olha's house. Though she had no reason to be terrified, Irena felt it building in her, instinct making her scream a warning. "Please. You don't understand. I am the American opera singer, Irena Sava, and I was kidnapped." She struggled for the right words. "He . . . he took me." She spoke loudly, hoping that all would hear and remember. Not much insurance, but all she had.

An hour later, she'd been given a hard roll and jam and some coffee, bitter from reused grounds but hot. They'd put her in a tiny, ill-lit room in the police station. It had a cot with a badly stained mattress taking up all of one wall, a table and two chairs in its center. She sat at the table, clutching the warm coffee cup as she told her story once, then again and again. Both local police heard it, but neither seemed to believe it until she switched from Romanian to English. They knew the language, enough to understand that she spoke it well.

"Call your superiors in Bucharest. They must have a description. If that isn't enough for you, I'll be happy to sing."

She actually made the three of them smile. "The papers say Irena Sava defected. Perhaps you had a change of heart?" the large man who'd brought her here asked.

Until now, he'd been kind, though a bit dense. Now she wondered if his kindness was an act, if her reported defection could not be undone. She shivered. The officer nodded as if he understood and went to get her more coffee, returning with a full cup. "It was a mistake," she muttered. "I did not defect."

"I called our superiors in Sibiu. Someone will be coming soon. Try to sleep in the meantime." The officer did not look at her as he spoke and his words seemed cold. When they left her, they locked the door. She decided she was thankful. He hadn't had to tell her anything and the matter would be sorted out soon enough.

She pulled the blanket she had come in up around her shoulders and, using her arms as a pillow, lowered her head to the table and slept.

# CHAPTER 41

## RICHARD

I woke to the feel of fur beneath my bare arms and chest, the familiar scents of musk and blood, and the welcome warmth of the body of the animal I had killed two hours before. I pushed away from the carcass, stripped off the shreds that had been my shirt and the charred remnants of the cuffs of my jeans. After, sitting on the ground, I peeled off the melted soles of my tennis shoes. They took pieces of my skin with them, but given what I'd just come through, the brief discomfort could be ignored.

My mental powers had returned as well and as I headed down the mountain, my mind sought Irena and Michael. She was gone but I sensed him heading north on the main road, felt the pain of his wounds, the grim determination that would have kept him limping for miles through the frozen night in pursuit of her.

And, of course, that same determination would have him fighting up to the very end when he was so obviously outmatched. I relished the thought of that.

He'd seen the bear attack me, and the inferno that had been the cabin, and so his thoughts were on finding Irena rather than escaping from me. I considered surprising him with my raw and uneaten self, then decided to play with him as he had with me. I touched his mind, softly, so softly that he did not notice my presence until I all but screamed hello.

My greeting had the desired effect. His heart rate doubled. He whirled so fast that his wounded leg gave out and he fell. His night vision was good, but far from perfect. Even so, he tried to see into the shadows looking for me.

I was almost a quarter mile away at the time, nearly at the limits of my mental range. Since I could walk faster than he could run, I took my time chasing after him.

A stupid mistake. I was still some distance off when I heard a car on the road, felt Michael's sudden surge of hope. I tried to touch the driver but there was no bond between us and he was a bit drunk. Michael flagged him down and jumped inside.

As the car sped away, I caught the destination. Teius. I consulted the map in my head. An hour's easy run for one like me, less if I went overland. I stepped into the shelter of the trees and moved my mind outward, scanning the terrain as I ran.

Teius was much like the small towns in western Canada: one minute there was wilderness, the next cleared fields. Then houses, a little church, a store, a police station, everything huddled together for comfort. Given the fact that there were a lot of people on the street for such a late hour and I was wearing the equivalent of a charred denim loincloth, I could not exactly enter the town. But this was apparently wine country, the fields surrounding the town lined with tall stakes supporting bare grapevines.

The sight of so many tall sharp sticks recalled the woodblock prints I had seen of the Impaler and his victims, a pleasant thought tonight. Keeping deep in their shadows, thankful that the moon had not yet risen, I moved as close to the houses as I dared. With my body flat on the cold ground, I shut my eyes and let my mind move through the town.

Everyone was asleep but a handful of people gathered close to a tiny house, all whispering together about the girl the old man, Olha, had found and could she really be that singer?

I moved closer to the shops and churches on the north side of town. With the blood bond still tight between Irena and me, my mind found her easily. She was asleep in a cell at the local police station. I felt her fear, her sorrow. I was not strong enough to leave the sleeping mind with a message, but I would also not disturb her peace. Besides, Michael was hiding among the dormant vines, as close to the police station as he dared go, waiting for his chance to reclaim Irena. I felt a pang of jealousy at his feelings for her, though they would make no difference in his fate. I told him so.

No surge of fear when I touched him that time; not even an argument. Instead, he retreated from the vineyard to a stand of nearby trees, backed up against a broad trunk, and gripped his knife. I had a reluctant respect for that and I didn't much like the feeling.

—Before you kill me, Old One, promise me that you will get her out of that jail before anyone comes to take her away.—

Old One. In our week together, the man had never once spoken my name. Perhaps he did not consider me a man at all, and to speak my name would somehow make what he had done to me seem less torture than expediency. Not likely. He'd done worse to Irena and now his thoughts were more on her than on his own end.

But he did think of me, and with grim irony. He would be killed by one of the creatures he'd hoped to become. We shared a similar emotion; mine, because in a family so concerned about their dwindling numbers, I was about to devour someone who, under different circumstances (and an incredible amount of re-education), might have made an admirable addition to it.

His thoughts and mine rolled around inside me as I moved closer to him, creeping in from his right on the snow-covered ground, hands and feet moving carefully so I would make no sound.

I stopped a few yards from him to take in the sweat-damp hair, the blood-crusted pants, his pain. Enough! Any more and I would would start to pity the lunatic. With my thoughts on Irena and the end he deserved, I stood and whispered his name.

I'd expected to have to repel an immediate attack. But all he did was turn toward me and lower the blade so that he held it only with the tips of his fingers. Our eyes met, his as steady as mine. Neither of us moved. He would force me to be the aggressor, and for all my instincts, all my fantasizing about vengeance, I did not want to be the one to initiate that battle.

I tried. I recalled the agony he had put me through. The way he'd brutalized Irena. The way he'd left me for the flames to claim. And last, that wonderful moment when I had broken free of the blade and the fire and lay beneath the winter sky knowing for the first time exactly what I am.

Michael should have been begging for his life now. But though I tried, I could not tap the necessary anger or even the cold logic that said that killing him was necessary. Instead, we stood as frozen as the snow-shrouded world around us, each waiting for the other to move.

Perhaps it was our kinship that kept me from ending his life. Perhaps it was instinct holding me back. He knew this country far better than I did. Irena and I would likely need his help. I liked that notion. Killing delayed, not denied. I felt better.

"Na'arige," I whispered, a word of compromise in a language I barely knew.

"Truce," he replied, as if he'd understood.

"What did you say?" I asked, though I had heard him perfectly well.

He didn't repeat himself. "Irena cannot stay in that cell," he said. "Someone will come for her. If we don't get her out, she will disappear merely because she has spoken to me. Before you kill me, let me know that she is safe. Please."

"How do you know this?" I asked.

"I was too late to get to her before the police did. So I got as close as I dared to the station. They have a number to call if anyone associated with me was found. I was on the side of their building listening while the man was on the phone. He was told to have her ready to leave in an hour. I heard the policeman here ask if she could be Irena Sava. I did not dare try to touch his mind. I am not strong like you, Old One—"

"Richard, damn it! The name is Richard."

"Very well. Richard. Though I could not touch his mind, I could hear him. Apparently the answer was no because his final words were an apology. Then they locked Irena in that cell as if she were a criminal."

"What do you believe is going to happen?"

"She told them she was with me. I am a dissident, a wanted man. They do not know what we discussed in our days together and will think it too dangerous to release her now. They might be merciful and send her to a labor camp, but more likely they will take the careful course and kill her. If her body is found and identified, they can claim she was murdered by us and use it as an excuse to round up anyone who has ever spoken out against Ceauşescu. I have friends in town who will help us. We can go to them as soon as everything is quiet. Please, let me be sure she is safe before you kill me."

"Hold out your hand," I said.

He did. In spite of his uncertainty about my intentions, his pulse stayed steady while he drank.

As I'd guessed, his blood was thick with the taste of my family. But if I were forced to, I could finish him off cold-bloodedly, as my father had done to Viktor Celac. Understanding that made me feel better, for I hardly had reason to trust him.

I would have held him longer, but the sound of an approaching car startled me. I looked up at Michael, then pointed to the south. A moment later, we saw lights bouncing along the edge of the vineyard trellises, heard an engine. It belonged to a jeep of sorts, far noisier than the one the family used in Quebec. This one had an extra set of headlights, a spotlight mounted on its roof.

"Securitate," Michael said.

I shut my eyes, my mind moving outward. As they got closer I could brush their thoughts, not enough to read them at such a distance but enough to sense the emotion behind them.

From one of the passengers, a sadistic excitement. From the driver, regret.

"You're right," I said.

"We have no time to get a car but we can get her out together," he said.

Together was a great exaggeration. Michael could stand and walk, but his leg was far too weak for a fight so I would have the bulk of the battle. There were two in the jeep, three in the station, and likely all were armed. I'd win but they would have plenty of opportunities to kill Irena during it. And the outcome would hardly allow me to keep the low profile my family preferred. I wondered if that would make any difference here.

"Give me your jacket," I said.

He understood and handed it over. With it covering my pale skin and him in a black flannel shirt, it was easier for the two of us to creep along the line of vines. When I was closer to the station, I touched the driver's mind as he leaned against the side of the jeep, smoking a cigarette and waiting for the others to bring Irena out.

—He is to drive her to Rimet. Uphill? A gorge, I think. Do you know how far it is?— I asked Michael.

"Ri . . ." —Rimet? Maybe ten, twelve kilometers.—

—Wild country?—

—Yes. And the road ends at it. There is an old monastery. Abandoned. It must be where they will take her. They will question her . . . discover what she knows, and kill her.—

—How are the roads going up there?— I asked.

—Steep. Dirt. Rutted. Probably icy.—

The jeep would not be able to travel fast. That was good because I did not know their exact destination and so I would have to stay close to them on the way.

I looked at Michael, wishing he were shorter and lighter. I'd pressed my limits hard in the last day. The next hour would be difficult but I would not leave Michael behind.

—Come,— I said and began working my way down the road so that when we crossed it we were out of sight of the town. We then backtracked until we were closer to the police station, enough that I could trap the driver's mind if he went the other way. While we waited, I told Michael what we would do. As we'd expected, when the truck pulled out, it turned right then took the left soon after: the road to the gorge.

I buttoned up Michael's coat and dropped forward, my hands flat to the ground, fingers and toes digging into the snow. Michael was heavy on my back, but balance, not weight, would be the problem. —Remember, hold tight, lean forward, and keep your knees up and bent,— I said and ran.

# CHAP+ER 42

Michael was bruised and both of us coated with snow before he trusted me enough to lean into my gait rather than fight it. As I moved through the thick pines that hugged the road, I could see the lights of the jeep off to my right, bouncing as it dodged pot-holes, moving carefully up the dark, slippery incline.

I thought of touching Irena's mind, of telling her that help was near, but I was afraid her reaction would give our presence away. I did merge with her mind briefly, but only to look through her eyes. She sat in the back between two men. The better dressed of the pair (the one in charge, I assumed) looked out the window. The larger of the two, likely the strong arm, had hit her at the sta-tion when she'd demanded to speak to someone in Bucharest. Now he rubbed the inside of her thigh. No display of that Sava temper now. Instead, she stifled a whimper.

Once I was certain that she would survive to the road's end, I quickened my pace. We got there ahead of them, hid in the bushes close to the crumbling stone wall of the monastery, and waited.

The last rise of the road was steep and the truck's tires spun in the snow. When the rear started sliding sideways, the driver gave up, braked, and turned off the engine. He pulled out a pack of cigarettes and began walking down the hill the way he'd come, stopping some distance away to light up.

He had no stomach for what would happen but that made no difference. —We can't let any of them escape,— I told Michael, who had far more experience with killing than I did.

The back door of the jeep opened. Strong Arm pulled Irena out. She slipped in the snow and fell. He kicked her then jerked her to her feet and began dragging her toward the building and our hiding place, his partner a yard or so in front of him. Irena struggled, but her soul wasn't in it. For the moment, thinking herself abandoned and about to die, she'd given up.

—Irena,— I called.

I was right. She did give a little cry of recognition. The man gripping her arm looked down at her, more curious than concerned as he dragged her forward. I touched Michael's arm, told him to take the smaller of the two when I gave the signal.

By then they were less than ten feet from us. —Now!— I ordered.

I took down the man holding Irena with one silent leap against his side, my fingertips and nails raking across his spine while my teeth ripped into his neck. He never even screamed. Irena looked at me, her face frozen in shock. Then her eyes seemed to lose their focus. Her legs buckled and she fell forward onto hands and knees, stomach heaving. I wanted to tell her she'd be all right. I doubted she would hear me or even want to.

With Michael wounded, the dead man's partner had a more than even chance. He'd managed to draw his revolver but Michael had gripped his wrist, keeping him from getting an aim on anyone. The force of my leap sent him crashing off Michael and against the wall of the monastery, hard enough that chunks of the weathered stucco broke off and rained down on him, ashes for tonight's dead.

The driver dropped his cigarette and reached for his gun as he ran for the cover of the trees. Michael took the unconscious man's gun and aimed at the driver's back. "No shots!" I told him and began walking toward the driver. He had his own gun aimed at my chest but never fired. On my silent order, he lowered his arm and dropped the weapon. Thankfully, whatever qualms I'd had about killing had ended with that first taste of blood. My hands brushed the sides of his face. His body went limp, and as he fell I snapped his spine.

I never touched his memories, never tasted him. It was a bless-
ing not to know his name or his age or whether he had a family or
children. Out there in the cold, his past made no difference. He'd
been the enemy and he was dead.

I scooped up a handful of snow and rubbed it across my face,
let the bloody water drip onto the snow, then washed my face a
second time before wiping it on the hem of Michael's coat. Now
that I didn't look quite so barbaric, I went to see to Irena.

She'd rolled away from the body and was sitting on the
ground hugging her knees as she looked from Michael to me. I'm
not sure which shocked her more—the way I'd killed the brute
who'd hit her or seeing me here with Michael. Understandable
that she must have considered us an either/or proposition, and did
not want him as an ally, however temporary.

I held her briefly, promised to explain his presence later, and
walked over to the man I'd thrown off Michael. He lay where
he'd fallen. His pulse was uneven but, as I'd hoped, he still had
one. I pulled him upright with his back against the wall, crouched
beside him, and rubbed his face with snow. His eyelids twitched.

—Open them— I ordered. More snow, a hard slap on his face,
and he obeyed.

His eyes were that cold shade of blue often seen on actors
playing Nazis in old B movies. I saw astonishment in them as he
looked at me, trying to determine how I had bested him so easily.

—You know how— I told him. And because the half-moon
brushing the tops of the trees threw enough light onto the hilltop
that he could see my face, I punctuated the remark with a grin.

The sight had the effect I'd hoped it would. He looked away,
heart pounding. I gripped his wrists with one hand, grabbed his
chin with the other, and forced him to look at me. His pale eyes
were silvered from the moonlight, mine full dark and revealing a
power so cold it froze even me. I caught his mind again, let his
wrists go. He didn't move. I heard Michael swear, sensed Irena
crawling up behind me. She touched my shoulder, her fingers icy.
I brushed her hand away.

"Do you come up here often?" I asked him.

He pressed his lips together. I was glad he struggled. I reveled
in the pounding of his heart as my cheek brushed his. My teeth
sank into the side of his neck, a pain I magnified until his head
fell back. His mouth opened but I denied him the release of a
scream.

—You will talk to me,— I told him, then, for the sake of the pair looking on, I repeated, "Do you come here often?"

I let him speak a reply. "Twice . . . twice before." His voice was loud. Perhaps he thought someone might be near. Of course, he was wrong. I'd already made sure of that.

"And you killed the prisoners you brought here?"

He pressed his lips together, not because he was particularly patriotic. No, he'd convinced himself that if he could keep silent he might somehow escape.

"Take Irena back to the jeep to keep her warm," I said to Michael without looking away from the man.

"No!" Irena's voice was soft but determined. "We should all hear what he has to say."

"This may be worse than what I did before," I replied, as much for my captive's sake as hers.

"But this time it won't be a surprise. Besides, I should see what I may become, yes?"

I looked over my shoulder at her, saw that she was standing, a bit unsteadily. Michael moved close to her, hands raised toward her; not touching but offering help if she wanted it. She glanced at him, her expression cold, and he backed away.

I turned my full attention on the man in front of me. —Answer my question,— I ordered.

"Go to . . . hell."

The gods were smiling on me. —You first,— I said and sent him straight into my memory of that burning room where Michael had left me to die.

He tried to scream. I denied him that release.

When he talked, I let him see through the illusion. When he balked, I sent him back to the flames. When he dared to hope I might let him live, I suggested that confession was good for a dying soul. He'd been given orders to ask Irena about everything Michael had told her, then about her friends, her family. He was to get names before he killed her. Last, and oddest, he was to take a sample of her blood back to the station. Someone would come for it.

He seemed anxious to make me understand that he was a small player in this drama. Higher-ups questioned the more serious cases. He did not know his superiors' names, but gave me a phone number where he called for orders. Before this, he had only questioned and killed four men and a boy; one of his comrades had killed eleven, including five women and a nine-year-old girl.

—Did you bring all your victims here?— I asked.

Tears rolled down his face, glittering in the moonlight. He could not move to brush them away and he sobbed too hard to speak but by then we had long since abandoned speech.

—The men, yes.—

—Where did you hide the bodies?—

He showed me the place with his mind. A thick stand of trees. The wooden cap of an old well.

—What were their names?—

I shared his reply with the others, heard Michael swear.

—And the others? The women and children? What were their names?—

He only knew three. One was a child, Michael's kin.

When I learned everything the man knew, I looked over my shoulder at Michael, then Irena. Irena was sobbing openly, one hand on Michael's arm for support. Michael seemed composed. Inside he was raging but at least now the rage was not directed at my kind. "Go back to the jeep," I told them, my voice so cold that this time neither argued.

Once I was alone with my meal, I freed that primitive part of me. And it was well satisfied.

A half hour later, body relaxed, eyes human, mind sharper than it had ever seemed before, and wearing a set of clothes that almost fit me, I returned to Michael and Irena. Michael was in the driver's seat of the jeep, Irena sitting beside him. I doubted they had spoken to each other at all. They were running the engine for the heat, so I slipped into the back and quickly shut the door. There was blood on my hands. I tasted more on my lips. It had shot into me hot with fear but all I felt now was an icy calm as if I had evolved into some avenging Old Testament angel. If a dozen of these barbarians came up that hill, I would face them and feel no remorse, no fear. And I would win.

Irena twisted around to look at me. She touched a trembling finger against the red on my lips then tasted him. A family gesture, disquieting from someone who was not one of us.

"Is he dead?" she asked.

"Yes."

"Good," she said, voice flat.

"We should hide the bodies," Michael commented, his voice as expressionless as hers.

I nodded. Michael and I got out of the jeep. Reluctant to be alone, Irena followed. As Michael and I began dragging the driver off into the trees, I decided there was something else we needed to do. I veered off to the left into a thicker stand of trees, following the memory my meal had left me, until I found the well where he had dumped the bodies. We dropped the body beside it then went back for the other two before I took the time to examine that mass grave.

The well's wooden cover was locked but its hasp had long since rusted. I broke it, lifted the cover, and inhaled the musty scent of old death, the sweeter more cloying scent of new.

"Are there more bodies down there than the ones he killed?" Michael asked.

"We can see," I said. I motioned Irena to stay back. Thinking that these were likely Michael's kin, I held out my hand to him. He took it, and let me into his mind. My eyes focused on the darkness at the bottom of the pit then I extended my mind, and his, straight into the horror of it.

I had never tried to extend into the earth before, but only because I'd never had reason to. As thought mimics speech, so this power mimicked sight. And the darkness was almost too much for my mind to grasp. With effort, I amplified the thin rays of moonlight along the sides of the well until I could discern shadows and shapes, white bones peeking through gray flesh. There was no motion other than the occasional silver flicker of light off the shell of the black beetles that thrived on the rot. In the tangle of decaying limbs and flesh and tattered clothes, I could not count the dead until I focused just on the skulls. Eleven. Judging from their clothing, three of them seemed to be women. If I had been able to touch them, I might have tasted a bit of dried blood, a pinch of flesh. Perhaps I might have touched a memory, acquired a name.

One skull, the smallest, drew my attention. I looked at the shape of the eye sockets, the teeth. The puzzle ended when I saw a second set of incisors, not nearly as long as mine, but in the same place.

How hard had this poor child fought? How hard had any of them?

Michael's grip on my hand had become tight enough to be painful, drawing me back to myself. As I retreated, he broke away from me. I opened my eyes and saw him sitting on the snowy ground, hugging his knees. He did not move when I touched his shoulder, just let out a sound trapped between a sob and a sigh when Irena did the same. Only the memory of what he had done to her kept her from drawing him into her arms. "How many?" she asked.

I told her. "They were like you, and Michael." I did not add that one seemed like me.

"There were no small children there," Michael said. "Where did they take all the little ones?"

Somewhere safe, where they were trying to control them. "We'll find them, Michael," I said. The gentle tone of my voice surprised me as much as it did him.

When he looked up, I saw the tears in his eyes. "I would have killed you," he said.

I wondered.

We dumped the bodies of the killers with their victims. As we did, Michael paused to look closely at the one I had questioned, noting the ripped shirt, the bites on the neck and chest, the slashes on the stomach. I was glad he looked. Let him know what kind of creature he hoped to become.

He offered me the gun that had belonged to the driver. I told him to keep it. In the last hour alliances had shifted. He was one of us now.

Irena rested her forehead on her palm, wiped back her hair. "We should go," she said, taking my hand, moving close as we walked.

On the way back to the jeep, I thought of my family. "I need to find a telephone," I said.

"There's one in the police station," Michael suggested, then gave a brief laugh so I would understand he wasn't serious.

"Cluf will be better," I suggested. "Stop just outside of town."

I had expected Cluf to be a smaller version of Bucharest rather than a crossroads village only slightly larger than Teius. It was five in the morning and still dark. I could have broken into the offices, little more than a house surrounded by other houses, but I would likely be heard and after there might be questions.

I walked slowly down the cobblestone street, my mind moving through the larger houses until I found the residence of Mihai Malita, the manager of our Cluf office.

Like so many long-term employees of the Austra firm, he had inherited his position when his father retired. He could have applied for a promotion—we have offices in Bucharest as well as the regional center in Cluj-Napoca—but his family was in Cluf. He loved his home, and his salary, twice what anyone else in the area received, assured them prosperity. He was also a party member, an active one, an expedient move we had encouraged.

A portly man, he looked all the wider in horizontal-stripped blue and white pajamas. When he answered my pounding and did not see anyone he knew, he started to close the door on me.

"I am Richard Austra," I said. "My family employs you."

"Go sober up," he replied and started to slam the door in my face. I held it open and began reciting the addresses where Tarda water was sent in Portugal and Chicago and Montreal and the name of his superior in Bucharest. Convinced I was who I said I was, he let me in.

"I've come to use your telephone," I said. "I need to call my family in Canada."

Malita rubbed the sleep from his eyes. "Easier to call Bucharest. I understand that one of the Austra family is there. They say his visit concerns trade." He paused and eyed me carefully, taking in the ripped and bloody coat, the tangled hair. "Perhaps it has something to do with you as well?"

No doubt.

# CHAP+ER 43

I returned to the jeep with a bottle of water and a sack of rolls and cheese, all Mihai had that would travel. I handed it to Irena and stretched out in the backseat. The last twelve hours had seemed like a week and even if I had not felt the familiar dawn lethargy, that daily tide that pulls at all my family, I needed rest.

I gave Michael directions to the start of the easiest path that led to the top of the Old One's mountain and told him to wake me when he'd driven as far as he could. With nothing more to be done, I rolled over so my face was against the back of the seat, covered myself with the blanket, and shut my eyes.

Light pulsed above me, the rising sun dappled by the branches of bare trees and pines. The hard shocks made the seat shudder. With effort, I moved beyond all of it until Irena shook me awake.

"Where are we?" I asked.

"West of Cîmpeni. We've been spotted!" Irena said.

I sat up quickly. "How?" I asked.

"A jeep like this one was coming the other way. I ducked down but the driver got a good look at Michael. He's behind us."

"How many?"

Michael answered. "A driver only. Should I try to get away from him?"

The road wound upward through the Bihors. It was narrow, potholed, and icy. "Let him catch up," I said, turning to look back.

We were rounding a curve in the road so for a moment I couldn't see the jeep. When I did, I noted that it was a lighter shade than ours and that the driver was keeping his distance.

"Slow down as if you're pulling over but don't stop," I said.

The maneuver took the driver behind us by surprise. He braked but not soon enough. At fifty feet it was an easy thing to grab his mind. He turned the wheel hard to the right, skidded off the road, and rolled twice. I felt shock but little pain. The man had died instantly.

Michael glanced over his shoulder to see. When he turned back, he all but ran head-on into an oncoming vehicle. Black but otherwise another match for ours with a driver and two passengers. I recalled that in Bucharest the darker the shade of an official car the higher the rank of the driver and wondered if it applied to every part of the country or only the capital.

Our jeep spun out. Michael turned into the skid and gave it more gas. Our turnoff approached and Michael made the right too quickly. The rear wheels lost traction, spinning us around to face back the way we'd come.

He'd just put it in reverse when the first bullet went through the windshield. Irena ducked while Michael gunned the engine. Again he moved a bit too fast, but he made the turn.

A second bullet came through the back. Then five more. I heard Michael swear, Irena give a soft cry. The scent of blood filled the space. Both of them had been hit but I sensed that Irena's was by far the worse. I wanted to see to her but I couldn't, not yet.

Three of them and now one of us to fight back. I recalled that Michael hadn't been much use before and we'd been all right but then we'd had the advantage of surprise.

"Pull over!" I ordered. "Then do what you can for her."

Michael hadn't even stopped when I rolled out the rear door and into the snow. The car behind us braked but too late. They were between Michael and me now, the guns in the backseat turned in my direction.

A shot just missed my shoulder. Two more thudded into the snowy ground in front of me. I ran toward the jeep, closing the gap enough to trap the driver's mind. He turned to the men in

the back and, following my orders, fired. As he did, I heard another shot, this one from Michael. It caught the driver in the back
of the head and the windshield in the front seat splattered red
from the blowback.

I ran to our jeep, saw Michael limping around to the passenger
door, blood dripping from beneath the cuff of his shirt, a minor
wound but enough to weaken him further. I reached him as he
pulled the passenger door open. Irena lay sideways on the seat,
her sweater red with her blood. The shot had taken her in the
chest, and she fought to breathe. I'd survived a chest wound
much like that but Irena was human and I could only take her
hand and tell her it would be all right. Michael had been to med-
ical school and interned in a labor camp. He knew what to do.

I helped him lay her on the backseat so he could examine the
wound. I didn't have to read his mind to know how bad it was.
His expression and the bubbles forming in the hole each time she
exhaled said it all. Her pulse raced, her breathing was shallow,
her face pale. Michael wrapped his hand in the edge of her
sweater and pressed the heel of his palm against the wound. "Rip
the blanket into strips," he said.

I followed his instructions, taking part of one strip and rolling
it tightly, creating a plug and pressure pad to stop the bleeding.
He pressed the plug into the wound, and wrapped the strips
around her chest to hold it in place.

"I'll watch her. You drive," he said.

I looked at him, sent a private question. Michael shook his
head slowly. —In a hospital with the right tools she would still
have only a small chance,— he replied.

So we were buying time. At least we both understood it.

The route we took could barely be called a road. In some
places it was so narrow that I prayed we would make it through.
Other spots were so rutted and uneven that even at a crawl Irena
cried out from the pain. While I drove, I did my best to keep a
part of myself in Irena, stealing the pain, feeling her pulse increase as her body fought for air. Five miles later, we had to abandon the car. As I helped Michael carry Irena from it, her eyes
fluttered open and focused on my face.

—It's bad?— she asked.

"Bad. Irena, what should I do?"

—What you must.— She leaned her head against my shoulder,
her long hair soft as a kiss on my bare skin.

We started to climb. Every time I got too far ahead, I stopped and waited for Michael to catch up.

"I slow you down. Leave me here. I'll shoot anyone who starts up the trail," he suggested.

"Stay with us. She's going to need you," I replied, not adding that I would, too.

The trail grew steeper and narrower until we reached a wide spot with a good view of the path we'd come up. Boulders protected us from being seen from the road and gave some shelter from the frigid wind.

I took off my jacket to pad the ground, laid Irena on it. The blood had soaked through the bandage we'd made. That racing pulse was gone, though. I thought it a good sign until Michael shook his head.

She was still alive but her mind was focused on the future, on death. I touched her, pulled her back to near consciousness and called to her. —Irena, stay with me!—

It took her a long time to reply, and when she did her thoughts were weak. —It's all right. Whatever happens is all right.—

—But I can save you.—

—I know.—

Hardly the clear answer I'd hoped for. I thought of the gesture in the jeep when she'd tasted the blood on my lips, her occasional comments about changing. I thought of my mother, my family. I brushed the hair back from Irena's forehead and kissed it. I had not come this far just to watch her die. Irena might have a long time to damn me for this later, but I made the decision for her.

"Come here, Michael. I'm going to need your help to heal her."

"You can do this?"

"If I can change her, then yes. To do this so quickly requires two of family, but I think your blood is enough like ours to do."

"She can drink from me?"

"She must drink from me. I will have to give back to her what she has lost." Which had been quite a lot. I had to trust the man to let *me* take from him. He might die in the process. I told him so.

"I'm stronger than you think. I will help you do it."

I bit into my wrist, deep enough that the blood dripped onto her face as I held my wrist against her lips. She choked, moaning from the pain. A trail of blood leaked from the side of her mouth. I brushed it away and rested a hand on her forehead. "Drink. Please, Irena, listen to me and drink!"

She heard the words, or she sensed them, or both. No matter, I felt a surge of need in her, a pulling back from that empty place where her soul had wandered. I ran my fingertips over the side of her neck, feeling her swallow, the reflex tentative at first, then stronger.

She drained my life through my blood. As it moved from me to her, her body became warmer, her skin seemed to glow. I looked down at that beautiful face, the russet highlights in her hair brilliant in the late morning sun, and I felt tender as a mother creating new life. Perhaps that was why my own instincts—so strong that I would kill a friend if need was hard on me—slept until I sensed myself growing dizzy, my own pulse slowing as the world faded around me.

Even then, I did not stop. Instead, I lowered my head onto Irena's chest, listening to her heart beating even and strong as my own began to fade. When the time came to call for Michael, I found I could not speak, but he was already beside me.

The physician first, he felt Irena's wrist and noted the pulse before unwrapping the strips of cloth from her chest, pulling out the bloody knot that had helped her breathe, examining the wound. And all the time, she continued to drink and my own need rose, as strong as my body was weak.

I felt his warmth as he stretched out beside me. His hand touched the side of my face, his lips brushed mine. From his kiss, I knew how close to death I had moved. Close enough that the incredible allure that is our last and most potent defense had drawn him to me. Had I become desperate enough in that little cabin, he would have done the same.

He kissed me again, and I felt him struggle to pull away from the unfamiliar attraction. "You did not have to do this, Richard. I had already given my word," he murmured, unable to tap any emotion but desire.

A drop of warmth fell on my cheek, then his blood filled my mouth, freely given. Like Irena, I was impatient, and bit deeper. He instinctively tried to pull away from the pain but my free arm grabbed his, holding his wound tight to my lips.

I wanted to remind him to trust me, but it would be a lie. I had gone so close to that eternal light that I could not trust myself. As I grew stronger, my lips moved to his neck. I bit deep and took what I needed. My body gave me no choice.

We lay close together as the sun rose, stealing the darkness from our hiding place. It burned and on instinct, I slithered sideways, drawing all of us into the comfort of the shadows, wondering vaguely which of us would be alive at nightfall. . . .

I drifted in the serene space between life and death, pulled back to earth by the sound of boots crunching on the frozen ground, a voice barking an order. Only my mind moved as I took in the situation.

There were three of them, all armed. It hardly troubled me. I had my most potent weapon in the trail itself.

The spot we had picked was sheltered but high, with a long drop only two yards away. Without understanding why, the largest of the three men walked toward it, crying out as he lost his footing on the ice and slipped toward the edge. His comrade went to help but as their hands touched the second man lunged forward, taking them both over the side.

The third guessed what had happened and came up on us quickly. A cold and lethal circle of steel pressed against the back of my neck but the man could not shoot. But my last minutes of mental effort had stolen much of my strength, and I was not sure how long I could hold him back.

No matter. That allure still clung to me. I felt the hunger in him, for me and my nature. Then the temptation to taste of an old one became too great. He lifted my arm from Irena's lips, kissed my palm, and licked the wound.

A fatal mistake. My blood was in him now, the bond I needed so simple to create. I moved and he did not react. I rolled over and, with eyes shut tight against the glare of the sun, I took the weapon from him and flung it over the ledge. Holding tight to his arm, I slid sideways and, making room for him between Michael and me, I pulled him down.

My instincts had not failed me.

Lunch had been delivered.

When I woke late in the afternoon, I was covered with blood. Mine. Irena's. Michael's and few seeping drops from that nameless pawn whose body lay beside me, his open eyes opaque in the glare of the afternoon sun.

Earlier, I'd drained the man halfway then nursed Michael,

then took the rest of my victim. I'd changed Irena; I could feel it when I touched her mind. I was less certain about Michael but would know soon enough.

Thinking a bloodless body should not be the first sight Irena saw when she woke to her new life, I stirred myself long enough to drag it some ways down the trail and threw it into a deep fissure in the rocks where hopefully it would never be found. Having done everything I could for Michael and Irena, I sat beside them, picking an angle that would shade their faces from the sun.

I heard a truck on the road far below us and knew we would not be alone for long. It made no difference. The sun was already low in the sky. Darkness belonged to my world, not theirs. They would not catch us tonight, or ever.

Michael woke at dusk and pushed himself to his feet. He'd expected to feel stiffness, pain, but there was none. I was hardly surprised when he extended the rips in his already ruined jeans and brushed away the dried blood from his skin.

The slashes should have been raw, possibly seeping. Instead he saw long streaks of whiter tissue. He took off his shirt. The spot where the bullet had grazed him had also healed over.

Then he saw the scars on his hands, felt the one on his face. He ran his tongue over his teeth and frowned.

I grinned, fangs brushing my lower lip. —You're better off keeping the teeth you have. Take care of them and carry a knife instead or . . . — I pointed to the pendant around my neck.

He laughed from astonishment at the strength of my thoughts in his head. His mental response, filled with all the effort he'd always had to use to tap his weak mental power, reached me at a point well past pain.

—There are men at the base of the trail,— I told him.

—Are there?— He laughed again. He'd been cocky before. Now he was going to be lethal. What a wonderous ally I had created.

He crouched beside Irena. His movements were awkward but grace would come soon enough. He rested a hand on her forehead, pulled up her sweater, touched the scar on her chest, then kissed her forehead, not with passion but with gratitude. I felt as if I were looking at Adam and Eve. If so, who was I?

"We should go. We're not ready to fight," I said.

"Aren't we?"

"She isn't awake yet. It may be awhile. She'd been much closer to death."

"Then it takes longer?"

"It did for my mother," I said.

"Your mother?" he asked.

"I'll explain all that later," I said and picked Irena up and put her over my shoulder. Burdened as I was, it was my turn to struggle to keep up. As we neared the summit, rocks began to jut from the barren earth. They resembled walls, so that the keep itself would appear to be one of them. I wondered if a pilot or passenger of some passing airplane had ever noticed the reflection of sunlight on the colored windows my father had created here and guessed what they saw in such a high and impossible location.

But not so impossible any longer. I stopped as we neared the top. The sun was beginning to set and I turned and looked at the valley below. In my father's memories there had been wilderness. Now there were towns, small ones but towns nonetheless. And on a lower peak nearby, I saw trails and a ski lift. What did the Old One think of his neighbors? Did they think of him at all?

Michael had paused some feet in front of me and looked up at the final rise to the top. "It's too steep," he said.

"But at least there are handholds, a bit of a trail. Someday I will show you the Rockies, Michael. Now those are real mountains. Not little hills like this."

I moved Irena from my right shoulder to my left and started forward. Michael followed and we went on until the trail grew so narrow and the drop-off so steep that he froze.

"You could fall that distance and not even bruise, Michael, but it would be painful and a long walk back up."

I lied about the fall, of course, but once I had him moving, things went better. Near the top, the trail vanished but we didn't need it any longer. Surrounded by rocky outcroppings, some taller than the keep itself, I saw with my own eyes the family's first and only real home.

I knew every stone of it from shared memory, but like the land around it, it had altered with time. The crack in the wall near the huge carved doors had widened, and there were other, smaller cracks as well. The roof, uneven slabs of shale made to mimic the rocks around it, had buckled and a section of it appeared to be missing. I recalled that this area was known for tremors. Perhaps those and not a violent storm had caused the damage. But the walls were so thick that the damage made no difference. A millennium from now most of it would still be here.

—Can you be so certain about the rest of this uneasy world, little one?—

Usually I can follow a thought back to the one who had sent it to me, but not here. The words seemed to rise from the barren earth around me as well as the keep we walked toward. They had a richness to them, an unhurried musical cadence as if this, not the spoken word, had been the Old One's first language.

The tall carved doors hung open.

The Great and Powerful Oz welcomed us.

# CHAPTER 44

## PATRICK

Of course, we never did go out that night. Instead we took Andrei back to our hotel suite. The four of us settled into the main room with a pitcher of water with a twist, made to look like a pitcher of martinis. Stephen sat beside Andrei, his hand on the man's thigh. Hunter turned on the TV and we made a pretext of getting drunk and watching an old movie while we listened to Andrei's silent answers to the equally silent questions Stephen asked. Andrei revealed more details on what they had planned for Richard and Irena but had no other useful information.

I thought of Richard somewhere paralyzed and in pain and I felt a need rising in me, a craving strong and unfamiliar. I wasn't certain this feeling was mine entirely or partly Stephen's. I didn't care.

Stephen leaned closer to Andrei. The man shut his eyes. I could feel the tension in him. The terror. Always in hiding, I had never tapped a human's fear and I longed to feast on it.

"Patrick, why don't you and Hunter go to bed?" Stephen all but ordered, his voice slightly slurred as if he were drunk.

I didn't want to move. Hunter touched my arm, motioned me toward my room. The cameras must have been rolling by then, trying to catch something on tape, but it made no difference once the outer room went dark.

I left my own lights out, took off my shirt and tie and hung them next to the suitcoat in the closet. It was late enough that I could have slept but I doubted I'd be able to until dawn claimed me. If I had dared, I would have spied on my father, but he'd be expecting it.

—Of course I expected it. Now come and take my place.—

I did, and quickly. —Why?— I asked when I sat down beside him.

—He is safer with you tonight. Just remember that he needs to be able to travel tomorrow.—

Stephen went to my room rather than his own. I understood. I took Andrei's good arm, pulled him to his feet, and all but dragged him into my father's room. "Please," he moaned, begging; but to the camera picking up the slightest whisper, that single word would have sounded like an invitation.

In spite of the leeway I had been given, I felt damnably prudish as I helped Andrei take off his shirt. It might have been the cameras catching our shadows in the dark or my feeling that my father would not trust my self-control enough to leave us completely alone. Nonetheless, I had a performance to give and I pushed him back onto the bed and pulled the covers over both of us.

"You are so beautiful," I said, my voice in the cadence of my father's. Then I kissed him, feeling his fear beating against me, its glorious temptation ripping through my conscience.

I had barely tasted him, barely begun to touch passion, when the phone rang. Solely by habit, Andrei's good arm reached for the light.

My hand closed over his wrist and jerked his arm back. I reached over him for the receiver, answering in my best imitation of Stephen's voice.

The Romanian reply was too fast for me to follow. Fortunately, Hunter got on a moment after I did.

Richard had been too clever to make the call himself, so it was Mihai on the line, calling from Cluf to tell us that it had been suggested that we pay a visit to our distant relation while we were in the backcountry.

I wanted to laugh from joy. Instead I lay back, my hand still gripping Andrei's arm. —It looks like we don't need you anymore,— I said.

He ignored my baiting, but rolled over and buried his face in the pillow to stifle his sobs.

I did not have to ask the question. Richard had escaped, so Michael had to be dead. —I owed him my life. No matter what they did to him, he never gave them my name,— he told me.

My hand brushed Andrei's, the marks I had made. —You're still alive,— I reminded him, wondering why I felt the need to give him any hope at all. I held him for the next hour, listening to his life unfold, a silent conversation that ended with the first dawn light.

We had a car waiting for us when we landed in Sibiu the following afternoon. Because we had Andrei with us and the car was too small for five, we had a fine excuse to dismiss the driver. With Andrei as our guide, we headed southwest, briefly touring a spot that would have been ideal for our operations. Ruse out of the way, we headed toward the high pass that led to the Old One's keep.

We saw the signs of my brother's struggle even before we made that final turn some miles from our destination. Police cars. Two closed trucks. A roadblock where we were pulled over.

Stephen got out of the car with Andrei, showed our papers and began a discussion with the officer in charge. I barely listened, my mind touching that of a young guard shocked by what he had seen.

One killed in an auto accident. Three shot. Two fallen from the cliffs of the Old One's mountain and the last one missing, and . . .

I had to stifle a laugh. For such a peaceful creature, Richard was certainly running up an impressive body count.

We did not try to get past the police blockade but instead drove back through Cîmpeni and headed for the more difficult north route to the peak. We parked the car in a stand of trees. Hunter and Andrei changed into jeans and mountain boots, my father and I into the loose knits that let us move freely.

Beyond the first quarter mile our path ceased being a trail at all. Stephen led and I brought up the rear as we headed upward through a forest of pine and beech that thinned to high meadow, then sheer rock. Andrei looked up at it. His knees buckled and he would have fallen if Hunter hadn't caught him. "We are going up there?" he asked in a terrified whisper.

"And we will reach the top by nightfall," Stephen told him and started walking. Hunter fell in behind him, then Andrei and me. The Romanian reeked of fear but he kept up for the first hour then lost his footing so suddenly that I had to scramble to catch him before he slipped off the ledge we were on.

"Dizzy," he mumbled.

"It's his ribs. His breathing is too shallow for this height," Hunter explained, adding that the altitude had begun to affect him as well. "Given his shape and my age, you may have to carry us both or leave us behind," he said, adding that he wouldn't mind a few hours alone with our reluctant guide.

There was a stone cottage halfway up the mountain, one Hunter had used before. Though almost in ruins, the old walls still offered shelter. We helped the men collect some wood for what remained of the hearth then left them with the promise to return the next day. Unencumbered by human companions, we finished the climb just before dark.

Richard was waiting for us there, leaning against a rock ledge. He wore black silk pants, Turkish in style, a red silk vest. His hair was finger combed, hanging in loose ringlets. He did not look like someone who'd gone through the adventure those soldiers had hinted at. Then I saw his eyes. They were wiser than I recalled them, steadier, but with an uneasiness that worried me. I also noted that he did not run to embrace Stephen as he usually would. He hid something.

"Is Irena all right?" I asked.

"Yes. She was badly wounded and . . ." Words failed him. He showed us instead.

"She made the choice, yes?" Stephen asked.

"She was dying. I had to guess what she would want."

"How did you do it alone?"

"The one who took her was our third. He was enough like family to allow it."

"You hid his body, yes?" Stephen asked, concerned about what the authorities would discover when they found it.

"He's still alive."

Stephen and I both thought the question. I asked it. "You changed him? Why?"

"It is difficult to explain in a few words. Much has happened that we need to discuss."

"We pay our respects first. That is our custom," Stephen replied, walking past him toward the tall closed doors, his anger so strong I could feel its heat.

# CHAP+ER 45

## RICHARD

We did not see the Old One when we arrived, only heard his command that we go below and wash. Carrying Irena, I'd followed his directions down a steep and narrow staircase that leveled off and widened into six large chambers. Each contained a platform large enough to hold three of us and more. These were softened with featherbeds and pillows, the stone walls made beautiful by silk draperies, the stone floor by Turkish rugs. The platforms were draped in scarves of brilliant color, the doors curtained with silk as well. In the first of these I saw clothes laid out for us, in the last a deep stone cistern. Its water, much warmer than the air, bubbled out of the bottom and sluiced off at the top into a trough that disappeared into the wall.

"A luxurious prison," Michael commented.

"This was where the Old One kept his personal slaves," I replied, wondering if this had been readied for us or if it was now Catherine's quarters. Thinking of Catherine's history, I vowed not to leave Irena alone for even a moment. I looked down at her, the ruined sweaters and jeans, the jacket I had bought for her caked with her blood. "Hold her," I said to Michael, giving up my precious burden long enough to take off my clothes. Then I began doing the same with hers.

Michael looked from her to me, then went and stood at the far end of the hall, his back to us. He seemed to be standing guard but in truth he was prudish, another surprise.

I brushed a lock of hair away from her face and studied her body. Darker skinned than my mother, she did not have the same translucent quality to her flesh but there was a similar glow. She had been pretty before, now I suspected that she would be beautiful, magnetic. Like her kin.

I bathed myself and Irena, then dressed us both. Her clothes were lavish, diaphanous silk scarves of pale pink and blue and cream, artfully arranged to both conceal and accentuate the body beneath. All one needed to do was push them aside to uncover a breast, a hip, or all of her. Her legs were bare but there were strings of bells for her ankles, a gold link chain for her waist. A crystal vial on a table near the bed held some exotic oil, a hint of pine and jasmine. I rubbed a bit into Irena's hair, into my own, then put on the pants and vest that had been left for me. I wanted nothing more than to lie beside her, kiss those full lips, and hold her through her long healing sleep. But the Old One called and said my family was near and, with Irena in my arms, I had rushed to meet them. I had stopped in the shadows inside the keep, handed my precious burden to Michael. "Give me a moment with them," I'd told him, and gone to meet them alone.

Now I held her close again and followed my father into the darkness of the keep and toward a distant pool of torchlight.

The hall was huge, well over a hundred feet in length, half that in width and as high to the vaulted roof above us. The two ends had small rose windows in brilliant hues, the south side from which we'd entered had a line of them along the top. These were the first of my father's windows, created in some tiny workroom deep in the walls. In others' memories I had seen them fill this huge space with light, giving it the feeling of some pagan church.

Twenty feet above us, a narrow balcony circled the space. I sensed we were being watched but did not look up. I'd met Catherine before, and did not wish to be distracted by her now, not when I could see the reality of the visions I had shared with the oldest of the family.

There were mosaics on the floor, thousands of glass tiles

forming asymmetrical patterns. A carpet covered its center. Denys's complex design, though the tufting had been done by all. It seemed to have faded only slightly over the centuries, as if the walls themselves repelled the ravages of time. Paintings covered the stone walls, tapestries softened them. The space was a museum, the private exhibit of my family's ancient talents.

The waist-high platform we approached had a base of stone and a top of polished wood some sixteen meters square, its edges rounded from age. High carved posts marked the corners and torches were mounted at the tops of those. A thick crimson carpet covered the dais's center, pillows strewn across it.

The floor surrounding the dais was bare stone, worn by centuries of struggle. It was here the family brought their conquests for pleasure or pain or death. I moved sideways to that spot, standing where my father had made his first human kills. I recalled the excitement of the family as they watched, my father's growing confidence, his thrill at his power. Having recently been tested, I understood the emotions all too well.

I took those last few steps forward, looked down at Irena still sleeping in my arms, bowed my head, and held her out as if she had been brought for sacrifice.

"Look at me when you present your gift, child." The voice was beautiful, the language Romanian. I raised my head and Frn'cs stood before me. The folds of his loose silk pants did not move, the golden bracelets on his wrists and chains around his neck had made no sound. As I'd assumed, he had always been there.

I knew what the Old One looked like as well as I knew my father's face but knowing and seeing are two separate things. Like all my family's, his hair was pure black. Longer than in my memories, it fell in thick curls nearly to his waist. His face was sharp-edged like my father's, the eyes wider apart and full-black as if he had never learned, or bothered, to hide his nature. His lips were only slightly darker than his skin, ivory on alabaster. The short torso and legs that were far too long to conceal made him stand well over seven feet. He could never walk among men and pass for human, yet one who could cloak himself even from his kin could walk where he chose.

He moved to the edge of the dais, sat cross-legged on it, and took Irena from me. Resting her on his knees, he cradled her shoulders with one arm as if she were an infant. Her head fell sideways against his chest. Her hair covered her face. He brushed it back, his hand lingering on her forehead, his lips touching her lips. I understood the intimacy of family greetings but Michael hissed in a breath. At that moment, he felt far more jealousy than I did.

"You have created this?" the Old One asked me.

"I changed her into what she could become. As to who sired her, I believe she is your grandchild. As is he."

Concerned about the state of mind of my other "child," I pulled Michael forward, drawing the Old One's attention to him.

The Old One fixed his gaze on Michael. Michael stared back as if they were equals while the Old One's mind moved through his, probing his weaknesses, his strengths, his desires.

—Michael Celac. Liberator. Now that you've been given the gift of centuries, what will you do with it?—

"I will go back to my people. I have promised to protect them."

The Old One laughed, revealing teeth longer and far more lethal than those of his children. "But your people are here, Michael. Some even believe they need you."

He handed Irena back to me then raised one arm. His bracelets fell down it, clinking together just before his elbow. —Come down!— he called, a thought so strong it seemed to echo through the space.

I heard rustling on the narrow balcony high above us, glimpsed fabric brush the ornate rail, a woman's body vaulting over to land on all fours at our right. Catherine, I thought, until I heard someone else land behind me, another in front. Two more walked down the narrow stairs at the back of the hall, all of them clothed as Irena was. I turned to look at the two who had used the stairs. Both were visibly pregnant. One carried a baby.

So many. And all had once been human except for the naked black-eyed infant girl that one of them handed to my father. My brother and I moved close to look at her. It had been over a thousand years since the family had welcomed a firstborn. Seeing the face and the limbs, feeling the grip of that delicate hand as I pressed one finger against her palm, sensing that unfocused mind brushing so easily against mine, I knew we welcomed one now.

Motion pulled me from my reverie. I saw Michael hurrying toward the woman who had landed beside me. She was pretty in much the same way Irena was, though thinner and darker haired.

"Ana?" Michael asked, not certain he could believe what his eyes told him was true.

"It is me." Her voice had the feel of velvet on my skin.

"Is my sister here? Your brother?" Michael asked.

She shook her head. "Marinka and I were separated before my brother and I escaped. Then the Old One found us. He only gives shelter to the women. I do not know where my brother has gone."

"I cannot mourn. This is more than I'd ever hoped for," he whispered.

She moved close to him. A petite thing, the top of her head did not even reach his chin. As they embraced, the child I held seemed to frown. I sensed primitive jealousy followed by a furious squawl. When Ana pushed away from Michael and came to take the infant from Stephen's arms, we saw a damp spot on the silk covering her breasts. "She is your child, yes?" my father asked.

Ana looked at Michael as she replied. "Refuge came at a price." I sensed the resignation in her thoughts, the fury in Michael's as he understood why her brother had been turned away.

Michael turned and moved toward the dais, legs stiff, hands in fists at his sides. Did he really think he could take on a creature who could kill with a thought?

But Michael had not survived so long by being rash. He stopped at the edge of the dais, fists clenched as he fought the urge to strike. "Why did you take them?" he asked.

—What I did centuries ago for myself, I do now for my children. Five women. One child and three more to come. All first-born. All with my strength.— He looked past Michael to Stephen, whose emotions swayed between elation and fury so quickly I could not grasp the logic behind them.

Then Frn'cs bowed his head. Though his eyes were shut, I sensed his thoughts had merged with Michael's and my father's. Loving words? Calming words? His mind was far more devious than that, something I only realized when I felt their anger tingling on my skin, brushing through my hair, crackling in the air itself. It whirled around us, building into a silent storm, as dark as it was lethal.

The Old One rose to his feet and drew himself to his full height, standing motionless as the pillars of his hall. Stephen and Michael stood in front of him. My father's eyes were black, his body taut, but Michael, with fists pressed against his thighs, jaws clenched, seemed the one most ready to explode. The only sound came from the infant, a shrieking that seemed to give voice to the silent fury in that hall.

Without looking, I sensed Ana handing her infant to someone, the women backing away from us. Irena stirred in my arms. I moved away from the dais and searched for a safe place to leave her.

Sensing my concern, one of the women touched my arm and looked up at me. Her eyes were a deeper blue than my mother's, her hair blond tinged with red. —I am Mai. If she wakes, I will call you, —she told me, her thoughts lingering in my mind as I handed Irena to her and walked back to the edge of that stone arena.

Nothing had diminished in those moments I had been distracted. If anything, the anger had increased to the point where it seared. As my mind filled with it, the Old One leapt between Michael and Stephen, backing away until the three formed a triangle, all of them silent, tense; the thoughts that flew between them private.

Michael was the first to explode, charging Frn'cs as if he could win. The Old One could have stopped him with a thought, but let Michael come. Michael hit him hard, with a closed fist not an open hand. Too recently changed, he did not understand what his own body did best.

Frn'cs struck back, four fingers raking down Michael's bare arm, leaving it bloodied, momentarily useless. If Michael had been trained to fight like one of us, he would have kept his distance and let the arm heal. Instead, impatient to win before the blood loss made him weak, he charged again. Two slashes this time, arm and side. Michael went down.

Ana screamed and started toward the fight. Patrick grabbed her around the waist, holding tight while she kicked and bit, trying to break free. "Frn'cs will kill him!" she cried, then slumped against him. I saw tears on my brother's arm. She was that human. I looked at my father, at Patrick. In a family incapable of harming each other, we had no idea how to respond.

Frn'cs backed off, giving Michael the minutes he needed. When Michael finally pushed himself to his feet, his arms no longer bled. His side was still open but he ignored the wound, attacking again, retreating with six new slashes.

As they fought, the stones became soaked in blood, all of it Michael's. Each time he went down, I prayed he would simply stay down but he was far too stubborn for that. I began to hope that this was not some slow and vicious kind of killing, but merely a painful lesson in self-defense. Then, mercifully, Michael slipped on his own blood, went down hard, and stayed there.

I thought the struggle had ended, but Frn'cs knelt beside Michael and pulled him to his knees. He pressed the back of Michael's head against his shoulder, exposing Michael's neck.

"You were the one wronged," Frn'cs called to me. "What life he has left belongs to you. If you wish to claim it, come forward. If not, as the one attacked, I claim my right to the kill."

I had no doubt that he would kill if I declined his offer, but if I accepted, I would be starting down a dangerous path. I wanted to run from the hall, from the barbarity of either choice. Instead, I forced myself to walk forward as Michael, helpless and waiting, watched me approach.

The hall went silent, except for Michael's labored breathing and Ana's soft sobs. I looked from her to Patrick, who let Ana go then shook his head slowly, a warning he did not need to give.

—I will not be seduced into doing this,— I told him.

*Will not. Will not. Will . . .*

I don't know if I actually surprised the Old One or if he let it happen, but as soon as I was close enough to take what was offered, I attacked. One quick kick sent him backward onto the stones. Without taking my eyes off him, I pulled Michael to his feet. Supporting him as best I could while keeping him behind me, I backed away, unaware of Patrick moving closer to me, of Ana coming to help Michael walk.

I had not drawn blood. I had not intended to harm, only protect. Everyone knew it, including Frn'cs, yet he had rolled onto hands and feet, body tense and close to the ground, ready to spring.

From the time we could walk, Stephen had taught us how to use our bodies as weapons. This could be an almost even fight if the Old One kept his mind in check. What I could not comprehend was how we could be fighting at all.

Then he moved, so quickly he was on me before I knew he'd attacked. I had never been sure what instinct was, but I felt it now. I retreated as he attacked, defending but doing no harm to him, then took a moment's respite to lower my arms and raise my chin, the family gesture of a child yielding to an elder.

I did not look as Frn'cs walked over to me. His deceptively delicate hands curled over my shoulders and he pulled me close. But instead of a quick, largely ceremonial drawing of blood, he bit hard and began to feed.

It was not like those youthful battles with my brother, those magnificent nights with Irena, or even the first family sharing that left me light-headed. It was as if Death kissed me, and I was no more able to defend myself than I had been in the little room with the knife in my back. My legs gave way and he held me, absorbing my life as my vision faded, revealing not darkness but that incredible final light.

I used what power remained in my mind to scream for help.

Patrick had been questioning his senses. My father stood frozen in disbelief. Michael, who had only a little more strength than I did, moved first. Lunging in low from the right, he swept Frn'cs off his feet. We all went down, but only Frn'cs had the strength to twist and land on hands and feet, ready to attack again.

Then Patrick moved beside me, and Ana went to defend Michael. One of the other women, Lili, moved close enough to brush my hand. Mai touched my mind, offering to join us if needed. Six to one. Not an even fight yet, not with two of us so wounded, but we would stand our ground. The Old One tensed, and as I looked into those lightless eyes, I sensed that he waited.

For me? My arms rose away from my body, my fingers curled and tensed, my bare feet were just as hard, toes digging into the stones. As I began to fall forward, to ready myself for that lethal leap, my father stepped between us.

Until he turned his back to me, I'd had no idea if he would support his father or his sons.

"—Stop!—" he ordered and with the word and the thought, I felt a calm fill the hall. I did my best to respond, to join my power with his.

—Stop?— the Old One asked, a ripple of laughter rolling through my mind.

—I will not attack you but I will not allow you to destroy our future or touch my sons.—

Frn'cs looked from Stephen to me, his expression amused and more. The calm in the hall increased. He stood and backed away. Beside me, Michael let out the breath he had been holding and swayed. He would have fallen had Ana not been close to catch him.

My father moved beside me. I leaned into his arms. As I did, I heard a comment from the Old One made only to me. —Do you think what happened here was about killing?—

—It never was,— I replied.

I was still bleeding, though only a little. Michael had been hurt far worse and his human flesh took longer to heal. But Ana sat on the blood-soaked stones, holding his head in her lap, her wrist against his lips, sharing her strength.

I looked over my shoulder at the dais. It appeared empty but I think that even my father could not be sure.

# CHAP†ER 46

With my father supporting me, and Michael walking with assistance from Ana, we left the great hall for our rooms. Our procession moved in slow silence, each of us deep in our own thoughts.

Because I was too weak to hold her, Patrick carried Irena. She was only half awake when he placed her on the bed in the first room we reached and covered her the way my mother always did for us even though we had no need of it. With part of my attention constantly on Irena, I let my father draw me away from her and down the hallway to the cistern.

Now that the danger had ended, I gave in to the weakness I felt, sitting on the ledge by the water, letting my father wash my blood from my neck and shoulder, Michael's from my arms and chest and hands. The water made me shiver, and the memories of the last day rolled through me—the physical pain a fraction of the anguish I had felt when I had seen the horrors in that well. "So much has happened," I said. I tried to continue but could not.

—Later. You need life now,— Stephen told me and as he started to draw me close, Patrick also came and sat on the other side of me. Comforted by my own, I drew them in.

Ana was doing much the same thing for Michael but he had

lost far more blood than I had and his need weakened her. She
started to call for Lili or Mai but my father reached her first.

Ana looked up at him, suspicious of his intent until his hand
brushed her cheek and their minds touched. Convinced then that
he meant no harm, she let him feed Michael, then both stripped
off his ruined clothes, lifted him over the cistern wall, and lowered him into the water. The overflow into the sluice ran red from
Michael's blood and he moaned when the water touched the
wounds. He could hold himself up, but barely. He was like my
mother had been just after her changing . . . human flesh takes
time to heal but when it did, he would be amazed at his added
strength.

"You have an infant to tend to. If you like, I will stay with him
while you go and get her," Stephen said to Ana.

—There is no need for me to leave.— She bowed her head.
Moments later, I heard footsteps on the stairs behind me, turned,
and saw Mai coming with the child. She moved past me, smiling
shyly as she did, and handed the infant to her mother. In the soft
torchlight of these rooms, Mai's hair glowed like amber and her
blue eyes took on the color of jade. She gave her name to Patrick
and touched his cheek, a family gesture.

"I am Patrick. My brother is—"

"Richard; and that is Stephen. Frn'cs speaks of him most often. Ana's child is called Iarna—'winter'—because she was born
on the long night. Frn'cs tells us that means she will be blessed
with uncommon luck."

We were silent then, all of us aware of the strangeness of our
meeting.

"I hope that we will get a chance to learn more about each
other before we leave," I finally said.

She laughed as she moved past me. "But that is why you are
here, to take us to our new home. Then we will have much time to
learn. The others will come down later, when you are all well."

I watched her start up the steep stairs, her long legs, her bare
feet, the thin silk that hugged her body. I thought of the next family sharing, her and the others part of our hunt, our nights. When
I looked away I saw my father watching me from the other end of
the hall, his arms holding Michael, his blood still feeding him.

—What happened here tonight . . . ?— He started to make
some comment, but the thought ended as a question.

I shook my head. I had no answer.

Some time later, my father and brother left me, heading down the mountain to bring Hunter and Andrei up. I heard Michael and Ana in one of the chambers, Lili singing to Iarna in another as I returned to the room where Irena lay. I pulled the curtain over the door, stretched out beside her, and, holding her close, called her name.

Perhaps she had been waiting to hear my voice inside her for it seemed to draw her out of sleep. She opened her eyes. They were still the same warm brown, a bit darker perhaps, but little changed.

"Hello," I whispered.

She smiled, but it faded as she saw her surroundings. "Is this the keep?" she asked.

"You've been asleep a long time. How much can you remember?"

"I . . . I . . ." She ran her hand over her stomach at the place where she'd been shot, then looked at me to verify what she already knew.

I held her close and told her about the long hours after she'd been shot. As we lay together, she drifted back into that healing sleep. I waited, not surprised to be summoned back to that hall.

The Old One waited, sitting cross-legged on the dais. All but one torch had been extinguished. Backlit by the fire, his body threw a sharp-edged shadow on the still bloody stones.

I jumped up beside him, sat as he sat, our knees nearly touching. "Where is Catherine?" I asked.

"She has never allowed rivals. To protect them, I sent her away. Perhaps she will forgive me and come back once I am alone. Or perhaps this world has become more appealing to her. If so, I pity those of you who must live in it."

"And the women? How long have they been here?"

"Let them tell their own stories. I summoned you so we could speak of our family." He picked up a pillow and handed it to me. "What do you know about these?" he asked.

"That they were tenyears gifts from the children born here," I replied. I looked at them. There were so many, but he kept the ones from those who had gone. Had he taken those away, only six would remain, and only three from his own children.

"Whose pillow do you hold?" he asked.

I looked at it, deep blue on blue, one pattern hidden by the next; mysterious and concealing.

"Rachel's," I replied.

"And this?"

Brilliant shades of royal and gold. Joyous designs.

"Elizabeth's."

"And this?"

It did not show the skill of the others and seemed to have been done too quickly, as if the mind of the one who had done the work was occupied elsewhere. There were bits of other cultures in it, some Arab, some Gypsy, some Tartar perhaps.

"My father's."

"He always seemed the most human of my children, and like those short-lived creatures, he can hide best from himself. You will see him do that. Over time, what he learned here will mean nothing to him and the day will come when you will have to remind him. When it does, the words I left with you years ago will come."

I didn't understand, and told him so.

"Gifts come with age, child. I divine the future from the past, see patterns in history that those experts you hire would never expect. Your family will be tested and soon. When it is, you will be ready to lead them."

Me? The idea was ludicrous and I wanted to tell him so, but he silenced me with a wave of his hand and drew me down beside him, his arm over my chest, holding me close.

We do not dream, but it seemed that I dreamed then—of places and events past and present, of family gone and family to come, of desolate worlds and the freedom of the stars. And I began to see that he had built this hall, large enough to hold his family five times over, for the day when the ones who brought him here returned.

I wondered if they would ever come.

Then darkness claimed me and I slept. When I woke, it was late in the morning and the hall was filled with light and the rainbows of our family glass. The Old One had gone and Irena lay beside me, her head upon Rachel's pillow.

"I was told that I would find you here," she said.

Since she sounded so much like herself, I rolled up on one elbow. "I'm sorry for what happened. I think you did not want it, but—"

"You had no choice." She took my hand and slipped it under the silk of the gown, over the place where the wound had been then up to her breast. "I would have had no choice either," she said and kissed me.

My mind extended to the space around us, the rooms beneath. The keep slept. Satisfied that no one would disturb us, I did what I'd wanted to do since I'd dressed her in those silks. I slipped the scarves aside and drew her in.

# EPIL⊕GUE

## PATRICK

Nicolae Ceaușescu has among his favorite private sayings: "Oil, Germans, and Jews are Romania's most valuable exports."

After much discussion with those who planned to leave the keep, we decided that the women and their children would have to be another.

We might have smuggled them out. It would have been possible but risky, especially with an infant, and had we been caught, things would have been worse than awkward. "Ransom" would be the safer method.

Andrei assured us that the purchase of exit visas was often done and that the more money offered, the fewer questions asked. In the end we negotiated a price of fifty thousand each. The government thought we were fools, but they did not draw our attention to that fact. And so, two weeks after we left the keep, our newest family members flew into Dawson then traveled north to our land on the Peace River. It is a wild place, far more remote even than our cabin in Dawson. But they have children to raise and our children need the wilderness to understand what they are.

As a fugitive with more than one murder on his list of crimes, Michael Celac had to be treated differently. My father's ability to avoid questions could only stretch logic so far.

Irena thought of the questions the authorities had used to identify him and offered a partial solution. I admit that her request to be the one to wield the knife had more than a bit of vengeance at its core but when she was through, the new strip of flesh that repaired her damage to Michael's face showed no sign of that jagged scar, and the tip of one finger that had been cut off during a particularly vicious round of questioning after his arrest grew back when the finger was cut through further down. Doubtful it would work when she'd begun, Michael had let her do it anyway. Seeing the result, he happily set about filleting his hands. Hunter suggested he leave the scars that didn't show as evidence.

At the time he did this, Michael still had not made a decision on where he would go. He and Andrei had spoken with Hunter and my father for hours. Hunter stressed that Michael would not be just another refugee, that the meetings he could arrange with American and British authorities would be taken seriously. Stephen provided far greater detail on the danger to the woman he loved if he were found and his nature revealed. But in the end, after Michael asked for some time to consider, it was Ana lying beside him that made him agree to leave the country.

"I am glad you made that decision," Stephen said when Michael told him of it later.

"And if I had wanted to remain in Romania?"

"You would have forced me to make a difficult choice." Stephen didn't elaborate. He didn't have to.

Irena, of course, "escaped" on her own. She staggered into our offices in Cluf, her clothes ripped and dirty. To assure that she did not disappear again, the firm released the story to the International press before they contacted Romanian authorities. She said she could not remember much of what happened to her and flew into New York five days later to a celebrity's welcome, an offer to sing at the White House, an agent overburdened with requests for interviews, her picture on the front page of the *Chicago Tribune* and in a number of other major papers. So much for the anonymity my family requires. She accepted the White House offer, did the interviews. Since her face was already well known, there was no reason for us not to grant her wish—her demand!—for her years of fame.

The story might have ended as it had begun—on a stage. But we still had the nagging problem of the glass house we had promised to build in Romania. After consulting with Michael, Andrei, and Hunter, the family decided on Oradea because of the easy access to the silica which we preferred for family windows, and its proximity to others like Michael and his kin.

We have no illusions that eventually the buildings and their contents will be nationalized and any formulae written down will be stolen. So it seemed best to put someone in charge who did not need any information in writing. I'd already spent months in Chaves. I knew more than enough and, abandoning formal education for the moment, I volunteered.

Of course, in Romania, every foreign-funded project has an intelligence officer planted on the staff, one whose sole purpose is to make certain that the state knows every miniscule detail of the operation. To address that reality, my father requested that Andrei join our firm.

Though Andrei protested, his superiors made it clear they would not listen to any argument. Stephen offered him the position of head of operations, and so he moved to Oradea to help in the construction.

As the work progressed, party officials involved in the planning often commented on my youth. Andrei provided a convenient explanation. "The Austras begin training their children when they are very young. Apprenticeships are how it has always been done by that family," he told them.

So when I suggested that I tour the local school to look for children that might show a particular aptitude for our work, the government agreed. And when I said that the hardest work might be best suited to convicts, they agreed to that as well. And so, I moved through the crowds most likely to contain others like Michael and Irena. I found one dark haired boy in an orphanage in Stei, and two more in a prison camp near Timisoara, but they are like Andrei rather than Michael. And that was all.

We hold numerous socials at the firm. Party officials have been invited solely so that I could draw them aside one by one and touch their minds. But though I have been thorough, and Andrei careful to invite everyone he suspects, we have not found the ones who took the missing children. Perhaps the children were killed, but if so we do not know who killed them.

There are no cameras in my house. I found and destroyed six

before the government gave up on hiding them there and contented themselves with eavesdropping instead. Andrei lives in the house next door. The party thought it brilliant when he suggested that as the perfect way of keeping tabs on me, and of making sure that my temptation remained close at hand.

I have not visited the Old One often, though I sometimes pause in my work to turn my face toward his mountain. And I inhale the scent of the forests and think of the promise of this land.

And at night, when the rest of the world sleeps, Andrei and I lie together and dream of a better world.

# WI+H THANKS

It is impossible for a writer to describe places she has never been, discuss professions she has never pursued, or set down phrases in languages she has never used without a great deal of assistance.

For their help with this book, I wish to thank Camelia Ray for her assistance with language and a bit of help on the Romanian social climate in those years and Diane K. Lane for her in-depth descriptions of auditions and the arduous requirements of those who wish to pursue a career in opera. I stretched the limits of voice markedly but, Diane, this is, after all, fantasy. I would also like to thank my Milwaukee workshop, the Redbird Refugees, for all their input and support over the last few months.

Since this novel is for me much like a homecoming, I would also like to thank those who have been with the Austra series from the beginning: Ginjer Buchanan, my editor at Berkley; the late Ray and Barbara Puechner, who allowed me the freedom to write while they handled all those annoying little details; and Don Maass, my current agent, who encouraged me to return to my roots.

This book begs a sequel. Muse willing, there will be one.

—Elaine Bergstrom